Praise for Benedict Jacka and the Inheritance of Magic series

"One of the most satisfying contemporary fantasies I have read in a long time; cozy and human, with some good fight scenes to boot.... An enchanting journey into a world where sorcery may be for sale, but agency is beyond price." —*The Wall Street Journal*

"Benedict Jacka is one of my must-reads."
—#1 *New York Times* bestselling author Charlaine Harris

"A world of magic usually known only to the rich and powerful is put to the test in the page-turning urban fantasy that launches an intriguing new series.... There's lots of promise to this eat-the-rich world. Readers will be eager to see where things go next." —*Publishers Weekly*

"Jacka has drawn a potent new world of magic controlled by a privileged few, and Stephen Oakwood is the sigl-wielding rebel we didn't know we needed." —*New York Times* bestselling author Chloe Neill

"Benedict Jacka is a master storyteller." —Fantasy-Faction

"Books this good remind me why I got into the storytelling business in the first place."
—#1 *New York Times* bestselling author Jim Butcher (on *Fated*)

"The new magic system introduced in this series, which began with *An Inheritance of Magic*, continues to fascinate, and the stories will remind readers of classic urban fantasies (such as the Dresden Files series from Jim Butcher), as Stephen's world gets more dangerous and he powers through each setback by learning bigger and better magic and paying a higher price each and every time." —*Library Journal*

"Benedict Jacka writes a deft thrill ride of an urban fantasy—a stay-up-all-night read."
—#1 *New York Times* bestselling author Patricia Briggs (on *Fated*)

"Fans of urban fantasy will enjoy the new take on London and the plucky character of Stephen is endearing. Readers will quickly imprint on Stephen and want him to succeed and rule the magical world."
—*Booklist*

"A combination of a coming-of-age story and a coming-into-power story set in an urban fantasy version of our world where magic hides in plain sight even as it magnifies the ambitions and the sheer reach of the rich and powerful. . . . I'm looking forward to seeing where Stephen Oakwood's adventures in drucraft lead him, and us, to next!"
—Reading Reality

BOOKS BY BENEDICT JACKA

THE INHERITANCE OF MAGIC SERIES

An Inheritance of Magic
An Instruction in Shadow
A Judgement of Powers

THE ALEX VERUS SERIES

Fated
Cursed
Taken
Chosen
Hidden
Veiled
Burned
Bound
Marked
Fallen
Forged
Risen

A JUDGEMENT OF POWERS

Book 3 in
the Inheritance of Magic series

BENEDICT JACKA

Ace

New York

ACE
Published by Berkley
An imprint of Penguin Random House LLC
1745 Broadway, New York, NY 10019
penguinrandomhouse.com

Copyright © 2025 by Benedict Jacka
Penguin Random House values and supports copyright. Copyright fuels creativity, encourages diverse voices, promotes free speech, and creates a vibrant culture. Thank you for buying an authorized edition of this book and for complying with copyright laws by not reproducing, scanning, or distributing any part of it in any form without permission. You are supporting writers and allowing Penguin Random House to continue to publish books for every reader. Please note that no part of this book may be used or reproduced in any manner for the purpose of training artificial intelligence technologies or systems.

ACE is a registered trademark and the A colophon is a trademark of
Penguin Random House LLC.

Library of Congress Cataloging-in-Publication Data
Names: Jacka, Benedict, author.
Title: A judgement of powers / Benedict Jacka.
Description: First edition. | New York: Ace, 2025. |
Series: Inheritance of magic; book 3 |
Identifiers: LCCN 2025004220 (print) | LCCN 2025004221 (ebook) |
ISBN 9780593956106 (trade paperback) | ISBN 9780593956113 (ebook)
Subjects: LCGFT: Fantasy fiction | Novels
Classification: LCC PR6110.A22 J83 2025 (print) |
LCC PR6110.A22 (ebook) | DDC 823/.92—dc23/eng/20250429
LC record available at https://lccn.loc.gov/2025004220
LC ebook record available at https://lccn.loc.gov/2025004221

First Edition: November 2025

Printed in the United States of America
1st Printing

The authorized representative in the EU for product safety and compliance is
Penguin Random House Ireland, Morrison Chambers, 32 Nassau Street,
Dublin D02 YH68, Ireland, https://eu-contact.penguin.ie.

A glossary of terms can be found at the end of this book.

A JUDGEMENT OF POWERS

CHAPTER 1

COLD WIND BLEW down the concrete halls, carrying the scents of stone and water. The rain had stopped at sunset, leaving the streets and walkways wet, but the air still carried its chill. Distant traffic and faraway voices blended into background noise, but here, in the heart of the city, I was alone.

I was standing on a concrete walkway. Lights along the walls cast glowing rings of orange that faded quickly into the sea of darkness all around. Lit windows looked down from the flats above and from the theatre complex across the water, but I couldn't see a single living person. I glanced up and down the walkway one more time; when nothing moved, I kept going.

The structure around me was the Barbican, a huge sprawling complex of brown concrete in central London. It was the first time I'd visited the place, and it felt to me like a richer version of the council estates I'd grown up around. The tower blocks were the same, the rows of flats were the same, but it all looked cleaner and posher—there was even a handful of plants and trees, though all they really did was draw attention to how cold and sterile everything else was. Scattered living things, dwarfed by the thick stone barriers made to contain them; the essentia in the air, muted and weak. It would be a terrible place to find a Well, but I wasn't looking for a Well. I was looking for my father.

Twelve days ago, I'd been attacked in Covent Garden by a man calling himself Vermillion. He'd tried to stab me to death and nearly succeeded, but in doing so, he'd also given me what I'd been searching for. Vermillion was a member of the Winged, the weird mysterious group who for most of the past year had been alternating between attacking me and trying to recruit me. According to them, my father had been a member. I wasn't sure whether to believe it, but I *was* sure they held the key to finding him, and Vermillion's attack had given me the leverage I'd needed to pressure one of their other members into handing over a letter from my father.

That had been three days ago. Two days ago, I'd sent a message to the email address the letter had given me. Two hours ago, I'd been told to come here.

But told by whom?

I slipped behind a concrete pillar, my back coming to rest against the cold stone. To my eyes, the essentia currents glimmered faintly as they drifted through the darkness, taking on tinges of colour as they passed through objects: reddish brown as they moved through the concrete, pale blue as they moved through the fluorescent lights, a hint of green as they gathered around the leafless trees down on the courtyard below. It was beautiful, in a quiet, peaceful way, but all it was really telling me was that there was no one with an active sigl nearby.

And even that wasn't much help. If there *was* someone out there, they could just have their sigls turned off. Like me.

Middle of the Barbican, I repeated to myself. I'd rushed out of the door as soon as I'd seen those words on my screen; only now was I realising how ambiguous they were. I'd studied the orange-grey-green maps posted at the Barbican junctions, and as far as I could see, this spot, around the southern side of the artificial lake, was as close as you could get to "middle." But there was no sign of my father.

When you show up for a meeting and no one's there, you start second-guessing yourself. What if my father had already been here and left? Maybe we'd both wandered around the Barbican, somehow missing each other? What if I'd got the time wrong, or the place, or . . .

A line from the letter floated to the surface of my thoughts. *The spirit is served by demons that give gifts to those they favour.*

I shivered, pushing the thought away. That letter had left me with a million questions, but now wasn't the time. The message that had led me here . . . had it *really* been from my dad?

If it hadn't, the best thing I could do right now was to stay hidden. But if it *had*, then my dad might be out there doing exactly the same thing. And if *I* was hiding and *he* was hiding, we were never going to find each other.

I hissed out a breath. *Screw it.* I'd been waiting for this chance for years. I wasn't going to lose my nerve now!

I headed for the nearest stairwell and trotted down the steps until I came out at ground level, next to the dark stillness of the Barbican's artificial lake. The breeze blowing off the water was cold. I walked out into the middle of the courtyard, then stopped. A hundred windows looked down on me, blank and shadowed and faceless. Any of them could be holding someone watching me.

I took a deep breath and channelled.

Essentia stirred inside me, flowing through my body. In the early days channelling my personal essentia felt like trying to pick up water between my fingers. Nowadays it feels more like flexing a muscle, the essentia an extension of my own body, my nerves extending through the flows to brush the surface of whatever they touch. I lifted my right arm and sent essentia surging through my hand and into the sigl ring on my fourth finger.

Blue-white light erupted silently into the night. The sigl was weak, made years ago when I was still fumbling my way through shaping, but it was still bright enough to make me shield my eyes. To anyone looking out of their window, I'd look like a figure holding up a tiny star. Most people wouldn't understand what they were seeing. A drucrafter would.

I held the sigl at full power for a slow count of five, then cut the flow. The light winked out, leaving spots dancing in my eyes. I jogged away across the courtyard, disappearing into the shadows beneath the walkways, then stopped.

Murmurs echoed, louder than before. I heard the scrape of a window opening, then another; questioning voices. A flicker of movement showed up on the walkway, though I couldn't make out the figure behind it. The Barbican seemed to stir, turning towards the source of the disturbance.

Using a sigl in public, as I'd just done, is a bad idea. Drucraft isn't something you're supposed to advertise, and if the wrong person notices you doing it, it can mean trouble. But London's a big place, and one weak sigl doesn't draw *that* much attention, especially one that doesn't actually do anything you couldn't duplicate with a good torch. Most of the time, if I get caught using drucraft, all I have to do is hurry out of sight, and that's going to be the end of it.

But that's if the people watching don't know who I am. For someone who did, and who knew what I could do, I'd just written *"Stephen Oakwood is here"* in letters of blue-white fire.

The Barbican came awake, scattered lights coming on, voices echoing around the courtyard. From down where I was hidden I heard the sounds of questions and answers. But as the minutes passed and nothing happened, they tapered off. One by one the voices ceased, until everything was quiet. The Barbican slept once again.

I stayed out of sight behind a concrete pillar, listening. Nothing came, and I clicked my tongue. Was I going to have to do something *more* obvious?

The scrape of a footstep sounded from nearby.

Instantly I was on full alert. You can tell a lot from a footstep. Normal footsteps are steady and rhythmic; the sound of someone with somewhere to go. This had been a single motion, followed by silence.

I stood very still, straining my ears. Nothing else came, and I focused on my sensing, reaching out. And this time, I felt something. It was faint—very faint—but beyond the currents of essentia drifting through the Barbican, the white-grey tendrils carrying with them echoes of water and concrete and earth and stone, was something else. Something . . .

—water, deep and crushing. Gold gleaming in the depths. Scales like mountains, rippling like the tide—

I wrenched myself away, the flood of images cutting off as if with a knife. I'd been about to stick my head out in the hope of seeing my father; instead I stayed where I was.

The corridor was silent for a while, then I heard quiet footsteps moving towards me, passing my hiding place without stopping. I reached out again with my sensing, more cautiously this time, and felt nothing—there was *some* kind of wispy essentia signature, but it was so faint that I might have imagined it, and as I watched it faded. The footsteps faded. I was alone once more.

I waited.

Doubts started to nag at me. Only minutes ago I'd been promising myself that I wouldn't let this chance slip away. Why had I hesitated?

I shook my head; this was getting me nowhere. I stepped out around the pillar, out of cover. I was going to have to come up with—

"Stop."

My head snapped around and I stopped dead.

"Stay where you are."

The voice was coming from behind the pillars a little way down the corridor. I couldn't see who was talking, but whoever he was, he was close. Without thinking, I took a step—

"I said *stay*," the voice repeated. "One more step and I'm gone."

I stopped.

"Good," the voice said, when I didn't move. "Now. I'm going to ask you a question. Just one. Think carefully before you answer. Answer wrong, this conversation is over, and you'll never hear from me again. Take another step, this conversation is over, and you'll never hear from me again. You understand?"

It was a man's voice, middle-aged, and in the time he took to finish speaking my hopes soared and plummeted, up and down like a roller coaster. I desperately needed to know if it was my dad, and I couldn't tell. It didn't exactly sound like him ... but it didn't sound *not* like him, either. It had been so many years ...

"You understand?" the voice repeated.

I swallowed, my mouth suddenly dry. "Yes."

"Good," the voice said. "Now. What was the number of the house where Stephen got his cat?"

I stared. "What?"

"You need me to repeat it?"

"What do you mean, 'Stephen'?" I demanded.

"Answer the question."

"... I can't."

"Don't know?"

"No, I *can't*, because there isn't an answer. I didn't get Hobbes from a house, it was from one of the ground-floor flats on that estate round the corner. I mean, I guess it had a number, but why would I care? It was just 'the flat with the old sofa out front.'"

The voice didn't answer.

"You there?" I asked. Subtly, I tried to crane my neck to catch a glimpse of whoever was talking, but all I could see was the concrete pillars. A few steps to the side would give me a clear line of sight, but . . .

"Yes," the voice replied. "Stay here for a slow count of fifty. Then go up the stairs to the level directly above. Ring the bell for flat 117. You'll be let in. Follow?"

". . . Yes."

"Repeat it back to me."

"Stay here for a slow count of fifty, go up a level, ring flat 117," I repeated. "Then what?"

"You'll find out. Start counting."

"Hello?"

Silence.

I started counting. I've had longer minutes in my life, but not by much.

As I counted, my thoughts raced. Who had I been talking to? It had to be whoever had sent me that email . . . which meant it had to be my dad.

Didn't it?

I desperately wished I could identify him from the voice. But the voice had been maddeningly vague, close to my memories but not quite a perfect match. Were my memories wrong? Or was it someone imitating him? Or was he disguising his voice? Or . . . or . . . or . . .

Forty-eight. Forty-nine. Fifty. I darted forward.

There was no one behind the pillars. I looked from side to side, trying to figure out where my stalker had gone. There was a small, blue-painted door, but when I tried the handle, it didn't open.

I took the stairs up.

The first-floor level was silent, lights winking in the darkness; if I'd stirred the Barbican awake, it had gone back to sleep. I walked along the walkway, my feet echoing softly on the tiles, then pressed the button marked 117.

There was a pause, then a metallic buzz and the door clicked. I slipped inside.

Flat 117 was at the end of one of the corridors. The door was very slightly ajar, and as I pushed it, it swung open without resistance. The inside was dark.

I hesitated. I could make out a few pieces of furniture in the shadows; all else was black. I felt stretched, like a taut wire, ready to snap forward or back. Was this what I'd been waiting for, or was it a trap?

The door yawned before me, inviting me to step through and find out.

Resolve flared up in me and I set my teeth. *I'm not backing out now.* I stepped through and swung the door closed behind me. The lock resisted slightly, then clicked shut.

I swallowed, then spoke into the darkness. "Show yourself." I could hear the tension in my voice.

For a moment everything was silent. Then there was the click of a switch and the room flashed into light. I blinked, squinting, as a man stepped out and turned towards me.

My father had my looks, matured and weathered. His jaw was a little squarer, his brow a touch heavier; still handsome, but in a more distinctively masculine way. He was a couple of inches taller than me and a little stronger, and brown eyes sparkled at me from beneath a head of wavy black hair. "Stephen," he said with his lopsided smile. "It's been a while."

I think right up until that last second I'd still been wondering if it was really him, whether the whole thing had been some sort of insanely elaborate trick. But the sound of his voice, steady but warm, with the trace of his old East End accent, banished all that in an instant. My doubts turned to smoke and I flew into his arms.

My father staggered as I crashed into him, then laughed, hugging me tightly enough to make me lose my breath and then ruffling my hair the way he'd used to do when I was a little boy. "You okay?" he asked. "Not hurt?"

I shook my head, not trusting myself to speak.

"Were you followed? Anything we need to deal with right now?"

I shook my head again, then spoke. "No." My voice wavered a bit and I had to swallow. "Nothing like that."

"Good." My father disentangled himself and pushed me back slightly to arm's length. "Let me take a look at you."

He studied me. I did the same to him, and as I did, I started to notice the differences that my first glance had missed. When we'd last met, he'd had a scattering of white hairs, mostly on his sideburns; now they'd spread upwards through his hair, which had left "jet black" and was teetering on the edge of "salt and pepper." There were small wrinkles at the corners of his eyes that I didn't remember. But his grip as he held my shoulders was just as strong, and the spark in his brown eyes was just as I remembered it.

"Good," my father said again. "Good." He was smiling, but a stranger probably wouldn't have recognised the warmth in his eyes. Only I could tell how happy he was. "You have no idea what a relief it is to see you."

"You think it's a relief for *you*?" I said. My voice wobbled a little bit at the end. "I was afraid you were dead."

My father laughed. "Not quite. Now come on. Sit down and tell me what's happened."

With the rush of seeing my father again, I'd been blind to where we were. Now that I finally looked around, I saw that we were standing in a cramped, expensive-looking flat. Books and papers were piled on cheap white IKEA shelves, and two mustard-yellow sofas filled the living room behind. The sofas backed onto a floor-to-ceiling window, but the blinds had been pulled down so that no light would escape.

My father walked into the kitchen as I sat down on one of the sofas and tried to lean back. The sofa looked like one of those you see advertised on the Tube, but it was hard and uncomfortable. On the wall opposite was a painting of a naked woman with oversized lips lying in a bed of garishly coloured ivy. "Do you live here?" I asked my father doubtfully.

"God no," my father called over from the kitchen. "Belongs to some fancy interior designer."

"Oh," I said, slightly relieved. "Are you renting it?"

"We've got a kind of time-share," my father said, walking back in with a couple of half-litre bottles. "He uses it while he's in London, I use it while he's in New York. I bring my own food, clean up after myself, make sure not to leave any sign I've used the place." He grinned. "If he knew I existed, he'd probably think I was the perfect tenant." He set down one of the bottles and pushed it over; it was a Coke. "Here. Used to be your favourite, right?"

"Actually I haven't drunk it in years."

"Really?"

"Too expensive. And after I quit soft drinks for a couple of months, I found I wasn't missing them."

"I've missed a lot, haven't I?" my father said. For a moment he looked melancholy, then seemed to shake it off. "All right, first things first. Here." He pushed a card across the table. "Memorise that address, then destroy it. From now on, you want to contact me, use that. Don't use your old email, it's compromised. Create a new one and use it for this and nothing else. No names."

The card was blank except for a handwritten address. "What do you mean, compromised?"

"As in, someone else can access it. They've been reading your mail for years."

"Wait, what? But I just used it to send you—"

"Why do you think I gave you such a hard time downstairs?" my father said dryly. "Don't worry, they haven't got the manpower to search the whole Barbican."

"There was someone else there," I said slowly. "Before I met you. Was it . . . ?"

"Someone trailing you?" my father asked. "No idea, but no reason to take the chance. Anyway, he didn't follow you."

"So we're safe to talk?" I asked. I wasn't sure exactly what "safe" meant in this context, but from the way my dad was acting, I figured it was best to follow his lead.

"For the rest of the night," my father said, flashing a quick smile. "Hopefully long enough for us to catch up. Now, how about you tell me why you sent me that email? Obviously you must have got my letter, but why now?"

"Because I didn't have your letter! I got hold of it on Monday and decoded it on Tuesday."

"How come you only got hold of it on Monday?"

"Byron had it."

My father's expression darkened.

"You didn't know?" I asked.

"I knew there was a chance he'd intercepted it," my father said. "But . . . I also knew there was a chance he hadn't. And that maybe things weren't so bad, and you didn't need me . . ." He sighed, and for a moment he looked old and tired, like someone weighed down by old choices and regrets. Then the next moment he was back to normal, the change so sudden that someone who didn't know him might have missed it completely. "Well, I'm here now. Tell me what's been happening."

I almost wanted to laugh. "That's . . . going to take a while."

"We've got the time," my father said, that smile of his flashing out again. "Come on. Start at the beginning."

This time I *did* laugh. "The beginning? Well, about a year ago, I looked out of my window one morning and saw a strange car at the end of the road . . ."

I started from there and kept on going. Meeting Lucella. The kidnap and escape. Tobias, the party, and Charles Ashford. What had happened to Hobbes. Becoming a locator and that long summer of work and training. Byron, and his house in Hampstead. The raid on the Well in Chancery Lane. Byron's increasing interest in me; the attack by Mark. The way locating had become harder and harder, leading to me dipping my toe into shadow work, which had led in turn to that raid in Moor Park that had nearly gotten me killed. Calhoun Ashford and my new job as a bodyguard. The deadly ambush by Vermillion in Covent Garden. How I'd turned the tables on Mark, extorting him into stealing that letter from Byron and giving it to me.

It took a long time. My father stayed nearly silent; he asked a few small questions to clarify things, but for the most part he just let me talk. It was an old habit of his; ever since I could remember, whenever he asked me what I'd been doing, he'd always listened with that same close attention. I've never been the kind to overshare, but growing up, I'd always known that if I *did* share something with my dad, he'd listen. Only when I got to the fight at the theatre, when I'd been stabbed, did I see him react; I heard a faint crackle as his hand tightened on the plastic bottle before he controlled himself again.

By the time I'd finished, the bottle in front of me was empty, replaced by a glass; my father had fetched it from the kitchen while I'd been talking. His own drink was opened but untouched. "... And from there it was just a matter of getting my old copy of the book from my aunt's and cracking the code," I said. "Then I emailed you, and ... well, you know the rest."

My father was silent.

I tilted my head. "Dad? Hello?"

My father didn't react for a few seconds, then got up, walked around the coffee table, and put his hand on my shoulder. "Well done."

I blinked, craning my neck to look up at him. "Why—?"

"I had no idea all this was happening," my father said. "If I had, I'd have done something. But I hadn't, and I didn't, and you handled it all on your own, and you did a better job than anyone could have expected. I'm proud of you."

A warm feeling spread through me. I put my other hand over my father's and gave it a squeeze.

My father stayed there for a moment longer, then gave me a last affectionate shake and let go. "All right," he said, returning to his side of the coffee table and dropping back down into the sofa, then giving me a piercing gaze. "We've got a lot to talk about."

I nodded.

"First is Vermillion," my father said. "He attacked you . . . what, two weeks ago? He's the priority. Everything else can come second."

"No."

My father looked taken aback. "Stephen, he just nearly killed you. That wasn't a joke."

"You don't have to tell *me* that," I said testily. "And we can talk about Vermillion as much as you want, but we're doing something else first."

"What?"

"You're going to tell me why you disappeared," I said. "The whole story, this time. What happened with you and my mother, your history with the Winged, why you had to vanish, all of it. I've been in the dark for years now. I've had to piece everything together bit by bit, working on my own with nothing but scraps, and it's been *really hard*. All those years, I wished over and over that I had you here to talk to. Well, now you're finally here, and you're going to tell me the things you *should* have told me from the start." My voice started to rise, heat creeping into it. "No more sweeping things under the carpet, no more 'when you're older.' All of it. *Now*."

My father took a deep breath. "Fair enough." He looked at me. "Where do you want to start?"

"The Ashfords," I said immediately.

My father nodded. He seemed to settle himself, as though deciding what to say, then began.

CHAPTER 2

"When I entered the service of House Ashford, I was younger than you are now," my father said. "I'd just left school and was looking for a job. My mates were going into all kinds of things—sales, building, the army. The economy was better then, but it was still hard if you didn't have the right piece of paper. I knew about drucraft by then—you know that story—so I thought I'd look for work with one of the Houses.

"Well, I learned pretty fast that most Houses weren't interested. They were snobby old-money types who didn't have time for a poor working-class kid from the East End. But I stuck with it, and eventually a woman I knew gave me a tip about a place called House Ashford. Still an old House, but they were up-and comers—they'd just bought a big mansion, and they had boots to fill. So I gave it a shot, and I probably wouldn't have made it, but as luck would have it, I managed to impress someone. The new Head of the House, Charles Ashford."

"You *impressed* him?"

My father grinned. "Sounds funny now, doesn't it?"

"I'm pretty sure that Charles absolutely *hates* you," I told him. "Enough that just us looking alike is enough to make him hate me as well."

"Yeah, that one's my fault. Sorry. Though the thing I did that pissed him off the most is also the reason you exist, so I'm not actually that sorry. Anyway, I served as an Ashford armsman for two years. Got tapped for drucraft training—usually Houses don't give you that until you've been there five years minimum, but rules don't matter when the boss likes you. In exchange I did off-the-books work for Charles, including bodyguarding his younger daughter. And that was where the trouble started."

"Okay, I know I said 'everything,' but you don't need to give me the details on that part."

"Good, because I wasn't going to. Anyway, short version is that it was a secret, until it wasn't, and then everything blew up. I went to Charles to talk things out and . . . let's just say it didn't go well."

"What did you do, tell him you quit?"

"Worse. Asked him if I could marry his daughter."

I blinked. "Really?"

"Wanted to do the stand-up thing," my father said with a shrug. "Plus, I thought he might say yes. He'd started almost treating me like a son, some of the time—he had two daughters and had never done the father-son thing, so I think he enjoyed it just a little, though he'd never admit it. So I thought, hey, give it a shot, maybe he'd be willing to let me join the family. Stranger things have happened."

"And you actually thought that would work?"

"I was twenty years old, and like all twenty-year-olds, I was a bloody idiot."

"Hey."

"Yes, I know you're twenty-one, and no, that doesn't make

much difference. Trust me, when you're my age, *you'll* think your current self was a bloody idiot as well. Anyway, that was when I discovered that rich guys only like you so long as you know your place. And that's how I got fired and your mother got disinherited and we both ended up living hand-to-mouth in Plaistow."

I sat quietly for a few seconds, taking that in. Was that why Charles had always been so harsh with me? Because he felt as though he'd trusted my father, and wasn't going to make the same mistake twice?

"You said you'd talked to your mother," my father went on. "How much did she tell you about that part?"

"That you two fought like cats and dogs. Then her sister died, and Charles came to her and invited her back."

"Yeah, I guess that's the part she'd have remembered," my father said. "For me . . . I came home one day and found her gone. Flat was stripped of all her things. All that was left was you." His mouth set in a hard line. "She never talked about it with me. Not once. Just walked away. I never forgave her for that."

I sat there uncomfortably, not sure how to answer.

"So, there I was," my father said. "Back where I started, with a couple of sigls that they missed when they tried to confiscate them, and with you. And that's how you ended up growing up in Plaistow, with me and your babysitters and your aunt."

I hesitated a second before speaking; I was afraid of hearing the answer to the next question. "Byron said you worked for him," I said. "For the Winged." With an effort I looked my father in the eye. "Was that true?"

My father met my gaze. "Yes."

I felt my heart sink. I think at some level I'd known it was true—it explained too much—but I'd still hoped Byron had lied.

"There were reasons," my father said when I stayed silent.

"These guys . . . seem like really bad news."

"Actually, they're probably even worse than you think they are."

"Then why did you work for them?"

My father sighed. "Like I said, there were reasons. Anyway, listen and you can judge for yourself.

"Things were okay for a while. Money was tight, but we scraped by, and it got easier once you started school and I could work through the day. I'd burned my bridges with the Houses, but I'd picked up a few contacts while I was with the Ashfords and I was able to find enough work to keep us going.

"But then the recession happened. Rent went up, hours went down. I'd never managed to get anything long term, so when the jobs dried up, I didn't have much to fall back on—I needed to have started saving years ago, and I hadn't. We started missing payments, having to go short on food. And then I meet this weird guy who says he wants to hire me. Better pay, better hours, and all I have to do is not ask questions."

"Did you know he . . ."

"Worked for the Winged? No. I could tell he was dodgy, but I thought his crew were just regular crooks. Stolen goods or something."

"You always told me to steer clear of all that."

"Yeah, I know I come across like a bloody hypocrite here. But . . . look, you said you were living on your own for about three years?"

"Plus a year with my aunt."

"I'm guessing it wasn't easy."

"No."

My father nodded. "Imagine doing all that, but with a kid to take care of. Sorting out babysitters and food and school. You were an easy kid—looked after yourself and didn't cause problems—but there's always something. And then the money started drying up, and . . . I'd look at you and think about how I could hardly even buy you food, much less anything nice. I'd wonder if you were getting enough to eat, whether you were getting picked on at school for having holes in your clothes. All the things other parents did for their kids, holidays and trips and nice restaurants—you weren't getting any of that."

"I didn't *care* about any of that," I protested. "I mean, yeah, having newer clothes and a console and TV that weren't made in 1990 would have been nice. But at least you always paid attention to me. I mean, look at Colin—his dad was so caught up in all that drama with his mum that there were whole weeks where he'd barely say a word to him. Or Gabriel, his dad isn't even *there*. I never felt like I was the unlucky one."

"And if the money had run out?" my dad asked. "If the landlord had thrown us out on our ear and we were living off charity? Moving from place to place, no real home, living out of a suitcase and a cardboard box?"

I hesitated.

"You see, it's not easy," my father said. "Knowing what I do now, yeah, working for Byron was a mistake. But knowing what I did then . . . different story. And Byron knew how to sell it. He'd dug up my history with the Ashfords and made the Winged out to be the underdogs. Rebels fighting against the rich Houses."

"Is that true?"

"Half true," my father said with a grimace. "But it's the other half that'll mess you up. Anyway, I didn't really need much persuading. I was pretty bitter about the way things had gone with the Ashfords—I was still in touch with your mother, and when you're scraping to find enough money to pay the gas bill, while they're going on summer holidays in the Mediterranean . . . well, working for the Winged let me feel like I was getting back at them somehow."

"Working for them how?"

"Grunt work, to start. Watching doors, driving people around, walking the floor at parties. I didn't have the shortcuts I had with the Ashfords, so I had to work my way up from the bottom this time. From time to time Byron'd hint that he could get me special treatment if I showed 'extra commitment,' but I'd always shut him down. But the work was steady and the money was good. And after a while I started getting given more sensitive stuff. Stakeouts, watching houses, sealed deliveries. Never anything blatantly illegal, but enough that you could tell something was up.

"And gradually I started to build up a picture of the Winged. At the lower levels they're less of a cult and more of a big patronage network. Really active in the arts, which was a new experience for me. I'd never been part of that world, you see. Then I started driving Byron around, and I'd take him to one of his parties and show him in the door and you'd see every artist in the room turn and stare like wolves at a hunk of meat."

"Why would they do that?"

"Because artsy middle-class kids are taught growing up that success is all about getting in with the right guy," my father said. "And back then, Byron was that guy. Could make or break a career with a phone call. Every party, all the young hopefuls would buzz around him like flies, hoping to be the one he'd pick. Was an education for me, I'll tell you that much."

"So the Winged spend their time . . ." I said with a frown, ". . . going to parties?"

"The ones I was hanging around with."

"And that turns into something else later?"

"No, they mostly just keep on doing the same thing."

"I thought the Winged were important."

"They are."

I gave my father a confused look.

"You're not thinking big enough," my father told me. "Listen.

I worked for Byron, driving him to parties. Byron would use the parties to meet up-and-coming artists. The artists he liked, he'd tap to make films. The films get funded by finance companies linked to the Winged. Eventually the film comes out and nudges the audience into whatever message the Winged happen to be pushing. Add in all the other guys doing the same thing as Byron, and that's hundreds of films a year. It adds up."

"It still sounds . . ."

"What?"

"I don't know. Ordinary."

My father laughed.

"What's so funny?"

"What did you think the Winged spent their time doing?" my father asked. "Trying to overthrow the government?"

"I guess."

"You know why they don't?"

I shook my head.

"Because they'd be overthrowing themselves."

I stared for a second. "You mean . . . ?"

"Well, not completely," my father said. "They have a lot of people in their pocket, but not everyone. But the point is, these guys aren't trying to overthrow the establishment, they *are* the establishment. A massive network, everything from artists to security to bankers to politicians. And not only in the UK. We're just one piece of their network, and not even close to the most important one."

I looked at my father dubiously.

"I told you, you're not thinking big enough," he said. "The Winged are one of the most powerful factions on the planet. They count support in countries, not men. Their only real rivals are the Order of the Dragon."

"Who are they?"

"The Winged's opposite number. If the Winged are about getting what you want, the Order are about holding on to what you have. Stability instead of freedom. They and the Winged have been fighting over who gets to be top dog for hundreds of years. Remember what I told you about the Cold War? The US and their allies on one side, the Soviets on the other?"

I nodded.

"That was one front in the Winged against the Order. Not the whole war; one front. That's the kind of scale these guys work on."

I tried to wrap my head around that.

"But at the time, I didn't know any of that," my father said. "And neither did the guys I worked with. There's a big cutoff in the cult. The patronage network, the money and the parties and the circuit . . . the bottom ninety-five percent of the Winged, that's all they ever see. It's only the ones on the upper level, the guys like Byron, who know the real story. They call themselves vanguards. Lower rankers don't have any clue about what the vanguards really do—all they see is that the vanguards have all the money they could ever want, people jumping to their feet when they walk in the room, and an entry pass to every VIP event in the city. So they spend all their time trying to get into the vanguards' orbit so that they can get some of that too."

I remembered what Father Hawke had told me about the Winged's "inner circle." "Was that what you did?"

"No," my father said, shaking his head. "I just wanted to take care of you. From time to time I'd get approached for shadier stuff, but the payment they'd offer would always be things like expense accounts at a club, so you could sit in a booth and pretend you're a high roller. Stupid shit like that. So I turned them all down. I had the feeling I was probably shooting myself in the foot, cutting myself off from the fast track, but I didn't care as long as I was earning.

"But I was wrong.

"You see, I didn't understand the Winged back then. I saw how most of the guys were just in it for the money and women and parties, and I thought that was all there was to it. What I didn't get was that the ones at the very top, the vanguards... they're *believers*. It's why the Winged are so powerful. The corps might be rich, but they don't care about anything but next month's bottom line. But the vanguards, they actually believe in the cause. And so when I didn't act as corrupt as the others, I got their attention without realising it.

"So I started getting given the sensitive jobs. And I found out what the people I'd been working for were *really* like.

"The world at the top of the Winged is totally different from the layers underneath. Think of it like a very exclusive club. Hard to get into, but once you're in, you can do whatever you want for the rest of your life. And when I say whatever you want, I mean it. They go in every direction you can think of. Some of them sit in their studies writing political philosophy. Some pull strings and move money around. Some are warriors—they fight the enemies of the Winged, and they're no joke, believe me. Some are sex-and-drugs hedonists. And most are some mixture of those things.

"My new job was 'cleaner.' As in, someone who cleans up a mess. And just like everywhere else, ten percent of the people cause ninety percent of the problems, so I wasn't seeing the ones holed up in their studies, I was seeing the bad ones. I did that for maybe two years, and I saw things that'd make your hair stand on end. Remember that movie we watched together the last Christmas before I left? Where some junkie hitman's in a car and he manages to shoot one of his own partners in the face? And now the third guy's driving a car that looks like a prop from a horror movie and he's trying to figure out what the fuck to do next?"

"Yeah."

"Remember how I didn't think it was very funny?"

I nodded.

"Because I'd been in pretty much the same situation as that guy driving that car. Trust me, it's not funny. And that was just an accident. I'm not going to get into the things that were on purpose."

"Like what?"

"I don't want to talk about it," my father said. "I'm not proud of what I did in those couple of years. I didn't murder anyone, or rape anyone, or torture anyone, but I drove cars and watched doors and cleaned up problems for people who did."

I stared at my father for a second, trying to figure out how to take that. It was a disquieting thing to hear. "Do all the Winged spend their time doing stuff like that?"

"No, thank God. But they all know about it. Every now and again it spills out into the news, and you'll see people on TV saying they're shocked, *shocked*, to find out that their dear friend and colleague was doing something so horrible." My father's expression was grim. "It's bullshit. They know. They always know."

"But why? What do they want?"

"They do dirty work because it gets them in with the rich and powerful. That gives them influence, and they use that to push their agenda."

"What agenda?"

"Freedom, progress, all that stuff," my father said. "There are a hundred subgroups and they all have a different emphasis. Mostly they pull in the same direction, but when you've got a group as huge as the Winged you get a lot of little variations, and those little variations make a big difference to whoever's on the receiving end. You told me Byron already gave you his recruiting pitch, but if you went to a different member of the Winged, they'd give you a different one. Probably be about three-quarters the same, but the disagreements over the last quarter can get pretty nasty. Some of those jobs I was doing for Byron, it was other members of the Winged who were the targets."

I couldn't wait any longer. I'd been holding off on this for a while, but I'd been waiting for an answer to this for a long, long time. "Why did you disappear?"

My father was silent for a moment. "Something finally happened where I couldn't look the other way," he said at last. "I had to choose. Stay with the Winged, or leave."

"What was the 'something'?"

"You're better off not knowing."

I frowned.

"I mean that literally," my father said. "You *are* better off not knowing. Because that way, if someone from the police or the Winged asks you about it, you won't have to lie when you say you don't know."

"The police . . . ?"

"Well, probably not the police," my father amended. "The Winged couldn't pin the whole thing on me—too much mess. So they had to sweep the whole thing under the rug. In the meantime, I was gone. Had just enough time to leave you that letter before I had to run."

"Why?"

"Because I knew that the first place the Winged were going to look for me was with you," my father said. "And if they couldn't immediately catch me, their next move would be to go *after* you. These are not nice people, Stephen. They do not play by the rules. Kidnapping a kid and threatening to hurt or kill them if the parent doesn't co-operate is absolutely in their playbook."

"Then why didn't they—?"

"Because I put a lot of effort into making sure that didn't happen," my father said. "As soon as I realised that you could be a target, I started preparing. Every time I was with other guys on a job and the subject came up, I'd talk about how badly you and I were getting on and how I was thinking about just walking out and never coming back. There are probably guys in the Winged who've never even met me who think you and I absolutely hate each other, that's how hard I sold it. So if you ever do run into them, they're probably going to assume you've got the biggest case of daddy issues known to man."

"Uh, thanks."

"You're welcome. Next step was to make sure they couldn't talk to me. Pretty hard to blackmail someone if you've got no way to get in touch. I couldn't hide or guard you well enough that they couldn't get you, but I *could* disappear well enough that they couldn't find *me*. So that was what I did."

"You could have taken me with you."

"No, I couldn't."

"I would have come if you'd asked."

"Yeah, and that was why I didn't do it. You don't know what you would have been signing up for. Look, Stephen, I know your life's been hard these last few years, but no matter how tough it was, no matter how much you had to go through, you still had a *life*. You had friends, a job, a normal place to live. You didn't have to sleep in hotel rooms with a gun under your pillow."

"You could still have given me the choice," I said. I could hear the resentment in my voice, but I couldn't help it.

"No, I *couldn't*," my father said, emphasising the word. "If you'd associated yourself with me, you'd have had no chance of a normal life, *ever*. I got into this whole stupid mess because I wanted to *help* you."

"And you didn't think to at least ask?"

"No," my father said flatly. "I knew you wanted me to stay. I knew that by leaving you, your life was going to be pretty hard and lonely for a pretty long time. But when you have kids, your job is to do what's best for them, not what'll make them happy right now. I hate that I had to leave you alone for so long, and if I could go back, there are a lot of things I would have done differently. But leaving . . . that's not one of them. Given the situation, I'd do the same thing in a heartbeat. No matter how much it hurt."

I opened my mouth to fire back an angry retort, then stopped. Why was I acting like this? I'd come to talk to my father, not to fight with him. I stared down at the floor, the feelings draining away.

The silence stretched out awkwardly. "Shall I go on?" my father asked.

I nodded.

"Once I'd left, I knew Byron was going to try to find me," my father continued. "I don't think he cared personally, but that didn't matter. And I knew the first thing he'd do would be to post men to watch you. It was the same job I used to get."

"Yeah, I know. That white Ford."

"White Ford Fiesta with 2009 plates," my father agreed. "Every time I showed up, it was there. You ever wonder why it was the same car?"

". . . No?"

"I mean, that was how you were able to spot it, right? Same car, same plates, every day?"

"Yes . . ."

"So if you're watching someone, that's not the best way to do it, right? Even someone who hasn't been trained to spot tails, they see the same car outside their house every morning, they're going to catch on eventually. And it's not that hard to fix. Most of the cost of putting men on a job is the men. Having them switch cars isn't much dearer." My father looked at me. "So why do you think they didn't?"

I looked at my father.

"If you just want someone watched, you send out a guy," my father said. "If you *really* want someone watched, you send out a guy, then you send out *another* guy where he can watch anyone watching the *first* guy."

I felt stupid. All this time, and that had never occurred to me.

"The first time I came back to our house, all I saw was that white Ford," my father said. "Second time, all I saw was that white Ford. Third time, all I saw was that white Ford, and by then I was getting impatient. I knew Byron wasn't going to give up that easily. But I also knew that you were on your own in that house, and you had no idea what was going on, and I wanted to talk to you. So that night, I came back. Hoped to sneak in and spend the night talking, just like we're doing now. If I'd been more careful, I'd have waited longer, taken more precautions . . . but I didn't. I figured maybe Byron's men had got sloppy." He rolled up the sleeve of his left arm and held it up to me.

I stared at my father's forearm. There was a faint, puckered scar that I'd never seen before running from just above the elbow to just below the wrist.

My father held his arm up for a few more seconds, as if to make sure I'd got the message, then lowered it again and began rolling down his sleeve. "It was close," he said. "If I hadn't had that one extra sigl Byron's guys didn't know about . . . well, let's just say we wouldn't be having this conversation. Anyway, I learned my lesson. I sent that letter, but when I didn't get an answer I went no-contact. I knew the more times I tried to contact you, the more likely the Winged would get suspicious. My best chance—*your* best chance—was if they believed I wasn't coming back."

"But I just emailed you," I said. "And you said my account was compromised. Does that mean . . . ?"

"That's the big question, isn't it?" my dad said. "But if I had to bet on it, I'd say probably not. The first few weeks after I left, I guarantee you there was a guy reading your emails every day. But that was four years ago and the Winged have a lot of people on their shit list. Very unlikely they're still watching you after all this time. Still, that's only going to be true so long as they don't realise anything's changed. If this Mark guy tells Byron what he did, they're going to start paying you attention again. So first thing you do, when you get home, delete those emails from your folders, and you make damn sure you never mention me or the Winged in any other communications you send, email or phone or letter or anything else. There has to be absolutely no visible link between the two of us."

"Why do they want you so badly? What did you *do*?"

"Well, it's not just a matter of what I *did*."

I looked at him with eyebrows raised.

"I haven't been just sitting around the last few years," my father explained. "Let's just say I've been giving the Winged other reasons not to like me very much."

"All right," I said. "That answers the first big thing I wanted to ask you about. What about the second?"

"What's the second?"

I looked at him with eyebrows raised. "You can't guess?"

My father shook his head.

"You told me in your letter that the Winged are a cult that worships some kind of a spirit and they have demons giving them gifts."

"... Oh. That."

"Yes," I said with some asperity. "That."

"Right now I'm a bit more concerned about the guy who stabbed you."

"I kind of think there might be a bit of a connection!"

For the first time in the conversation, I saw my father hesitate. "What do you want to know?"

"I want to know the truth," I said. "Do these things really exist? Is that how the Winged get those weird powers?"

"... I'm not sure."

"What do you mean, you're not sure?"

My father was silent for a few seconds before answering. "The Winged vanguards have some abilities that are hard to explain," he said at last. "A couple of times I saw Byron talk people into things they should never have been willing to do. He didn't seem to use a sigl to do it. Maybe he was using some new kind I'd never heard of, but..."

"When I was there for that raid last year in Chancery Lane, I heard my half-brother talking to Byron about that," I said. "He claimed mind-controlling someone with drucraft was supposed to be impossible. Well, I looked it up afterwards, and as far as I can tell, he's right. Every expert says magical suggestion is something drucraft just can't do."

"Yeah, I got told the same thing. Still, a lot of Drucraft Houses have secret techniques. And the Winged have more resources than any House."

"You think that's all it is?"

"It's as good an explanation as any."

"That wasn't how you made it sound in that letter."

"That was a while ago."

"So what happened since then?" I said with a frown. This wasn't at all how I'd expected this conversation to go. I'd come here braced to hear something completely crazy. Now my dad was walking his claims back, and I wasn't sure how to take it.

"Like I said, the Winged aren't the only cult out there," my father said. "And they're called 'cults' for a reason. They don't think they're just a bunch of drucrafters. They think they're agents of some kind of god."

I hesitated a moment before replying. "Are they?"

"Who the hell knows? If you listen to these guys, they'll all try to tell you they've got some kind of secret knowledge or special power. They're the chosen ones, they're on the right side of history, whatever. It's all bullshit. As soon as your back's turned, they're giving the same speech to the next guy, trying to convince *him* that he'll have everything he wants if he just does as he's told."

I gave my dad a dubious look.

"You don't believe me?"

"I do. I'm just . . . having trouble squaring all this with what you wrote."

"When I wrote that letter, I'd been working for the Winged for nearly ten years," my dad said. "It changes your thinking, being in a cult that long. You start believing stuff that an outsider would think was crazy."

"Is that really why?" I asked. Something about my father's manner seemed off, as though he was trying to convince himself more than me.

My father looked to one side, staring at the wall of the flat. "Maybe," he said at last.

"Maybe?"

"When I started working for the Winged, I thought they were just a bunch of criminals who used the whole cult thing as a con," my father said. "Keep the gullible in line, that sort of thing. By the end, I thought they were a bunch of demon worshippers. Back then, I thought that the worst case was that some of those demons might actually be real." He paused. "Want to know what I think the worst case is now?"

I nodded.

"That we're all playing pieces on a game board the size of the universe and there are gods looming over us playing a game of death chess where the moves are our lives."

I couldn't think of how to respond to that.

"Anyway," my father said, and shook his head, seeming to throw off the thought. "I wouldn't worry about it too much. If you're trying to deal with someone more powerful than you, how they got that way doesn't really matter. That fight you had with Vermillion—does it make *that* much difference where his powers came from? If you're lying there bleeding to death, is your last thought really going to be 'Wow, I wonder how he did that'?"

"He didn't use any really special powers. Just a pair of high-tech goggles and a transparency sigl."

"He'll have more up his sleeve than that," my father noted. "So let's not give him a second chance to use them. Now I want you to go through that fight with him again, in more detail this time. After that we'll look at your home setup, so we can start making some contingency plans . . ."

CHAPTER 3

DAWN WAS BREAKING when we said our goodbyes. I didn't want to leave, and when my dad tried to shepherd me out of the door, I dug in my heels. He tried to argue that I might have been tailed and would be safer somewhere else, that I needed to wipe my old email account and set up a new one, and finally that we'd both been up all night and needed to sleep. None of it worked and I still refused to go. Only when he faithfully promised that he'd be sticking around this time, that I could come and see him whenever I wanted, and that he was never going to disappear the same way again, did I reluctantly agree.

I slipped out of the door and stood blinking on the Barbican walkway. All around, I could hear the bustle and noise of the London morning; doors opening, calls and shouts, the slow beeping of a delivery lorry backing into a bay. The sun was hidden behind grey clouds, and the air was damp and cold.

I joined the people filing out of the Barbican, heading for work. I was a little wary that someone might notice that I didn't belong, but no one looked at me twice; they all seemed distracted and isolated, too busy with their own lives to notice the boy walking quietly ahead of them. I gave the block of flats containing my father one last look, then the walls closed in around me and it was gone.

Once I made it onto the train, I relaxed slightly. The car was packed with night workers returning from their shifts, half of them slumped asleep, the rest staring blearily at their phones. Drivers from Bangladesh, cleaning women from South America and the Philippines, night watchmen from Africa; all the people who do the invisible, low-status jobs that no one above a certain income ever thinks about. There are millions of them in London, cheap labour shovelled in from all around the globe like coal into a furnace. Fuel for the machine.

I was glad to be ignored. It gave me time to think.

I'd stayed up talking with my father all night. First it had been me talking, with him quizzing me about my interactions with the Winged. He'd made me go through every meeting I'd had with Byron, as well as my fights with Mark and Vermillion. He'd broken down each fight and meeting, sometimes praising me in a way that gave me a warm flush of pride, at other times giving criticism that had made me wince.

From that point on he'd shifted into explaining/teaching mode. So many times over the past few years I'd wished I'd had him around for advice, and now I did. In fact, there had been so much advice that I was having trouble remembering it all. I'd taken notes, but I could already tell that it was going to take me days to process everything.

Eventually my dad had noticed that I was getting overwhelmed, and we'd shifted into just talking. It had been just like those old, rambling, freewheeling conversations we'd used to have, and I hadn't realised until today just how badly I'd missed them. Some of it had been connected to my work, about sigls and locating and how I'd been managing with money and with rent. Some had been more general, like our different experiences with Houses and drucraft companies. And some had just been simple catching up. Apparently my dad had a new girlfriend, though he was evasive about the details.

Still, now that I'd left, what my thoughts kept coming back to wasn't sigls, or my dad's history, or his love life. It was the part where we'd been talking about where the Winged's powers came from.

On one level, I knew it was a weird thing to get hung up on. Vermillion's attack on me had been less than two weeks ago, and it had left me bleeding to death; if I hadn't been able to stay focused enough to use my mending sigl, and if the ambulance hadn't made it in time, I'd be dead. So it wasn't really a surprise that my dad was tunnel-visioned on that, and it did make sense to focus on it instead of on weird metaphysical questions. But for some reason, those were what my mind kept drifting back to.

I remembered my dad's expression when I'd asked him if those things were real. It had been the only time in the whole night when he'd looked truly off balance. When I'd told him about Vermillion and the Winged, he'd shifted almost instantly into what I remembered as his problem-solving mode: figure out the scale of the threat, deploy short-term measures to stop things from getting worse, then start working on a long-term answer. But when I'd pressed him on the things that the Winged worshipped, he'd suddenly looked unsure. Why?

Maybe because only one of those was a problem he knew how to handle.

But did it matter? Like my dad had said, if I ended up getting stabbed to death by Vermillion, it wouldn't matter very much whether I believed in the Winged's strange cult. And I wasn't at all sure I *did* believe in it. Yesterday, while I'd been searching the

Barbican in the silence of the night, it had been easier to believe that all this crazy stuff might be real. In the grey drabness of the London morning it all felt very far away. I was on a Tube train full of commuters, going home tired from a night of no sleep, and I was already starting to wonder what I might have for breakfast. It was all very ordinary and mundane.

The train went around a bend, wheels screeching against the rails, and the lights flickered and went out. The darkness only lasted a couple of seconds, but for that brief moment the inside of the Tube carriage was black, the only illumination the scattered phone screens, their glows turning their owners' faces into eerie, inhuman masks. Then the lights came on and everything was normal again.

I shivered and looked out of the window at the blackness of the tunnel.

IT WAS SEVEN thirty when I finally stepped back through my front door. The house was quiet but for the distant sounds of the London morning. Ignas, Matis, and the others had already left, leaving the house silent and empty.

I trailed upstairs, opened my door, and was nearly knocked off my feet by a large and muscular grey tabby cat. "Ow," I told him.

Hobbes looked up at me, ears slightly flattened, and gave me a loud, complaining "mraow."

"Okay, okay, I'm sorry I left you shut in. I'll get you some food."

"MRAAAAOW."

"*Yes*, I'll let you out. Give me a second!"

Hobbes disappeared into the back garden, reappeared and head-butted me vigorously as I poured him out some cat food, then buried his face in it as soon as I put it down. I stroked him as he ate, feeling the slight kink in his hips. His bones have healed from where they were broken, but they're not quite symmetrical, and you can feel it if you run your hands over his fur. It doesn't seem to bother him.

Once Hobbes had finished eating, he hopped onto the bed, meowed at me until I scratched his head, then curled up next to me and went to sleep. I kept stroking my cat, feeling the strength of the Life essentia radiating out from the sigl at his neck, and wondered what to do.

In a way, Hobbes was where this whole thing had started. Or not started, but grown deeper and weirder and stranger, that one night last April where for a few brief hours everything had fractured and come apart. I'd seen things I shouldn't have been able to see, and made a sigl I shouldn't have been able to make, and at the end I'd passed out and slept for most of the day. And that could have been the end of it. I saw some crazy things, but honestly, if there'd been no lasting effect, I would have put the whole episode down to hallucinations caused by hunger and sleep deprivation and forgotten about it.

Except there *had* been a lasting effect.

I focused slightly, emptying my thoughts, and colours sprang into view. Grey-white wisps of essentia trailed through the air, twining down in a spiral into the tiny spark of green fire at Hobbes's neck. It took in those airy wisps and ignited them, turning them into lines of power that spread out through his muscles and limbs. They were slow, lazy, but they were always there, giving Hobbes more strength than any living creature of his size should have.

I blinked and the image was gone. I was finding it easier to call up my essentia sight these days. It was as though every time I used it, I grew a tiny bit closer to that other world.

I'd learned a lot of things in the past year. I'd learned about the Houses, about the power and privilege they commanded, and how they used it to pass their holdings down to their chosen heirs. I'd learned about the corporations who occupied the same world, sending out armies of downtrodden locators to find the Wells that they used to mass-produce the sigls that they sold to the Exchange. I'd learned about the drucraft economy, the mask that you saw in the daytime, and the dark side that took place in the shadows. And gradually, I'd learned how I fitted into it all. How I was a manifester, a drucraft rank prized among the House aristocracy but seen as a curiosity by everyone else. How my mother had been from that same aristocracy, and how she'd left and never contacted me, so that I wouldn't be in the way of the Ashford succession. And now I knew my father's part too. The mysteries that I'd been puzzling over . . . I didn't understand them all, not completely, but I thought I could finally begin to see how they fitted together.

Except one. My essentia sight.

It hadn't bothered me so much last year because I'd had so much else to worry about. Between the Ashfords and my new career, I'd been out of my depth and struggling to stay afloat, and the mystery of why I suddenly had this strange ability hadn't seemed very important compared to questions like "How am I going to stop the Ashfords from abducting me?" or "How am I going to pay my rent?" So I'd focused on immediate problems and assumed that the other one would eventually sort itself out.

But it hadn't. And I was starting to get the feeling that it might be important.

When Vermillion had attacked me the week before last, he'd said something. Right before slipping down those goggles over his eyes, he'd made a casual comment about how if I was what "they" said I was, the two of us were going to go up against each other sooner or later. It had stuck in my head, and I'd found my thoughts going back to it. The elites of the Winged were important people; my dad had said they counted support in countries, not men. Why would someone like that care about someone like me?

It wasn't because of my looks. It wasn't because I was a drucrafter. It probably wasn't because I was a manifester. It *might* be because I was in the line of succession to House Ashford, and given that my mother had specifically warned me about people trying to exploit my family status, that was probably the explanation I would have settled on . . . except that Byron had one member of House Ashford under his thumb already, and when a second had tried to join, Byron had practically laughed him out of the room. What did I have that Lucella and Tobias didn't?

No matter how I looked at it, the only thing I could think of that really made me special was my essentia sight.

But why? My essentia sight was useful—very useful—but while I was proud of what I'd accomplished this past year, I had no illusions that it made me a big fish. For all my hard work and training, anyone with enough money could just walk into the Exchange and buy a sigl that would blow my homemade ones out of the water. To make top-grade sigls, you need more than drucraft skills, you also need know-how and Wells. And that was where I came up short.

Which brought me back to where I'd started. Why did the Winged care about me?

There was one person who might know.

I'd yet to tell anyone about my essentia sight. I'd sort of vaguely brought it up with my father, in a "my sensing's much better now" sort of way, but he hadn't followed up on it—he'd been focused on the Vermillion problem, and to be fair I hadn't emphasised it very hard. But there was one person who'd as good as told me that he knew what I could do. His name was Father

Hawke, and when he'd visited me in hospital last week, he'd told me to come to him if I wanted to know more.

I hadn't taken him up on the offer. Father Hawke had helped me several times over the past year, and at this point I more or less trusted him . . . but I was afraid that if I started down this particular rabbit hole, I wouldn't like the answers.

But I was starting to think I might need them.

WEST HAM CHURCH loomed up in the darkness, a monolith of ancient stone. The wind had dropped off and the sky overhead was clear, piercing stars bright in the darkness. The air was hushed and cold.

I'd reached the churchyard and had taken a few steps onto the paving stones when I realised I was no longer being followed. I turned and looked back at Hobbes.

Hobbes was standing just outside the low churchyard wall, flicking his tail from side to side. He'd followed me tonight, as he sometimes does, but right now he was acting as if the border of the church grounds held an invisible barrier. As I watched, he backed away a couple of steps and sat.

"Well, fine," I told him. "I guess I'll see you when I come out."

The inside of the church smelled of old stone and candle wax. Lights shone from near the altar, but the rest of the great church was dark.

"Stephen," Father Hawke said. He was sitting at the other end of the nave. A book was resting on his lap, but it was closed and he was looking towards me. "Welcome."

I closed the door behind me.

"Bolt it, please."

I looked at Father Hawke questioningly. When he didn't elaborate, I reached back and pulled the cold iron bolt into its socket.

Father Hawke watched me as I approached, dark eyes glinting from a sharply planed face. He's tall enough that, even sitting, his head was only a little below mine. I sat opposite.

"I've been wondering how long it would take you," Father Hawke said.

"To come here?" I asked. The church was very quiet; the sounds of the cars going up and down Plaistow Road were muffled by the stone walls.

"To ask the right questions."

"You told me to come when I was ready to hear the answers."

Father Hawke nodded but didn't speak. He looked at me. I looked at him.

"Why do the Winged care about me?" I said at last.

"You already know the answer, I think," Father Hawke said. "You remember last year, when you came to me asking about those strange abilities certain members of the Winged seemed to have?"

I was silent.

"What did I tell you?" Father Hawke asked.

"You told me they came from spirits."

"Gifts from spiritual entities," Father Hawke corrected. "Though if you're referring to the patrons of the Winged, you should really call them demons."

"You're telling me that Lucella and Byron, the rest of the Winged . . . they've got special powers granted by demons."

"The inner circle of the Winged. Yes."

I started to answer, then stopped. To me, a "demon" was a monster you fought in fantasy games. Now Father Hawke was telling me they were real?

"How did you gain your gift?" Father Hawke asked.

"What do you mean?"

"You don't need to keep pretending, Stephen," Father Hawke said. "It's good that you're cautious, and you should *continue* to be cautious, but I've known the truth about your particular ability for some time. What I don't know is how it was granted. You aren't under any particular obligation to tell me, but I'd be very interested."

I hesitated. I'd never told anyone this story, not even Colin or my father, and I felt reluctant to start now. Part of it, as Father Hawke said, was caution—I'd had some harsh lessons last year about what could happen when I let the wrong things slip. But another part of it was that it was just too personal. I wasn't even sure that I *could* explain what had happened that night.

But I'd come too far to back out now.

"It was last year, in the spring," I told Father Hawke. "After I came to you with my cat. You told me that my best chance of saving him was a mending sigl. So I went searching for a Life Well..."

Haltingly, I told Father Hawke the story. Going out, day and night. Watching Hobbes decline as my infusions of essentia had less and less effect. How I'd stopped eating to sharpen my focus. How at the very end I'd found a temporary Life Well, but one that had been too weak to make the sigl I needed; how I'd tried anyway and failed.

When I got to what had happened afterwards, though, my story became disjointed. Thoughts splintering like glass. Stars blazing with colours beyond sight. Falling into the sky, held to earth by a thread.

"Then when I tried the second time, it felt . . . easy," I said at last. "I made the sigl, went home, and used it. Then I fell asleep for a long time."

Father Hawke had been listening in silence. Only the intensity of his gaze and the way he'd been leaning forward at a slight angle betrayed how focused he was. "Fascinating," he said at last. "And afterwards?"

"That was it," I said. "When I woke up the next day, everything was back to normal. Except I could see essentia. I don't think it's actually made my sensing ability any stronger—my range is the same, the kinds of essentia I can pick up are the same. But instead of just feeling them, I see them as well."

"Do you know why sensing is so difficult to learn?"

"I always just thought I was bad at it."

"The answer's in the name," Father Hawke said. "It's literally its own sense. Your other senses seem natural because you've spent your entire life practising them; when you start learning drucraft, you're starting from scratch. But *why* do you think it takes so much work? A baby doesn't need to be taught to hear. Why do you think everyone can't do the same with essentia? Just detect it naturally, from birth, the same way they can hear sounds?"

I shook my head.

"The short answer is that it's because humans simply aren't very good at it," Father Hawke said. "For all of our other senses, we have a dedicated part of our brain that interprets the information the sense gives us, and then presents it to us in a format that our mind can understand. For instance, there's a section at the back of our brain called the occipital lobe that takes in and processes the raw data from our eyes. And it's actually fantastically sophisticated. Have you ever thought about just how *much* information your eyes give you? Take one glance at a room, and you can take in its shape and colour and size, see how bright it is and how many people are inside, and even identify them, just from their faces. And yet, you can do all that in less than a second. It's an amazing ability."

I'd never thought about it that way. "I . . . guess it is."

"Humans don't have any such equivalent for sensing essentia," Father Hawke said. "There's no part of our brain that does all the hard work of processing and organising the information. And so we have to learn it all by ourselves. Slowly, patiently, bit by bit.

And even then, we're forever limited by our natural capabilities, in the same way that our sense of smell can never match that of a dog, even if we train our entire lives.

"Your particular ability, I think, gives a way around that. It takes the raw data from your sensing and transfers it to the occipital lobe in such a way as to let your brain use all that sophisticated visual processing apparatus to translate the information into a form you can quickly and easily understand. The more you improve your sensing, the more useful it'll become. It's quite a remarkable gift."

"Huh," I said. I sat thinking for a little while, going over what Father Hawke had said. "So it . . . routes my sensing through the part of my brain that lets me see, even though I'm not really seeing?"

"Correct."

"But you just said human brains *don't* work like that."

"Correct."

"So how come I can do it?"

"You've been altered."

"Altered?"

"Possibly by direct modifications to your brain, possibly something more subtle," Father Hawke said. "The brain modification theory is rather an obvious one, though, so as I said, I'd very much recommend that you continue to keep the details of your ability a secret. Modifying human subjects to more effectively use or perceive essentia has been a dream of Life drucraft researchers for quite some time, and there are plenty of companies who'd happily pay millions for the chance to study your gift. And when I say 'study,' I mean take your brain apart to see how it works, preferably while you're still conscious."

Well, *that* was a horrifying little image to keep me up at night. I pushed it out of my mind. "Altered by who?"

"By *what*," Father Hawke corrected. "And I already told you."

I hesitated. "A demon," I said at last. I'd meant to sound sceptical—the idea of some spirit floating around and just deciding to "alter" me seemed ridiculous—but now that I actually said it out loud, it didn't sound ridiculous. It sounded kind of terrifying.

"Perhaps. But whatever entity gave you your particular gift, I don't believe it was one of the patrons of the Winged."

Well, that was a relief, but . . . *No! I don't believe in this stuff.* "Why?"

"Because of the nature of the gift," Father Hawke explained. "Spirits are mysterious, and even the lowest of them is an entity we could never truly comprehend. But we can, to some extent, understand the gifts they bring. And with all of the major cults, their patron spirits give gifts that tend to follow certain patterns." Father Hawke leant back in his seat slightly. "In the case of the Winged, their gifts always seem to grant power in a *social* context. The ability to charm, to seduce, to dominate. It's hard to imagine a servant of—a demon of the Winged ever granting one of their followers the ability to better perceive the immaterial."

"If it wasn't from the Winged, what was it?"

"Ah," Father Hawke said. "This is where we get into the realm of guesswork. Spiritual gifts seem to fall into two categories . . . or perhaps it's more accurate to say that they're granted for one of two *reasons*. The first kind, the more common, are granted to those who embody something. Think of the subject of a cult's worship as representing a . . . state of being, a concept. Those chosen for gifts are those who approach that state most closely. In the case of the Winged, it's the rejection of limits. The desire to be more, to do more, to be capable of anything . . . those who draw attention are those with the greatest ambitions, the most intense desires. It's a similar story with the other cults. It's not always easy to say why one is chosen and another isn't, but they're always extreme personalities.

"The second kind of gifts are rarer. They might be granted to those who embody a particular quality, but they might just as well be granted to those who seem quite ordinary. What marks these people out isn't what they are, but what they do. Or, to be more accurate, what they're *going* to do. They are gifts granted for a purpose." Father Hawke looked at me. "I believe your gift is of this second type."

"A purpose?"

"I believe so."

"What purpose?"

"No idea."

"What?"

Father Hawke looked at me cheerfully.

"Wait, after all that, you can't tell me the one part that actually *matters*?"

"Stephen," Father Hawke said, "I'm afraid that the people granted these gifts typically go their entire lives without ever being quite sure of their purpose."

"But this doesn't make any sense," I said in frustration. "You're saying this . . . thing, whatever, it granted me this ability because it wanted me to do something. If it actually wanted that, wouldn't it just *tell* me?"

Father Hawke looked at me for a few seconds. "You still don't understand."

"Understand what?"

"When you walked to this church tonight," Father Hawke said, "how many insects did you pass on the way?"

"What?"

"Insects. Ants, beetles, woodlice. How many?"

"I don't know. A lot."

Father Hawke nodded. "Imagine that, on your way here, you saw an insect struggling in a puddle. If you reached down, picked it up, and placed it somewhere dry ... would you have explained your reasons to it? Would it have been able to understand you if you had?"

I tried to think of how to answer that.

"The entities that grant these gifts are as far above you as you are above an ant," Father Hawke said. "Their motives are unknowable to us, just as our motives are unknowable to an ant. They are older than we can imagine and exist on a level none of us can truly comprehend. All we can do is piece together what we can from the glimpses offered to us."

I looked back at Father Hawke's dark eyes. All of a sudden, the church seemed very cold.

"Look at what you've been given, and at the challenges you have faced," Father Hawke told me. "In time, I believe your purpose will become clear."

I sat there for a few seconds more, then rose to my feet and walked away. Halfway to the church door, I stopped and turned. "Why should I do what this thing wants?"

"All of us serve something greater than ourselves," Father Hawke replied. "The only choices given to us are what to serve, and how willingly to do so." He smiled slightly. "Choose wisely."

I started to turn away.

"Oh, Stephen?" Father Hawke said. "While you're deciding ... take a moment to consider what would have happened if that entity *hadn't* reached down to you that night." Father Hawke nodded towards the door. "Until next time."

THE SOUNDS OF the city returned as the church door swung closed behind me, distant but clear. Stars shone down coldly from above.

Hobbes was waiting for me just beyond the churchyard boundary, his tail curled around his legs. "Mraow," he announced as I walked out.

"Hey, you," I said tiredly. I sat down on the low wall, on the boundary between the churchyard and the street. Hobbes rubbed his cheek against me, and I reached down to stroke him, letting him twine around my legs.

"I still don't think I really believe any of this," I told Hobbes.

Hobbes blinked up at me, eyes gleaming in the darkness. Around him, hovering at the edge of my vision, a green aura glowed.

I sighed and scratched his head. Hobbes closed his eyes happily.

Take a moment to consider what would have happened . . .

Hobbes would have been dead. I might have been too. Instead he'd survived, all because I'd changed.

No, not changed. Been *altered*.

"Why?" I said aloud.

Their motives are unknowable to us, just as our motives are unknowable to an ant.

"I didn't ask for any of this," I said into the night. "All I wanted was to save my cat, and find my dad, and . . ."

I trailed off, an answer coming unbidden to my mind. *And you got both those things.*

What would the price for them be?

A chill went through me and I shivered. The wall I was sitting on was old and cracked and, on an impulse, I leant down close. After a few seconds I saw movement: a tiny ant, scrambling its way along the pebbles and cracks of the wall.

I looked at the insect for a moment, then placed a finger down to block its path. The ant came up against the side of my finger and stopped, antennae probing. It wavered for a few seconds, then changed direction, working its way around my fingertip. Once it was clear, it carried along the way it had been going, crawling along the top of the wall until it disappeared into the darkness of the night.

I stared after it for a few seconds, the cold breeze blowing through the churchyard and ruffling my hair. At last I rose to my feet, took a final look at the church tower reaching up into the sky, then turned my feet towards home, Hobbes trotting at my side.

CHAPTER 4

THE NEXT DAY, I was back to work.

For a couple of months now, I'd had a part-time job bodyguarding Calhoun Ashford, the current heir of House Ashford and my first cousin once removed, as well as his fiancée, Johanna Meusel. To be honest, calling myself a "bodyguard" is stretching it—when you hear that word, you think of some ex-squaddie built like a brick shithouse, not a slender twenty-one-year-old who's five foot eight at a stretch. But Calhoun wasn't complaining, and given the current state of my bank balance, neither was I.

Tonight would be the fifth time I'd be escorting Calhoun and Johanna on one of their dates, and by this point I had it down to a routine. First, I called Hendrik, Johanna's chief of security, to get the venue details and confirmation of booking. Next, I looked the place up online to get an idea of the layout and how crowded it was likely to be. It was a restaurant this time, a French place just north of St. Paul's. Its hours were six to nine thirty, and the table was booked for seven. I left at five.

The restaurant was a huge, blocky thing of weathered stone, with gold-and-purple lettering and awnings. I got a chilly reception from the doorman, but he thawed a bit once I dropped the name "Ashford." I took a quick look inside, asked for Calhoun and Johanna's table, checked it for cameras (long story), then thanked the rather bemused-looking waiter and went back outside to wait.

Calhoun's car pulled up outside the restaurant at seven p.m. on the dot. It was a long, sleek saloon, navy blue with silver trim. He gave me a nod as he got out of the back seat but didn't come over to chat. A little cold, but, given what we'd been up to last time we'd met, I was happy for him to keep his distance—I really didn't want anyone asking too many questions about what had happened last Sunday.

Watching Calhoun show up for these events always makes me feel a bit inadequate. I grew up being told I was good-looking, but Calhoun looks like a prince out of a fairy tale. He's ridiculously handsome, six feet tall with snow-white hair, and dresses like someone out of a period drama. He's also got more sigls than me, is a better-trained drucrafter than me, has a higher essentia capacity than me, and is the heir to House Ashford, who are rich enough that I've never bothered to find out exactly *how* rich because the number would be totally meaningless. I don't think I'm an especially envious person, but when you run into someone who's got all the things that make you special and is better than you at literally *all* of them, it's hard not to find it a bit annoying.

Walking at Calhoun's side was Johanna, blonde and blue-eyed, as beautiful as Calhoun is handsome. Johanna's my age and the only daughter of House Meusel, a drucraft house from eastern Germany with connections to the Ashfords. The relationship between Calhoun and Johanna had been floated from the start as a marriage alliance, and I still didn't know how the two of them actually felt about each other. Johanna gave me a smile as they passed.

Behind them both was Hendrik, bulky and dark-haired, with eyes that moved constantly over the surroundings. Unlike the other two, he didn't give me a smile or nod; his eyes swept over and past me, scanning for threats. He followed Calhoun and Johanna into the restaurant, closing the door behind them.

And after that, there was nothing much to do.

Working security is weird. You're paid to stop trouble, but ninety-nine percent of the time there isn't any trouble to stop, meaning that it doesn't actually make any difference whether you do your job well or badly. It's easy to get bored and let your mind wander... which means that when that one percent chance *does* come up, all too often you aren't paying attention. And it didn't help that in my case I didn't have a very clear job description in the first place. Although Calhoun had never quite come out and said it, the real reason he'd hired me was to guard against his own family. Problem was, while he was definitely right to worry about his family moving against him, it was hard to figure out how they'd do it. My half-brother and Calhoun's half-sister had, between them, made three different attempts to ruin Calhoun's life over the past year, and those were just the ones I knew of. But they'd all been completely different plots that had worked in completely different ways. Off the top of my head, I couldn't see how someone standing guard outside the restaurant Calhoun was eating in would have stopped any of them.

But it was his money, so as long as he was paying me to stand out here, I wasn't arguing. Instead my thoughts drifted back to what Father Hawke had told me last night.

I've never believed in anything supernatural. I suppose that sounds weird, given what I do—most people think of drucraft as some crazy out-there conspiracy theory, in the same ballpark as ghosts and UFOs and angels sending messages to your phone. But I grew up with this stuff. To me, essentia is as real as light or gravity, and drucraft is as real as any art or skill. Saying you don't believe in drucraft is like saying you don't believe in boxing. I know it's real, and I'm good at it.

But, as I was only now starting to realise, one result of that was that I'd never really had to grapple with these sorts of questions. My dad hadn't brought me up to be religious—I had the general impression he was agnostic, though I'd never asked. School had mostly avoided the whole subject; the main message I got from there was that the purpose of life was to get high marks so you can go to a better school. And so I'd grown up focused on things that were tangible, that felt real. Drucraft, sigls, my friends, my dad, my home, my cat. And that had been enough.

Now Father Hawke and my father's letter were suddenly telling me that *wasn't* enough, that there was this other world of spirits and demons. And I had no idea how to deal with it. Had I really been given my essentia sight by some kind of spirit? How could I know for sure? And what was I supposed to do about it?

I let out a frustrated breath and shook my head. This felt impossible. I was totally out of my depth with this stuff, and I knew it. Maybe I should be worrying about problems I could actually do something about, such as money.

The money problem was one that I'd been dealing with ever since my dad left, a constant voice in the back of my mind asking *how much does this cost? What bills are coming up? Is the number in my bank account going up or down?* Working for Calhoun earned me £45 an hour, which was the highest hourly wage I'd ever earned—far better than my average per hour from locating, and more than four times what I'd earned in the Civil Service. And I could charge for the time I spent researching the venues and travelling, which I did. But even if I was claiming for a full six hours per date, that only earned me £270.

£270 a week was enough to pay my rent and bills. Add in my income from locating Wells, and it put me in the black... as long as nothing went wrong. Trouble was, for the past year "and then something went wrong" had pretty much been the story of my life. The armour vest had been £600, the drone I'd bought with Colin had been a hundred more, and then there had been those vet bills... my bank balance wasn't plummeting, but it was fluctuating enough to make me worry.

Times like this, it was hard not to resent Calhoun and Johanna. Rich people get to ignore this stuff. If food prices go up or the boiler breaks or there's no work for a couple of months, then oh well, no big deal. For me, any of those things is a potential disaster, and I'm painfully aware that it'd really only take a couple of them one after the other to push me into debt-and-overdraft territory. I don't *like* tallying up costs for everything and measuring them against how much I'm earning that week and always keeping an eye on the number in my bank account. But unless I want something worse to happen, I don't have a choice.

And so I waited.

Around eight thirty, my phone buzzed, and I glanced down to see a text from Hendrik saying that they were coming out. I pushed myself off from the wall I'd been leaning against and stretched, working the kinks out of my muscles.

Calhoun's car pulled up in front of the restaurant. The driver got out, then hurried away across the road, disappearing into the shadows of the trees at the centre of the square.

I watched the man go, absent-mindedly thinking over the money problem. There *was* an alternative. Up until now, with my locating work, I'd more or less followed the crowd. Even when I'd gone on raids, I'd only done so on other people's orders. But for a couple of months, I'd been turning over in my mind the thought of striking out on my own.

It was dangerous. There's a reason most people follow the crowd: it's a hell of a lot safer. But in a lot of ways, it felt as though my locating career had gone as far as it could go. Launching my own raids was risky, but if I kept going the way I had been, I'd just end up in a holding pattern, hoping something would change when there was no reason to expect that it ever . . .

. . . wait. Why had that driver left the car?

I frowned, coming awake. The car sat in front of the restaurant, fifty feet away from me. There was no sign of the driver. Shouldn't he be waiting for Calhoun and Johanna?

I took a step towards the car . . . and stopped. The car hadn't moved, but all of a sudden some warning had gone off inside my mind. I replayed the last couple of minutes in my mind. The message from Hendrik, the way the car had pulled up, the driver—

The driver. Why had he hurried away?

Behind me, I heard the door open, the sounds of clinking glasses and cutlery swirling out into the night. Johanna's voice sounded, clear and amused with her German accent. "—have to have *something* you like," she was saying with a hint of laughter. "All you've been telling me is what these other people prefer. You haven't said—"

I hesitated an instant, then held out my arm. "Wait."

Johanna and Calhoun paused. They'd been walking out of the restaurant, Johanna in the middle of donning her fur-lined coat; now they turned their attention towards me. "What's wrong?" Calhoun asked me as the door swung closed behind him.

"The driver's gone," I told him.

I felt foolish as soon as the words were out of my mouth. This wasn't my job. Hendrik had told me right at the beginning: he'd handle all the *real* security, all I had to do was watch out for Tobias and Lucella. I was going to look really stupid if—

Hendrik stepped up next to me. "Gone where?"

"I don't know. He just pulled up, got out and crossed the road, and . . . didn't come back."

"Was it the same driver?"

"I don't know."

"The driver who brought us here was an Ashford armsman," Hendrik said. Although he was talking to me, his eyes were fixed on the car, and I suddenly noticed that he was standing exactly between it and Johanna. "English, buzz cut, one ninety, black suit with Ashford coat of arms on left breast. Was that the man you saw get out?"

I hesitated, thinking back over the few seconds in which I'd seen that driver. ". . . No. He was shorter, and he wasn't wearing a suit. And he looked Indian or Pakistani."

"Back inside," Hendrik told Johanna.

Johanna didn't hesitate for an instant. "Come on, Calhoun," she said, slipping her hand into his, then backing up to the doors. Calhoun frowned but let himself be drawn inside.

"Stay with them," Hendrik told me.

Something about Hendrik's tone of voice made me obey instantly. It was the tone my dad had used when I was helping him with a job—do it now and don't ask questions. In the last glimpse I caught of Hendrik as I followed Calhoun and Johanna back inside, I saw him slip his hand inside his jacket.

The inside of the restaurant was warm, with wooden floors lit in yellow and gold. A waiter in a spotless outfit came up to us instantly. "Ah, Lady Meusel. Did you forget something?"

"No, no, nothing like that," Johanna said with a smile. "We're just having some problems with our transport. Could we use your back door?"

"Of course! It's an unmarked door, very discreet."

"Thank you very much."

The waiter moved away. "Stephen?" Johanna asked me. "Where *is* the back door?"

"Ah . . . through the dining area, down the hall." We were still watching the front door, waiting for Hendrik. I ran through a mental inventory of my sigls. Slam and light on my left hand, flash and haywire on my right, strength and lightfoot on the cord around my neck. I sent a pulse of essentia into my strength sigl and felt it activate.

"What's going on?" Calhoun asked Johanna with a frown. He glanced at me as he did, and a moment later I saw the green glow of Life essentia spring up around him as well.

The front door stayed closed. There was no sign of Hendrik, and all of a sudden the silence was starting to feel ominous. What was—?

There was a deep echoing *bompf* from out in the street, like a giant's cough.

Hendrik burst through the door, not quite breaking into a run, his right hand still inside his jacket. "Move," he told Johanna, his voice clipped.

Johanna pointed towards where I'd told her the door was. Hendrik strode past. Calhoun and I shared a look and followed.

We hurried through the restaurant. A few of the guests and waiters were looking towards the street, but their expressions were puzzled rather than alarmed; no one seemed to be quite sure what was happening. I had a brief impression of circular tables, huge gold-edged plates with tiny morsels of food laid out on them, then we were at the back door, unmarked and nondescript with a fire exit sign. "Where's the nearest train station?" Hendrik asked me.

I had to think, but luckily we weren't far from where I'd met my dad. "Barbican. Out through that door and keep going straight until you get onto Long Lane."

"Wait twenty seconds, then follow," Hendrik told me. He slipped through the door, letting a gust of cold air into the restaurant before it swung closed behind him.

What had that noise been? I didn't quite ask. *An explosion? What was Hendrik doing out there?*

A moment later I realised: he was looking for the next threat. I was still behind, but I was catching up. I looked at Calhoun. "You ready?"

Calhoun gave a curt nod. He'd slipped a gauntlet onto his right hand. "Ready."

I took a breath, then stepped outside.

Cold air hit me, the chill feeling stronger after the warmth of the restaurant. The back door led out into a dark courtyard, tree branches casting alternating patterns of light and shadow on the flagstones. I couldn't spot Hendrik at first glance and focused on my essentia sight; the green glow of Life essentia sprang out in the darkness and I turned my head to see him pressed up against the tree trunk.

"Stephen, Calhoun." Hendrik's voice was low, pitched to carry. "Get her to the station."

I hesitated. Behind me, Calhoun did the same.

Hendrik's voice sharpened. "Go!"

Then Johanna was there, slipping in between us as casually as if she were out for an evening stroll. "Come on, Calhoun," she told him. "Aren't you going to walk me home?" She strode off towards the corner of the courtyard; I couldn't make out where she was heading, but she moved confidently, and Calhoun moved quickly to stay ahead of her.

I hurried after them. Hendrik stayed very still as we passed, his head turned towards the restaurant. Our footsteps rang on the flagstones; I could hear chatter from the direction of the street, but there were no shouts or raised voices. As we reached the edge of the courtyard a huge church loomed up out of the night, dark and silent. A gate led into a side street.

I followed Calhoun and Johanna out into the street, trying to watch in all directions at once. The sounds of the night city pressed in, making it hard to listen for danger. Hendrik had disappeared in the darkness behind us; if he was still there, I couldn't see—

I felt a flash of essentia from behind us, there and gone.

I stopped at the corner of the church, looking back. The gate back into the courtyard was open, and just for an instant my feet itched to take me back through it. Somehow I felt as if my place was *there*, fighting that thing, not running away—

"Stephen?" Johanna's voice floated out of the darkness. "Let's not hang around, all right?"

I shook myself and the moment was gone. I turned to rejoin Calhoun and Johanna, and the three of us moved quickly away down the narrow street, leaving the restaurant behind.

IT TOOK US maybe three minutes to make the journey to Barbican station, and I spent every second trying to look in every direction at once, wondering if someone would try to finish the job that explosion had started. Once we reached the station, I breathed a little easier. The station entrance was narrow, a square concrete cave mouth with a walkway above, and there was only one way in. Calhoun and I took up positions flanking the entrance. Johanna waited a little further inside.

"I don't like running away like this," Calhoun said.

"You get used to it," I told him without looking around. I was still watching the entrance. Men and women were passing in and out, giving us the occasional curious look, but none stopped to talk. There was no sign of Hendrik.

"We don't even know if anyone was there," Calhoun said.

"Hendrik told us to go," Johanna said.

"You have a lot of faith in him," Calhoun said.

"He's been my bodyguard since I was a little girl," Johanna said. Her voice was absent, as if she was trying to figure something out. "He doesn't give orders very often, but when he does, you should listen."

I glanced back to see that Johanna's eyes were fixed on the entrance, just as mine had been. Her face was calm, but as I took a second look I saw that her right hand was gripping her dress.

Minutes passed.

"I'm going back," Calhoun said.

Johanna took hold of Calhoun's arm. "No."

Calhoun frowned at her. "I'm not helpless, Johanna."

"Hendrik knows what he's doing," Johanna said. Her voice was steady and clear; if I hadn't seen those clenched fingers, I would have thought she was calm. "If he needed your help, he would have said so."

Calhoun looked as if he wanted to move, but Johanna didn't let go of his arm. I saw his eyes flick between Johanna and the entrance, but in the end, he stayed where he was.

Time ticked by. With every passing minute, I grew more tense. What was going on back there? Maybe I should leave Calhoun with Johanna and go to—

And then Hendrik came striding around the corner. I glanced back just in time to see a flash of relief on Johanna's face, there and gone in an instant. "What happened?" Calhoun asked him.

"We're clear," Hendrik said, and nodded towards the tunnel behind us. "Let's get downstairs."

We passed through the ticket gates and then down the escalator towards the platforms. Hendrik talked as we travelled, relaying the story in as few words as possible.

"How do you know there were two?" Calhoun asked. He had to raise his voice slightly to be heard over the noise of the escalator and the departing train below.

"At least two," Hendrik said. He didn't look at Calhoun; he was watching the top of the escalator behind us. "Driver and one other."

"One other?" I asked, wondering if Hendrik would reply. He'd answered Calhoun's questions, but I wasn't Calhoun.

"On the roof."

Calhoun frowned. "Who?"

"Dunno."

"What?"

"Didn't see 'em."

"Then what *did* you see?" Johanna asked.

"They moved when you crossed the courtyard," Hendrik said. "I waited to see if they'd follow. They didn't."

We reached the bottom of the escalator and stepped off onto the platform level. The fading roar of a departing train was echoing through the tunnel, warm air gusting past to fill the wake of the train's passage. "So they . . . what?" Calhoun asked. "Just watched us go?"

"That doesn't make sense," I said. "Why would they set off a bomb then watch as we walked away? It *was* a bomb, right?"

Hendrik nodded.

"Maybe they'd accomplished their objective?" Johanna said thoughtfully. She wasn't acting at all the way I'd have expected her to react to nearly being blown up. "Two different factions, maybe? One setting the bomb, one just watching . . . ?"

Hendrik gave her a look.

"All right, it's a bit unlikely," Johanna admitted. "Maybe a probing attack, then. When they saw they couldn't get an easy kill, they backed off rather than get into a serious fight."

Hendrik didn't look convinced. We walked out onto the westbound platform. The dot matrix indicator read HAMMERSMITH—3 MINS, CHECK FRONT OF TRAIN—6 MINS.

"Who do you think they were after?" I asked.

"I was just wondering that," Johanna said. She gave Calhoun a cheerful look. "Want to compare lists of who wants us dead? See whose is longer?"

Calhoun frowned at her. "This isn't funny."

"Oh, lighten up," Johanna said with a smile.

"Bomb location," Hendrik suggested.

I gave him a puzzled look.

"He means we can check to see where the bomb was placed," Johanna explained. "If it was under the right rear seat, that's where Calhoun sits. If it was under the left rear seat, that's my usual place. And if it was under the front passenger seat, then that would be Hendrik, but I don't *think* there's anyone in London who wants to kill you?"

"Not at the moment," Hendrik told her.

"Let's get you home," Calhoun told Johanna.

"Why don't I go back with you?" Johanna suggested.

"I think we should get you somewhere safe."

"While you go and talk with your uncle?"

"Yes . . ."

"If I'm going to be joining your family," Johanna said, "don't you think I should be in the room for discussions like that?"

"That's..." Calhoun looked harassed. "Let's just get you back to the hotel safely, all right?"

Johanna folded her arms with a frown. The air stirred and I glanced down the tunnel to see the glint of headlights on the rail.

CALHOUN AND JOHANNA were still arguing when the train pulled into King's Cross. Calhoun, Johanna, and Hendrik disembarked, and Hendrik (who'd been staying out of the argument) drew me aside to tell me that he'd take it from here. I watched the three of them disappear into the Saturday night crowds, then crossed to the other platform and took an eastbound train home.

The train ride back let me gather my thoughts a bit. It was only finally sinking in that I'd just survived a bombing. London's got a long history of being bombed by some group or other, but it was the first time I'd actually experienced one myself.

It hadn't been anything like I'd expected. When you see bombs going off on TV, there's always this long build-up. You get warnings about what you're about to see, leading up to some huge dramatic explosion, followed by long drawn-out shots of blazing wreckage and people running around and shouting. Now that I'd actually been in one, the main thing that struck me was how *confused* it had been. I hadn't even realised the bomb had been there until well after it had gone off, and I was pretty sure that none of the people in the restaurant had clocked what was going on at all. The explosion had been over in an instant, leaving people looking around in puzzlement and trying to figure out what had just happened. I'd been right at the centre of the whole thing, and I hadn't even seen what had happened to the car!

Was this what it was like dealing with this sort of thing for real? One brief flash of danger, then thirty minutes of running away? Even Hendrik, who'd been the first to figure out what was really going on, hadn't seemed to know much more.

I spent the rest of the journey back turning it over in my mind, without coming up with any insights. I had no idea who'd set the bomb or why; all I was left with was a feeling of disconnection and unease. I went home and collapsed into bed.

I WOKE UP the next morning to Hobbes's meows. As I fed him, I opened my old laptop and went to the BBC news website, clicked on UK, then when I didn't see anything clicked on Regions, London and South East, and then London. Corrosive liquid had been thrown at a girl in Tower Hamlets. Construction on the HS2 line was being delayed yet again. A man had raped and killed an NHS worker in West London. No mention of explosions.

I tried social media sites. There were a handful of posts asking about a disturbance near Smithfield. Some people were reporting that the area had been closed off with police tape, but that was all.

I frowned, leaning back from my laptop. Why wasn't there anything in the news? Maybe the police were keeping it quiet while they investigated? If that was the case, they might come and question me too . . .

My phone buzzed with a message. I glanced over.

REPORT TO CHARLES ASHFORD IMMEDIATELY

I grimaced. *Might have been better off with the police.*

CHAPTER 5

THE ASHFORD MANSION is on The Bishops Avenue, north of Hampstead Heath. It's several storeys high, with carefully tended gardens that extend to the front and back; the buds on the rhododendrons were showing, and the trees formed a leafy green umbrella that muffled the sounds of the road. If you look at it from the outside, it's really beautiful. Unfortunately, I have to deal with the people who live inside it.

"Tell me what happened last night," Charles Ashford ordered.

"What, just me this time?" I said, glancing around the study. The last time I'd been pulled in for one of these interrogations, Tobias and Lucella had been here too. The shelves filled with books and the map of the United Kingdom were much as I remembered, though I had a feeling there were a few more pins in the map.

"Were you hoping for someone else to take the blame?" Charles said. "Too bad. Now get on with it, I don't have all day."

I told Charles the story. It was easier than usual since I didn't have to hide anything.

"... and then I went home and didn't hear anything else until you called me in this morning," I finished.

Charles continued writing at his desk.

"So is that it?" I asked.

"For the moment."

"Kind of surprised you're not trying to accuse me of planting that bomb."

"You didn't have the opportunity," Charles remarked without raising his eyes. "I checked."

Charles is the head of House Ashford, neatly dressed, with a square grey beard and cold blue eyes. He looks in his mid-fifties, but according to my mother he's sixty-nine, and his age is the reason for a lot of what's been happening over the past year. Charles needs an heir to take over the House Ashford leadership, and, as of last autumn, that heir is Calhoun.

For now.

"Calhoun reported his version of events last night," Charles said. "Johanna Meusel and her head of security, Hendrik Wolf, supplied a joint statement a few hours later. The detective chief inspector gave me a summary of the police's findings this morning." He glanced at me, eyes sharp and clear. "Fortunately for you, your account doesn't contradict any of them."

"So if you're done trying to blame me for this," I said, "any chance I could find out what actually happened?"

"A small explosive device was detonated in Calhoun's car. According to the DCI, it was an improvised bomb with no casing, resulting in no fragmentation and the blast being largely contained. There were no injuries. If the car had been occupied, it would have been a different story."

I wondered whether my warning had made a difference. I didn't bother bringing it up to Charles. Knowing him, he'd probably say it was my fault for not noticing faster.

"Now, think carefully before you answer this next question," Charles said. "Did you tell anyone that Calhoun and Johanna would be at that restaurant last night?"

"No."

"Are you sure?"

"I didn't find out where they were going until yesterday morning," I told Charles. "I had less than seven hours between finding out and setting off. So no, I didn't spend that time rushing around telling people about it."

Charles stared at me. I met his gaze without flinching.

In the end it was Charles who looked away. "You can go."

"... Really?"

"I'll get around to looking at your employment status at some point, since Calhoun seems to have decided that it's an appropriate use of House funds to hire you as a bodyguard," Charles said, picking up his pen and returning to his papers. "But right now I've got more pressing matters." He waved his hand in the direction of the door. "Off with you."

I took a step towards the door, then stopped. I stood there for a moment, thinking, then turned back, walked to the chair in front of Charles's desk, and sat down.

The scratching of Charles's pen stopped, and his eyes rose to rest on me. "Is there something wrong with your ears?"

"Who planted that bomb?" I asked.

"I don't really see how that's any of your business."

"We had a deal, remember?" I said. "You'd spend an hour or two telling me about the drucraft world every month or so. It's been more than a month."

Charles gave me an exasperated look. *"Now?"*

"You don't think this counts as important?"

"It's why *you* see it as important that I'm wondering about. As I recall, you spent most of our last conversation questioning me about shady jobs for your old corporation. Given that you don't get paid for investigating crimes, I'm struggling to see why it's any of your business."

"I do care about things other than money," I said with some asperity. "And even if I didn't, you might have noticed that your family has a bit of a track record of dragging me into their problems."

Charles sighed. "The answer is that we don't know."

"What are you going to do?"

"Nothing."

I looked at Charles.

"You seem confused," Charles told me.

"I just..." I said. "Okay, look. How many times now has something like this happened? Someone tries to hurt or kill or generally ruin the day of someone in this family—usually me, by the way—and I end up in this study telling you about it. And you do... nothing."

"Is that what you think I do all day?" Charles asked.

"You're always saying how busy you are," I said. "But I never seem to see you actually *do* anything."

"And what do you think I should be doing?"

"I don't know. Finding out who did it?"

"The police are investigating the attack from their end," Charles said. "Our men are investigating it from ours. How do you think I should be contributing to that? Ringing them up every hour?"

"... I don't know."

Charles looked at me with faint contempt. "You don't know."

Something about his tone pushed me over the edge. It was how *patronising* he sounded, like I was a stupid little child. "Okay, you know what? I think you have no idea of anything that goes on outside this house. Scratch that, I don't think you have any idea of what goes on outside this *room*. I have to go out every day and work my arse off just to earn a living. Meanwhile, you sit behind that desk and give orders and act like everything's going to work out the way you want it to."

Charles looked back at me, and I clenched my jaw, suddenly wishing I'd kept my mouth shut. That had been a really stupid thing to say. But I was just so *tired* of being pushed around, kept in the dark, and bullied and threatened. I could have been killed last night, and this guy was treating me like a stupid child.

. . . I still should have kept my mouth shut. *He's going to be angry.*

But when Charles spoke, his voice was calm. "Are you talking about Tobias and Lucella?"

I didn't answer.

"You said 'orders.' As I recall, they're the only two other people you've seen me issuing orders to. So I presume they're the ones you're thinking of?"

". . . Yes."

Charles nodded. "Until a year ago, you didn't even know that Tobias and Lucella existed. Since then, you've had less than a dozen encounters with them both. So go on, Stephen, give me the benefit of your great experience. What do you know about them that I don't?"

"I know that your big threat to them last year did sod all," I told Charles. "Remember when you told them you'd disinherit them if anything happened to Calhoun? Well, it's been barely six months and Tobias is right back to his exact same tricks, he's just being very slightly more subtle about it. As for Lucella . . . you don't even want to *know* what's going on with her."

"Stick a pin in that one, we'll be coming back to it. But let's not get distracted. Are you saying Tobias or Lucella are responsible for last night's bomb?"

"Why shouldn't I? You're right, I've only known them for a

year, but you know what? In that time, they've made three tries at getting rid of Calhoun, one way or another, and those are just the ones I know about. One of which, by the way, involved Lucella trying to get him shot in the head. When a bomb goes off in his car . . . yeah, I'd say they're a pretty obvious place to look."

"So you think Tobias and Lucella are trying to murder Calhoun, and I'm doing nothing about it," Charles said. "Does that sum it up?"

"They've also tried to murder *me*, not that you seem to care," I said. "But yeah, it does. They're basically the evil relatives out of a fairy tale where it's *incredibly obvious* that they're trying to get their family member killed so they can take his place, but for some reason they're allowed to keep on getting away with it no matter how many 'mysterious accidents' seem to happen."

"Do you know how that bomb got into Calhoun's car?"

"No."

"Then listen, and once I'm finished, we'll see if you can figure out the culprit yourself. Calhoun's car left this house yesterday at 6:30 p.m.; at that time, it had been checked and had definitely not been tampered with. After dropping off Calhoun and Johanna, the driver took the car a short distance away and parked. He remained in the car until 8:25 p.m., at which point he received a text message telling him that plans had changed and that he was to leave the car and travel to a new location. Since the message was—apparently—from our head of security, he saw nothing suspicious about this. As soon as he was out of sight, a third party entered the car and drove it to the restaurant. We can reasonably assume that the bomb was planted at this point."

"Where in the car was it?"

"Under the left rear seat. The car pulled up outside the restaurant, at which point you saw the driver exit the vehicle and hurry away. At this point we get into technical discussions about whether the bomb was timed or remotely detonated, and, if so, whether it was triggered by the person on the roof reported by Hendrik Wolf or by some third party, all of which are irrelevant for the moment since none of that relates to the actual placement of the bomb. Now, you have the relevant information. What conclusions can you draw?"

I thought for a few seconds. "The timing was really precise. Whoever did this knew exactly when to send that text and when to steal the car."

"Obviously."

"So, they had to know in advance. To have the bomb ready, and that driver, and everything ready to go . . ." I looked at Charles. "That was why you were asking me whether I'd told anyone about the venue."

"Also obvious. Hurry up."

"They knew the driver's phone number," I realised. "And they knew how to spoof a text to fool him." I looked at Charles. "They'd have to know a lot about House Ashford."

"And?"

"Okay, maybe I'm being stupid here, but I don't see how any of this is evidence *against* Tobias or Lucella."

"You're not being stupid, but you're not being particularly perceptive, either. Look at it from the perspective of an investigator. If you were trying to find out who did this, what leads would you follow?"

I had to stop and think again. My earlier anger had melted away at this point; this was *hard*. "The phone that sent the text . . ."

"A burner, already discarded. Dead end. What else?"

"You could try to figure out everyone who knew that Calhoun and Johanna were going to be there that evening," I said slowly. "Which . . . I guess you're doing already. Or you could try to trace the driver. Or the person on the roof."

"And what do all those avenues have in common?"

I shook my head.

"They're difficult," Charles said. "Slow and unlikely to work. This was a very carefully planned, very *cautious* attack. After it had become clear that the bomb had failed, the operative on the roof could have pursued and engaged you directly. Instead they allowed you to withdraw. Maintaining secrecy was, to them, a higher priority than eliminating their target."

I frowned.

"Now compare and contrast," Charles went on. "In their previous plots against Calhoun, how thoroughly did Tobias and Lucella cover their tracks?"

"Not very. Either they used House Ashford armsmen, or they did it all themselves."

Charles looked at me with raised eyebrows.

I finally saw where he was going. "You're saying it couldn't have been Tobias and Lucella because they're too incompetent."

"Next is motive," Charles said. "As you already mentioned, Tobias and Lucella are under notice that should anything happen to Calhoun, they'll suffer for it. You're correct that this hasn't stopped them from causing trouble, but you may have noticed that the types of trouble they have caused since then have been very specifically designed not to cause Calhoun direct physical harm. Do either of them strike you as the type to be particularly willing to risk sacrificing their family position?"

I was silent.

"And finally, we come to means," Charles said. "Neither Tobias nor Lucella has the resources for this kind of assassination attempt. They don't have access to explosives, and they don't know the kinds of people who would."

I wouldn't be so sure about that. "So if they didn't do it, who did?"

"Someone with a motive to see Calhoun removed," Charles said. "You would be an obvious suspect."

I glared at him. I'd been wondering how long it would take him to get around to me.

"But fortunately for you, the restaurant's camera footage places you outside its front door at the time that the bomb was being planted," Charles continued. "So that brings us back to the suspect pool of anyone who would benefit from Calhoun or Johanna's death or injury, which is a large one. Still, we'll probably find out eventually. Particularly if they try again, which seems likely."

"And that doesn't bother you?"

"Once you ascend beyond a certain point, assassination attempts are part of the landscape," Charles said. "If Calhoun can't deal with that, he has no business being a Head of House."

And as far as you're concerned, that's that. I wondered if Tobias and Lucella's more messed-up personality traits were a consequence of having this guy as the head of the family.

"I think that's enough," Charles said.

"I thought you were going to tell me what's going on?"

"I thought *you* just told me I had no idea of anything that goes on outside of this room?" Charles said dryly. "Next time, choose your words a little more carefully. Now get lost."

For the second time I started to leave, then hesitated. I felt embarrassed, but there was a sense of disquiet there too. Should I say anything, or . . .

Screw it. Let's find out. "Okay, I was wrong," I admitted. "But *you're* wrong about something too."

"Which is?"

"You said that Tobias and Lucella don't have access to explosives and don't know the kinds of people who would. That's true for Tobias. It's not true for Lucella."

"And who does she know who'd be able to do that?"

I paused for a second, but I was committed now. "The Winged," I said at last.

Charles's expression didn't change. "And her relation to them would be . . . ?"

"She's one of them," I said, and braced for a reaction.

I didn't get one. Charles just looked at me.

Uh-oh. Was he angry? Did he not believe me? Charles had never acted as though Lucella was his favourite relative, but it belatedly occurred to me that he was still her uncle, and telling him something like this might not have been the smartest of moves. Maybe I should back off and—

"Well, well," Charles said. "So you aren't completely ignorant."

"I'm not—" I started to object, then blinked. "Wait, you believe me?"

Charles just looked at me without reaction.

Absolutely no reaction. He hadn't asked "Who are the Winged?" He hadn't challenged me for proof. Which meant . . .

"You knew already," I realised.

Charles raised his eyebrows slightly.

"Wait. Did you know from the start? All the time last year that Lucella was . . ."

"They recruited her around four years ago," Charles said. "The same year she moved back in. Now, how did *you* know she was a member?"

"I've had to spend a lot more time dealing with your niece this past year than I'd like."

"Don't waste my time with evasions." Charles looked at me with narrowed eyes. "Tell me how you found out about the Winged and Lucella's affiliation with them. *Now.*"

I flinched slightly; that last word had been delivered in a voice of steel. Charles hadn't made any threats, but all of a sudden I knew I was on thin ice. "They helped set up the raid last year."

"What, and they were wearing name tags? I asked you how you *found out*."

I hesitated, the thought of lying flitting through my mind, but I knew I wouldn't be able to come up with a good enough story. "They approached me."

"And offered you what? Money?"

Why is that always the first thing he assumes I care about? "They wanted me to join them."

"And did you?"

"No."

"Why?"

"I didn't trust them." *Or you.*

Charles stared at me.

"Why do you care anyway?" I asked when he still didn't speak. "I mean, if Lucella's been a member for four years and you haven't done anything about it, it obviously doesn't bother you that much."

"That isn't your concern."

And I was right back to pissed off again. Why did no one in my family *ever* tell me the whole truth about *anything*? I opened my mouth to make some sarcastic remark . . .

. . . No, I'd made that mistake once already. I hated feeling ignorant and out of my depth, but I had to learn to control my temper. Getting angry with this guy didn't work.

"I said I'd turned the Winged down," I told Charles. "I didn't say they'd given up."

Charles watched me without expression.

"Also, the way they sell it, they're the good guys and you're the bad guys," I added. "Maybe you should tell me your side of the story?"

"And everything else I know about them as well, I assume," Charles said dryly. "Subtle manipulation isn't really your strong suit, is it?"

"I'm going to find out about this stuff from someone."

"Yes, yes," Charles said with a wave of his hand. "To answer your question, it's a matter of degrees. For an organisation like the Winged to recruit one member of a Noble House is routine. For them to recruit, or attempt to recruit, *three* members of a particular Noble House indicates something quite different."

"What would—wait. Three?"

"Oh, you thought it was just you and her? Sorry to disappoint you, but you were their third choice. But what's interesting about that is that they approached you *after* recruiting Lucella. Can you see why?"

I frowned.

"Approaching one member of a Noble House indicates an interest in that person," Charles told me. "Approaching a second indicates an interest in that family. Approaching a third, after the second already told them yes . . . that indicates something more."

"Don't they want as many members as they can get?"

"The Winged's resources are large, but not infinite. Why do you think they're spending so much of them on us?"

". . . Because they think you're important?"

"Then why not go after one of the Greater Houses?" Charles said. "House Ashford is only a Lesser House, and we didn't even qualify for that until a quarter century ago. So?"

Why does he expect me to be able to answer this stuff? I was tempted to say that I had no idea, but something in me balked at that. Charles was annoying as hell, but something about the way he provoked me made me want to impress him, if only to prove him wrong. "Maybe they *do* go after the Greater Houses," I said. I had only a vague idea of who the Greater Houses were, but luckily Charles wasn't asking me to name them. "If they have that many resources, maybe they just try to recruit every heir of every House just on the off chance that it works."

"Not a bad guess, but wrong. The Winged are in constant competition with their rivals, especially the Order of the Dragon. Trying to suborn one of the Greater Houses too obviously could lead to the Order responding in kind and the two being drawn into a direct conflict, which both prefer to avoid. A Lesser House is another story. We're important enough to be a target, but not so important that going after us would upset the balance of power."

I tried to make sense of that. "So . . . did the Winged plant that bomb?"

"Possible, but it's not their usual style," Charles said. "The Winged's favoured approach is subversion. If they want to take over a House, they target key figures within its leadership to recruit or blackmail. It's only when that fails that they turn to assassination."

"You're saying they don't want to blow you up, they want to take you over."

"To take over this House and use it as a base of operations, yes. Presumably to help support their perpetual revolution, though quite frankly I don't much care what they'd do with it afterwards."

"Are you going to let them?"

Charles raised his eyebrows. "What do you think?"

I looked back at Charles. I still didn't know my grandfather particularly well, and I didn't know his long-term plans. But if I had to guess at what he cared about, House Ashford seemed to be at the centre of it.

"Probably not," I said.

"I will do whatever is necessary for this House to prosper and survive," Charles said. "Which does not include being taken over by the Winged. They despise Houses on principle, and if they controlled House Ashford they'd end up running it into the ground purely out of spite."

"Why?"

"Because they hate the whole idea of a social order. They can't stand that you can have privileges and obligations based on where you're born into society."

"They say they just care about freedom."

"Freedom for the pike is death for the minnows. If someone tells you their highest value is freedom, it means they see themselves as a pike."

I HAD A lot of thinking to do on the journey back.

I'd learned a lot over the past few days, but I was still struggling to fit it all together. My dad, Father Hawke, and Charles all agreed that the Winged were incredibly powerful, but they didn't seem to agree on much else. My dad made them sound like a secret society, trading in patronage and favours. Father Hawke called them servants of demons. Charles acted like they were just another player in his political world. Which way of looking at it was right?

Maybe it was like the story of the blind men and the elephant. Everyone was seeing a part, not the whole.

The problem was that which one I listened to made a really big difference in regards to how I could expect the Winged to act towards *me*. If I listened to my dad, the Winged were mostly interested in me as a way to get to him. If I listened to Father Hawke, the Winged wanted me for my essentia sight. And if I listened to Charles, I was just a way into House Ashford. If I assumed they wanted me for one thing when they actually wanted me for something else, it could end very badly...

I sighed. I missed the days when my biggest worry had been finding enough time to practice my drucraft. When did my life get so complicated?

I got off the train at Plaistow, trudged up the stairs to the ticket gates, then turned down the long hill that'd take me home. I turned into Foxden Road, took two steps, and stopped.

There was a man standing outside my front door, leaning against the gatepost. He was in his mid-twenties with light brown hair, dressed in black trousers and a red silk shirt. His arms were folded and his eyes were closed, as though he were trying to sleep.

I knew he wasn't trying to sleep. I'd met this guy exactly once, but when someone cuts you open with a knife, you don't forget their face afterwards. This was Vermillion, who'd introduced himself as "Knight-Apostle of the Brotherhood of the Winged."

I stayed still.

After a few moments Vermillion opened his eyes and looked at me. When I didn't react, he straightened up and began strolling in my direction.

CHAPTER 6

It took Vermillion fifteen seconds to cross Foxden Road and amble over to where I was standing, and I spent most of that time deciding whether to stand my ground or run. This guy had very nearly killed me last time we'd met, and I had no reason to believe a rematch would go much better.

But we were literally in front of my home. Where would I run *to*?

I called up my personal essentia, focusing on my strength and shadowman sigls, the ones that had proven most effective in our last fight. I didn't actually trigger either; I knew that Vermillion's sensing was just as good as mine, and I didn't want to give him any warning. Instead I held the sigls ready, on the verge of activating. Then I stood my ground.

Vermillion came to a stop, not quite close enough to be threatening. "Hey."

I looked him up and down. I couldn't see any weapons.

"I'm just here for a chat," Vermillion said.

"Last time we had a chat, you tried to knife me."

"Don't worry, I won't do it this time. Unless you start something first." Vermillion glanced around. "Want to get a coffee or something?"

I stared at Vermillion, trying to figure out what to make of him. His stance and the way he was looking at me were casual. Was this guy for real?

Well, only one way to find out.

"All right," I told him. "Follow me."

WE HEADED NORTH through Stratford Park and up West Ham Lane. I kept a wary distance from Vermillion as we walked, watching him from the corner of my eye, but he just kept wandering along, humming to himself. He didn't seem to be paying me much attention; he was looking at the park and the people on the streets with apparent interest.

The plaza outside Stratford station is probably the single busiest spot in all of Newham. When I was young it was much emptier and plainer, but the whole place got rebuilt for the Olympics and now it's this huge expanse of concrete with skyscrapers and the steel-and-glass station front looming over it. At the north end is a wide staircase that leads up and over the railway lines to Westfield, and at the south end is the bus station. At rush hour it's so crowded that you can't see from one end to the other. This was one of the quieter periods, meaning that there were only a hundred or so people crossing the plaza instead.

To one side of the plaza were a set of low stone benches, made out of bricks and metal wire. I led Vermillion over to them and stopped.

"Here?" Vermillion said with raised eyebrows.

"Seems like a good place to me," I told him.

One of the more to-the-point bits of advice my dad had given me two nights ago was that if I absolutely had to meet with someone from the Winged, I should do it in as public a place as possible. Our current spot was right next to the main entrance and exit to Stratford station, and there was a constant stream of people flowing in and out of the station concourse. They weren't paying us any particular attention, but any movement we made would be in plain sight of maybe twenty or thirty people, not to mention the CCTV cameras watching from above. According to my dad, the higher-ups in the Winged didn't like publicity. Being in the middle of a crowd wouldn't protect you if they wanted you dead badly enough, but it *would* stop them casually dragging you off.

I saw Vermillion's face change as he figured it out, and he laughed. "I told you, I'm not going to start anything unless you do," Vermillion said, but he was grinning and seemed to find the whole thing funny. He sat down on one of the benches and leant back on his hands. "So, you look healthy. What kind of treatment did you get?"

"None of your business."

"Don't take it so personally. I was just looking to see what you could do."

"You stabbed me in the back!"

Vermillion shrugged.

We stood looking at each other for a few moments. The plaza was filled with chatter and the noise of footsteps. Over on the other side, a street preacher was calling out to the uncaring crowd.

"Byron been in touch?" Vermillion asked.

"Why do you care?"

"I mean, he's been trying to sign you up, right?"

"Is that what this is about? You trying to make sure I don't take Mark's spot?"

"Eh, that's Mark's problem," Vermillion said. "Actually I was going to suggest a compromise. You join the Winged under me instead of under Byron. Mark gets to keep his place, you get to stop being harassed, and Byron takes the credit. No one's totally happy, but everyone can live with it."

I stared at Vermillion. "You're actually serious."

"Sure."

I had to laugh. I knew it shouldn't be funny, but I couldn't help it. Vermillion sat calmly, waiting for me to finish.

"You people are unbelievable," I said at last. "First Lucella tells me she's going to kill me if I get too close to Byron. Then Byron tries to recruit me after seeing me with Lucella. Then Mark tries to beat the crap out of me for talking to Byron. Then Byron chews out Mark for messing up his pitch to me. Then Mark calls you in to stop me from saying *yes* to Byron, because Byron's forbidden Mark to come close to me, which is only a problem because Mark was trying to attack me, which only happened because Byron wants to replace him." I looked at Vermillion. "Did I get that right? Because there are soap operas less complicated than this crap."

Vermillion considered it for a second, then shrugged. "Eh, close enough."

"I mean, at least with the other three, they're consistent," I said. "Lucella and Mark want to kill me, Byron wants to recruit me. You . . . apparently think you can be in Column A and Column B at the same time. Pick a lane!"

Vermillion leant back and stretched, crossing one leg ankle to knee. "You got the wrong idea about how this whole thing works."

"Then explain it to me."

"I don't want you dead," Vermillion said. "That dust-up at Covent Garden? That was just part of the job."

"I didn't sign up for any job that involved invisible knife-wielding psychos trying to stab me!"

"Actually you kind of did. But even if you hadn't it wouldn't matter, because it *is* part of *my* job."

"What job?"

"Apostles," Vermillion said. "We're the soldiers of the Winged. We handle the fighting."

"So go fight someone else."

"I mean, I mostly do. But you're kind of on my turf. Figured I'd check you out."

"How the hell am I on your turf?"

"You're a gifted from a faction that's not us," Vermillion said matter-of-factly. "That means you're in the game."

My heart sank. I'd been hoping against hope that the Winged might not know about my gift. "I don't know what you're talking about," I told Vermillion.

Vermillion studied me for a few seconds, then grinned. "You're a really shitty liar."

Damn it.

"Don't beat yourself up over it," Vermillion said. "Byron had you made first time he met you."

"How?"

"Dunno, but he's pretty good at that kind of thing. Most of the recruiters seem to be able to tell."

"Can you do it?"

"Do what? Tell if you're a gifted?" Vermillion grinned again. "What, you're wondering if you've got an invisible mark on your forehead?"

I was silent.

"Don't worry, it's not that obvious. You pretty much look like a normal kid to me. At least, you did before the fight. Was pretty clear that you weren't one *after*."

Well, that was something, but . . . "Why?"

Vermillion gave me a curious look. "You really are new to this, aren't you? For a start, you've got way too many sigls. A soldier or a raider, they'll have maybe two or three, max. You used, what, six? And those were just the ones I saw."

Oh. Right. I really should have known better than to do that...

... except that using every trick in the book was the only reason I'd survived at all. "Buying a bunch of sigls from the Exchange doesn't make me special," I told Vermillion.

"Most kids your age wouldn't have the skill to use sigls from that many branches, and I'm pretty sure you *didn't* buy them from the Exchange."

"How do you know?"

"Guys fight differently with stock sigls than homemade ones," Vermillion said. "Hard to explain, but you know it when you see it. Like I said, I wanted to see what you could do."

My heart sank again.

"So that makes you a House elite, corp special forces, or a gifted. You're not old enough to be special forces, and no House elite would be caught dead in those trainers. Plus, you know, Byron *said* you were a gifted. I mean, I could have just taken his word for it, but where's the fun in that?"

Yeah, definitely no chance this guy was going to leave me alone.

"I'm kind of curious about who you're with, though," Vermillion said. "Most of the time, when I'm up against another gifted, we both know the score. We're going to talk it out or we're going to fight it out. You, though? You really don't seem to have any idea what you're doing. Even your sigls feel more like ones you came up with yourself."

For someone who'd seen me so briefly, it was a little disturbing how good Vermillion's guesses were. I opened my mouth, trying to think of some cover story or deflection or...

... oh, who was I kidding, I've always been terrible at

bullshitting. Besides, weird as it sounded, I didn't get the feeling that Vermillion was trying to manipulate me. Out of all the members of the Winged I'd met, he actually felt like the most likely to tell me the truth.

"I'm not really with anyone," I said.

"Yeah, I figured," Vermillion said with a nod. "Castaway, right?"

"What?"

"As in, not raised up through the ranks. You just got handed your gift, sink or swim."

"... Yeah."

"So you're going to have to join up with someone. Why not us?"

"Who says I have to join up with anyone?"

"I mean, you do get the odd gifted free agent. But—no offence—they're usually guys who've been around the block a few times. You obviously haven't."

I would have taken offence, but it was very clearly true. "Isn't there a bit of a problem with your plan?"

"What do you mean?"

"You guys in the Winged, you get your ... gifts ... from the same place, right?"

Vermillion gave me a confused look.

"Your demons," I clarified.

"Daimons."

"What?"

"Daimons," Vermillion said. He pronounced it like "diamond," but ending in an S. "If you're going to talk about this stuff, at least get the name right."

"Your ... daimons," I stumbled over the word a bit, "I don't think they were the ones who gave me my gift."

"Oh," Vermillion said. "No, obviously. But why does that matter?"

"Because I'm not on your side?"

"Your daimon isn't."

I looked at Vermillion, puzzled.

"Yeah, you really are kind of clueless about all this," Vermillion said. "Look, when a daimon touches someone, it's like . . . I dunno, sticking your arm into muddy water. They're not over here, we're not over there."

I tried to figure out what that was supposed to mean.

Vermillion waved a hand. "Yeah, okay, I'm not really the guy to explain this. Point is, finding someone on the other side? It's *hard*. So they usually don't. Most of the time, they'll just check in on you ten, twenty years later—see if you're still alive, that sort of thing."

"I don't see what you're getting at."

"Just because your daimon gave you a gift doesn't mean you have to do what it wants," Vermillion explained. "It's not like it's hovering over your shoulder. Once they touch you, that's it. You can go off and do your own thing. And people do. There are vanguards in the Winged who got their gifts when they were part of the Order of the Dragon, there are Dragons who were gifted by daimons of the Winged. It happens more often than you think."

"You make it sound like they're footballers changing clubs," I said sceptically. I wasn't at all sure Vermillion was telling me the whole truth here. "You sure it's that *easy*?"

"Well, if you tried that with us, you'd get a few assassins after you," Vermillion said with a shrug. "But you ought to expect that, really. Point is, right now, you're free to join whoever you want."

"Wait," I said. "Our fight two weeks ago . . . was that some sort of *tryout*?"

"Hey!" Vermillion said with a grin. "You're starting to get it!"

I hesitated. I had no intention of saying yes, but I did want to find out more. "Your position, being an 'apostle' . . . what do you actually do?"

"Whatever I like, mostly."

"I thought you said it was a job."

"Well, yeah, fighting the enemies of the Winged. But, you know, everyone in the Winged has different ideas about who those enemies are. There's a lot of wiggle room."

"Can you be a bit more specific?"

"Hmm, okay. Mostly it's culture war stuff. Someone wants someone else to be saying something different. All pretty low stakes. It's mostly about pressure—let the guy know he'd better change his tune if he knows what's good for him, that kind of thing. I had one of those last week. Some journalist who writes about Israel-Palestine. One of the other vanguards wants him to change his tune because he's supporting the wrong side."

"Which one's that?"

"Fuck knows, I can't keep track of that shitshow. Don't really care to be honest."

"Did you do it?"

"Hell no. I've got better things to do."

"Like?"

"Well, the big ones are to do with the Order of the Dragon," Vermillion said. "We fight with them over castles and stuff, and that's actually serious. The Warband as well, though they're not so important these days. But if there's a fight with *those* guys, you actually have to show up."

I had no idea what he meant by "castles," and this was the first I'd heard of the "Warband." "Who are the Warband?"

"Let's just say you should be glad you ran into us first. The others aren't as welcoming as we are."

I really didn't think "welcoming" described the Winged very well. "So is that what Byron's been trying to recruit me for? A foot soldier?"

"Nah, Byron's with the Cathedral," Vermillion said. "They're the politics-and-culture crowd. If you signed up with him, you'd be going to parties and hanging out with the artsy set. As well as, you know, doing the *other* things he wants, but I'm guessing you already figured out that part. I'm not really into that stuff. Like I said, I'm just there for the fighting."

"And you think I'd *want* to do that?"

"Why not? You obviously enjoy it."

"... What?"

"I mean, you're no Bruce Lee, but you did land a couple of hits on me. Guys as young as you don't get that good without a lot of practice. Why not get something out of it?"

"Yeah, there's a bit of a problem with that."

"What?"

"I told you already," I said. "Pretty much everyone I've met in the Winged wants me dead."

"I don't want you dead."

"You've got a funny way of showing it."

Vermillion sighed. "Okay, this is getting annoying. How about I prove it to you?"

"You're going to prove you *don't* want me dead?"

"Uh-huh."

I thought about making some snarky remark about proving a negative but decided against it. "Okay."

Vermillion uncrossed his legs, rose to his feet, stretched out his arms, and ... began to dance?

He was ... good. *Really* good. I've never been the type to go to shows, so mostly when I hear "dancing" I think of what you'd see in a club. Vermillion blew those guys out of the water. His movements were like liquid, each movement flowing into the next.

Dimly I was aware of other people stopping to watch, but I didn't turn to look. I was too busy staring, watching Vermillion glide from pose to pose. I'd forgotten his face; all I could see was the motion. It was as close to perfection as anything I'd ever seen, and I felt a rush of admiration, a desire to keep watching, to drink in the sight of someone who could do something so—

Vermillion's voice broke my train of thought. "—And cut."

I snapped back to reality. A scattered circle of people were standing around us, watching. Vermillion was standing right in front of me, and something sharp was pressing up under my chin.

I froze.

"Get the point?" Vermillion said. He was smiling, but there was a glint in his eyes.

My eyes darted left and right. At least twenty people were looking straight at us; they had to be seeing exactly what Vermillion was doing, but they weren't reacting to it at all. They were all staring at Vermillion, rapt. Whatever Vermillion was holding under my chin, it was sharp and was on the verge of breaking skin.

I tried to lift my chin slightly; Vermillion moved with me and the pressure remained the same. I could sense some kind of essentia, but—

"I can push things a little harder if you like," Vermillion told me.

"I get it," I said through clenched teeth.

Vermillion pulled away, stepping back; I caught a flash of metal as he slipped something back into his pocket. All around us people blinked, seeming to come awake. Vermillion turned away from me, spread his arms, and took a bow. "Thank you, thank you!" he called to the crowd. "I'll be here all week!"

There was scattered applause, but mostly people just seemed to be trying to figure out what they'd just seen. Vermillion returned to his seat on the bench. "So," he told me. "Believe me now?"

". . . Yes," I told him, trying to keep my voice steady.

"Hey, why'd you stop?" someone called from around us.

"Yeah, do it again," another said.

"Ladies, gentlemen," Vermillion announced. "I love meeting my fans, but we're done for the day. Come back another time."

There was a murmur from the spectators, but no one moved. Some were taking out their phones.

Annoyance flickered across Vermillion's face, and he swept his eyes over the crowd. "Leave."

I felt a tingle of something; just for a second Vermillion's face looked cold and intimidating, a mask sculpted in marble. It was gone in a second, but the effect on the watchers was much greater. They backed away, lowering their phones and looking scared. The crowd dispersed, and in seconds we were alone.

Vermillion turned back to me. "So where were we?"

I took a deep breath and sat down. "Okay," I said. "You've made your point."

Vermillion just smiled.

I was trying hard not to show how shaken I was. I'd known that being in public didn't make me safe, but I'd thought it would at least slow Vermillion down. It hadn't. "So you want me to be a soldier in your war."

"You don't actually spend that much time being a soldier," Vermillion said. "Most of the time you can do what you want."

"What happens if I say no?"

Vermillion shrugged. "Nothing?"

"Really?"

"I mean, I'm not going to press-gang you. That kind of thing's fine for cannon fodder, but vanguards need to actually believe in the cause. That's why Byron's been making such an effort with you."

"And afterwards?"

"What do you mean?"

"If I say no and we run into each other afterwards?"

"Oh, right. I probably end up killing you. Nothing personal, but everyone has to pick a side, and if you're not on ours..." Vermillion shrugged again.

I felt a chill run down my spine. Vermillion was leaning back on his hands, casually tapping his foot against the stone, but all of a sudden I was very aware that there was a real chance that I was going to end up dead because of this guy. He wouldn't do it because he resented me or disliked me. He'd just stick a knife through my ribs because he wouldn't see any particular reason not to. And once he decided to do it, nothing I could say to him would make the slightest difference.

"Well, that's about it," Vermillion said. "I'll leave you a way to get in touch."

"Wait," I said. "Tell me something. Why do you do all this? You said that once these . . . things . . . give their gifts, they're hands-off. They don't control you afterwards."

"Yeah."

"So why do *you* work for the Winged? What's stopping you from leaving?"

"Well, they wouldn't pay me, for one thing. The Apostle package is pretty generous, even without the incentives."

"Is that really it?"

"Doesn't hurt," Vermillion said. "But . . . no, that's not it. I'm guessing Byron gave you the whole spiel about what we stand for? Freedom and individuality and stuff?"

"Yeah."

"It's actually true," Vermillion said. "Don't get me wrong, Byron's an arsehole, but he's telling the truth about that part. You want to be independent, right? Make your own choices, do what you want?"

"I guess."

"So do we," Vermillion said. "And if you do want that, there's no group in the world that'll give you more freedom than the

Winged. The Houses, the corps . . . they have money, but you're always going to be under someone's thumb. Our vanguards aren't. All you need is to be gifted, and you've got that already. There are guys who'd kill for that. Come to think of it, you've already met one." Vermillion pushed himself off the bench and stood. "Think it over." He walked away across the plaza.

For the third time in as many days I went home with my head whirling with thoughts. After meeting my dad, I'd been thinking about demons and powers. After Calhoun's car had been bombed, I'd been thinking about attacks and assassination attempts. This time, I was worrying about Vermillion and the Winged.

Ignas and the others were in the living room, but I avoided them. I headed upstairs to my room, shut the door behind me, and locked it. Hobbes was out, leaving me alone in the room. I sat down on the bed and tried to think.

It was hard. My dad, my job, the Winged, demons and gifts, factions and alliances and assassinations in the dark. So many things to worry about, all pressing in on me at once. How could I even keep track of them all?

I took a deep breath and shook myself. That, at least, I could do something about. I dug around for my notebook and pen, curled up on my bed, and began to write. My first couple of attempts were too disorganised to make any sense. The third try came out better. I kept going until I'd filled up the page, then stopped.

Problems
1. My father's still in hiding from the Winged, and has to stay that way.

2. The Winged still want to recruit me, and probably aren't going to take no for an answer.

3. My essentia sight makes me noticeable to these people. It's probably the biggest reason the Winged are so interested in me. Others might be too.

4. My essentia sight might or might not be a gift from some kind of demon/daimon/spirit/whatever, which might or might not be using me for some purpose I don't understand.

5. Someone's trying to assassinate Calhoun and/or Johanna.

6. I'm not earning enough money.

7. Vermillion says that if I don't join the Winged, he's probably going to end up killing me.

It wasn't the first time I'd done something like this. I'd written a very similar list a year ago, but back then my problems had been immediate ones, with (mostly) immediate solutions. These ones were a lot murkier and harder to solve. In fact, looking at it, some of them might not even be *possible* to solve.

Okay, so maybe that should be my starting point. If there was literally nothing I could do about a problem, there was no point worrying about it.

Thinking about it that way actually helped. For a start, I could probably cross off number one. The Winged hunting for my dad was obviously bad, but he'd managed to stay hidden so far, and the only way that would be likely to change would be if I gave him away. I had to make sure that didn't happen, which meant telling absolutely no one that we were in contact and being very careful about when and where we met. It was going to mean seeing less of him than I wanted, which sucked, but better that than the alternative.

Number five—the bombing—also fell into the "nothing I can do about it" category. I didn't especially *like* the idea of someone trying to murder Calhoun and Johanna, but from the way they were acting, this kind of thing wasn't exactly unheard of in their world and was something they knew how to deal with. So, cold as it sounded, I should probably leave them to it. It wasn't like I could do much to protect them anyway.

Number six was the money issue, and while that *was* something I could do something about, it was also the one that was least likely to get me or anyone I cared about killed. Running out of money was bad, but survivable. Getting stabbed to death by Vermillion wasn't.

With that settled, I went back to the notebook and crossed out one, five, and six. I moved my pen to number three—my essentia sight—and hesitated, the point hovering above the paper.

Three and four were . . . hard. Honestly, my first impulse was to write them off as well. I still wasn't at all sure that these demons or daimons that Father Hawke and Vermillion talked about were real, and if they were, I couldn't see what I was supposed to do about it. Even if I believed everything they said . . . if there really *were* these spirits, or daimons, hovering around granting powers to people and then disappearing . . . then how did knowing about it even help? I couldn't do anything to change it, so what was the point in thinking about it? It was tempting to shelve the whole thing and worry about the more immediate problems, like Vermillion. That was basically the advice my dad had given me, after all.

But something about the idea of shelving it made me uneasy. After all, that had been more or less what I'd been doing for the past year. And while it hadn't yet blown up in my face, I was starting to wonder if it was making me miss the big picture.

What if all the problems I hadn't crossed out were different sides of the same thing?

I went back to the list and tapped the numbers two, three, four, and seven. Winged recruitment; my essentia sight; the things that gave it; Vermillion.

I have to pick a side.

That was it, wasn't it? Pretty much everyone I'd met over the past year was on a team. House Ashford, the corporations, the Winged. That was why I'd been struggling. They had support and I didn't.

But which side should I pick?

I leant back against the wall and closed my eyes. Imagined futures danced in my mind. Stephen Oakwood, Knight-Apostle of the Brotherhood of the Winged. Stephen Ashford of House Ashford. And a third possibility, something vaguer.

Joining the Winged was the option I liked the least. So far, I'd met four active members of the Winged—Lucella, Byron, Vermillion, and Mark—and in every case, there'd been something about them that just felt *wrong*. I didn't know whether you needed to be broken somehow to join the Winged, or whether being a member made them that way, and I didn't really want to find out.

But what if I didn't have a choice? I remembered what Charles had told me. The Winged liked to recruit, to manipulate; only when that failed, when they'd been completely rejected, would they kill. So far, every time, I'd turned them down . . . but would I do it again, if the other choice was Vermillion's knife?

I wasn't sure. And I had to admit that last thing Vermillion had said had made an impression. The idea of being independent, having the power and freedom to do whatever I wanted . . . that was tempting.

Though I had the feeling that being with the Winged wouldn't be quite as independent as they made it sound. It certainly hadn't worked out that way for my dad.

The other option—joining the Ashfords—was probably more realistic. They *were* my family, and I didn't hate *all* of them, and they did seem to be coming around to not treating me like complete garbage. On the other hand, they also had a track record of causing me a lot more problems than they solved, and I wasn't at all sure getting closer to them would improve the ratio. Calhoun had helped me out with Mark, but there was a big difference between coming to him with a very clear and specific request like that one, and asking for something vague and open-ended like "protect me from Vermillion." And even if they were willing to do it, I wasn't sure they could.

There was another problem with joining the Ashfords. Even if I signed on with them in exchange for protection, there'd be nothing to make them hold up their end of the bargain. It was the "no leverage" problem that had caused me so much frustration last year. Whether it was House Ashford or the Winged or a corporation like Linford's, I had no way to force any of these people to keep their word. If I asked them for something, and they said no, what was I supposed to do? Complain? Threaten to quit? There was nothing I could give any of them that they couldn't get just as easily from somewhere else, and that meant they'd always have the upper hand.

There was a third option.

Father Hawke had told me I'd been given my gift for a reason. I could lean into that. Instead of begging others for protection, I could use what I'd been given already. An image hovered at the edge of my mind, a figure of shadow and light. Strength that wasn't borrowed from others but was drawn from a purpose.

But I couldn't see how that would help much against Vermillion, either.

I sighed and opened my eyes. "Pick a side" had sounded good, but the more I looked at my options, the less I liked any of them.

Maybe I was looking at this the wrong way. Now that I thought about it, all of these "pick a side" options were really coming down to the same problem. And it was exactly the same one as last year, wasn't it? The last time I'd done one of these lists, my conclusion had been that I needed to work on my drucraft. I'd come a long way since then, but the basic problem hadn't changed. I needed to be stronger.

How?

But as soon as I formed the question, I realised I already knew the answer. *The raiding plan.*

With a rush of energy, I turned to a new page in my notebook and began to write, lying half curled on my side as I filled up one double-page spread after another. Outside, clouds drifted through an overcast sky.

CHAPTER 7

It was one week later.

"All right, we're in the air," Colin said over the phone.

"How long?" I asked.

"Few minutes. I'll tell you when it's clear."

"Got it." I hung up and slipped the phone back into my pocket.

It was Sunday night, and I was in Elephant and Castle, a part of south London a little way down from the South Bank. I'd been to Elephant and Castle a few times as a kid, mostly to visit the Imperial War Museum, and I remembered it as poor and grimy but familiar-looking, a lot like Stratford and Plaistow. It didn't look familiar anymore. Sometime between my last visit and today, the old town centre had been torn down and turned into a vast building site. A high barrier kept out visitors.

Somewhere beyond that barrier was a Matter Well. I was here to find it, drain it, and get out again.

I was on the barrier's north side, hidden in the shadows of a trio of concrete-and-metal structures that I didn't recognise.

They were old, boxy things the size of small cars, built long ago for some unknown purpose, then abandoned to the rust and graffiti artists. Standing nearby was an ancient tree that towered over both structures and the barrier. Everything else was bare. I vaguely remembered that there'd been a hotel here once, but it was gone; all the remnants of the past had been stripped away, the metal boxes and the tree the only survivors. All cleared to make space for a new block of flats and shopping mall.

The rush of traffic was all around. A main road did a loop around the cleared land and the building site, the white-and-red lights of cars flickering through the darkness. Occasionally a pedestrian would come by, and when they did, I tried to keep out of sight; there really weren't many legitimate reasons for someone to be loitering in my current spot. I'd wanted to do this on a weeknight, when fewer people would be around; Colin had wanted us to go on a Friday or Saturday night, when he wouldn't have classes in the morning. We'd compromised on Sunday.

My phone buzzed and I fished it out of my pocket. "Yeah."

"Okay, looks clear," Colin said. "Lots of people moving around the outside, no one within the barrier."

"Any security?"

"Not that I can see. But there are a bunch of things that look like shipping containers. One of them might be a security hut."

"All right, I'm going in. Keep watch and buzz me if it seems like I've stirred anything up."

"Got it. Good luck."

I hung up and pocketed my phone. *Okay, let's do this.*

I sent essentia flowing into the sigls at my forehead, chest, and waist. The one on my forehead was a vision sigl, the one on my chest a lightfoot sigl that reduced my effective mass. Most important, though, was the one at my waist, causing visible light to curve around my body without quite touching it. This was my diffraction sigl. Of all my sigls it had been the hardest and most complicated to make, but it gave me invisibility . . . more or less.

The world darkened into shades of blue, and my stomach lifted upwards as my weight dropped to less than half of what it should be. I jogged forward.

The barrier fencing off the construction site was ten feet tall, covered in bland geometric patterns and messages urging you to **DISCOVER**, **CONNECT**, and **INSPIRE**. I jumped up, grabbed the top, and hauled myself over, giving the **INSPIRE** message an extra kick as I did. I've always hated that corporate management-speak, and growing up in London these days you get it shoved at you *everywhere*. Honestly, it made me even more motivated to raid the place than I had been already.

I dropped down on the other side of the barrier onto dirt and sand. The inside of the building site held shipping containers and construction materials, excavators and cranes standing still and silent. It wasn't pitch dark, but it felt that way compared to outside, and I waited for a few seconds until my eyes adapted and I was able to make out paths in the dirt, running south.

The blue tint to my vision made it hard to see. My vision sigl is designed to take ultraviolet light (which my diffraction sigl very specifically *doesn't* bend away) and shift it just far enough down the spectrum that I'm not blind. I didn't do the best job with it, which is why it only lets me see in blues: it's a pretty kludgy setup, and times like this made me feel it. The Ashfords use what are called "active camouflage" sigls, which duplicate and reproduce outgoing light (and only outgoing light) so that when anyone looks at the wielder, they see what's behind them. Near-perfect invisibility without hampering your own vision, all contained in one sigl, instead of in two. It's better than my diffraction sigl in every way . . . trouble is, it also requires you to be a master of shaping Light sigls and have access to an incredibly powerful Well.

Which, ultimately, was why I was here. This Well wasn't Light, and wasn't powerful, but it was a step in the right direction.

Once my eyes had fully adjusted, I set off into the darkness, sand crunching under my shoes. I could make out trails of essentia in the darkness, heading south. I hadn't managed to get all the way in when I'd scouted this place during the daytime, but I'd had a good enough look to be sure that there had to be a Well right about . . .

There! The threads of essentia converged to a glowing halo. Back when I could only sense essentia, Wells felt to me like a presence; now that I can see it, they look as though the land's suffused with light. Every part of the area glowed a deep, vibrant red, the light welling up from the ground and twining lazily in the air. To a random passerby, this spot would have looked like an ordinary building site: shipping containers piled in the dirt, with an excavator and cement mixer parked nearby. The only thing that might have struck them as a little bit strange was the square of empty dirt at the centre, marked off with bollards and tape.

Those bollards and tape told me that the Well was claimed. I couldn't actually check, of course; doing so would require access to the Well Registry, which I no longer had. But there was no other reason for this particular spot to be marked off, except that someone in the not-very-distant past had found this Well and, in exchange for a small finder's fee, sold the right to exploit it to a House or corporation.

Until recently, the fact that this Well was claimed would have made me turn away. Back when I'd been a locator, I'd followed the rules ... mostly. Okay, I'd strayed into grey areas a couple of times, but I'd never actually found a claimed Well and just decided to walk up and take it. What I was doing here was crossing a line, and no matter how much logic told me I needed to, some part of me wasn't completely comfortable with this.

I was still going to do it, though.

Keeping all three of my sigls active was becoming a strain. I let them wink out; weight returned to my body, the night around me brightened, and I felt an easing sensation as my personal essentia recovered. I stepped into the shadow of the excavator and rang Colin.

Colin picked up immediately. "You in?"

"Already at the Well."

"I didn't see—oh, right."

"Yeah, that's the idea. Any movement?"

"Can't see a thing. FYI, battery life's down to ten minutes."

"Okay, I'm going to start. Keep watch over my area. You see someone heading my way, buzz me. Otherwise, fly it back once you're in the red and save the other battery for when I get out."

"Got it." Colin hung up.

Colin was watching from overhead via a camera drone. The plan was that he'd act as my eyes in the sky, giving me advance warning of anyone headed my way so that I'd have time to evacuate or hide. Unfortunately, we were still relatively new to this and were still working out the kinks, and one of said kinks was the drone's flight time. It turns out that camera drones have absolutely terrible battery life, and ours (bought off eBay) kept running out of charge at the worst possible moments. We'd come prepared with a second battery, but coverage was still going to be spottier than I'd like.

I spent a couple of minutes selecting my spot. I would have

liked to stay in the shelter of the shipping containers, but the Well was far enough out in the open that I eventually decided it would be too tricky. I ducked under the tape, crouched in the dirt, and began to draw out the Well's essentia.

Shaping a sigl is sort of like sculpting with threads spun from air. The first step is gathering, where you pull in the Well's essentia and concentrate it. Since it's not yours you can't control it directly, so instead I extended my personal essentia from my body, close enough that it wouldn't lose attunement, and began to sweep it in circles. Gradually the glowing red essentia around me began to respond, slowly at first, then faster and faster, forming a spiral centred on me.

If I were really shaping a sigl, the next stage would be to form the essentia construct, the blueprint that would become the sigl's kernel . . . which, given that this was a Matter Well, would probably take hours. Matter essentia seems to take forever to shape for some reason; maybe I don't know the proper way to do it, maybe the essentia just works that way, but whichever it is, the only times I've made a viable Matter sigl have been the times when I've taken more than three hours to do it. Whenever I try to do it fast, I end up with a lump of aurum.

But tonight I wasn't trying to shape a sigl; I just wanted the essentia. Which meant that a lump of aurum was exactly what I was aiming for.

I pulled the essentia down into a spot in front of me, concentrating it more and more densely. I was going much faster than normal, and a part of me cringed at how sloppy this all was; had this been a real sigl, I'd have botched it already. Instead I kept on pouring in more and more essentia, watching as the "light" grew brighter and brighter until it felt almost blinding. A tiny glint appeared in the air, visible to my real eyes this time, and I reached up to cup it in the palm of my hand . . .

Something flickered at the edge of my vision. I turned my head.

There was something moving behind one of the excavators. For a moment I thought it was some sort of darting light, then it clicked and I realised what I was looking at. The beam of a torch.

Shit! I hesitated, looking between the torch and the forming sigl. The essentia flow was fluttering, slowing. Cutting off the process now would make the sigl fail . . .

. . . but it *wasn't* a sigl. The torch beam was coming closer. I snapped off the flow of essentia and scrambled to my feet, ducking under the tape before darting into the shadow of the containers.

I was only just in time. As the cone of the torch beam splashed over the area of the Well, I sent essentia flowing into my diffraction and vision sigls, watching as the world darkened to shades of black and blue. The cone of the torch beam changed from white to a deep sapphire as it kept coming, drawing closer and closer. And then the person carrying it rounded the excavator and the light was shining right on me, dazzling in the night.

I held very still, squinting. I was exposed against the container, but whoever was holding the torch shouldn't be able to see me. Key word: *shouldn't*. There are a lot of ways to beat invisibility, especially if the invisibility sigl's a weak one, and mine is about as weak as you can get. The beam of the torch stayed on me, painting a circle on the shipping container with me at the centre, and I held my breath . . .

. . . The beam moved on. I heard the crunch of boots on dirt as the man began to circle the containers. My eyes were still dazzled, swimming with colours, and I couldn't get a clear look at him; all I saw was a shadow in the night as he tromped back and forth. The beam of the torch swept over me twice more, but didn't stop.

To my sight, the Well was obviously disturbed, its essentia swirling and ragged. I wondered if this guy was a drucrafter. If his sensing was any good, he should be able to tell that someone had been here. Would he notice?

Apparently not. The man finished his circuit and turned away. The *crunch, crunch, crunch* of his boots faded away into the night and was lost in the sounds of traffic from the A-road around us. The light of the torch dimmed and vanished. Silence fell.

I kept still and quiet for another minute, then let my invisibility drop. I walked back to the Well and started to draw in the aurum again.

Colin buzzed when I was close to finished. "Yeah," I said into the phone.

"There's someone moving around the south of the site," Colin told me. "Looks like some guy with a torch."

"Now you tell me."

"What do you mean?"

"Never mind." The Well was mostly drained by now, the red light reduced to a dim glow. "Have I got a clear path out?"

"Long as you head north."

"All right. Keep an eye out and buzz me if you see anything. I'm moving out."

I hung up and stuffed the phone back into my pocket, while in my other hand the last trails of essentia spiralled down to merge into the tiny sphere of aurum. It was almost funny how small it was.

I looked down at the item in my palm with mixed feelings. It was invisible in the darkness, but I knew it would be a deep ruby red. It could have been a sigl; now it was just an inert piece of matter, only valuable as something to be sold. I'd succeeded, but knowing that I'd drained the Well to make something useless took a lot of the satisfaction out of it. I'd have preferred to make something real.

Of course, if I'd tried, it would have been ruined anyway...

I shook off the thoughts and looked around. The Well was almost gone; the only sign that it had ever existed were the traces of red light surrounding the area. They'd been far enough away that I hadn't been able to draw them in, but they'd fade, too, with time. This had been a temporary Well, and temporary Wells don't refill. In a few weeks, there'd be no way of knowing it had ever existed.

I slipped the piece of aurum into a box I'd brought for the purpose, sealed it, and put it into my pocket. Then I set off north, letting my invisibility sigls cloak me from sight. It took me only minutes to make it back to the barrier, at which point I pulled myself over, dropped down on the other side, and walked away into the night. My first solo raid was over.

". . . BUT IT'S FLIGHT time that's the issue," I said to Colin. Half an hour had passed, and we were sitting on a pair of concrete benches in a nearby park. A streetlamp cast a pool of light around us, towering blocks of flats looming up from all around. "Doesn't matter how good the camera is, if it isn't up there in the first place."

"I mean, I could hot swap the batteries," Colin said. "But that still means flying the drone all the way back."

"Can't you just put in a bigger battery?"

"No, because batteries are heavy. If you want a bigger battery, you need a more powerful electric motor to lift it. But that draws more current, which means you need an even *bigger* battery to power the motor, which means you need an even *more* powerful motor to lift the battery, which draws even *more* current, which means—"

"I get it," I said with a sigh.

"It's the whole tyranny of the rocket equation thing," Colin said. "Everything that makes your drone fly makes it heavier, which makes it harder to make it fly. Plus, don't forget I need somewhere where I can launch the drone and control it while it's in the air. Doing this on the pavement isn't going to cut it."

The spot we were in was called Elephant Park, advertised on the maps as a "leafy local space with a hip takeout." It had probably been built when they'd demolished the dirty-but-cheap council estates that I remembered from the old Elephant and Castle. The new tower blocks that had sprung up in their place were clean, modern-looking, and filled with flats that probably cost about half a million pounds each.

We'd picked the park because it had been only a couple of hundred yards away from the building site. Looking across the train lines towards the building site, I could see a huge skyscraper rising up just next to it. As the apartment blocks dwarfed us, so the skyscraper dwarfed the apartments, made from sloping steel and glass with three wind turbines on the angled roof. I don't know its real name, but people call it Isengard.

"But you got the stuff?" Colin asked.

I tapped the pocket with the box. "Yep."

"So what's the problem?"

"That security guard came up on me right while I was in the middle of it. I had to stop halfway through."

"I thought that didn't matter."

"It didn't matter *this* time. It would have been a total failure if I'd been trying to make a proper sigl."

"You are so anal about this stuff."

"Yeah, there's a reason for that."

"Still wouldn't kill you to relax a bit," Colin said, then waved his hand. "So you're definitely going through with this?"

"Yes," I told Colin.

The plan I'd come up with last week had five steps. After a good deal of false starts and crossings-out, the last page on my notebook read as follows:

1. Test run raid
2. Put together team
3. Raid for sigls/aurum
4. Get into the black
5. Raid for powerful sigls

Tonight had been Step One. Next was Step Two.

"Who'll it be?" Colin asked.

"Pretty much the ones from that raid last Christmas," I said. "Pavel, Anton. Bridget. Might as well ask Ivy, though she'll probably say no." I glanced over. "And you. If you want?"

"Yeah, of course. Who's Bridget again?"

"My half-sister."

"Oh, right, the rich girl." Colin thought for a minute. "You think they'll all show?"

"Maybe?" I said. I was nervous about this next part. It had been one thing to plan all of this out when it was something I could do on my own. Having to pitch the idea to a crowd of people and sell them on it was something else.

We sat for a little while in silence. A couple of people went by along the edges of the park, but not many. It was probably a popular place during daylight. "Can I ask you something?" I said.

"Sure."

"If you were given something really rare and useful, but that you didn't ask for ... how would you feel about the person ... thing ... that gave it to you?"

"What kind of thing? Like a laptop, or a guitar, or ... ?"

"Like some kind of supernatural ability."

"Like one of your sigls?"

"Okay," I said. "So you know how in our old D&D games, there were these outsiders, like demons and angels, with a bunch of supernatural abilities? Imagine if one of them granted you one of those, some sort of mid-level power you could use at will. Would you feel some sort of obligation to whatever did it?"

"Obligation to do what?"

"To do what it wanted. We're kind of assuming it gave you that ability for a reason."

"What kind of reason?"

"You don't know."

"How can I not know?"

"Because you've never seen this thing or talked to it or interacted with it. You just wake up one day with this ability."

"Then how do I even know I got it from an outsider?"

"You don't. After looking into it, you eventually come to the conclusion that the outsider explanation is the most likely one, but you're not sure."

"Oh, okay," Colin said. "So in this hypothetical scenario, this outsider might have given me this magical power for some reason, but I'm kind of left to guess at what it is."

"Right. So would you try to do what it wanted?"

"Honestly?" Colin said. "My instant reaction here is that it'd completely depend on the kind of outsider."

"What do you mean?"

"I mean, if I was in that position I'd drop everything and start trying to figure out exactly what this thing *was*. As in, is this supernatural gift coming from the equivalent of Jesus, or the equivalent of Nurgle?"

"Huh," I said. Now that I thought about it, of course that was how Colin would see it. "I want to know more" was his first reaction to *everything*.

"As for whether I'd feel obligated to this thing . . ." Colin said. "I don't know, I could see that going both ways? I mean, on the one hand, this thing didn't actually enter into any kind of agreement with me. It just did it without giving me a choice or anything. On the other hand, I do believe in reciprocity and stuff, so I guess I'd feel some kind of obligation. But it'd depend on what the purpose was, you know?"

"Yeah, okay," I said. It's useful, talking about these things. For so much of the last year I'd been trying to do everything on my own. It's a lot easier to think clearly when you aren't completely bottled up in your own head.

"So . . ." Colin said after a pause, "is this all just hypothetical?"

I didn't answer, and we sat for a little while longer in the darkness. I gazed up over the railway lines at Isengard. The wind turbines spun on its roof, their movements deceptively slow and lazy. Down here, hemmed in by the blocks of flats, there was little wind. It was different up there.

London is a city of layers. Colin and I had spent the night down on the ground, scurrying around in the dirt. The men and women who lived in the flats here and in the Barbican, they were in the layer above. But the corporations in their towers and the Houses in their mansions were just as far above them as they were above us.

Then above the corporations and the Houses were the groups like the Winged.

What was above *them*?

I looked up, past the wind turbines on the tower, to the darkened sky. It was overcast, thick clouds shrouding everything in grey. We sat there a while longer before leaving to catch the last train home.

CHAPTER 8

Monday and Tuesday were spent preparing for the first meeting of what I hoped would be my raiding team. Then on Wednesday I went to meet my mother.

I've only known my mother for six months. My dad told me a little about her while I was growing up, and of course she'd been with me when I was a baby, but that doesn't let you *know* someone. A couple of times over the winter I'd found myself looking at her, trying to call up those old memories, but it hadn't worked. I could see echoes of myself, but they were all on the surface—the way she moved, little mannerisms and ways of speaking. Her thoughts and feelings were a closed book to me.

This was maybe the sixth or seventh of our meetings, and, like all the others she'd arranged, we were on Hampstead Heath. It was in the West Heath this time, a patch of woodland with dirt paths running through trees and leafy bushes; the first shoots and buds were starting to sprout, but it was still quite bare. The West Heath isn't as deep in the Heath as the bridge that we'd met at before, although in the cold spring weather it was still mostly empty. Apparently my mother was slightly less concerned about being seen with me nowadays.

Slightly.

"Stephen," my mother said as I walked up to her on the earthen path. As usual, she was wearing smart business clothes, with heeled shoes that didn't look very practical for a walk in the park. "Are you all right?"

"Why wouldn't I be?"

"With what happened. You're not hurt?"

I paused, trying to figure out which of the things I was doing she was talking about. Had she found out about the raid? Or . . . oh, crap, had she found out about the stabbing? I'd done my best to keep that quiet because I *really* did not want her to start asking questions . . .

"The *bombing*," my mother said.

"Oh," I said with a flash of relief. "Right. No, I'm fine."

"Honestly, Stephen! You were right next to a car bomb!"

"I wasn't *right* next to it." Now that I thought about it, it was kind of funny that I'd actually managed to forget about the whole thing, but once you've had someone stab you full of holes, a bomb going off in the street outside just isn't as scary anymore. "And from what Charles said, I probably could have been next to the car and I wouldn't have been hurt."

"Good grief, your head really is in the clouds," my mother said. "If this is how casual you are about things like this, I'm glad Calhoun's stopped using you as a bodyguard."

That soured my mood. I'd had a message from Calhoun to that effect on Monday. According to him, he was happy with the work I'd done, but because of the attack they were tightening up their security and it would be a while before he could start bringing me along again.

The frustrating thing about it was that I was pretty sure that

Calhoun didn't even understand why I might be upset. His message had been apologetic, and he'd kept emphasising that I'd done nothing wrong, like he was worried about me feeling insulted. But it had apparently never occurred to him that it was nothing to do with hurt feelings; I just needed the damn money! I'd been counting on that extra income, and with it gone I was back in the red again.

Part of the reason I was going forward with my raider plan was because, if it worked, it'd give me my own source of income, one that wouldn't leave me dependent on the whims of the Ashfords. But to set that up I needed time! That piece of aurum I'd made on Sunday was worth more than any bodyguard gig, but it would only be worth anything if I could *sell* it, and while Felix claimed he could find me a buyer, he still hadn't got back to me . . .

"Anyway," my mother said, interrupting my thoughts. "You're all right, and that's the important thing. What I actually wanted to talk about was something else. You've been getting to know your grandfather, haven't you?"

"I mean . . . sort of."

My mother nodded. "I think you should start taking lessons."

"Lessons?"

"You've done very well with what you have, but there really are a lot of holes in your education. I think it's time you started filling them in."

"I mean, I've been *trying*," I said. "But finding people who'll tell you about this stuff isn't easy."

"You don't need to find them. You've got me."

I gave her a sceptical look. "How much is it going to cost?"

"Oh, come on, Stephen, give me some credit," my mother said, looking offended. "I know I haven't been there for you very much, but I'm not going to make you pay for things out of your own pocket."

Well, that was something. "Any chance you could find me a Dimension tutor?"

"A what?"

"Dimension drucraft," I explained. "I'd like to start learning it." According to Maria, the essentia analyst I'd met last year, it was one of my affinities, and from what I'd heard it was supposed to be very versatile. Unfortunately, those same sources *also* said it was far and away the most difficult branch to learn. If I wanted to get anywhere with it, I'd need help.

"I'm not talking about drucraft lessons."

"Why not?"

"Because your drucraft skills are already far above average. Honestly, they might be better than mine at this point. Don't get me wrong, I'm very impressed with how far you've come, but you don't need to be quite so focused on it."

Yes I do, I didn't say. I *had* to keep honing my drucraft skills, because they were the only advantage I had. But I couldn't say that without inviting a lot of questions I didn't want to answer. "So what *are* you talking about?"

"You must have noticed by now that when you talk to your grandfather, he takes a lot of things for granted," my mother said. "The Houses and the political landscape of the United Kingdom. Corporations and the current economic climate. Foreign policy and the US empire. You are going to have to learn those things sooner or later."

"I'd much rather be able to make a good Dimension sigl."

My mother sighed. "You sound like Calhoun when he was a little boy. Do you really think that's what makes your grandfather the head of House Ashford? Having the strongest sigls?"

"No, I think he was born that way."

"And what do you think lets him *keep* it? Your great-grandfather turned House Ashford from a minor family that nobody had ever heard of into a Lesser House. Your grandfather turned us from a Lesser House into a player on the European scene. Now we're one of the top ten providers of Light essentia to the NATO militaries, to the point that we supply more by weight than most of the Greater Houses of the UK. Why do you think I spend so much time travelling? It's not because I like the plane trips!"

I had no answer to that. This was a world I knew nothing about.

"Also, your etiquette could use some work," my mother said, looking me up and down. "How to conduct yourself at society events, when to talk and when to stay quiet, that sort of thing. And we really should do something about your clothes. That fleece and those trainers make you look like a dog walker."

"What am I *supposed* to look like?" I demanded. "I'm not *part* of your family. You and your dad remind me of that every time I see you. Why should I act like I am?"

My mother hesitated, about to answer, then seemed to change her mind. There was an awkward silence.

What am I doing here? I wondered. Every time I spoke to my mother I felt this disconnect, as though we were from different worlds that always had to stay a certain distance apart. Our conversations never seemed to go anywhere, and I always seemed to come away from them feeling worse. Why did I keep coming back?

Because she's my mother. I hadn't wanted to come today, but when she'd asked, I'd done it.

"Anyway," my mother said, seeming to recover. "What if I got you a job with our supply office?"

"Your what?"

"Supply of sigls," my mother explained. "They track the essentia level of all our Wells and when they're scheduled to be used. The idea is to match up customers with Wells so that each one's used as soon as possible after it fills. We used to run it out of our home office, but now that we own those floors in Chancery Lane, we've moved the whole operation over there."

"And that would involve..."

"Fielding calls from our clients, scheduling shapings, coordinating shapers with clients, keeping the Wells supplied with whatever resources the overseer needs. It's just office work, but it's a good way to learn the business. You'd be working with Clarissa—we moved her over to doing it, but it's not really her specialty and they've been a bit swamped."

I remembered Clarissa from some previous phone conversations. I really did not like the idea of working with her. "Yeah..." I said. "I'm not sure."

"I know it's not the most glamorous job, but you can't expect to start at the top. Calhoun did a stint in the supply office between school and university."

"It's not that," I said. Honestly, compared to the office jobs I'd had in the past, it actually sounded relatively interesting. "It's just that I wouldn't be working with Wells, would I? Or making sigls, or anything like that?"

"No..."

"So it wouldn't give me much drucraft practice."

"This again?" my mother said with a sigh. "Look, you don't need to be so obsessive about drucraft. The actual day-to-day work of running a House isn't drucraft, it's management."

"Why does that even matter?" I shot back in a sudden flare of irritation. "I'm not *going* to be managing your House, your dad made that clear. And *you* obviously think the same way, given that you won't even talk to me unless it's at some place hidden away in the woods where you don't have to worry about us being seen together."

Consternation flickered over my mother's face. "I don't—it's not about being seen with you. We went over this last year."

I didn't answer. We *had* gone over this last year, and the memory still made me angry.

"Look, I'd just feel a lot better if you were somewhere I could keep an eye on you," my mother said. "There are . . . some political developments going on. I can't really go into the details. But I'd be a lot happier if I knew you were a little more prepared."

Prepared for what? It felt as though she was trying to hint at something, but I had no idea what it was. "I'm doing my own preparations, thanks."

My mother looked frustrated but let the matter drop. We talked in a desultory sort of way for a little longer before parting.

As I walked back through the park towards Hampstead Heath Overground, I thought about what my mother had said. The truth was, if she'd come to me with this same offer a year ago, I would have said yes. I wouldn't exactly have been enthusiastic about working for the Ashfords, but the security of a steady income would have counted for a lot.

But some of the things that had happened over the past year had made me realise that while a steady income was security, it could also be a trap. My job at the MoD had given me enough money to live on, but it had taken up so much of my time and energy that I hadn't really gotten better at anything. And so when Lucella had shown up with her two goons, I'd been caught completely off guard.

My biggest worry right now wasn't having enough money to pay my rent; it was being stabbed to death by someone like Vermillion. Working in an office wasn't going to help with that.

Earning a higher salary wasn't going to help with that. It'd just fool me into thinking that I was safe when I wasn't.

No, if I wanted to actually make a difference, I had to do more. All the pieces were in place and I'd spent long enough preparing. It was time to make the jump.

THE ADMIRAL NELSON was noisy. I got there early, found a corner table, and waited.

Colin, Pavel, and Anton all arrived at about the same time. I waved Pavel and Anton over, and there was a moment of confusion when they and Colin approached my table together until they realised that he was supposed to be there as well.

"Hey, little prince," Pavel told me, gesturing to Colin. "He with you?"

"Yes," I said, trying not to show my annoyance. I hated that nickname and wished Pavel would stop using it. "Anton, you okay?"

Anton nodded. He and Pavel were from Romania, heavyset with a weather-beaten look. Anton was taller, Pavel more talkative. I'd met them last year while I was learning the ins and outs of locating, then again during that disastrous raid on Christmas Eve.

"This all?" Pavel asked, glancing around. The pub had enough people that we didn't stand out, but not so many that we were at risk of being overheard.

"We're waiting for two more," I told him.

Bridget showed up next, pausing at the door and giving the whole pub a doubtful look before spotting us and walking over. I saw the bartender giving her the side-eye. My half-sister is small, pretty, delicate-looking, and very obviously underage—she's sixteen and looks younger. The bartender took his eyes off her as she came over to our table.

"Oh, hey, it's you guys," Bridget said to Pavel and Anton. Her eyes rested on Colin. "And you'd be . . ."

"Colin," Colin said, shaking her hand.

"Another locator?" Bridget asked.

"Call me the tech support," Colin said with a grin.

"We're meeting here?" Bridget said, glancing around.

"What were you hoping for?" I asked. "A conference room?" The truth was, Bridget was right—this *was* a pretty crappy place to plan an operation—but it wasn't like I could pack everyone into my bedroom, and every other public place that I'd been able to think of was worse. I wondered how real raiders handled these things.

Bridget sighed and pulled out a chair, giving the seat a doubtful look before perching on it gingerly. "I hope you didn't bring Leo this time," I told her. The Admiral Nelson's a dog-friendly pub, but there are limits.

"He's out in the car."

Ivy was the last to arrive, and she looked ill at ease right from the start. She glanced around uncertainly, and I think if I hadn't caught her eye and given her a wave, she might have walked right back out again. Instead she picked her way over and, after some hesitation, pulled out a chair a little way from everyone else.

"Oh, hi, Ivy," Bridget said. She looked at me. "So are you going to tell us why we're here?"

"I want to put together a team," I told the others around the table. I saw a couple of sideways glances, but not many. I hadn't been too specific in my invitations, but everyone had probably come here with a fairly good idea of what this was going to be about.

I was keeping an eye on the other people in the pub. No one

had sidled over, but we were definitely getting looks, and it wasn't hard to guess why. Our group consisted of me and Bridget (English, young-looking), Anton and Pavel (thirty-something, Eastern European), Colin (college age, half-Chinese), and Ivy (college age, African). People will tell you that London is "diverse," and that might be true if you only look at the numbers, but if you actually live here you notice how segregated it is. The Bangladeshis hang out with other Bangladeshis, the West Africans hang out with other West Africans, the rich kids in their semi-detached houses go to school with other rich kids in semi-detached houses. Some groups mix—the working-class white kids and black kids in my old school would play football together—but most don't. Our group looked like a poster from an HR department.

"Why?" Ivy asked.

"We've all been on raids before, right?" I said. Not strictly true, given that Colin and Bridget were at the table, but I didn't want to get into that. "How do they go? A corp recruits us, they tell us where to go and what to do. If we're lucky, everything goes to plan and we get paid a tiny little fraction of what the Well's worth. If we're not, we get sold out. Either way, we run all the risk, they get all the profit."

I paused to see if anyone would speak up. They didn't.

"So why not cut out the middleman?" I went on. "Do the whole thing ourselves. Pick a Well, raid it, and either use the essentia for sigls, or turn it into aurum and sell it."

"Sell it where?" Pavel asked.

"We find a buyer," I said, trying to project more confidence than I felt. "The demand's there."

"Is it that easy, though?" Bridget said. "The whole reason drucraft corporations run these raids is because they're the ones who buy the aurum."

"So we find a different corporation. Or someone who sells to a corporation."

"It's illegal," Ivy said.

"I mean, yes," I said. "Raids generally are."

"The one we went on wasn't," Ivy said.

"Well..." Bridget said. "It kind of was."

"But if someone had called the police, they wouldn't have shown up," Ivy said. "If we just pick some random B-class Well and break in, they *will*."

"The police don't give a shit about break-ins these days," Colin said.

"They don't care about *regular* break-ins," Bridget corrected. "Some middle-class person getting their house burgled, sure, they'll ignore it. A big corporation's another story."

"Only if they know something's happening," I said. "Invisible people don't show up on security cameras."

"You realise Houses and corporations *know* about drucraft invisibility, right?" Bridget said. "You try to break into a corp HQ or a House's mansion and count on basic invisibility to keep you hidden, you're in for a really nasty surprise."

"I'm not talking about HQs or mansions, I'm talking about low- to mid-level Wells. They can't afford to have cameras and security *everywhere*."

"Well, that's true," Bridget admitted.

"It's still stealing," Ivy said.

"I thought you were a locator?" Bridget asked Ivy curiously.

"A locator. Not a raider."

"Aren't they pretty much the same thing?"

Ivy gave Bridget an indignant look.

"I mean, I thought they kind of overlapped," Bridget said. "You know, they're the people who find you Wells or aurum, and you're kind of not supposed to ask too many questions about where it's coming from . . . ?"

"Locators do it *legally*," Ivy said. "Raiders don't."

"So why were you on that raid?" Pavel asked.

"It was a legal raid."

Anton made a scoffing noise. Pavel rolled his eyes.

"It's true," Ivy insisted.

"I think legal versus illegal is kind of a grey area for these things . . ." Bridget began.

"You too good for us?" Pavel said to Ivy. "That how it is?"

"I didn't say that."

"Then what?"

"Okay, okay," I said, waving my hands. "Let's cool it, all right?"

Pavel gave me a look but settled back in his chair. Ivy looked as if she was on the verge of getting up and walking out. "She doesn't like us, go get lost," Pavel said, gesturing towards the door.

"Enough," I told him. "Okay?"

Pavel subsided. Anton was frowning but said nothing.

"Look," I said, turning to Ivy. "I don't really like doing this either. But it feels like these days, trying to do things the law-abiding way . . . it just means getting exploited. If you haven't got the right connections, you get stuck at the bottom of the barrel on minimum wage forever. And if you try something risky, like we did over Christmas, it's even money you get sold out. I mean, you remember how that ended, right?"

Ivy looked unhappy but didn't answer.

"Okay," Pavel said. "This is fine, but . . ." He rubbed his thumb and first finger together. "Who's paying?"

"No one, yet," I said. "We get the aurum from a Well and sell it. Split the money."

Anton and Pavel glanced at each other, and Ivy leant back in her chair. All three looked dissatisfied. I'd had the feeling the three of them would be the hardest to persuade. Colin's my friend and Bridget's my family, but Anton, Pavel, and Ivy were practically strangers. Unfortunately, they were also the only other actual locators at the table.

"We don't have to only sell Wells," I said. "We could use them ourselves."

Now it was Pavel's turn to make a scoffing sound. Anton asked something in Romanian and Pavel replied in the same language.

"What?" I asked.

"Who makes the sigls?" Pavel asked.

"Me," I said. "I've done it before." I didn't mention that so far, the only other creature I'd made a sigl for had been my cat.

"Sigls don't put food on the table," Pavel said.

"Not directly," I argued. "But each sigl you add makes you a bit more versatile, a bit more able to defend yourself. You and Anton, you told me you've had to run from raiders before, right? Maybe if you had a few more sigls of your own, things might have gone better . . . ?"

I noticed that Ivy seemed to be paying more attention all of a sudden. But Anton and Pavel didn't look persuaded. When I'd rehearsed this in my head, I'd tried to think of how to say this in a way that would convince me, but it didn't seem to be convincing them . . .

"Maybe tell them that you've already got a target," Colin suggested.

"Right," I said. "Look, this isn't just theoretical. I've got a Well picked out."

"Where?" Pavel asked.

"What class?" Ivy asked.

"C," I told Ivy, then looked at Pavel. "And I'll tell you when we get there."

"So why you don't take it yourself?" Pavel asked.

"It's in an office building," I admitted.

I got a bunch of blank looks.

"It's a big building, and it'd be a lot safer with people watching the front and the back," I explained. "Besides . . . think of this as like a trial run. I want to try this out on a not-so-difficult target so that we can scale it up to harder ones."

"I guess that makes sense," Bridget said.

I squared my shoulders and looked around at everyone. "So? You in or out?"

Twenty minutes later, I watched the door swing closed. Bridget, Ivy, Pavel, and Anton were gone. Only Colin remained.

"You think they'll show up?" I asked.

Colin looked thoughtfully towards the door. "Some of them?"

I sighed, letting the tension go out of my muscles a little. "Was it just me, or did they not look very convinced?"

"It wasn't just you."

"What was I doing wrong? I mean, I wasn't expecting them to jump at the chance or anything, but . . ."

"Well, no offence, dude," Colin said, "but you don't exactly come across as an experienced criminal."

"How do I come across?"

"Like a fresher recruiting for the dance team."

I grimaced. I shouldn't be surprised, really. I might be good-looking, but in a "pretty" way, not in a "natural leader" way. And I'm not great at acting like I know what I'm doing when I don't.

"Your end goal here's still sigls, right?" Colin asked. "That's Step Five of your five-step plan?"

"Yeah."

"Then why'd you pitch it to them like a business plan?" Colin asked. "You made it sound like the money came first and the sigls were an afterthought."

"Did you see how Pavel and Anton reacted?" I asked. "I could barely get them to agree on this. After we do a few successful raids, then maybe I can talk them into thinking a bit bigger."

"Don't you mean *if* we do a few successful raids?"

"Well, the first one went fine."

"Mm."

"So what do you think?" I asked.

"I think you'd better tell Felix to hurry up with a buyer for that aurum," Colin said. "Because it doesn't sound to me like your locator friends are going to work on credit."

CHAPTER 9

THERE ARE TIMES when everything goes well. You'll be playing a pickup game of football where the teams might look equal at first, but for some reason yours just clicks. Everyone works together, passing when they should, playing their role and putting the team first. Your team scores goal after goal, and it all feels effortless, and everyone gets confident, which makes them play better, which makes them *more* confident, until it's obvious to everyone that you're going to win. It's a comfortable feeling, like having the wind at your back, and when you get it, you just want to enjoy the moment while you cruise to victory.

And then there are times that are the exact opposite.

Things began going wrong right from the start. Bridget was delayed because of her driver, and while we were waiting, Pavel started asking for money. He and Anton wanted some sort of down payment in case the raid didn't work out. I told him there wasn't anything to pay him *with*, but the argument dragged on.

Next I found out that Ivy wasn't coming. She'd sent the text message earlier, but the argument with Pavel and Anton had distracted me and I didn't see it until she was already supposed to be there. She was vague about the reasons, only that she "couldn't make it"; I wanted to phone and ask what the hell that was supposed to mean, but knew that it wouldn't actually change the answer. Anyway, the whole reason I'd picked this place was that it was low security; we should be able to manage without her.

I hoped.

We met up with Bridget near the Well. It was an office building off High Road Leytonstone, a blocky building with a sign saying "LVS Services," and somewhere inside was a Matter Well. I'd known about it for a year, but the fact that it was very obviously claimed had always stopped me from making a move. Now that I'd already crossed that particular line, it was a natural place to start.

The Well was inside the building's walls, meaning that if I wanted to reach it I was going to have to break in. The place was solidly built, with walls partially topped with barbed wire, but I'd scouted it out during the daytime and I had a plan. There was a row of shops backing onto the office building; if I could get on top of them, I should be able to cross over and climb up onto the office roof. From studying satellite photos, I saw that the office roof looked to have a door, meaning I could descend to the Well, tap it, then go back out the way I'd come in. While I was inside, Pavel and Anton would watch the front and back, while Colin would provide eyes in the sky. Bridget and her dog would provide backup, but since I would be the only one actually doing the break-in, I couldn't see any way in which this could go seriously wrong. If someone raised an alarm, I could just turn invisible and run. It should be completely safe.

I hoped.

At first everything was easy. Colin got his drone in the air, Anton and Pavel took up their positions, and Bridget found a place out of line of sight to wait (with complaints about being bored). My strength and lightfoot sigls made it an easy climb onto the roof of the shops, and from there I was able to get across onto the roof of the LVS building.

Then things stopped being easy.

My phone buzzed while I was studying the door, and I fished it out of my pocket with a frown. "What?"

Pavel spoke over the shared line. "Police."

I'd been in the middle of figuring out how to get through the door, but that brought my thoughts to a screeching halt. "What?"

"At the front."

I crept to the front of the roof and peered cautiously over the edge. The office building fronted onto High Road Leytonstone; fluorescent streetlights painted the pavement in pools of orange, and parked in front of the building was a Met Police car. The yellow and blue checks would have made it obvious even without the big letters painted on the roof.

Shit!

I pulled back quickly. "How long's it been there?"

"Couple of minutes."

It was *right* in front of the building. High Road Leytonstone is busy, but it was close to midnight and there was only a scattering of cars and people. There was no reason for a police car to be loitering here.

"Colin, you seeing this?" I said into the phone.

"Yeah."

"What are they doing?"

"I dunno, just sitting there. You trip an alarm or something?"

"No! . . . I mean, I don't think so." Had I triggered something without realising it?

I looked at the door behind, dark and shadowed in the night. It was locked, but I was pretty sure I could force it, and back when

I'd been planning this I'd thought that wouldn't be a big deal—by the time anyone noticed and called it in, I should have had more than enough time to make it to the Well. But that had been assuming there wasn't a police car right outside the front door!

"They're not getting out," Colin said.

"So?"

"So maybe they're not here because of you? Maybe they just picked this spot to park while they're eating their doner kebabs."

"They just happened to pick this *exact* spot?"

Bridget chimed in on the shared line. "You might have hit a silent alarm."

"This doesn't make sense," I said. I was getting frustrated. "This Well's only a mid-C, that was the whole reason I picked it. It shouldn't have this much security!"

"Didn't you say it was full, though?"

"So?"

"People usually beef up security on a Well when it's full," Bridget explained. "Especially if they've got a shaping scheduled."

"You couldn't have mentioned that *before*?"

"I thought you knew that already."

"All right, all right," Colin asked. "What's the call?"

I hesitated. I could feel the Well beneath me, overflowing with essentia. It was strong—at least twice as strong as the one we'd hit at Elephant and Castle. I could probably pull the essentia from it in only twenty minutes.

But to do so I'd have to break in and get through any other barriers between me and the Well. What were the chances that I could do all that before the police responded?

Maybe I should wait for them to go away? They couldn't stay out all night . . . but neither could we. How long before someone was spotted, or got impatient?

"Hey," Pavel said. "We doing this, or what?"

I took a breath and closed my eyes, slipping into the state of mind I used to sense essentia. I could feel the currents around me, tinted red with the light of the Well underneath. How did this feel?

Chaotic. Spinning out of control.

"Hey. You going?"

I opened my eyes. "No."

"What?"

"We're calling it off," I said into the phone. The Well was so close, but . . . no. "I'm coming back."

"Hey, hey," Pavel objected. "What the hell? You can't just—"

I hung up, activated my sigls, and watched the world shimmer into shades of blue as I started back the way I came. I knew I'd be able to get back down safely. I also knew Pavel and Anton were not going to be happy.

"Unhappy" was an understatement.

"What the hell?" Pavel demanded. "Why?"

"Because the police were right outside," I told him.

"So? You go in, get the stuff, run. Right?"

We'd retreated down High Road Leytonstone to a tiny park by the side of the road; it was a strip of grass about the size of a train carriage, with three sad-looking trees. It was a terrible place to have a meeting, but it had been hard enough dragging Pavel and Anton even this far.

"It takes *time* to tap a Well," I said. "The police would have shown up before I was halfway done."

"How you know?" Pavel demanded. "Your friend, he say they're busy eating kebabs. Maybe they don't get out."

"I didn't actually see them eating kebabs," Colin said. He'd packed up his drone and had it slung over his shoulder in a carrying case. "I just said for all we knew—"

"Who gives a shit?" Pavel pointed back up High Road Leytonstone. "Stop being a pussy and go!"

"No," I said. "That's a terrible idea."

"Why?"

"Look, it *can't* be a coincidence that they showed up like that. And if they noticed something the first time—"

"Stop being little bitch."

"Did you hear a word I just said?" I told him in annoyance.

Anton said something aggravated-sounding in Romanian.

"What is it?" I asked.

"He says, the police come, you set the dog and chew them up," Pavel said. He gestured towards Bridget. "Yes?"

"Hey," Bridget objected. She'd been standing quietly at the edge of the group until now. "Don't drag me into this."

"We're not having her dog chew up any police!" I said.

"So why you bring her?" Pavel demanded.

"Look, I don't know how things work in Romania, but you don't *do* stuff like that over here. The police might not care about regular London street crime, but they're going to start caring pretty fast once you sic a hellhound on them!"

"We could have been earning tonight!" Pavel said, his voice rising. "You think we have money to hang around when you talk and talk and—"

"Hey, hey," Colin interrupted. "Let's keep it down."

Pavel, Anton, and I all reflexively glanced around. It was past midnight, and High Road Leytonstone was mostly empty... but a couple of people were walking on the pavement opposite and there were lights in the windows. No one was obviously listening in, but they might be.

A few seconds ticked away as everyone took a moment to reset. Anton said something to Pavel.

"Have you guys forgotten what happened at Christmas?" I asked Pavel and Anton. "When I told you to be careful, and that we should bail? Remember? You didn't listen, and if I hadn't come back and cut you loose, you both would have got it in the neck. You can't give me a little bit of credit?"

That one hit home. Pavel looked embarrassed; he turned to Anton and they spoke for a few seconds, then he turned back to me. "Credit doesn't pay bills."

I didn't have an answer for that.

"Look," Pavel said. "You're a good kid. But . . . this isn't working." He nodded towards Bridget. "You go back to your family. Okay?"

I stared at him, but Pavel didn't wait for an answer. He and Anton turned and walked away.

The three of us stood for a few seconds in silence.

"I need to go too," Bridget said at last, then hesitated. "I'm going to be honest, I'm not sure I'll be coming next time, either. I mean, if I'm just going to be sitting around, I don't think there's much point."

"You were the one who *wanted* to go on raids," I said in frustration. "You were twisting my arm to do this for months!"

"Well, yeah, but that was when I thought they'd be exciting," Bridget complained. "Not hanging around waiting for something that never happens. Tomorrow's a school day, and if Mummy notices how late I got in, I'm going to have a lot of trouble coming up with a story, you know? I don't want to risk it unless it's for something important."

I wanted to throw up my hands. "Fine! I'll . . . see you around. I guess."

Bridget left. Colin and I were the only ones remaining. "Well," Colin said, "that didn't go very well."

I sighed. "I'm going home."

It was an hour and a half later.

". . . and then there was a huge row and everyone left," I finished. "Well, everyone except Colin. I went home and then came here."

"You sure you didn't get caught on camera?" my father asked. "Or followed?"

"Caught on camera doing *what*?" I demanded. "Standing around on a roof? We didn't *do* anything. The whole night was a total bust."

My father nodded. "You were lucky."

"That's what you call being lucky?"

I was with my dad in the same Barbican flat. Just like before, the blinds were down; unlike before, a couple of bottles of apple juice were sitting opened on the coffee table. He'd asked me last time what my favourite drinks were these days, and I'd mentioned a brand that I liked but couldn't usually afford. There'd been a stock of them in the fridge when I'd shown up.

I'd arranged this meeting in advance. My hope had been that I'd arrive with an impressively big piece of aurum that I could show to my dad and ask him for advice on where to sell it. Instead, all I'd brought him was a thoroughly unimpressive story.

"Most raids are busts," my father told me. "The Well gets used first, there's too much security, something goes wrong at the last minute . . . it doesn't take much. At least, not if the raiders are careful. And if they're not, then they're a bunch of idiots who are going to end up dead or in prison."

"That's why you think I'm lucky? Because it wasn't a total disaster?"

"No, because what you were doing was doomed from the start," my father said seriously. "When you do that, the best thing that can happen is that it falls apart straightaway. If things had worked out tonight, you would have come away pleased with yourself and thinking that you were on the right track. Long term, that would have been worse."

I sighed. "Okay, so I screwed up. Can we skip to the bit where you tell me how?"

"You screwed up because you weren't being selective enough," my father said. "Usually the way you start something like this is with people who know each other already. Went to school together, were in the army together, are cousins or brothers or something. Anything that lets you know them really, really well, so that you know you're starting with the right people. You started with the wrong people."

"What was wrong with them?"

"They were the wrong type," my dad said. "Look." He pulled over a piece of scrap paper and started sketching a diagram. "Whenever any new thing gets built, it's always a certain kind of person who does all the heavy lifting. The ones who come up with the ideas and work the hardest and are the most committed. Different fields have different names for them—officers, founders, partners. They're always a bit weird, a bit obsessive. Then you have the rest. The ones who just want to get paid and have a laugh and leave work behind when they go home for the day. They don't really commit, not in the same way.

"When you're building something new, something big, you want the first type *only*. You're looking for fanatics, not followers. Later, once the groundwork's been built and you need extra hands, *then* you bring in followers. But with them, it's always a bit transactional, you understand? Cash up front."

"You're saying Pavel and Anton are those kinds of guys."

"I knew plenty like them when I worked security," my father said. "Good guys, could trust them in a fight, but you don't ask them to work for free, you understand? It's just a job for them."

"And Bridget?"

"Same story, except it's entertainment instead of money. I mean, she basically *told* you that she's just doing this for fun. She's not going to be pulling all-nighters."

"So that leaves . . . who? Just Colin?"

"When you're doing something like this, if you're not rejecting most of the people you look at, you're doing it wrong," my dad said. "The most important decision isn't what you do, it's who you pick, and the absolute *worst* thing you can do is saddle yourself with guys you can't count on."

"I guess."

"One bit of advice, though," my dad added. "If you're serious about doing this with Colin, tell him the truth."

"I did tell him the truth."

"Not *all* the truth. For something like this to work, you and your mate have to be on the same page. If the two of you want something different, then you'd better have that out right at the start. Because, if you don't, you'll have it out later, and you can bet your arse that if you do it that way it'll cause ten times as much trouble."

I was silent. I hadn't been completely honest with my dad, either. I'd told him about Vermillion and about Father Hawke, but not about my gift. Or my half-formed suspicions of what might be behind it.

"Anyway," my dad said. "Back to Vermillion and the Winged. I want you to go through that conversation at Stratford."

I did. My dad listened closely, asking questions and making me repeat Vermillion's exact words as well as I could remember them. There was a second bottle of apple juice sitting open on the coffee table by the time I finished.

"All right," my dad said at last. "That's not as bad as it could have been."

"The guy put a knife to my throat right in front of Stratford station."

"I didn't say it was *good*. Just that it could have been worse. The biggest thing I've been afraid of this whole time is that the Winged might just out and out snatch you. If they're still trying to talk you into joining them, you've got some breathing room."

"And what happens when I say no?"

"Are you going to?"

"Yes," I said. Of all my options, joining the Winged still felt like the worst one. I wasn't going to consider it unless I had absolutely no other choice.

"But *they* don't know that," my father said. "So you want to keep that ambiguous as long as you can. As long as they see you as a prospect, they'll hold off."

"Will that work forever?"

"No," my father admitted. "You have to remember that manipulation is these people's specialty. You won't be able to trick them forever, but you can buy yourself time. As of two weeks ago, you're on a clock. You have a significant, but *not* unlimited, amount of time before the Winged run out of patience. Spend it wisely."

"Don't suppose you've got any great ideas as to how?" I said. My father wasn't really telling me anything I didn't already know.

"Honestly?" my father said. "Your raiding plan? It's not a bad one. I can show you how to defend yourself and make yourself a harder target, but you're going to find it really hard to stand up against Winged vanguards without better sigls. And I hate to say it, but this is the most realistic chance you've got of getting them."

"You think I could make it work?"

"Yes," my father said. "You might not realise it, but you're actually a long way ahead of the competition. Your average raider gang has a couple of finder's stones and one extraction sigl between them. The ones who've been around a bit, they might have a scattering of combat sigls. But you literally carry more sigls on your fingers than most entire raider groups." He glanced at me. "You never did tell me how you got so good at shaping so fast."

"Extraction sigl?" I asked, avoiding the question.

"Primal sigls that turn Well essentia into aurum. Raiding kit 101. They've got legitimate uses, so they're not *completely* illegal, but you don't want to get caught with one."

"They're a substitute for shaping, like a finder's stone's a substitute for sensing?"

"Pretty much. Anyway, point is, your average low- and low-middle-grade Well has security intended to keep out your average raider. They're not equipped to keep out someone like you, who can turn invisible and climb like a cat. A C-class Well produces a sigl that'll sell for what, £40K, £50K? That puts a hard limit on how much security the corp or House can keep on it while still turning a profit."

I'd expected my dad to push me harder on the shaping thing. Maybe he figured that I'd tell him when I was ready. "So what went wrong tonight?"

"What went wrong is that number's an *average*," my father said. "The actual amount of security you're going to find at a Well is going to be different each time. What happened tonight could have been a hundred things. Maybe the Well was more valuable than you thought. Maybe there was a laser sensor on the roof. Maybe someone was looking out of their window and saw you and called 999. Maybe they just happened to be doing a random inspection. Maybe the new chief of security was being overzealous. Maybe it was something completely different. The point is, *you don't know.* Every time you go out on a raid, you're rolling the dice. You can do everything the same way and have ten milk runs in a row, then do exactly the same thing the eleventh time and everything goes to hell. This is the reason I'm not especially happy about you doing this, because it's *dangerous.* You can reduce that danger, but you can't make it go away."

I was silent.

"Another thing to remember," my dad added. "When you go on a raid, you're stealing. Yeah, it's easy to tell yourself that the corps and the Houses have it coming. But what about the night watchmen you run into? The random guy on the street who sees you and shouts for you to stop? The copper who starts chasing you? You going to fight them? How much are you willing to hurt them if you do?"

I hesitated.

"When you do something like this, you're opening yourself up to a lot of things going wrong," my dad said. "Sometimes *very* wrong. What you did tonight, feeling like things were getting out of control and calling it off? Keep doing that. If you have to choose between being too brave and being too cautious, always be too cautious, because nothing you can get from a successful raid is worth what a failed one can cost you. Stay jumpy and always be ready for the worst-case scenario, because sooner or later it'll happen."

I remembered my mother's story from last year, of how her sister had been killed in a botched raid when the raiders had blundered into more security than they'd been expecting. It wasn't a pleasant thought.

"Next point," my father said. "You need to realise how you're going to come across to other drucrafters. You remember what Vermillion said about you having that many sigls?"

"He said it made me a House elite, corp special forces, or a gifted."

"Most people haven't even heard about cults, much less a 'gifted.' And no one's going to look at you and believe you're a veteran. So that only really leaves one choice."

"So they're going to think that I'm . . . what? Some rich kid from a House?"

"A rich kid that's slumming it," my dad corrected. "Or the son of some corp executive. Oh, and they're going to assume your sigls are a present from Daddy or bought from a trust fund."

"I worked my arse off for those!"

"You tell them that, they won't believe you."

I frowned.

"That's where things like that 'little prince' nickname come from," my dad added. "Your looks don't help, either."

"So how do I get people to *stop* seeing me like that?"

"Mostly, you don't," my father said. "People judge you, that's just how it works. They see what you've got, but not what you did to get it. And they don't really care. Best advice? Lean into it. If someone calls you a prince, laugh and play it up. Say that if they do a good job, you'll put in a good word for them with the king."

"I don't *know* the king," I said. I knew that arguing about this was kind of ridiculous, but it was *really* annoying. "As far as the Ashfords are concerned, I'm already the poor relation. Now you're telling me I'm going to get it from both sides?"

"Pretty much. Anyway, try not to let it bother you. You've got bigger things to worry about."

It was a good point, and I shook off my annoyance, turning my attention to what was actually important. "Vermillion didn't think my sigls were from a trust fund," I said. "He figured out that I'd made them, just from watching me use them."

"Okay?"

"He called me a gifted." I watched my dad's face closely as I spoke, looking for a reaction. "Actually, he didn't call me one so much as he just took it for granted. Like it was so obvious there wasn't even any point discussing it."

"I told you, manipulation is the Winged's specialty. They want you to believe something, they can make it very convincing."

"You're saying he's lying."

"Not lying. Like I said, the Winged are believers. This Vermillion, he probably really *does* believe that he's an elite warrior of his god. But just because he believes it, doesn't make it true."

I was quiet for a moment. So what *was* true? If the story that Vermillion and Father Hawke had told me about my gift wasn't true, then what was?

I remembered what my dad had said about being on the same page. Maybe it was time to stop hiding things.

"What if he's right?" I asked my dad.

"About what?"

"You asked how I got so good at shaping so fast," I said. "It's not shaping. It's seeing."

I told him then. I didn't go into the details of the night that I'd gained my gift or Father Hawke's speculation, but I did go into the details of exactly what it could do. "And it looks like Vermillion and the Winged know about it," I finished. "Even if they don't know exactly what I can do, they know I can do something."

My father frowned.

"So?" I asked nervously when he didn't speak. "What do you think?"

"It fills in a few holes," my father said slowly. "I'd been wondering why they'd been quite so interested in you. Now it makes a lot more sense." He nodded, seeming to come to a decision. "Well, I can see why you went with the raiding plan."

I waited for him to go on. "So?" I said when he didn't.

"What?"

"Don't you think this changes things?"

"Not really. The Winged are still trying to recruit you as a vanguard, you're still going to say no. All this means is that you've got an extra trick up your sleeve."

"But . . ." I tried to figure out how to say what was bothering me. "What if it's true?"

My father sighed. "Sometimes there isn't an answer to that question."

"What does that mean?"

"Vermillion told you that you got your gift from a 'daimon,'" my father said. "For some unknown reason, it reached down out of the sky, picked you, and handed you this random, seemingly impossible power. Then it disappeared just as mysteriously as it came. It hasn't talked to you, and according to him, it probably never will. From your perspective, you don't really know where the ability came from. All you know is that before, you didn't have it; now, you do. Right?"

"Right."

"Now turn that around," my dad said. "Let's say that there's some plateau of sensing skill where, if you're talented enough and you work hard enough, you eventually tip over the edge and you can see essentia instead of feeling it. It's not well known because hardly anyone reaches it, but it's there. One night you push yourself harder than you've ever pushed yourself before, and you tip over. And once you've done it, finding your way back is easier. Again, you don't really know where it came from. All you know is that before, you didn't have it; now, you do. Okay?"

"Okay . . ."

"So which one of those is wrong?"

"I don't know. That's the point."

My father shook his head. "No, it's not."

"So what's the answer?" I asked.

"The answer's neither."

I frowned.

"They're *models*," my father said. "Different ways of seeing the world. The Winged would say your ability's a gift from a daimon. A drucraft researcher would say that it's some aspect of sensing we don't understand. And someone who didn't know anything about drucraft wouldn't think it needed explaining at all. And all those models *work*. They all explain the world just fine."

"But I don't want something that works. I want to know what's *true*."

"That's because you're twenty-one," my father said with a slight smile. "But here's something to think about. Look at the story Vermillion was telling you. According to him, you're not just a talented drucrafter, you've got a special gift. More than that, it's a gift which comes with absolutely no strings attached. It's like those action movies where the hero's some sort of government super-assassin, but for some reason he doesn't have to follow the government's orders. All the power, none of the restrictions. Right?"

"I guess," I said slowly.

"So take a think about the fantasy he's selling," my father said. "In his world, you get to be divinely gifted, *and* incredibly powerful, *and* free to do whatever you want. You get to be a part of this elite brotherhood, having a life filled with luxury and danger and excitement, and all you have to do is sign on the dotted line. Now think for a second. If you wanted to talk a young man into joining you, someone smart and restless, but without much to anchor them . . . isn't that exactly how you'd sell it to him?"

I was silent.

"I told you," my father said. "The Winged are *good* at this. They know how to tell you exactly what you want to hear. Just like they did with me."

"So what do you think I should do?"

"Exactly what you're doing," my father said. "Build up your strength and abilities, and keep the Winged at arm's length. You won't be able to do that forever, but buy yourself as much time as you can. And I'll do what I can to help."

I nodded reluctantly. I could see the logic. Vermillion and the Winged were the big threats; I didn't have the luxury of hanging around overthinking things. For now, the priority was keeping myself safe.

But was that enough? I remembered my decision after that conversation with Vermillion. *I have to pick a side.* The raiding plan would make me stronger, but was it really an answer?

I pushed it out of my mind. But something was telling me that I might not be able to put it off much longer.

CHAPTER 10

I WENT HOME that night with mixed feelings. My talk with my father had left me feeling better, but things were a long way from solved.

Our group (if you could call it that) was supposed to be meeting again on Tuesday, and I spent most of Monday seriously considering just calling the whole thing off. I was sick of arguing with Pavel and Anton about money, sick of hearing Bridget complain about being bored, and was feeling (especially after my father's advice) like just writing off the whole thing. But Colin texted me on Tuesday afternoon saying that he was coming, and he was the only one I actually wanted to talk to, so as the sun started to dip behind the tower blocks of Plaistow I left my home and wandered over to the Admiral Nelson, secretly hoping that Colin would be the only one who'd show up.

But when I walked into the pub, I got a surprise. Colin was there . . . and opposite him was Ivy.

"Hey, dude," Colin said as I walked over. Ivy gave me a nod but didn't say anything.

"Uh," I said. "Hey." Colin had a pint in front of him and Ivy some sort of soft drink. Both were three-quarters empty. I looked at Ivy. "I thought you weren't coming."

"I asked her to come early," Colin chipped in. "Why don't you grab a drink?"

I gave him a dubious look, went to the bar and ordered, then came back and sat down facing Colin and Ivy. Both were looking at me. I glanced at Colin and raised my eyebrows.

"So," Colin began, "I think we can say Sunday night didn't go to plan."

"That's one way to put it."

"So I invited Ivy over and we've been sharing stories. About where to go from here."

"Yeah, about that," I said. "I'm starting to think this whole raiding group wasn't the best idea."

"But you already said that you can't do it all on your own," Colin countered. "If you're going to be shaping sigls, you need someone watching your back while you do it, right?"

"Didn't we just try that?"

"But everyone wasn't exactly on the same page. You made it sound like some sort of startup business. Raid Wells, sell the aurum."

"Yeah..."

"Except you didn't have anyone to sell it *to*," Colin said. "So your whole story was kind of bullshit, wasn't it? If you'd been serious, you'd have twisted Felix's arm to find you a contact first. You made it sound like it was about money, then it turned out you *didn't* actually care about money. That was why those Romanian guys got pissed off."

"I told you. I'm not just looking for aurum, I'm looking for sigls."

"Yeah, but you've never actually explained why this matters to you so badly. I mean, you've got how many of these things already? But you still want more?"

"Not want. Need."

"Okay, so . . . why?"

I hesitated, my natural caution pushing me to keep my mouth shut. A lot of this stuff was verging on secrets that I shouldn't be sharing. It would have been one thing if it were just Colin, but Ivy was practically a stranger . . .

I remembered my father's advice. *Tell him the truth.*

"Okay," I said. "You really want to know? You're right. I'm not in this for the money. What I'm hoping to get out of this is sigls. As many as possible, as powerful as possible, so that I can protect myself. You remember that guy who attacked me last month?"

"You're worried about him coming back?"

"No," I said. "I mean, yes, but . . . honestly? My feeling is, the way things are going, that's going to become the new normal for me. I'm going to end up in more situations like that. I can't really get into the details, because I don't know most of them. But the short version is, I have to get a lot more powerful."

"When you say, 'a lot more powerful' . . . ?" Ivy asked, speaking for the first time.

"I mean something like 'one-man army,'" I said. "As in, able to take on a squad of armed soldiers or a SWAT team, and win. And yeah, I know that makes me sound a bit like a raving psycho, which is one of the reasons I haven't talked about this. But I've seen what I think I'm going to be facing, and that's the sort of level I need to be playing on."

Colin and Ivy looked at each other.

"Is this putting you off?" I asked.

"Maybe a bit," Ivy admitted.

"I mean, after last month, it's less of a surprise," Colin said. "I didn't tell her the details about that, by the way."

"Thanks," I said, and looked at Ivy. "If you want to back out, now's the time."

"These people you're worried about," Ivy said slowly. "Are they—?"

"I can't tell you the details," I interrupted. "No offence, but I don't know you well enough."

I'd thought that might offend Ivy, but she only nodded. "So," I said, turning back to Colin. "That's the long and short of it. You still interested?"

Colin and Ivy shared another look. "I mean," Colin said to her, "it kind of fits?"

Ivy hesitated, then nodded.

"Fits how?" I asked.

"Here's the thing," Colin said. "The two of us have been talking, and . . . honestly, neither of us are really motivated by the money angle either. I mean, it'd be nice, but it's not why we're here."

"Then why *are* you here?"

"I want you to keep teaching me drucraft, for a start," Colin said. "Beyond that, though . . . Ivy, you want to tell him?"

Ivy sat silently for a few seconds before speaking. "I want what you've got."

I looked at her with a frown.

"To be able to do everything you can," Ivy explained. "Make the same sigls as you."

"But you're already a drucrafter."

"I want to be better."

"You've got your own sigls."

"I've got *two*," Ivy said with a sigh. "Okay? Made *for* me, by my family. I couldn't make them on my own. I want to be able to."

"Same," Colin added.

"Okay, back up, back up," I said. The way Colin and Ivy were looking at me was starting to make me uncomfortable. "Look, I think you guys have got the wrong idea here. I'm good at drucraft, but half the time I'm figuring it out as I go along. I am really not qualified to be a teacher."

"We're not stupid, Stephen," Ivy said. "We're not expecting you to turn us into manifesters overnight. But you seem to be able to work with essentia and spot Wells better than anyone I know. I thought when we first met that you must have someone making all those sigls for you, but Colin says you made them yourself. Is that true?"

"Yes."

"So whatever you're doing, it's obviously working. All those sigls you used at the raid at Christmas? I want ones just like them. Invisibility, so that I can hide from people; and Matter ones, to speed me up; and Life ones, to make me stronger; and—"

"Whoa, whoa, whoa," I said, raising both hands. "You do not know what you're asking. It took me nearly a year to make all of those. Years *more* to learn how to do it."

"But you know how to make them *now*."

"Yes..."

"So you can show me," Ivy concluded. "Figuring that out's supposed to be the hardest part, right?"

I gave Ivy a dubious look. I still wasn't sure what to make of the slightly built, dark-skinned girl. We hadn't met many times, and, when we had, we'd spent half our time arguing. Ivy hadn't trusted me, and she hadn't been shy about showing it. Now, all of a sudden, she was proposing some sort of partnership. "Can you even shape your own sigls?"

"Well, not exactly," Ivy said defensively. "But I'm getting close. I could do it if I had someone showing me what I'm doing wrong."

"And I'd like a sigl or two of my own," Colin added. "They sound really cool. You can make ones that don't need the user to actually be a drucrafter, right?"

"Continuous ones, yeah," I said, rubbing my forehead. "It's just... You understand how much *time* this is going to take?"

"We're not asking you to work for free," Ivy said. "I can help you out too."

"How?"

"Well, you know I'm a locator, too, right?" Ivy said. "Maybe my sensing's not *quite* as good as yours, but I still find plenty of Wells. If you tell me what kind you're looking for, and I make note of them and save them for you, then you're going to find the Wells you need twice as fast."

Huh. That made me stop and think. Right now, Wells were my big bottleneck. If Ivy really was willing to pool her findings with me, it'd speed me up massively...

But that was a big "if." "You realise the ones I'm interested in are the most valuable ones, right?" I asked Ivy. "You sure you want to be sharing those?"

"I do want the money. But I want to be a powerful drucrafter more."

"And you're not going to be tempted to fail to mention the best ones?"

For the first time in the conversation, Ivy looked offended. "I *said* I'd tell you."

"And I can help out as well," Colin added. "I mean, maybe I'm not going to be able to sense Wells anytime soon..."

"Learning the drucraft disciplines takes something like one or two *years*," I told him. "Each."

"Okay, fine. But I can run the drone for you, and I can help out with Felix trying to find a buyer for your aurum. Sigls are your number one goal, but earning a living from this is number two, right?"

"Yeah," I said, then paused, looking at the two of them.

Did I actually want to do this? A small, dedicated team was

pretty much exactly what my dad had told me I should be looking for. No matter how skilled or careful I was, there were some targets I couldn't handle alone.

To be honest, if this had just been Colin making the offer, I would have already said yes. It was Ivy that I had doubts about. The other locator was very much an unknown quantity, and I had the feeling there were still a few things she wasn't telling us. Sure, she seemed capable enough, but what if she wanted something I couldn't give? Or if she turned out to be so obnoxious that I couldn't stand working alongside her?

What Ivy and Colin were really asking here was for me to invest in them. Which would mean that, in the short term, I'd actually accomplish *less* than if I spent the same amount of time working alone. In the long term, it had the potential to be more... but only if it worked out.

Would it work out? Did I trust them?

I understood now what my dad had meant about the most important decision being who you picked. This was a big one.

"What are you guys looking to get out of this?" I asked Colin and Ivy. "What do you want?"

"I want to be a master drucrafter," Ivy said.

"And I want to learn as much as I can about it," Colin added. "This is way more interesting than leaving uni and becoming a management consultant."

I looked at the two of them. Both looked back at me.

They've been thinking about this for a while, I realised. This wasn't something they'd come up with on the spur of the moment. How long had they been turning it over in their minds?

Time to choose.

"All right," I said. I held my hand out over the table. "We'll give it a try."

I shook Colin's hand, then Ivy's. Then the three of us sat back and looked at each other.

"So," Ivy said. "Where do we start?"

AND SO OUR group was founded.

We kept things small in the early weeks. We restricted our targets to D and D+ Wells and scouted each one carefully before making a move. A couple of times we began our raid only to see signs that might have been an alarm or approaching police; both times I called things off. I remembered my father's advice.

I also remembered how much trouble Ivy had given me in the past. In our previous encounters, the African girl's attitude towards me could best have been described as "default suspicion" . . . to be fair, we hadn't exactly gotten off to a good start in either of them, but that was then and this was now, and, if this was going to work, that had to stop. So in that early period, I kept a close eye on Ivy. I was keeping in mind what my father had said about starting with the right people—if she wasn't going to trust me, it would be best to end things.

But if Ivy didn't trust me, she kept it to herself. I did notice that she had a tendency to watch me out of the corner of one eye, and the few times the two of us were alone together, when Colin was off running the drone and it was just the two of us breaking into a Well, she seemed a little tense. But she never said anything out loud, and I didn't either. She did maintain a certain distance—after that first time in the pub, she never talked about what she wanted to get out of this, and in the aftermath of a successful raid, when Colin and I would relax and kick back with a drink, she'd generally make her excuses and disappear. But that was fine—I was looking for a raiding partner, not a girlfriend, and as long as she pulled her weight she could be as standoffish as she liked.

And she did pull her weight. It was the first time I'd really worked with another locator, and I was surprised at how big of a difference it made. I think at some level I'd been assuming that, compared to me, other locators would be sort of crap. Luckily, I'd been wrong. Ivy's sensing wasn't as good as mine, but she made up for it with persistence and the willingness to work long hours. After the second time she forwarded me a Well location in the early hours of the morning, my respect for her went up a good deal. Ivy might have her faults, but being a slacker definitely wasn't one of them.

Compared to Ivy, Colin couldn't contribute as much. To begin with he'd had some plans of getting a finder's stone and going locating as well, but after Ivy and I had explained to him exactly how *bad* finder's stones were, and after he'd run the numbers on the relative ranges, he'd reluctantly agreed that there wasn't much point. His final-year exams were also coming up, limiting the number of late nights he could pull. But he was still able to help out with sigl research—he couldn't do the actual shaping, but he could look through the Exchange catalogue, dig for information online, and generally take some of the work off my shoulders, as well as operate the drone on the raids.

The situation with the Winged stayed tense. Vermillion didn't contact me again, but Byron was still pushing for another meeting. I didn't want to risk provoking him by saying no, and I wanted to meet him in person even less, so I stalled. But I knew I couldn't do that forever.

On the Ashford front, things were mixed. Calhoun got back in touch and started giving me bodyguard jobs again. But they weren't as frequent as they had been, which was probably at least partly due to the fact that his security had been bumped up—now, every time that we went out, there'd be at least one grim-faced bodyguard. And instead of going through Hendrik and Calhoun's PA, I now had to deal with Anderson, the Ashford head of security, an unsmiling, shaven-headed man with absolutely no sense of humour. Whereas before I'd been free to watch over Calhoun and Johanna as I saw fit, now I was getting instructions to patrol very specific locations, with strict orders not to leave without permission. Quite often the locations didn't seem particularly important, and I started to suspect that Anderson was giving me make-work to keep me out of the way. I thought about complaining to Calhoun, but I didn't want to go running to my cousin with every little problem, and anyway, compared with some of the bosses I'd had in the past, this guy really wasn't that bad.

My mother kept on pushing the supply job, and I kept on resisting. Part of it was logic—I'd pinned my hopes on the raiding plan, and I simply didn't have the time to do an extra job on top of it—but there was also an element of stubbornness to it. My mother had never really given me a very good explanation for *why* she wanted me to take the job, and the more she pushed me to do it, the more I started to feel that she had some reasons she was keeping hidden. I didn't like the feeling of being manipulated, and I didn't want to be any more dependent on the Ashfords than I was already. So for now, I kept her at arm's length.

APRIL TURNED INTO May. Flowers bloomed across London, bare branches becoming lush and green.

Colin, Ivy, and I kept going on raids. There were still more failures than successes, but with each Well our skills became a little better, our teamwork a little smoother. Colin got his first sigl, a continuous strength enhancement which he was very excited about. I got a new Matter sigl for myself and made a flash sigl for Ivy.

I kept putting my mother off about the supply job, but I finally agreed to try out her "lessons."

After each raid I'd meet up with my father. We'd do a post-mortem, with him reviewing the operation, noting which parts had gone well or badly, and pointing out things that we could have done better. He also started giving me some combat sigl training.

I stayed away from Father Hawke. My father's words had planted a seed of doubt in my mind, and now I wasn't sure who to believe. And underneath that was something else: a fear of what I might find out. Raids were difficult and dangerous, but they were something I understood. When I thought about that last conversation with Father Hawke . . . it made me feel small and helpless, a tiny boat on a huge dark sea. So I pushed it away to the edge of my mind, where it could be almost (but not quite) forgotten while I thought about Wells and sigls and essentia, things that I was good at and could control.

May became June. Summer came to London.

CHAPTER 11

"I don't like this," Ivy said.

"Relax," I told her.

It was a summer night in Tower Hamlets. The sun had set not long ago and the hum of the city drifted in from all around. We were a little way north of Whitechapel Market, but the stalls had packed up as darkness had fallen, and any remaining voices from that direction were drowned out by the rush of traffic from the A11. Right now the three of us were on a little side street, dark and deserted. It was a scummy-looking place, but we weren't here for the scenery. We were here for a meeting.

The main goal of my raids with Colin and Ivy had been sigls. We'd identify a Well, figure out what sigls we could make from it, then carry out the raid. But very often it wouldn't be practical to use a Well for a sigl; either it'd be too weak, or too dangerous, or something would go wrong, and when that happened we'd turn the essentia into aurum instead. By this point we'd been doing this for nearly three months, and we'd built up quite a stockpile of aurum as a result—more than five carats' worth. I was hazy on the value of raw aurum (apparently it varies based on the size of the piece), but I was pretty sure that even at black market prices it was worth thousands.

But it doesn't matter what something's worth if you can't find a buyer, and that was what I'd been pushing Felix for. Last week, he'd finally got back to us with the news that he'd found one: a group willing to buy aurum by weight, no questions asked. They'd demanded to meet in this area—apparently it was their home turf. And that was why we were here right now.

"When you said Whitechapel, I thought you meant the market," Ivy said. "Not an alley that looks like a hangout for serial killers."

"It's not an alley," I told Ivy. Privately, I kind of agreed with her; between the high, windowless walls, the bollards cutting off vehicle access, and the scattered rubbish bags, the street didn't exactly give a good impression. "And given what we're here for, I don't know what you were expecting."

"I was expecting somewhere that didn't look like the set from *Candyman*."

"I didn't pick the place."

"You agreed to it."

"It was hard enough getting them to meet us at all," I said, trying to stay patient. Ivy had been skittish about this from the start, and it had taken a long time to talk her around. "You really want to cancel the whole thing because you don't like the look of the street?"

"They probably want to rob us," Ivy said.

"If they do, better to know early."

"Easy for you to say when I'm the one they'll be going for."

"Hey," Colin objected. "What am I, chopped liver?"

Colin and Ivy were standing in the middle of the street. I was a little way away, in the shadows of a garage door. Unlike them, I was hidden from sight by a diffraction sigl. Ivy and Colin were the bait; I was the backup.

We were talking over wireless earbuds. Our first couple of raids had made me realise that it's really awkward to do a raid while holding a phone to your ear, and so we'd eventually upgraded. There had been some teething troubles, but with Colin's help all three of us had now got to the point where we could call each other, have a conversation, and hang up again while keeping our hands free. For such a small thing, it had made a surprisingly big difference.

"Why are we even meeting these guys?" Ivy asked.

"'Cause they're the only ones Felix could find," Colin said.

"There has *got* to be someone better."

"Nice people don't usually buy stolen goods," I told her.

"You sure it isn't worth giving that Mr. Smith guy of yours a go?" Colin said. "At least we know he's in with your old corp."

"Yeah, and he sent me and Ivy on a raid that turned out to be a setup. These guys *might* screw us over, he already *did*."

"Shh," Ivy said. "You hear that?"

Colin and I fell silent, and I took a step back into the shadows. A moment later I heard what Ivy had: echoes from around the corner. The echoes turned into footsteps, growing louder and louder until those who were making them came walking into view.

There were four of them, dressed in trainers and baggy clothes. It was too dark to get a good look at their faces, but from the way they swaggered I pegged them as in their teens or early twenties. As they came out into the open part of the street, a couple turned to scan the area; one looked straight at me and I held very still, but the guy's eyes swept over me without stopping.

The four of them came to a ragged stop, spread out in an irregular line facing Ivy and Colin. The two groups looked at each other for a second.

"Hey there," Colin said.

"Whatcha got?" the guy at the front said in a British-Asian accent.

"Some aurum," Colin said.

"Let's see."

Colin reached into his pocket, and I watched the four closely to see if any of them would tense up or reach for anything. None did. They weren't radiating any essentia, either.

Colin pulled out a small box and held it up to view. There was a pause.

The leader held out his hand with a "give" gesture.

"So what are you paying?" Colin asked.

"Let's have a look."

"What are you paying?"

The leader rubbed his fingers together.

Colin and Ivy shared a look, then Colin put the box back in his pocket.

I sensed the temperature of the meeting drop a few degrees. "What?" the leader said, suddenly sounding a lot less friendly.

"We're not handing out free samples," Colin said.

The leader made a rude noise. " 'S'n empty box."

"Did you bring an aurum scale?" Ivy asked suddenly.

I felt the leader frown. "What?"

"An aurum scale," Ivy said. "They confirm something's aurum and measure its weight."

The leader gave Colin a look, as if to ask why he was letting Ivy open her mouth.

Colin made a gesture that said: *answer the question*.

"I haven't got a fucking aurum scale," the leader told Ivy.

"Then how are you going to tell what it is?" Ivy asked.

The leader stared at her. "You think we're measuring your shit out in the street?" He turned to the others in his group and laughed. They laughed too. The leader turned back to Colin.

"Well," Colin said when they didn't speak. "I'm glad we're all having fun here..."

"You hand that over," the leader told Colin. "We'll check it out. Then we get in touch, tell you what it's worth."

Colin paused.

"You got a problem?" the leader asked.

"That... doesn't sound like a great deal to us," Colin said.

"You calling me a liar?" the leader said. His voice was suddenly cold.

"No," Colin said quickly.

Shit. I was suddenly sure where this was going. "Get ready," I said quietly over the phone link.

The leader held out his hand. "Then hand it over."

Colin hesitated again.

A couple of the men took steps forward. Colin's on the small side, and so's Ivy; the shortest of the strangers was taller than either of them. "Come on," the leader said. He sounded like he was smiling. "All friends here, right? We take a look, tell you what it's worth. Then you'll get your money."

"Yeah, I'm not so sure about that," Colin said.

The men closed in a little more. A couple more steps and they'd be surrounding Colin and Ivy. "Let's do this the easy way," the leader told Colin.

Colin reached his left hand over to his chest, making a small twisting motion. To my eyes, the green light of Life essentia started to spread outward through his body.

"Ivy," I said quietly through the link. "Flash."

The leader's head turned as I spoke. He stared at Ivy.

"Okay," Ivy said loudly. "You want to see some aurum?" She held up one hand. "Take a look."

"You wired?" the leader said.

"Look," Ivy repeated. The ring on her finger glinted slightly in the darkness.

The four guys looked at her.

I felt Ivy channel, essentia surging through the ring.

It didn't work.

I'd already shifted my weight onto my toes, my muscles coiled; I had my target picked out. I sent threads of essentia into the strength sigl at my chest and the new Matter one on my right hand.

"Who are you talking—?" the leader demanded.

Ivy channelled again, and this time it worked. Light bloomed like a star.

Shouts echoed, but I was already moving. Cut essentia to my diffraction and vision sigls, redirect into strength and shadowman. Six steps to the guy on the left. I poured essentia into the sigl on my middle right finger and felt my fist lock up as I reached him.

My new sigl was a Matter one. Like all Matter effects it was designed to take a single physical property of a piece of matter and alter it; in this case the property was hardness, and the piece of matter was my right hand. I'd run into a guy using one last year and knew from personal experience that it felt like being hit with a lump of iron. This was my first time using it for real.

The guy was still rubbing at his eyes from Ivy's attack, and he didn't even see me coming until my fist smashed into his ribs like a wrecking ball. His breath went out with a gasp, and he crumpled up around the punch; from the way he fell, I already knew he wasn't getting up. I spun to face the next guy, getting a confused glimpse of Ivy and Colin struggling with the others, then I saw the glint of a blade and my focus narrowed to the one in front of me.

The guy facing me had pulled a knife, but his eyes as they looked towards me were wide with fear. I had my shadowman sigl running, converting outgoing light to essentia. To the guy facing me, I knew I'd look like a humanoid mass of darkness, a living shadow. Even in daylight it looks creepy; jumping out at you at night, it's terrifying.

The guy—a kid, really, now that I could see his face—backed away, his movements scared and jerky, holding up the knife like a shield. I advanced and he backpedalled, staying out of range. I lifted my left hand and triggered my slam sigl, sending a blast of air into his face. At this range the impact was puny, but it was enough. The boy turned and fled.

"Stephen!" Colin shouted.

I whirled to see the leader advancing on me. He had a knife, too, but unlike the other boy his teeth were bared and he was holding the blade in a stabbing grip. He lunged, grabbing with his free hand.

I skipped aside; the leader stumbled past, groping blindly in the darkness. He tried again and I hit him with a slam that knocked him back a step. Somewhere off to one side I could sense Colin starting towards us, but all my attention was on the leader, time stretching out as the two of us faced each other. It was only the second time I'd been in a knife fight, but I could read the guy's stance; he was looking to grab with his left hand and stab with his right, just as Vermillion had done. I didn't feel any fear. Adrenaline was surging through me, filling me with the thrill of the fight.

The leader feinted once, then again. I watched his body, looking for the shift in weight that'd signal a lunge. He stepped in cautiously, knife held back for a stab, and I smacked him in the face with a slam blast, compressed air knocking his head back with a *whuff*. He tried to back off and I hit him again. *Whuff, whuff.* The blows weren't hard enough to stun but they were rattling him, and as the fourth one hit, he sank a couple of inches, legs tensing. It all seemed to be happening in slow motion and as I saw him lunge I twisted aside, letting the knife go between my body and arm before snapping my left arm in to trap him and punching with my right. It was a clumsy hit, but my Matter-enhanced fist landed like a hammer and the boy's head jolted back; I ducked, slammed two shots into his ribs, drew back for a punch that would finish the job—

—and realised that he was slumping against me. My arm squeezing against the other boy was the only thing holding him up. I loosened my arm and he crumpled, the knife clattering on the paving stones.

I straightened up, looking around for the others, but they were gone. Two were on the ground, and for a moment I had the confused thought that the fight must have lasted so long that Ivy and Colin had chased the others away, then I saw Colin slowing to a halt and realised that the whole duel had happened in the few seconds it had taken for him to close the distance. Ivy, Colin, and I were the only ones standing.

"Where'd the others go?" I asked.

"Legged it," Colin said. "You okay?"

"Stephen?" Ivy said.

Both of them were looking at me uncertainly, and I wondered for a second why before remembering that my shadow cloak was still running. I dispelled it with a moment's thought and glanced down. The leader was stirring, the knife lying a few inches from his hand. "I'm fine," I said, and kicked the knife, sending it skittering away out of reach. "Come on!"

I took off down the street, and Ivy and Colin followed. By the time the two boys on the ground recovered enough to pull themselves upright, we were long gone.

"ALL RIGHT, FELIX," I said an hour later. "What the bloody hell was that?"

We were back at our corner table in the Admiral Nelson. Ivy, Colin, and I were clustered together, talking over the phone to Felix on a group call. Usually by this point Ivy would have disappeared, but I'd suggested she stay with us, just in case. It was a measure of how badly the evening had gone that she'd agreed.

"It's not my fault!" Felix protested. "You wanted some guys who were in the aurum business."

"Yeah, the *aurum* business." I lowered my voice slightly as I said the last bit, glancing instinctively around, but there was no one close enough to overhear. "*Not* some guys who'd try to mug us at knifepoint. What, did I need to spell that out or something? 'WTS aurum, looking for buyer, PS: buyer should not *try to murder us*.'"

"I told you they were a bit dodgy."

"Pulling knives is not 'a bit dodgy'!"

"Okay, okay," Colin said. "So things didn't exactly go to plan."

"Did you really have to beat the shit out of them?" Felix complained. "What am I going to do if Syed gets back to me?"

"Oh, I'm *sorry*," I said. "Next time one of your friends tries to stab us, I'll try to shoo them off in a nice way, shall I?"

"All right, all right."

There was a pause.

"So got anyone else?" I said.

"Oh, yeah, sure, I'll just go right back to my guy and tell him you want a new lot! You know how long it took me to set this up?"

"Yeah, four months! To find a bunch of muggers! If I'd known that was all we were looking for, I could have just gone for a midnight walk through Stratford Park with my phone out. Would have been a hell of a lot faster!"

"Okay, okay," Colin said again. "Felix, I'm guessing that was a no on having anyone else lined up?"

"Wow, you think?"

"Let us know how it goes, okay?"

Felix made a disgruntled sound. There was a little more talk, then he hung up.

"I mean, he's got a point," Ivy said once the phone had gone dark. "You were kind of asking for it."

"Asking for it *was* the point," I said. "We needed to know if we could work with them."

"Well, maybe we *could* have if you'd been standing next to us."

"Sure, and what would we have done the next time, and the time after that? Shown up ready for a fight again and again? What would have happened the one day we didn't? We needed to know if we could trust these guys *not* to rob us as soon as they had the chance."

"Would still be nice if you didn't use us as *bait*."

"Fine, next time *you* get an invisibility sigl and—"

"Would you guys quit it?" Colin said in annoyance. "Look, I don't know why you're even arguing. You said it—they didn't bring an aurum scale. They were never going to pay us."

Ivy seemed about to keep going, then she paused and sighed. "Yeah."

"So why are you blaming me?" I asked.

"It's not that," Ivy said. "It's just . . . I was counting on this working out."

I looked away. I was feeling the same.

We'd done a lot in the past months. We'd picked up a sigl each, we'd laid the groundwork for making several more, and we'd learned lessons that would stand us in good stead when we moved on to raiding more difficult Wells. But there was one area where we hadn't made any progress at all, and that was earning money.

Colin spoke up, echoing my thoughts. "Step four of your plan was getting into the black, right?"

"Yeah."

"So if Felix can't find us a buyer, the backup plan is . . . ?"

"There isn't one," I said with a sigh. "Unless you guys can think of something I can't."

"Try your family?" Colin asked.

"I don't think they buy aurum," I said. I didn't add that, even if they *did*, handing them physical proof that I'd raided a Well sounded like a terrible idea.

"You still work for a drucraft corporation, right?" Colin said to Ivy.

"That's not going to work."

"You don't know someone who . . . ?"

"No."

Colin looked between me and Ivy. "Well," he said when neither of us spoke. "I guess we could start selling the next few temporary Wells we find."

"The whole reason I was even willing to consider the raiding plan in the first place is that most of the *good* Wells are already taken," I said. "And the more Wells we sell instead of using, the fewer sigls we'll be able to make for ourselves. We'd basically be locators again, which puts us right back where we started."

"Okay, I'm out of ideas," Colin said with a shrug.

We sat in silence for a little while. At last I sighed and spoke. "Maybe we give up on step four."

"You mean skip to the part where we're raiding bigger Wells?" Colin asked.

"I mean, there's nothing exactly stopping us," I said. "I'd have liked a couple more months' practice, but . . ."

"I still don't have an invisibility sigl," Ivy said.

"We should be able to get you a shadowman at least. Didn't you say one of those Wells you found last month was due to fill?"

"I'll have to check, but it should be."

"So are we giving up on the money angle?" Colin asked.

Ivy and I looked at him, then at each other.

"Okay, cards on the table here," Colin said. "Personally, I'm fine with going straight to step five. Like I said, the money'd be nice, but my mum and dad are still paying my way and I don't actually need it. But I get the feeling the two of you do. So . . . I think it should be your call."

Ivy and I looked at each other. I was reluctant to talk about this with Ivy—it felt like making myself vulnerable—and from the way Ivy had never mentioned her own situation, I had the impression she might feel the same way . . .

But it was Ivy who finally broke the deadlock. "I do need it," she told Colin. She sounded unhappy, but determined. "I'm pretty much broke. But I want this more. I vote yes."

"If you're broke—" Colin began.

"There are people I can go to," Ivy said, cutting him off. "I don't *want* to, but it's fine." She looked at me.

I hesitated, thinking of my bank balance. It was currently sitting a little below £3,000 and had been declining since the spring. I was still getting a steady trickle of money from the Ashfords, enough that, up until last year, I would probably have been okay, but living costs had gone up brutally in the last twelve months. *Everything* was more expensive—bread, margarine, chicken, vegetables, gas, electricity, and most of all rent, which ate up almost my entire income all on its own. As it was, the number in my account was trending steadily downwards, and it would really only take one bad emergency to put me underwater.

But at the end of the day, my position hadn't changed. The

threat from the Winged hadn't changed. The sigls I could get from raiding were still my best chance.

"It's going to be tight, but I'll manage," I said. "Step five it is."

The three of us sat quietly for a few seconds. "So, that iron-hand sigl of yours..." Colin said. "Can I get one?"

"No."

"Why not?"

"Because you can't channel."

"But my strength one—"

"Your strength sigl is *continuous*," I said. Colin had picked up on how to use his new sigl quickly, but I still didn't think he really appreciated what it could and couldn't do. "If I made a continuous iron-fist sigl, it would go active whenever it touched your skin, and if it got stuck it would *stay* active. That would be *very bad*."

"Why?"

"Because your body isn't supposed to be hard and rigid," Ivy said.

"When I turn that sigl off after using it, my hand tingles a bit," I said. "And I only use it for thirty to sixty seconds, max. I've heard some real horror stories about what can happen if you leave it on too long." It was one of the reasons I'd held off on making the thing.

"I bet there's some way to make it work," Colin said.

"I am not doing Matter sigl experiments with you as a guinea pig! I don't want to have to explain to your dad and brother why you've got a stump where your hand used to be!"

"Fine, fine. I still want another sigl, though."

"Then put in the bloody work and learn to channel like the rest of us."

"All right," Ivy said, setting down her empty glass and straightening up. "I'd better do the rounds of my Wells. If that one in Kew's ready, we could do the shaping tomorrow?"

"Whoa, whoa," Colin said. "I've got my last physics final on Tuesday."

"That's fine, we shouldn't need you for this one," I said. "But it'll have to be evening, I can't do morning."

"Why?" Colin asked.

I sighed, getting to my feet. "Lessons."

THE ASHFORD MANSION was a busy place. Charles lived there, as well as my two half-siblings, Tobias and Bridget. Lucella had thankfully moved out sometime last year, but Calhoun was still there, along with my mother when she wasn't off on one of her endless business trips. There was also a rotating staff: a butler, a housekeeper, a cook, a gardener, any number of maids and cleaners, and (according to Bridget) one woman who was her governess and a man whose job it was to train the dogs. Then on top of that there were the people who weren't servants but who were still employed by the House full-time: the security staff, the tenders for the massive Light Well at the mansion's rear, and all the people connected to the family business. The first time I'd visited the mansion it had been on the night of a party, and I'd assumed that all the activity was a one-off, but the more times I came back, the more I came to realise that the average for the place was closer to "crowded party" than "empty building." It was very different from the silent flat in which I'd grown up.

There was one inhabitant of the mansion, though, that I'd never seen. Or, at least, hadn't seen before my mother scheduled me an appointment with him. My stepfather, Magnus Ashford-Grasser.

Right now Magnus and I were sitting in a room on the mansion's second floor, in a sort of self-contained flat that, as far as I could see, was reserved for Magnus and my mother's use. The room was a study, though one with a very different feel from Charles's. Charles's study was big and spacious and open, with maps and a clear desk. Magnus's was a third of the size and so cluttered that I had to pick my way from the door to the chair; piles of paper, computer equipment, and boxes filled with knick-knacks all jostled for space with a sofa, two armchairs, and an old exercise machine. Every flat surface was piled with reading material, as well as half a dozen houseplants and a scattering of old tea and coffee mugs. The one thing the two studies had in common was the number of books on the shelves. Comparing Magnus's study to Charles's, Magnus's felt cosier, but I had the feeling that if I had to actually live here the mess would drive me a bit crazy after a while.

". . . as part of the general trend in the British economy towards financialisation," Magnus was saying.

"What's financialisation?" I asked.

"I thought you said you'd read the book I gave you last week?"

"Uh," I said. "Parts of it." I *had* tried, but the thing had been incredibly boring, not to mention confusing enough to make Father Hawke's theology homework look simple. Either finance is really complicated, or the kinds of people who write books about it are just really bad at explaining things.

Magnus settled back slightly into his chair. My stepfather was in his mid-forties, thin and a little below medium height, with black hair that was showing the first traces of grey. He had a careful, precise way of speaking, each word clearly separated from the next, and blue eyes that had a way of resting on you when he spoke, as though measuring your reactions to every word. "In this context," Magnus said, "financialisation means that the Drucraft Houses and corporations began to gain less and less of their income from sigls, and more and more of it from finance. Partially in the form of sigl payment plans, but also from directly buying and selling securities. During the 1990s, many corporations and Houses came to feel that the returns they could get on these financial instruments were higher than anything they could get by trading in tangible things such as sigls and Wells."

"Okay..."

"This continued until the financial crisis of 2008. Many Houses and corporations had accumulated enormous amounts of debt under the assumption that they could keep leveraging that money into greater and greater profits. When the markets collapsed, that fell apart."

"So what happened?"

"Read that book and you'll find out," Magnus said. "But as regards the drucraft world, the main *long*-term effect of the crash was to establish a high-water mark. Houses and corporations came to accept that they couldn't just keep on increasing the size of their finance departments and expect to automatically bring in greater and greater profits. But financialisation didn't significantly recede, and so over the 2010s things mostly continued on as before. While the crisis did affect the entire economy, it generally affected the richest the least, and very few of the major players in the drucraft world actually went bankrupt. There was House Egmont, of course, and a couple of middling-to-big corporations had to file, but they were the exceptions, not the rule. The Bank of England cut interest rates to nearly nothing, meaning that many Houses and corporations which should have had unsustainable levels of debt were able to carry on. The Board provided large sums of money to some of the worst-off corporations in exchange for stakeholdings. And interest rates were kept low throughout the 2010s."

"So... they got bailed out."

"Yes."

I thought of what my dad had told me back in the spring,

about how much he'd struggled during that recession, and of the sleepless nights he'd had trying to figure out how to support me. Meanwhile the people who'd caused the whole thing had got off scot-free. "Glad things turned out so well for them," I said tonelessly.

Magnus gave me a sidelong look, and I wondered if I'd let too much of my feelings show. "Well," Magnus said after a pause. "I think that's enough for today. Next time we'll cover the current state of the drucraft economy and House Ashford's role in it. Oh, and Stephen? You do actually need to *read* the material I give you. There is absolutely no way you're ever going to understand the current state of the economy without understanding the financial crisis and its aftermath."

"Okay," I said, but didn't get up. "By the way, I was wondering. Is there anything . . . unusual about House Ashford?"

"Unusual how?"

"Anything that'd make people take a special interest in it. More than the Great Houses. House Ashford is a Lesser House, right?"

"Great House status only means that the House in question owns a permanent Well of S-class or higher within the boundaries of the United Kingdom. It makes them important, but doesn't necessarily make them the *most* important. In the case of House Ashford, we are somewhat more influential than our Lesser House status might suggest."

"Why?"

"As I mentioned, many Houses and corporations let the sigl sides of their businesses lapse during the 2000s and 2010s, which often involved selling off surplus Wells. House Ashford took the opportunity to acquire them." Magnus paused for a second, frowning slightly as if remembering something. "Some people at the time considered Charles Ashford's actions in this respect to be unwise. Certainly it caused him to miss out on a good deal of the profits from the mid-2000s bubble... that said, it also allowed House Ashford to build up a significant market share of Light Wells, while simultaneously insulating them from the worst of the recession."

"So... they own a lot more Wells than normal?"

"Yes, and that's caused an increasing number of people to pay this House an increasing amount of attention. Particularly in combination with the political developments of the past few years... but we'll get into that next week."

I nodded and got to my feet.

Magnus spoke just as I was reaching for the door handle. "Is there someone you know who's been taking a particular interest in House Ashford?"

I paused, my hand on the handle. "I don't think I said anything like that."

"Ah," Magnus said. He was watching me steadily, and waited a beat longer before nodding. "My mistake."

I left, closing the door behind me.

ONCE I WAS safely out of the Ashford mansion, and I was sure I wasn't being followed, I let out a breath. That had been a little too close.

It wasn't that I felt actively threatened by Magnus. This had been our fourth lesson, and he'd been consistently cool but polite—if he felt annoyance or resentment about having to teach a stepchild he'd never met, he hid it well. He wasn't exactly a captivating speaker, but he knew what he was talking about, and so far I'd found his lessons reasonably interesting. As teachers went, I'd had worse.

But although Magnus didn't know it, I'd encountered him

before. Last year, during my first visit to the mansion, I'd overheard a brief conversation between Magnus and my half-brother. It hadn't meant much to me at the time, but in the time that had passed since then I'd managed to piece enough of it together to get a sense of what he'd been saying. And the Magnus of that conversation had been a *lot* less friendly.

He'd also seemed very interested in the House Ashford inheritance and whether his own children would get it. Maybe interested enough to sabotage someone who wasn't a rival right now, but might be in the future...

I wasn't sure. But until I had a better read on my stepfather, I was going to be very careful about what I let slip to him.

I glanced at my phone, checking the time. Locating in the afternoon, then I needed to go for a run, then there was Ivy's shaping in the evening, then I was supposed to meet my dad. It was looking like a busy day.

CHAPTER 12

Twelve hours later.

"Okay, try it again," I told Ivy. "And remember, the aperture section has to be completely clear."

"I *did* make it clear."

"No, you didn't. Come on, let's go."

We were at the southern end of Kew Gardens. The temperature had risen a few degrees since yesterday, enough to make the summer night comfortably warm, and the air was filled with the scents of grass and leaves and exotic plants. Above, stars glittered down out of a clear sky. Working as a locator can be tough, but it also takes you to parts of your city that you'd never have seen. Landmarks, weird isolated corners that no one knows about, places that have long since been abandoned and forgotten. And every now and again, you end up somewhere really beautiful.

The Well was a little distance away, in the middle of a grove of trees. Ivy and I were sitting cross-legged on the grass next to a thick leafy bush covered with huge sweet-smelling flowers, their blooms a white-pink blur in the darkness. I couldn't make out

Ivy's features or follow her movements, but I could see what she was doing just fine.

Wisps of essentia stirred in the air, strands of light twining into threads. The threads began to interlock and take form, becoming a pattern. The pattern expanded as the essentia construct grew larger and more complex, taking the shape of the sigl it'd become...

"There!" I said, pointing. "Stop."

The construct froze. "What?" Ivy said.

"There, you see that?"

"No, I *can't* see that."

Oh, right. "Your aperture section's got some trailing threads. If you shape the sigl like that, then, when you channel, it's going to bleed through *here*. That'll mean that the one-way filter won't work and the field will convert incoming light as well as outgoing."

"So what am I supposed to do?"

"You gather in all the essentia from that part until it's completely clear, like I showed you."

"I *did* do it like you showed me."

"If you had, it would have worked. Start again."

Ivy sighed and let the essentia construct dissolve into nothingness. This was why we weren't practising at the Well; the more ambient essentia you have around you when you're shaping essentia constructs, the harder it is to feel what you're doing. Ivy began to regather the essentia, starting from scratch.

"You know, this would be a lot faster if I just shaped it myself," I told her.

"I don't *want* you to shape it yourself," Ivy said. From the angle of her head, I could tell she was staring at the air where the construct was; the glowing lines of light wove together, taking form once again. "You did that with the flash sigl and that's why it's so buggy."

"It's not buggy. I keep telling you, you're not channelling into it right."

"Why couldn't you make it activate the same way as my Life sigls?"

"Because it *isn't* a Life sigl. Also, you've messed up the aperture again."

Ivy made an angry noise and let the construct dissolve. "You want to take a break?" I asked.

"No!"

We sat in silence for a couple of minutes as Ivy's twenty-third essentia construct slowly grew above her hands. "How many of these did you make to get this sigl working?" Ivy asked.

"Maybe a couple of hundred," I said. "Plus one prototype. But most of that was trial and error. You're getting the easy version."

"'Easy,' he says," Ivy muttered. "If we're going to spend this long, can't you just teach me how to make an invisibility sigl, like I wanted in the first place?"

"Your regulator's wrong."

Ivy made a frustrated noise and let the essentia construct drop. I heard her take several deep breaths. "Okay," she said once she'd calmed down. Essentia construct number twenty-four started to materialise out of the night.

"*This* is why I'm not showing you how to make an invisibility sigl," I said once Ivy had had the chance to calm down a bit. "All this sigl does is convert light. Bending light's harder than converting it, and shifting its wavelength is harder than bending it. If you're having this much trouble with something this basic, there's no way you're going to be able to handle a vision-and-diffraction setup."

"So how long before I can?"

"The way you're going, a really long time. You've messed up the aperture again."

Ivy gave a small growl, then let the construct dissolve and started on number twenty-five.

"Look, are you really set on learning how to make these?" I asked after a couple of minutes of silence. "It took me the best part of a year to figure out my invisibility sigl. Yeah, some of that was trial and error, but most of it was me building up my skill with Light essentia, and... there just aren't really any shortcuts for that. I could probably make you one without too much trouble."

"I told you, I don't *want* you to do it for me," Ivy said. "Anyway, attunement ratios, remember? Anything you make for me's going to be a lot weaker than anything I make myself."

"Oh, right," I said. Attunement was something I'd read about in the Exchange catalogue but had never really understood until Ivy had explained it. Apparently when you made a sigl for someone else, you had to split the strength between the two of you. If you made the kernel with thirty percent of your essentia and seventy percent of theirs, the sigl would only work for them at seventy percent power. It explained why Colin's strength sigl was so much weaker than the one I'd made for myself.

"And there's a minimum strength for these things," Ivy added. "If you need a C-class Well to make an invisibility sigl for yourself, you need maybe a high C or a low C+ to make one for someone else. And you know how much harder it is to find a Well even a half grade higher. No matter how long this way takes, it's still easier."

I wasn't sure that was Ivy's real reason, but didn't say so. "But what if you're just really bad with Light essentia?"

"Oh, screw you."

I looked at Ivy in amusement. "Wait, *that's* what it takes to get a rise out of you?"

I couldn't tell in the darkness, but I had the feeling Ivy was blushing. "So is this right?"

I took a look at the construct hovering in front of Ivy. A glowing tracework of light to me, an invisible presence to her. "Looks... good, actually. Practise that a few more times, then we can do it at the Well."

We kept going until essentia construct number thirty, then took a break and rested on the grass to give Ivy some time to recover before the actual shaping. "You act a lot more relaxed around me these days," I told Ivy.

"Do I?"

"Our first few raids, you were always watching me out of the corner of your eye."

"You were a strange boy I was alone with after dark."

"Wait. You seriously think I went to all this trouble to set up this raiding team just to have an excuse to get you on your own to assault you or something?"

"You threatened me the *first* time we were on our own."

"I wanted the Well, not you. Anyway, is this your way of saying you're finally over that?"

"Well, you're not a stranger anymore," Ivy said. "Though I still think you're strange." She picked something from the grass and examined it. "Are you ever going to tell us who these people are that you're so scared of?"

I'd been expecting that question and had a reply lined up. "Are you ever going to tell us why you want to become a powerful drucrafter so badly?"

Ivy was silent.

"Just tell me one thing," I said when Ivy still didn't reply. "Is this anything Colin and I need to be worried about? Angry debt collectors chasing you down, or...?"

"No," Ivy said instantly, shaking her head. "There are just... some things I have to do back home. That's all."

I wondered where "home" was. I'd never asked Ivy—I knew that her surname was Mintah, and based on that I could probably figure it out with a bit of research. But she obviously didn't want to talk about it, and I didn't especially want to push her. I had more than enough other problems to worry about.

"All right," Ivy said, straightening up. "Ready?"

I nodded and got to my feet. "Let's do it."

"Okay," my father said. "Is this right?"

"Stance was the other way around," I told him.

My dad shifted his feet. "Now?"

"Yeah, like that."

It was the early hours of the morning. We were in the same Barbican flat, except that we'd moved the sofas and coffee table out of the way to create a training area in the middle of the living room.

"Okay," my father said. He was holding a comb in his right hand, in a stabbing grip. "So he lunged like this..."

In slow motion, my dad reenacted the attack that boy had tried the other night. I twisted aside, letting the "knife" pass between my side and left arm, then clamped the arm down on it hard. "And then I did that," I said.

"And then you punched him?"

"And then I punched him."

My dad nodded and stepped back. "That'll work. But try not to do it again."

"Why not?"

"You're not controlling the knife hand well enough. Here." My dad took up the same stance with the comb a second time and I mirrored him; again he lunged in slow motion, and again I let the arm go through and trapped it. "The other boy pulled back, right?" my dad said.

"Yeah."

"Okay, I'll pull, you resist. Ready?"

I nodded and my father tried to draw back. I kept my arm clamped down on his; squeezed between my arm and my side, his arm got stuck at the wrist. "So most guys, you grab their weapon hand, their instinctive reaction is to pull away," my dad said. "Which just makes things worse, because now you've got their wrist trapped instead of their arm, so their weapon's got no play." He wiggled the comb around; it brushed weakly against my back. "Right?"

"Right."

"Okay. Someone who knows what they're *doing*, though . . . they'll do this."

We disengaged and my father took up a fighting stance once again. Again he did a slow-motion lunge, and again I trapped it with my arm . . . except this time, my dad pushed in, stepping through so that our bodies were touching. His arm slid under mine, and now all of a sudden it wasn't trapped anymore. The comb poked me in the small of the back.

"Oh," I said, feeling foolish.

My father stepped away, lowering the comb. "Now, that's an aggressive move. Your standard gang kid, as soon as you clamp down, they'll panic and pull away. But a *good* fighter'll move into your space and stab you. Just because something works in Sunday League doesn't mean it'll work on a professional. Never forget that."

I nodded.

"All right," my father said, slipping the comb back into his pocket. "Give me a hand putting this back and tell me how the shaping went."

"Pretty good," I said, taking one end of one of the sofas and waiting for my dad to lift it before doing the same. Lift, not push—there were flats all around and we didn't want to make noise. "Ivy's got her own shadowman sigl now."

"She working out?"

"She's prickly, but I think I can trust her."

My dad nodded as we set the sofa down. "And your mate Colin?"

"He's working hard..."

"But?"

"But he's not a prodigy," I admitted. "I mean, it's the same with Ivy. They're smart, they learn fast, but the rate they're going they're both going to take a good year to reach the next discipline."

"That's pretty normal."

"I know, but it means I can't count on them to bail me out. The heavy lifting's going to be up to me."

"Well, as far as that goes, I might have something for you," my father said, moving the last couple of things back onto the coffee table. There was an empty pizza box from our dinner, and he sealed it back up, checking to make sure we hadn't left any crumbs. "Grab a drink and come and take a look."

I fetched a bottle of apple juice from the fridge and sat down facing my dad. "All right," my father said. "So the reason you're doing this raiding plan is you want some sort of sigl that'll give you a fighting chance against Vermillion and guys like him. Right?"

"Yeah, and I still think it needs to be a weapon," I said. We'd talked this over a couple of times. "I know you keep saying the most useful sigls are mobility ones, but the problem I keep running into with these guys isn't mobility, it's that I can't really fight back. It's a lot harder to hold someone off when you can't actually threaten them."

"And you also said you want something nonlethal."

I nodded.

"You sure about that?" my dad asked. "You said you were going to think it over."

"I did," I said. "And . . . yeah, I'm sure. You remember that raid I told you about, the one I did over Christmas? There was a moment there where I'd taken a gun off one of those men, and I was thinking about using it. And I decided I wasn't going to. It felt wrong." I paused. "I think . . . if I carried something like that, I'd end up never using it. Because there'd always be some other option I'd rather take instead. I'd have to be absolutely bloody desperate to pull it out, and by the time I got to that point it'd probably be too late." I looked at my father, suddenly nervous. "Do you think I'm being stupid?"

"No, I don't," my father said with a shake of his head. "Something a lot of people don't realise—the instant you draw a weapon, you're escalating the situation. Now, most of the time, when you do that, the other guy'll back down. But every now and again he *won't*, and when that happens you're going to have maybe half a second to decide whether to pull the trigger. And if you aren't *absolutely sure* about that decision, you shouldn't be carrying in the first place."

I nodded.

"That said . . ." my dad continued. "You need to understand that by choosing a nonlethal weapon, you're putting yourself at a disadvantage. Any nonlethal weapon is always going to be weaker than a lethal one."

"Yeah, but having a nonlethal weapon also means I'm free to actually *use* it," I pointed out. "If I'd had some kind of instant-death sigl for that Whitechapel fight, then it would have been completely bloody useless, because I'd have never pulled the trigger."

"True enough. All right. So you're looking for something powerful enough to put an attacker down, but safe enough that it won't actually kill them. And ideally it'd be something using Light essentia, because that's what you're best with. Sound right?"

"Right. So does it exist?"

My father dug into his pocket and pushed a piece of paper across the table. "Take a look."

I unfolded the paper. It looked like a printout from some sort of reference manual, coloured in green and white. It read:

NEURAL-TARGETING OPTICAL DISABLING (NOD) SIGL

PEO Soldier | Fort Belvoir, VA

Description

The Neural-Targeting Optical Disabling (NOD) sigl is a nonlethal weapon system designed to disable individual enemy combatants and suspects. The operator wears the sigl in a standard-issue hand mount. When activated, the sigl projects a rapidly firing strobe light over a narrow cone with a wavelength of 520 nm to 565 nm. If focused on a subject's eyes at sufficiently short range, this light strikes the back of the subject's retina, causing the subject's optic nerve to transmit an overload of information to the vision center and forcing the brain to temporarily shut down as it attempts to manage the surge of neural impulses, causing unconsciousness for five to thirty minutes.

The NOD-A is designed for single-target application, while the more powerful NOD-B is capable of projecting light over a sufficiently wide cone as to affect multiple targets at once. Eye protection will reduce the sigl's effectiveness.

The NOD sigl can function either at optimal or at extended range. At optimal range, the NOD sigl causes unconsciousness due to neural shock. At extended range, it causes dazzling and flash blindness but will not cause unconsciousness. Use at sufficiently short range may result in permanent eye damage due to retinal burns.

Benefit to the Soldier

The NOD sigl provides the Warfighter with a precise, reliable method of disabling targets where lethal force is forbidden by ROE or is otherwise considered inadvisable, with low chance of permanent injury or collateral damage.

Specifications

- Weight (sigl only): 2.6 g
- Weight (with mount): 8.9 g
- Range (Optimal): 20 m–60 m
- Range (Extended): 60 m–450 m

(NOTE: all measurements are for NOD-A)

Program Status

- FY87: Technology Readiness Level 6 (system/subsystem model or prototype development in a relevant environment). Scheduled Production Year One of the FY88–FY92 contract
- FY88: Technology Readiness Level 7 (system prototype demonstration in an operational environment)

- FY88: Production paused; Technology Readiness Level unchanged
- FY90: Program reviewed; Technology Readiness Level unchanged
- FY95: Program reviewed; Technology Readiness Level unchanged
- FY00: Program reviewed; Technology Readiness Level unchanged
- FY05: Program reviewed; Technology Readiness Level unchanged
- FY10: Program reviewed; Technology Readiness Level unchanged
- FY15: Program reviewed; Technology Readiness Level unchanged
- FY20: Program reviewed; Technology Readiness Level unchanged

PROJECTED ACTIVITIES

To be reviewed

CONTRACTORS

Tyr Aerospace & Defense (Tucson, AZ)

I looked at my dad. "It's a . . . light sigl that knocks people out?"

"So back in the Cold War, the US military funnelled billions of dollars into military research," my dad said. "Including drucraft. I reached out to a guy I knew and asked him to look up nonlethal ones that used Light essentia. This was what he came back with."

I went back and reread the first paragraph, stopping on the part where it said *"unconsciousness for five to thirty minutes."*

"Does it work?"

"My guy claims they tested it," my dad said with a shrug. "He gave me an explanation, something about overloading the trigeminal nerve. Don't know enough about neurology to tell you whether that makes sense."

"So how come no one uses it?" I asked. I'd read plenty of war stories when I was younger, and I'd never heard of anything like this.

"Ah, that I can make a guess at," my dad said. "There's a big difference between a weapon that *works* and a weapon that's *useful*. First problem: for this thing to work, your target has to be looking straight at you. Soldiers generally prefer to shoot their enemies in the back."

"Oh."

"Second problem." My dad pointed at the specifications. "That."

"Which . . . wait. 2.6 grams? Just for the sigl?"

"Yep."

"Oh, what the hell? That's, what, thirteen carats? That's all the way into A-class!"

"And I'm pretty sure that's why the thing never got rolled out for widespread use. R&D is one thing, but once you get into mass production, contracts go to the lowest bidder."

"Yeah, but how does that help? If this thing's too expensive for *them* . . ."

"So I don't think it's quite as bad as that," my dad said, tapping the specifications again. "You see the range?"

"Yeah, four hundred and fifty metres. What's it supposed to be used against, aircraft?"

"Sounds to me like they wanted big numbers to impress the generals who'd be signing their cheques," my dad said. "I don't think cost-effectiveness was on their radar. I bet if you tried you could make a shorter-ranged version for a lot less."

"You've got a lot of confidence in me."

"You managed to reverse-engineer an invisibility sigl from an Exchange catalogue," my dad said seriously. "This is just projection. High-level projection, but it's not actually any more complicated than what you've done already."

"The power, though..."

"Yeah," my dad said with a nod. "General rule of thumb for these sorts of offence sigls is that if you want a weapons-grade one, you need at least B-class. I think you should be able to get it down to the bottom end of B, but probably not lower than that."

I looked down at the piece of paper with mixed feelings. On the one hand, it was nice to know that my father had such a high opinion of me. On the other hand, a B-class sigl was a hell of an ask. My two most powerful sigls at the moment were my diffraction and lightfoot ones, and both were C-grade... and on the low end of C, at that. Going from C to B meant multiplying the mass by a factor of four, and the price by a factor of *ten*. There was no way in hell that I could afford access to that kind of Well legally.

Which meant a raid. And the kinds of Wells strong enough to produce that level of sigl were not easy targets.

"I don't suppose there's some other way?" I asked.

"Not that I can think of," my dad said. "I mean, you could just do what the corp soldiers do and carry a gun, but you've already said you don't want to go around shooting people. Besides, if it's the Winged you're worried about, a gun won't help very much. The foot soldiers, sure, but someone like Vermillion will have faced down men with guns before."

I sighed. Well, I'd just have to see what I could do.

"Oh," my dad added. "We're not going to be able to meet up here starting from next week."

"What, the guy who owns this place wants his flat back?"

"That too. He's coming back from New York end of the month. But I'm going to be out of the country."

"Why?"

"Business."

"What kind?"

"You're better off not knowing."

I looked at him with raised eyebrows.

"No, I'm not going to tell you what it is."

"What exactly is it you're doing these days?" I said with a frown. My father had disappeared for a while last month too.

"I told you, I can't talk about it," my dad said. "I'll leave you a way to get in contact if worse comes to worst. But don't use it unless you have to. Remember, you absolutely cannot let the Winged know that we're in contact."

I nodded reluctantly.

I GOT HOME as dawn was breaking, my mind filled with sigl designs. I scribbled down some of them in my notebook, then collapsed into bed. I woke up a few hours later to the sound of Hobbes meowing outside the window; bleary-eyed, I let him in and fed him, then passed out again.

When I woke up for the second time, the sun was streaming through my window and painting the walls in bright yellow. Hobbes was curled up asleep on my duvet.

I disentangled myself from Hobbes, then picked up my notebook and went back to drawing sigl designs. The square of light from the window crept slowly around the room as I worked, the only sound the scribble of pencil on paper.

It was past noon by the time I finally sighed and set my pencil down. I went down to the kitchen, made myself a stack of toast, added an apple and a carrot and a big glass of water, then took it all back up to my room and began crunching on one of the bits of toast, flipping through the diagrams I'd drawn.

Hobbes stretched, opened a yellow-green eye, and meowed.

"Hey, you," I told him, and considered. "I think I should go for it."

"Mrrraow?"

"It's what I've been looking for from the start," I told Hobbes. "A way to take on someone like Vermillion and actually win. If it works, it'll be a game changer. And I think I *can* make it work." I tapped the paper. "Keeping it narrow enough is going to be the hardest part, but I think I can see how I can make a focusing lens to handle that. I mean, it's just bending light in a different way, right?"

Hobbes rose to his feet, stretched, then walked over to rub his head against me. I scratched him behind his ears, staring out of the window as I thought. "The tolerances are going to have to be tight, but my dad's right. None of the principles are any different from what I've done before."

"Mraow?"

"You just want my toast, don't you?"

"Mraow."

I broke off a bit and handed it to him. "I swear there's something wrong with you," I told him as he chomped on it with his sharp teeth. "I thought cats weren't supposed to eat bread? Hey, stop dropping crumbs on the sheet!"

Hobbes was too busy munching to answer. "All right," I said, brushing the specks off onto the floor. "Let's say I can get the design to work. How the hell am I going to find a B-class Well?"

"Mraaaow?"

"Well, I don't need it right now. I'm going to have to shape constructs and then find some minor Wells to use as prototypes. But if I want an actual, scaled-up, working version, then I'm pretty sure my dad's right and B-class is the minimum. *Maybe* C+."

"Mraaaow."

"Even the absolute most cheap-arse B-class sigls you can get start at something like £50,000," I told Hobbes. "And those are probably threaded to hell. A good quality one is more like ten times that. I guess just getting access to the Well would be a different story, but . . ."

"Mraaow?"

"No, I don't know anyone who has one. Well . . . actually, I do. The Ashfords have more Light Wells than they know what to do with. Maybe . . ."

Hobbes watched me with bright eyes.

"No," I said, shaking my head. "Bad idea."

Hobbes looked at me, swishing his tail.

"I mean, I could try to pass it off as some sort of family favour," I said. "Calhoun *might* say yes." I tapped my pencil against the notebook dubiously. "But even if he did, I'd end up owing them, a lot."

"Mraaow."

"Raiding probably makes more sense. The Well at Moor Park was about that strong, and I think I could have handled the security there. The problem's finding it. Only reason I knew about that one was because the corp told us." I tapped the notebook again. "I could tell Colin and Ivy to keep an eye out, but it has to be a Light Well that's not too weak *or* too strong. What we really need is a list of all the Light Wells in England . . ."

I stopped.

Hobbes looked at me with interest.

". . . Wait," I said slowly.

Hobbes nudged me again. I fed him a second scrap of toast,

not paying any attention this time to how many crumbs he dropped. Then I stared up at the ceiling, thinking. About House Ashford, and that map in Charles's study.

Hobbes finished his scrap of toast and looked at me.

I sighed, putting two and two together. *I'm going to have to read that stupid book.*

CHAPTER 13

THE BOOK WAS just as boring as I remembered, but by the time next Monday rolled around, I was ready.

Now that I was actually doing the work, my lesson with Magnus went smoothly. It was hard to read my stepfather's reactions, but he seemed happy enough. I'd spent a while trying to think of ways to subtly steer the conversation towards what I wanted to ask about, but, as it turned out, Magnus did it for me.

"... and since then our House has primarily focused on selling to the various bodies of NATO," Magnus said. "Particularly the UK, Germany, and the United States. We do still sell to private clients, but we no longer advertise in the Exchange or the Borse."

"Why to the armed forces?" I said. It wasn't what I actually wanted to know, but I was trying to lead in gradually.

"The main use for Light essentia is in the military and security sphere," Magnus said. "A little ironic, given that Light is so often considered the 'softest' of the branches. But it's by far the strongest branch for stealth and detection."

"So all the other Houses and corps that specialise in Light essentia, they sell to the military too?"

"No, some specialise in private sales. Personal invisibility sigls are still very popular. Which naturally leads to a corresponding market in vision sigls designed to counter them."

"So our rivals," I said, "our . . . competitors . . . they'd mostly be other Houses and corps that sell to the military?"

"Exactly."

I kept my voice casual. "Like who?"

"About half of the Great Houses, for a start. Barret-Lennard. Hawker, of course. De Haughton and Reisinger, though it's not really their focus. But mostly it's the big US corporations. Tyr Aerospace, Schumann-Kraus Heavy Industries, Lumen Group. They're enormous, far larger than any House, and they can get quite forceful with rivals. You've had some experience with that, as I understand."

"Are they usually that hostile?"

"It's a little more complicated than 'friendly' or 'hostile,'" Magnus said. "Tyr and Schumann-Kraus are our biggest competitors, and most of the time, if we're bidding on some military procurement, they'll be bidding on it too. At the same time, they're also our clients—we sell almost as much to them as we do to the British armed forces. And at the same time as *that*, they often try to raid our Wells. Usually through third parties, but they'll send their own teams if they want something badly enough. That raid last autumn wasn't the first time Tyr's raided us, and it won't be the last."

"Do we ever raid them back?"

"That would be illegal."

Yeah, I thought. *Right.* I wanted to keep going, but Magnus was looking thoughtfully at me, and I decided not to push my luck. I steered the conversation into safer territory, then once we were done made my excuses and left.

As soon as Magnus's study door shut behind me, I headed for Charles's office. When I asked to see him, I was told that he was in a meeting. I told them I'd wait.

I still didn't know much about how rich people did things, but I was starting to learn the meaning of certain phrases. "In a meeting," for example, generally means "doesn't want to talk to you." I was pretty sure Charles would give me an extra-long wait as payback for showing up unannounced and had come prepared with a book Father Hawke had lent me back in the winter. I took it out and started to read.

It was an hour and forty-five minutes before one of the Ashford armsmen poked his head in and told me that Charles would see me. I was starting to recognise some of the staff by now—this guy was called Fred and seemed to act as Charles's secretary. I thanked him and headed for Charles's study.

"Just because your stepfather has decided to use our family residence as a work-from-home private tutoring business," Charles said as I walked in, "does not mean you have an open invitation to drop in whenever you feel like it."

"I haven't seen you all month."

"I agreed to see you once a month, not to be a one-stop shop for all of your remedial education. Maybe I should give Magnus some more duties to occupy his time."

"I don't think we could have had four lessons over the last four weeks without you knowing about it," I told him. "And I don't think you'd have let them go on if you *really* wanted to stop them."

"Don't confuse toleration with encouragement," Charles said, and nodded to the chair. "Sit."

I sat. "Well, since you're here," Charles said. "I understand Calhoun has still been employing you as an escort for social events?"

"Less than he used to."

"The case has been made to me," Charles said, "that having a member of the family in a security role, standing outside restaurant back doors, could be considered to be bringing the House into disrepute."

I felt a flash of anger. "Standing outside doors" was how my dad and I used to earn a living. "It's just a job."

"Regardless, they have a point," Charles said. "I've instructed Calhoun to stop employing you in this capacity."

I stared at Charles. That was it? All because he thought I was bringing the House into "disrepute"? A wave of fury rose up inside of me. I *needed* that job! With my locating income down to next to nothing, bodyguard work from Calhoun was the only money I had coming in at all! Dimly I remembered my resolution not to let myself get provoked, but this was too much. I drew in a breath—

"That said," Charles said, "I do recognise that you are, in your limited way, trying to make yourself useful. It's also been claimed to me that your skills are being underutilised. I'm told you have some ability with sensing?"

It took me a few seconds to realise Charles was waiting for an answer. "What?"

"Do you know how to survey a Well?"

"I have no idea what that means," I said. My anger was still rolling, and it was a struggle not to show it. "But if you mean 'can I feel the essentia in a Well and tell how strong it is,' yeah, better than you or anyone else in your family."

"So that's a no, then," Charles said. "Well, I suppose putting it off isn't going to catch you up any faster. You'll be attached to

Calhoun to assist on Well evaluation duties, starting next week. Someone will be in touch to give you the details."

I opened my mouth to tell Charles to go fuck himself. This high-handedness was infuriating. Who the hell was he to take away the job I was depending on and just expect me to—

No. No. Hadn't I promised myself that I would stop doing this? I needed to control my temper.

Besides . . . I *wanted* something from Charles. I'd spent much of the last week trying to figure out how to make him agree. And he'd just handed me the way to do it.

"I suppose I might be willing to do that," I said.

Charles snorted. "If you want us to keep paying you, you will."

Again I felt a flash of anger; again I forced it down. "I said 'might,'" I told Charles. "In exchange for a favour."

"What kind of favour?"

"I'd like all the information you have on Light Wells in the London area held by corporations that specialise in Light sigls. Tyr, Schumann-Kraus, Lumen, ones like that. Anything within an easy journey, thirty miles or so. With strengths . . . say around B? Let's say anything from C+ to B+. I'd like to know their exact strengths and when they're scheduled to fill or be used. Oh, and what kind of security arrangements they all have."

Charles stared. I think it was the first time I'd actually caught the old man off guard. "Why . . . exactly . . ." Charles said, ". . . would you need to know this information?"

"Research."

". . . Research."

I nodded.

"That is *extremely* specific research."

I looked back at him blandly.

"Research" was obvious bullshit. There was exactly *one* reason anybody would want this particular information, and I was damn sure Charles knew exactly what that reason was. The question was whether he'd call me on it.

Charles tapped his fingers on his desk. "What makes you think we would have access to that kind of information?"

Bingo. Not "there's no way in hell we're telling you because you're blatantly going to use it to do something illegal." Just "why would we know?" "Those companies are your competitors," I said. "So you'd have an idea of the sigls they sell, right? And the Wells they use to make them?"

Charles continued to stare, and I continued to look back at him. "We do, in fact, keep records of the Well holdings of other Houses and corporations," Charles said after a pause. "Given that we frequently attempt to acquire them, it's clearly in our interests to do so. Of course, when we *do* acquire such Wells, we also become responsible for their security. So it would also be legitimate . . . if slightly questionable . . . for us to have some idea of how well protected they are."

"So you can do it?"

"I'll have someone put together a dossier," Charles said. "I expect it'll take them a couple of weeks."

I nodded. "Then I'll start your new job when I get it."

Charles looked sharply at me, and I wondered if I'd gone too far, but the moment passed. "Oh, and Stephen? You remember what I said about bringing the family into disrepute?"

"Yes?"

"Having a member of the family be caught committing a crime would bring that family into much *more* disrepute." Charles's eyes rested on me. "In fact, if the crime were sufficiently serious, said family would be best advised to cut all ties with the family member going forward."

I looked back at the old man. "Sounds like anyone doing that would have to be careful not to get caught."

Charles held my eyes for a moment longer, then gave a nod. "That would be wise."

I WENT HOME in a good mood. The wait time didn't bother me—I still had plenty of work to do for the new sigl, and Colin was busy with his finals anyway. I went to sleep looking forward to a quiet fortnight of research and enjoying the nice summer weather.

I didn't get it.

THE CALL CAME in the early afternoon.

I was lying on my bed with my back propped up against the wall, sketching in my notebook. I'd more or less settled on the design I was going to use for the projection element, but I was having a lot of trouble figuring out how to incorporate the focusing lens while keeping the sigl's mass down. Hobbes was lying sprawled on the duvet with his legs splayed out, fast asleep. When the phone rang, I let it ring for a few seconds while I finished up the bit I was working on, then glanced over, expecting it to be Colin or maybe Ivy—

It was a video call from Byron.

Shit. All thoughts of the sigl went out of my head. It had been months since Byron had last phoned. Him calling like this meant nothing good.

I hesitated, trying to decide what to do. Let it ring? But I'd left his last couple of texts unanswered—refusing to take his call would make it obvious I was avoiding him. Answer on audio? That would be safer. But he'd been pushing me to meet in person. Maybe if I took it on video, I could claim that was just as good...

The phone kept ringing.

All right. I propped up my laptop on the bed, checked to make sure that the camera wasn't showing anything except the blank wall behind me, took a breath, and pressed the green button.

The window on my computer expanded into a black void. It stayed dark and silent for a few seconds as the "Connecting" message displayed, then the black screen vanished to reveal the image of Byron. "Stephen," Byron said, raising his eyebrows. "I was starting to think you weren't going to pick up."

Byron's a man in his mid-forties. He has blond hair, light skin, and dresses in dark, expensive-looking suits that always somehow look as though he's gone to sleep in them. His features are sharp, though slightly pouchy; still handsome, but with the look of someone whose past indulgences have started to catch up to him. Still, the eyes that focused on me were as penetrating as ever.

Byron's always made me nervous. Vermillion and Charles are threatening, but with both of them I have some idea what they care about. Byron's a black box. I know what he wants, but not why.

"Well, here I am," I told Byron.

"So you are," Byron said. He was indoors, in what looked like a living room. He studied me for a long moment. "You've been avoiding me."

To my side, Hobbes had woken up. He looked at the screen of my computer, his ears flattening, then turned and jumped down from the bed, turning to stare up at the laptop from a safe distance.

"I've been busy," I told Byron.

"What with?"

"Work. Stuff. You know."

"I hear you've been in contact with an old friend of mine."

It wasn't really a surprise that Byron knew about Vermillion. "You know the guy, huh?"

"Of course I know him," Byron said, raising his eyebrows. "Used to be one of my protégés. Quite a talented young man. Though sometimes a little aggressive . . . I hope there wasn't too much trouble?"

"Wait. You trained him as well?"

"I was his mentor."

Jesus. First Lucella, then Mark, then Vermillion. "Is there a single member of the Winged you *haven't* 'mentored'?"

Byron smiled. "I do admit I've had a better success rate than most."

I wondered what that success rate really was. From a throwaway comment Mark had once made, I knew there had been at least one more boy between Mark and Lucella. "So how's Mark doing?"

"You don't know?"

"I haven't seen him in months."

"Oh?" Byron studied me. "He hasn't been in touch?"

I tensed, thinking fast. The last I'd seen Mark had been at the beginning of March, and I did *not* want Byron to find out about that. From there it would be far too easy for him to connect the dots to my father. "The last time we met, you made a big deal of telling me that Mark definitely *wasn't* going to keep hanging around outside my door and then following me to ambush me in a dark alley. Now you're asking if he's been in touch. Aren't *you* supposed to know that?"

"There have been some changes in Mark's position of late."

"Changes?"

"He's going to be pursuing other projects."

I remembered Father Hawke's estimate of how much longer Mark would last. "What does that mean? You got rid of him?"

"Things weren't working out," Byron said with a shrug. "It happens."

"Is that why you called? To see if he'd come to take out his frustrations on me?"

"I'm afraid that now that Mark's gone his own way, he's not really in my sphere anymore," Byron said with a smile. "Just like you. Of course, if you were to join the Winged . . ."

"Right," I said sourly.

"I understand Vermillion made you a similar offer."

No point denying that. "It involved you getting less of the credit."

"And what were your thoughts?"

"I think . . ." I said, ". . . that if you're the one responsible for Vermillion, Lucella, and Mark turning out the way they are . . . then I'm not sure I really want to be following in their footsteps."

"Oh, come on, Stephen," Byron said. He actually looked slightly offended. "You can't blame me for *all* of that. They came to me, you know. I didn't headhunt them."

I gave Byron a sceptical look.

"Don't you want to find out the truth about what happened with your father?" Byron asked. "I promise you, there are things you'd learn from us that you absolutely are not going to discover anywhere else."

"Yeah, I'm not questioning *that* part. I'm just not sure it's worth the price I'd pay."

Byron studied me for a few seconds. "You can't keep stalling forever, you know."

I hesitated.

"Was that your plan? Keep drawing this out and hope

something would turn up?" Byron shook his head. "Don't get too full of yourself. Vermillion and I agree that you show promise, but you're not irreplaceable. And there are some political changes on the horizon. If you don't make a choice soon, it'll be made for you."

That sounded very close to something my mother had said. "What 'political changes'?"

"I'm afraid that as long as you're outside the Winged, that's not really your business," Byron said with a slight smile. He studied me for a few seconds longer, then shrugged. "But I suppose it's not really a secret. There are elements of the Winged who have an interest in your House Ashford. One of them is a man called Oscar. He leans towards a more active interpretation of our philosophy and tends to be . . . forceful . . . in dealing with obstacles. If he decides to make a move, and you happen to be caught up in it . . . well, I think you'll very much regret your hesitation."

I looked at Byron, unsure of how to answer.

"Think it over," Byron told me. He wasn't smiling this time. "But not for too long." He reached for something out of my view, and the call ended.

I TRIED TO get back to work, and didn't. Colin was supposed to be having his last chemistry final this afternoon, and I'd meant to go out with him to celebrate, but I didn't do that either. Byron's words were going around my head, and I couldn't concentrate.

One thing in particular he'd said stayed in my mind. *"Keep drawing this out and hope something would turn up."*

It wasn't as though I was doing nothing. I'd been working hard. But there *was* one thing I'd been avoiding. And maybe part of the reason I'd been working so hard was so that I didn't have to think about it.

I let out a long breath. Maybe I couldn't keep doing that any longer.

I arrived at West Ham Church with the setting sun. Yellow-and-gold light stretched out from the west, painting the scattered clouds and fading behind me into dusky purples and blues. I hesitated for a while at the door, wishing that Hobbes were here, but he'd been sleeping on the bed and hadn't stirred as I'd left.

I straightened up and braced myself. *All right.* I tried the church door, found it unlocked, and stepped inside.

How the hell does he always seem to know I'm coming? was my first thought as I saw Father Hawke waiting at the front. "Stephen," Father Hawke said, his voice clear in the empty church. "It's been a while."

"Yeah," I said. I walked forward, my footsteps echoing on the stone.

Father Hawke watched me approach. "Why?" he said when I was close enough.

"Why what?"

"The last time you visited was in March," Father Hawke said. "That was three and a half months ago."

I came level with Father Hawke and stopped. "Sorry."

"I didn't ask for an apology. I asked why."

I was silent for a minute, trying to marshal my thoughts. I find this sort of stuff hard to say out loud. "I feel like I have to make a big decision."

"What decision?"

"Which side to join . . . I guess."

Father Hawke nodded.

"My mother wants me to join the family," I said. "Well, not join. Commit. My—friends think I should stay neutral, keep my distance. Vermillion and Byron want me to join the Winged. They said being a free agent was an option, too, just not a good one..." I trailed off, realising that I was rambling.

"And why is that a problem?"

I thought for a second and answered honestly. "It's a really big decision and I don't know what the right choice is, and it feels like really bad things are going to happen if I get it wrong."

Father Hawke nodded again. "In that case, I have good news and bad news. The good news is that out of those options you just listed, three of them *aren't* big decisions. Joining your family, staying neutral, being a free agent. Oh, don't get me wrong, your relationship to your family will always be important. But it's also not something you get to make irrevocable decisions about. They're your family; you can be close or distant, but you'll always be connected, like it or not."

"Oh," I said, and paused. "What's the bad news?"

"The bad news is that the fourth of those options—joining the Winged—*is* a big decision. And making the wrong choice *is* going to lead to very bad things. And no, you don't get to call yourself a free agent and shelve it."

"Why not?"

"Because you have been marked," Father Hawke said. "And in doing so, you've been brought into the spiritual war that is fought in this world and all others, every year, every month, every day. Most people can afford to ignore it and pretend that it's nothing to do with them. It's a lie, but they can pretend. You don't get to pretend. You will have to choose a side."

I have to pick a side. I pushed the memory away. "But why?" I said in frustration. "I didn't ask for any of this. I don't want to be drafted into some kind of war. I don't even know what this war's about! Why can't I just be left alone?"

"You *aren't* alone," Father Hawke said. "You didn't spring into being out of nowhere. Your nature and talents are inherited from your parents and ancestors. Your skills were taught to you by your teachers and all the people you've ever met. The home you sleep in, the city you live in, the roads and trains and lights and running water you use every day were all built by others. And the beliefs you hold and the ideals you value trace back to the words of long-dead poets and prophets and philosophers influenced in turn by entities like the one that gave you your gift. You exist as a part of the world around you, not some isolated entity."

I was silent.

"To whom much is given, much shall be required," Father Hawke told me. "Your gift, your talents . . . if not to accomplish something, why were you given them?"

"I'd still like to have the choice," I muttered.

"You could join the Winged."

"I'm not joining the Winged."

"Why not?"

I hesitated before deciding to just tell the truth. "They seem kind of evil."

"Of course they're evil. But if all you're concerned about is your own freedom, why would that matter?"

I gave Father Hawke an annoyed look and asked him something that had been preying on my mind for a while. "How do I know whatever gave me my gift isn't just as evil?"

"That's actually a very good question," Father Hawke said. "We could look at the immediate effects of it—it saved your cat's life, and quite possibly your own. But that on its own doesn't mean anything. You can choose to spare someone for bad reasons, as well as good ones."

I nodded. That had occurred to me as well.

"More useful, I think, is to look at *what* you were given," Father Hawke said. "You were given the ability to see essentia. Not as a substitute for your own sensing, but as an enhancement of it. An ability of perception, of insight. Compare that to the gifts of the Winged. You remember what those were?"

"You said they were social ones. Influence over others."

"Yes. Why do you think their gifts are social?"

I frowned.

"What is the central belief of the Winged?" Father Hawke said. "The rejection of limits. In the modern world, where do those limits usually come from? If something's stopping you from doing what you want, what's that something typically going to be?"

Oh. Now I saw where he was going. "Other people."

"The gifts of the Winged allow the recipient to exert control over others and so bring the world into line with their desires. Some believe that the entities that guide the Winged can *only* give such gifts, as those are the only ones in accordance with their nature. Others argue that they do so by choice—that by giving the recipient the power to reshape the wills of others, it changes the mortal in turn, causing them to see others as instruments to be used. In either case, the gift is a reflection of what their god embodies. A demon of the Winged might give you the ability to make someone else see you as the most beautiful person on Earth and fall in love with you. It would *never* give you the ability to see the beauty in someone else and fall in love with *them*."

I thought about it for a minute. So whatever had given me my ability, it was something connected to . . . what? Perception? Insight? Thought? Something that wanted me to be more like that?

That was . . . well, actually, it was a little reassuring. It did make me feel a bit better that my ability wasn't something like "absorb the strength of things you kill" or "raise people from the dead as zombie servants," even though I still wished I knew more about what this thing was or what it wanted—

No. I checked myself. Not "what this thing was." *If* this thing was real. This was all still just hypothetical.

"In the end, though," Father Hawke continued, "none of that really answers the bigger question. Will you accept the task you've been given, or reject it?"

"How can I accept it if I don't even know what it is?"

"Presumably figuring that out is part of the task."

"Oh, come on," I muttered. "Could it just send me an email?"

"Sorry, the heavens seem to be leaning towards a more hands-off approach these days," Father Hawke said with a smile. "But stop dodging the question. What's your answer?"

"I can't answer until I know what the question is!"

"And have you been trying to figure it out?" Father Hawke asked. "Have you been spending some time each week turning it over in your mind, the way I suggested before? Thinking over your abilities, and what is within your capacity, and the position you've been placed in? Or have you been avoiding the whole subject and hoping it'll go away?"

I was silent.

"I think perhaps," Father Hawke said, "you haven't been trying too hard to find the answer because you're afraid of what might be asked of you once you do."

I opened my mouth, hesitated, and spoke. "Yes. Okay? I'm a random kid barely earning enough to live on. I've got some decent drucraft skills and that's *it*. I am not qualified to handle something like this! If I mess up shaping a sigl, the worst that happens is I get a dud sigl. If I mess *this* up, what the hell then? I don't even know what I'm supposed to be doing in the first place!

If this whatever-it-is wants something done, why doesn't it pick someone who knows more or can do more? There's *got* to be someone better than *me*!"

"God works in mysterious ways."

"That's not an answer!"

"Yes, it is. Just not one you like."

"You already admitted you don't know where this gift of mine came from. It could just as easily have come from a *different* evil demon, just one who's a bit more subtle about it. Right?" When I'd asked Colin about this, his joke about the gift coming from the "equivalent of Nurgle" had seemed funny at the time. It was a lot less funny now.

"Possibly."

"So how am I supposed to know which it is?"

"I told you," Father Hawke said. "You can think about your gift and the circumstances in which it was given. You can think about where you've been placed and where your abilities have led you. You can trust your intuition as to whether your particular patron feels good or evil. And if that's not enough . . . perhaps you'll simply have to have faith."

I had nothing left to say. I rose to go.

"Stephen," Father Hawke said, and I looked to see that his expression was sober. "It's understandable to be afraid. This will probably be the biggest decision you will ever make in your life. Just know that you're not the first to have faced it. Many others before you have stood where you are standing now."

"So how did they decide?"

"Usually, they prayed for guidance," Father Hawke said. "I'd suggest that, or whatever equivalent you've found works best. Whichever way you decide, good luck. Oh, and do feel free to come back to continue our chats. I promise that I won't pressure you on this particular subject until you're ready to discuss it further. Feel free to ask me any more questions, but your final choice on this matter is between you and God."

I LEFT THE church, stared back at it for a while as the last light faded in the western sky, then turned and walked slowly home. It took me a long time to get to sleep.

CHAPTER 14

THE PACKAGE I'D been waiting for arrived ten days into July.

Colin and Ivy were already in the Admiral Nelson when I walked in that evening, seated at our usual table. "Hey, dude," Colin said as I walked over.

"So what's the big news that you couldn't tell us over the phone?" Ivy asked.

I opened the folder that I'd been carrying, took out a slim sheaf of A4 paper, and dropped it onto the table. Then I sat back and looked at them expectantly.

"Dude," Colin said. "I know you like writing out lists, but this is getting a bit much."

"Take a look," I said.

Colin and Ivy shared a glance, then each picked up a page and started reading. I sat back and watched.

It took only a few seconds for their eyebrows to go up. "Wait," Colin said. "Are these—?"

"Yup."

"Is this real?" Ivy asked.

"I only got them this morning," I said. "But they look pretty real to me."

Charles had delivered on his promise. The sheaf of A4 was a printout of data on Light Wells in the Greater London area. Locations, strengths, estimated time to fill, ownership details . . . and security arrangements.

Colin picked up a second sheet of paper, then a third. "*How many of these things are there?*"

"Fourteen."

"Wow."

"This is from your family, right?" Ivy said. Her brow furrowed as she paged through the sheets. "How did they get this stuff?"

"I guess they've got people on staff."

"No, seriously, *how*?" Ivy said, putting the papers down to look at me. "I thought your family were a bunch of rich guys sitting around in a mansion?"

"My mother's family," I corrected. "But . . . well, I've been learning some family history. Turns out the guy who made House Ashford rich was my great-grandfather. He fought in the Second World War and stuck around in West Germany afterwards. And somehow, while he was there, he went from being a poor aristocrat to a multimillionaire."

"Somehow?" Colin asked.

"General impression I got was that he did not do it in a squeaky-clean way," I said. "It was right after a war, lots of people were dead, and a lot of those dead people's properties ended up falling into his pocket. The guy telling me the story didn't give me too many details. But Charles was the favoured son, so I'm guessing he grew up handling that stuff too. His brother Edward—that's my great-uncle—went off to Africa as a mercenary."

"So?" Ivy said with a frown.

"So I think my mother's family were less 'rich guys living off family money' and more 'pirate adventurers.' At least back in that generation. Raids seem like something they're really familiar with."

"You think that's why your granddad doesn't want to hand over the House to his grandkids?" Colin asked with interest. "He thinks they're all a bunch of wimps?"

"So . . . are you one of the grandchildren who might end up inheriting?" Ivy asked.

"No," I said curtly. "So what do you think?"

"I mean, the info looks good," Colin said, leafing through the pages. "These 'security' sections, though . . ."

"These Wells are B-class," Ivy said. "That's the point at which Well security starts getting serious."

"B-class sigls go for anything up to half a million at the Exchange," I said. "Not sure how much of that money the corps spend on security, but it's probably a fair bit."

"Jesus," Colin said, paging through. "Some of these security listings read like bloody dissertations."

"I'd be more worried about the ones that *don't*. They probably have just as much security, just stuff we don't know about."

"You're really going to do this?" Ivy asked.

"Yes," I said. "I am. This is the reason I put all this together. If I can't, this whole thing's been a total waste of time."

Ivy didn't look happy, but stayed quiet. "Are we going to have to check out every one of these?" Colin asked.

"Well, I think we can probably cross off some," I said. "Two of the Wells on that list are B+. We should probably rule those out right from the start."

"Why?" Colin asked.

"Going up half a grade multiplies a sigl's price by three," Ivy said.

"Which means three times better protected," I said. "I only

need a low B or a high C+ to make the sigl I want. No reason to get greedy."

"So the ones you've circled in pencil . . ." Colin said.

"Are the best prospects. At least that's how it looks to me."

Colin and Ivy pored over the papers for a couple of minutes. "Six?" Ivy said at last.

"Three permanent, three temporary," I said. "These are the ones that are about the right strength and are either full or close enough to it."

"Hey, the Moor Park Well's on here," Ivy said. "You didn't shortlist it?"

"Check the 'estimated time to fill.' I think they must have used it right after our raid."

"Two southeast, one southwest, one northwest, one north, and one west," Colin said.

"Yeah, would have been nice if any were in East London."

"Why have you underlined the bits in the security paragraphs where it says 'Time to HTR'?" Ivy asked.

"I'll get to that later," I said evasively. I didn't want to explain what 'HTR' stood for in a pub with other customers. "Short version, that's how long we're likely to have once the alarm gets raised."

"All right," Colin said, putting the papers down. "So what's the plan?"

"We divide these up and scout them out," I said, tapping the sheaf. "Remember, it's only a matter of time before all the Wells on this list get emptied, so let's not hang around."

SCOUTING THE WELLS was a two-part job.

Some of the work could be done online—searching for references to the postcode and name, and studying photos and satellite images. The locations might have security, but they weren't military black sites or anything, and simply plugging the postcode into Google Maps got us a wealth of information. Figuring out the Well's strength, though ... that meant visiting in person, and, as the one with the best sensing, that job mostly fell to me. So I spent the rest of that week travelling back and forth across London.

It was slow and time-consuming work, but it was exciting too. I knew that whenever I strayed near to those Wells, there were men and cameras watching specifically for people doing exactly what I was doing right now, and it added a constant low-level tension to the job. Not only did I have to scope out the areas and gauge the Wells; I had to do it without giving anyone reason to notice me or remember I was there.

Six Wells; six targets. Bounds Green, Norbury, Mill Hill, Dulwich, Camberwell, and Greenford.

Bounds Green was the first one I ruled out. It was a temporary Well in a car park at the intersection of several streets, its access restricted by barriers and a bored-looking security guard. It was a shame, because it seemed the least well secured, but it was also the weakest—the Well was on the low end of C+, wasn't close to filling, and might never ever even make it to the minimum strength the sigl would require.

The Well in Norbury was much stronger, but it was situated in an apartment building called Anderson Heights. The building was access-restricted, and walking around the outside, I could tell that the Well was somewhere deep within. Getting in would be simple, but once I did, I'd be deep inside a fully occupied residential building, and I didn't like that idea at all. If things went wrong, I could be trapped.

If Norbury was crowded, Mill Hill was the opposite: it was a permanent Well situated within a huge, mostly deserted cemetery. The landscaping seemed designed to make it very hard to approach without being noticed—there was lots of open green space with no paths, meaning that anyone walking up would stand out like a slug on plate glass. But, again, the Well was on the weak side, and it wasn't full. I crossed it off the list too.

Three choices were left. Dulwich, Camberwell, and Greenford.

SCOUTING THE WELLS was slow, painstaking work, but it did give me plenty of time to think.

When we'd met in June, Father Hawke had called me out for not thinking through the implications of my gift. So, during that week in July, I did exactly that. As I travelled on the Tube and studied satellite maps and walked the streets, I kept thinking over the problem at the back of my mind.

The more I thought about it, the more it felt as though this was less about what my gift *was*, and more about how I *saw* things.

The first way of seeing it was Father Hawke's. I'd been given this ability as a gift, and that gift had been for a purpose. It was a mindset I wouldn't really have understood before, but from the theology books he'd had me reading over the last year, I could at least follow it, if a bit hazily. If I believed them, then no matter what this entity was, God would act through it. No matter what I chose to do with my gift, it was *meant* for something; I could use it for evil, but God would ultimately turn that to good. Everything was meaningful; there were no accidents.

The second way of seeing it was Vermillion's. The way he'd talked about it, these gifts were given out casually, almost at random, by things that took no more than a passing interest. At most they might check in a few decades later to see if the gifted was still alive. If I believed *him*, then whether my gift had a purpose didn't matter. What I did with it didn't matter. It was mine and I could use it however the hell I liked. I wasn't a part of some greater plan.

And then there was my father's take, which you could call the sceptical one. I didn't *really* have any hard evidence that these spirits (as Father Hawke called them) or daimons (as Vermillion did) actually existed. Lots of people obviously believed in them, but people believe a lot of things. Just because the gifts were real didn't mean that the giver was. If that was right, then my gift didn't *have* a purpose; it was like looking for meaning in a vast machine.

There was one final way of seeing it.

Father Hawke had said these entities were as far above us as we were above an ant. I'd read some stories where, when the characters finally found out the truth about the supernatural things they were dealing with, it drove them insane. In those settings, the more you learnt about the supernatural, the crazier you became, and the worst thing that could possibly happen to you was that you saw something and correctly understood the implications. Mark had made a passing comment last year that one of Byron's failed students had ended up in a mental institution . . .

Four possibilities; four very different directions.

And the scary thing was that it felt to me as though any of the four could be *right*. I remembered what my father had said about models. Based on what I knew and what I'd seen, I had the disturbing feeling that all four explanations fitted the facts just fine.

Which should I believe?

THE WEEK CAME to a close. The three of us met again.

"I still say we go for the one in Dulwich," Colin said. "Least security, and it's the closest to full."

"It's got the least security for a reason," Ivy argued. "Stephen said he's not sure it's strong enough."

"Is it?" Colin asked me.

"*If* we go by the numbers on the report," I said. "But it didn't feel like it budged between Thursday and Saturday."

"So it's plateaued?" Ivy said.

"I think so."

"If we hit it right now," Colin said, "would it be enough to make the sigl you want?"

I hesitated. "Probably."

We were back in the Admiral Nelson. The more we kept meeting here, the more obvious it was becoming to me that a busy pub really wasn't the best place to plan a raid or a break-in, but we didn't have any better options. My own room was way too small, and neither Colin nor Ivy seemed particularly keen on offering up their own bedrooms as a replacement.

"It feels too exposed," Ivy said.

"That also means it's the easiest to reach," Colin said, looking at me.

"Maybe," I said reluctantly. The Dulwich Well was right beside a railway line. "My invisibility sigl can get me there easily enough, but that's not going to work once I start shaping."

"We're going to have that problem everywhere," Colin pointed out. "At least with the railway line there aren't cameras everywhere."

"That we know of," I reminded him. "They might have set ones up that I missed."

"IITR time is the lowest," Colin said. And neither Ivy nor I had any answer to that.

Between online research and some cautious questioning of Magnus, I had by this point picked up a general idea of how Well security worked. Houses and corporations had a problem: they needed to guard their Wells against raiders, but properly guarding a mid-rank Well required professional security, and professional security costs money. They couldn't put that kind of guard on every Well 24/7, because paying that much overtime would cost more than the sale price of the Well's sigl. On the other hand, if they hired from the security equivalent of the 99p store, then they *could* afford to keep the place staffed 24/7, but any serious raid would blow right through it.

According to Magnus, this problem was well understood in the House and corporate world, and they'd had plenty of time to work out a solution. The most common security protocol at this point, and the one that all of the Wells on our list were using, was what Magnus called "frontline HTR." "Frontline" was the obvious and visible part—minimal security at a minimal price. D-class Wells got a fence and a padlock; C-class Wells got a fence, a padlock, and some cameras. C+ and B-class Wells, like the ones we were looking at, got a security guard with a radio and a torch. The guard wasn't expected to fight off raids, just to keep an eye on the place.

But if there *was* a raid, the guard's job was to call in HTR. And that was when things got dangerous.

HTR stood for "High Threat Response." For the smaller Houses and corporations, that meant a priority line to the local police station. Medium-sized players tended to contract the job out to specialised security companies. The bigger names did it in-house. I hadn't been able to find many firsthand accounts of what an average HTR callout looked like, but the general impression I got was that they were like that Russian team I'd run into over Christmas—specialists who carried out and defended against raids for a living. Messing with them did not sound like a good idea.

Which meant that the "time to HTR" number on each Well

was essentially a doom tracker. If the alarm got raised, we really, *really* needed to be out of there before it ticked down to zero.

"All right, I'm going for a drink," Colin said. "You guys want anything?"

Ivy and I shook our heads. Colin pushed his chair back and headed for the bar.

"Are you sure about this?" Ivy asked once he was gone.

"Well, it's either this one or the one in Camberwell," I said. A man wandered past, close enough to see the papers on our table; I casually reached out and flipped them over. "And the Camberwell place has security cameras covering every last inch."

"I mean doing something like this at all."

Oh, I thought. *Right.* "Is this about you not liking the idea of stealing? I know you've never been keen on that part of the job..."

"I'm still not," Ivy said. "But no, it's not that. You know what 'HTR' means, right? It'll be something like those guys we ran into in Moor Park."

I grimaced slightly. "Yeah."

"And you're okay with that?" Ivy said. "Because I still have nightmares about that evening. Those guys were *terrifying*. They had guns and they had sigls and when they ran into us they just started shooting, straightaway. No warnings, nothing. I don't even want to think about what would have happened if they'd caught us. Arrested and thrown in prison if we were lucky."

"Probably worse," I admitted. "The UK police don't do much about burglars these days, and from what I've heard, Houses and corporations really don't like raiders coming back for another try."

"And you actually want to deal with that?"

"It's not that I *want* to," I said. "It's just... Look, you said you want to be a powerful drucrafter, right?"

"Yes."

"Ever wondered why there aren't many of those around?"

"Because most people don't have the opportunity," Ivy said. "They don't know drucraft exists, or they don't have the talent for it, or they don't have time to study it or teachers to show them what to do or sigls to practise with."

"Sure, that's part of it," I said. "But I know people who've got all those things and are still pretty average. Yeah, they're good compared to a guy off the street, but if you look at the opportunities they've had, they're nowhere near as good as they could be."

"Which people?"

"Doesn't matter. Point is, it's not just about opportunity."

"So what is it?"

"If you want things that other people don't have," I said, "then you have to do things that other people won't do."

"Have you considered that maybe the reason people don't do stuff like that is because it doesn't *work*?" Ivy said. "Maybe the ones who try end up getting dragged into the back of a van and never seen again."

"Maybe, but I think we've got some things going for us that most raiders don't. Better sigls, better information, an idea of what we're facing. I've spent a lot of time thinking about this, and I think we've got the tools to pull it off."

"You say 'we,' but what about us?" Ivy asked. "Colin and I don't have as many sigls as you. If things go wrong, you might be able to get away when we can't."

"If that happens, then I'll make sure everyone gets out."

"Will you?"

"I did before."

Ivy looked at me, her eyes searching mine. There was a long moment's hesitation, then slowly, she nodded.

"All right," Colin said, walking up to the table. He set his drink down with a clunk, then paused, looking between the two of us. "Did I miss something?"

I kept looking at Ivy until she glanced away. "It's fine," I told Colin.

"Okay," Colin said, sitting down and flipping over the top sheet of paper. "So. Dulwich?"

"Dulwich."

CHARLES'S INFORMATION HADN'T been free, and so it wasn't a surprise when I got marching orders the following week. What *was* a surprise was the location.

I got to the Bromley-by-Bow Gasworks in the late afternoon. The sun was shining from between puffy white clouds, bathing London in golden light and giving the air a warm, sleepy feel. Although the gasworks was in an industrial area, it was leafy and green, tall sycamores forming patches of dense woodland. I arrived early and wandered along a path into the trees.

The path led to a small clearing in the woods with a grassy lawn, a small garden, a statue, and a rotunda with ornate white columns. A stone slab held a metal plaque titled **TO THE MEMORY OF THOSE MEMBERS OF THE COMPANY WHO GAVE THEIR LIVES IN THE WAR OF 1939–1945**. Underneath were hundreds of names. Above it was a second, similar plaque from the previous war. The list of names on that one was even longer. To one side was a tall, black gas lamp, burning with a steady flame.

It was a peaceful place—quiet, with the surrounding trees—but also sad. I wondered if my dad's grandfather would have been friends with some of the men on that plaque. He'd fought in the Second World War, and my dad had told me that he'd lived around here. Ivy carpeted the trees and ground, painting everything in green.

Calhoun showed up a few minutes before we'd been scheduled to meet, walking into the shade. "Stephen," he said with a nod, gave the memorial a glance, then looked at the statue. "Woodall?"

"What?"

Calhoun nodded to the base of the statue, where an inscription read "Sir Corbet Woodall, Governor."

"There were a couple of Woodalls at my school. Descendants, maybe." He paused. "Why are you looking at me like that?"

I shook my head. Every time I met Calhoun I got a reminder of just how far away his world was from mine. "Nothing."

We walked together out of the shade and into the bright July sunlight. Looming up above us were the gasholders, huge, rusting skeletal cylinders of metal. I'd seen them hundreds of times, but this was the first time I'd come so close. There was a ten-foot steel fence between them and the access road that we'd emerged out onto; lurking discreetly to the side were a pair of House Ashford security.

I'd shaped one of my first sigls within sight of these gasholders. It had been a tiny little Motion Well, on the other side of the railway lines and the Channelsea River. Apparently I should have checked over the water afterwards... though, given House Ashford's interest in the place, maybe it was just as well I hadn't.

"You said this place was a 'cluster Well,'" I said as we walked up the access road. "What's a cluster Well?"

"An area where you get lots of small temporary Wells constantly re-emerging," Calhoun said. "They tend to form in places strong in two different branches instead of one. This one's Matter and Motion."

"Is the essentia close enough that you can use two Wells to make one bigger sigl?"

"Not usually. So they're only really good for producing large numbers of weaker sigls. Still, it adds up."

A gate in the fence was surrounded by large warning signs: **DANGER—DO NOT ENTER**. A guard was slouching against the fence waiting. The front-most House Ashford security man walked up; they exchanged words and the guard pulled out a key and unlocked the padlock on the gate. It swung open with a screech of rusty hinges.

"So do you guys own this place?" I asked as we walked in.

"No, it belongs to House Meath," Calhoun said. Beyond the gate was an old industrial road, winding between the gasholders. The place was overgrown with sycamores, all reaching up towards the light, their leaves casting dappled patterns on the concrete. "Usually they lease it to some corporation, but for some reason this year they're offering it to us instead."

"For some reason?"

"They didn't say why. Let's see if we can find out."

Now that we were actually right in the middle of the gasholders, they were even more intimidating: colossal, alien-looking structures covered in rust and peeling paint. I hoped none of them were going to fall on us. The air swirled with essentia, Matter and Motion blending together. We picked our way across the old industrial site, searching for Wells.

It was the first time I'd worked with Calhoun on something like this, and I was curious. According to everyone I'd talked to, the House Ashford heir was supposed to be a drucraft prodigy. So as we worked our way across the old gasworks, I watched my cousin closely, paying careful attention to what he could do.

And it didn't take me long to realise that he was very good. Calhoun could pick out Wells instantly, and distinguish Matter from Motion ones at a glance. In fact, after the second Well, I was forced to admit that, despite what I'd claimed to Charles, Calhoun was actually better at Well analysis than I was. Some of the Wells at the site were weak because they were new, but others were weak because they'd been over-drained in previous cycles. I couldn't tell the difference, but Calhoun could.

But when it came to raw sensing ability, I was better. Even without my essentia sight, I could spot Wells from further away than he could, and I was better at following the trails that led to them. I wondered if that might be because he'd grown up on a ridiculously strong Light Well—the times I'd been in the Ashford mansion, I'd always found that the essentia levels were so high that it was hard to pick anything out from the background noise. I'd grown up learning to sense in an atmosphere of relative quiet. Whatever the reason, it was nice to know that there was at least *one* thing I was better at.

"All right," Calhoun said at last. "Is that the last of them?"

"There's the one under the far eastern gasholder," I said. "But that's not even close to being a Well yet and might not turn into one at all. I wouldn't count it."

Calhoun nodded. "Then we'll take a look at the site from across the river and call it a day."

I followed Calhoun out of the gasworks, his two security men still bracketing us, one up ahead, one behind. The guard on the gate locked up behind us.

We went west and descended from the bridge onto Three Mills Island, a long spit of land bracketed by the Lea and Channelsea rivers. The rivers—canals, really—ran north to south, quaysides made from pebbled concrete. It was cooler down here, the breeze casting rippling waves and blowing across the strip of land between the water.

"Your mother spoke to me," Calhoun said as we came down the steps and turned north on the riverbank.

I glanced at him. "About?"

"You, mostly. How you were doing, whether I was happy with

you being around." Calhoun looked out over the water, where a coot was swimming with her chicks. "Today's orders came from Charles, but I think the decision might have been hers."

"Did she say that?"

"No, but she does seem to want you to take more of a family role."

Out on the river, the mother coot swam with quick bobbing movements, picking bits of food out of the water. Some she kept for herself; others she fed to her children. The chicks were juveniles, grown as big as their mother, but they still followed her lead and took food from her beak.

"I won't ask why you stayed away so long," Calhoun said. "I assume you had your reasons. But it does seem as though your situation has changed."

I was silent. When I'd met my mother again last year, I'd asked a very similar question: *why did you stay away?* Her answer had been that it had been for my protection; that anyone who knew of my connection to the Ashfords might try to use me.

I'd never completely believed that answer, but I'd seen enough since last year to know that there was some truth to it. The Ashford name was a double-edged sword, and the closer I was, the more attention I'd draw. So why had my mother suddenly changed tack?

We passed under a pair of railway bridges. A train roared by overhead, briefly putting our conversation on pause.

We came out from under the bridge and into the sunshine. "In any case," Calhoun said, as the rumble of the train faded behind us, "I wanted to ask what your plans are."

"With what?" I said guardedly. I had a lot of secrets to keep from Calhoun: the Well we were going to hit in Dulwich, my father, the Winged . . .

"Our family. Whether you're intending to keep doing things like this."

"Oh," I said. That was much safer ground. "I mean . . . probably. Charles kind of twisted my arm on this one."

"He made it sound as if there'd be more."

"Charles doesn't much like me."

"I'm not sure what your relationship is with Charles," Calhoun said, "but if he really didn't like you, he wouldn't be having you accompany me here."

"No, he just knows I'm good at what I do," I said. "Plus it probably helps that unlike Tobias and your crazy half-sister, I'm not going to stab you in the back. Wasn't that pretty much the reason *you* hired me?"

Calhoun frowned slightly. "And where do you think this is going?"

"Haven't a clue," I said. We'd left the bridges behind us and were passing a trio of barges moored up against the quayside. A long-haired black cat looked up at me from one of the decks.

I heard Calhoun sigh. "You know, you're not making this very easy."

I didn't look at Calhoun. The cat blinked at me, and I gave it a wave. I wondered how its owners kept it from wandering off.

"Do you understand what I'm asking here?" Calhoun said.

"Not really."

Calhoun stopped; ahead and behind, I was vaguely aware of his security men doing the same. We'd come to an area of the riverbank overgrown with huge wildflowers and weeds; they'd been growing unchecked for years, and some of them were taller than me. Up ahead was a weeping willow. Bindweed had latched on to the willow's leaves where they trailed down into the grass, white trumpet-shaped blooms reaching towards the sky.

"You're visiting Charles once a month, and Magnus once a

week," Calhoun said. "You're being sent out on Well surveys. And from what I hear, your mother's trying to get you a job in the supply office. Put that together, and it could mean a role in the family business. It could also mean a candidate for heir."

"Oh," I said. "So you're wondering if I *am* going to stab you in the back like Tobias and your crazy half-sister."

"If I really thought that, we wouldn't be having this conversation. But I would like to know your intentions."

I thought about it for a second. "Answer me one question first." Calhoun nodded.

"How do you feel about all this? The inheritance, our family, your cousin and half-sister trying to stitch you up. Do you have, like, such a burning desire to be heir that it doesn't bother you that there are people in your own family who'd happily see you dead just so they can pull the shoes off your feet and step into them? Because I'm pretty sure it would bother *me*. But every time I talk to you, you seem really . . . I don't know. Emotionless."

Calhoun looked back at me for a moment. "Is that how I seem?"

"I don't know, but you do seem freakishly calm about the whole attempted-murder thing. I guess I'm just wondering what could possibly make anyone so casual about it. Do you really want to be heir that badly?"

"To answer your second question," Calhoun said, "I wouldn't say I'm especially calm about it. I just tend not to show my feelings very much."

That seemed like a bit of an understatement. By this point I'd known Calhoun for the best part of a year, and I still had no idea what made the taller boy tick. I wondered what kind of upbringing would make someone *that* good at hiding their emotions. "And the other part?"

"I don't have any burning desire to be heir. It's a family duty."

"That's it? Duty?"

"Yes."

"And if Charles just decided tomorrow to give your position to someone else . . . ?"

"If I felt that the other candidate was more capable, I'd accept it."

I gave Calhoun a curious look.

"I've answered your question," Calhoun said. "So?"

Man, this guy is weird. "Oh, right," I said. "Well . . . this is a bit awkward, after what you just told me, but the truth is, I don't really have any investment in your family. I'm just interested in what you can give me."

Calhoun gave me a quizzical look.

"I'm not a leech," I clarified. "I'll pay for what I get. But . . . that's as far as it goes. Like, today's job? I only took that to pay back a favour from Charles."

"So you're not interested in working for our family?"

"Not really."

"Why?" Calhoun asked. "That supply office job you turned down might not seem like a high-status post, and it isn't. But if I advertised for it, I'd have a hundred applicants within the week. Jobs like that are a stepping stone to a permanent position in a Drucraft House."

"I don't want a permanent position in a Drucraft House."

"Again, why? Obviously, there are members of our family who'd be happy to give you one. You might think you're being canny, demanding payment up front, but in the long term you'd do far better as an insider. From what I've seen today, you're definitely good enough. In five years you could be one of the family shapers, and I promise you that the pay you'd get from that is *vastly* better than any kind of security work."

I sighed. "It's not about the pay."

"Then what is it about?"

I tried to figure out how to make Calhoun understand without giving too much away. We were standing in the middle of Three Mills Island, just off the main path. Calhoun's security men loitered to the north and south.

"You know what I was doing last year before Lucella showed up?" I asked.

Calhoun shook his head.

"I was working in the Civil Service," I said. "Before that was a bar. Then before that it was car insurance. Then there was another bar. Then secondary school. Then primary school. You know what they all had in common?"

"What?"

"I spent all my time getting told what to do."

Calhoun gave me a quizzical look. "That's . . . sort of how it works?"

"Yes," I said, and stopped.

"I don't understand," Calhoun said when I didn't go on. "Were you expecting that you'd be able to do whatever you wanted?"

"My point is," I said, "that I've spent most of my life in some random institution following random instructions given to me by some random adult to do some random thing which may or may not make any kind of sense but which I'll be expected to carry out to the letter. All while following about two hundred different rules, about half of which you get told, and about half of which you *don't* get told but you're expected to figure out anyway. Oh, and on top of that, when you look around you start to notice that lots of other people *don't* have to follow the same rules, but when you try to ask why, you're told to shut up and not ask questions. Right now, I don't have to do that. Yeah, being a locator isn't the best job. But I don't have anyone telling me what my hours are or how to dress or what to say. If I need to do something different that day, or if I have to protect myself or someone I care about, I can take the time off to do it. I don't have much but at least I don't have a boss, you understand?"

"I do understand," Calhoun said slowly, "but I think you're being foolish. A lot of those rules that you think are so arbitrary are there for a reason. And a lot of those people giving you orders started out in the same position you're in now. There's such a thing as working your way up."

I looked at Calhoun for a second. "It's a lot easier to talk about rules being there for a reason when you know someday you're going to be the one making them."

"I still have to obey them *now*."

"Yeah, maybe you do. But you know what? Every single time in your life that someone's looked at you and thought about giving you an order, there will have been a little voice at the back of their mind reminding them that someday, you're going to be the head of House Ashford."

Calhoun frowned.

"You talked about working your way up," I said. "Maybe to you that's how it seems this world works. Like a well-functioning machine where the guys who do well get promoted up through the ranks and everyone who does their job gets rewarded. You know how it looks to me?"

"How?"

"Like a huge, lumbering, mindless *thing* that sucks people in at one end and spits them out the other," I told him. "Half the time it doesn't work or makes things worse, and nobody seems to care. All those rules . . . they're to help the machine, not you. Keep it running smoothly. Most of the time the best you can do is just avoid getting crushed under the wheels." I looked at Calhoun. "You think you can trust House Ashford to be on your side. I don't."

Calhoun looked back at me for a long moment, and, when he

spoke, his voice was quiet. "I think I might understand that . . . better than you."

I frowned at Calhoun. He seemed to be looking at me, but there was something distant in his eyes, as if he were seeing something else.

Then all of a sudden Calhoun's eyes returned to focus, and the moment was gone. "Well. I suppose given your history with Lucella, I can see why you'd have reason to be suspicious. But if your previous jobs have left that bad an impression, I think that's all the more reason to look for something better."

"I suppose," I said. I'd shared about as much as I could without getting into dangerous territory. "But I've got my own problems to deal with. Working up the ladder at House Ashford won't help with that."

"I imagine this is connected to that issue you had back in February."

The "issue" had been Mark. Calhoun had helped me deal with that. "Yes."

Calhoun thought for a second, then nodded. "I still think you're making a mistake, but I suppose now I can understand where you're coming from, a little. Just promise me you'll think it over."

"All right."

Calhoun glanced out across the water at the gasholders. "We've seen all we're going to. Let's head back to the car."

Calhoun started back the way we'd come, and I followed. The riverbank was green and gold in the July sunshine, warm and lazy, and for a moment I was tempted to give Calhoun's offer a try. I'd meant everything I'd said, but . . . I had to admit, doing things aboveboard like this, not having to be underhanded all the time . . . it was nice. If every day was like this, would it really be so bad?

But... no. Even if I *did* trust the Ashfords, the Winged weren't going to go away. I needed to be stronger, and I wouldn't get that way by taking things easy.

Maybe sometime in the future that would change. For now, I had a Well to raid.

CHAPTER 15

BACK AT THE start of the year, if you'd asked me what I'd find hardest about raiding, I would have had several guesses. I might have said danger—my one previous raid, at Moor Park, had come with a very real risk of death. I might have said that it was the morality of the thing—like Ivy, I still wasn't completely happy about stealing other people's stuff for a living, even if the other people *were* giant soulless corporations. Or I might have said the risk of getting caught by the police.

But now that I'd been doing it for four months, I was coming to realise that what bothered me the most about raiding was the uncertainty.

I'm an organised sort of person. When I decide I'm going to do something, I plan it out. I can handle having to improvise and change plans on the fly, but I *hate* it when all that time I spend planning turns out to be totally useless because of something that's completely out of my hands. And that was exactly what happened with the Well at Dulwich.

We spent the Wednesday and Thursday of that week planning out how our raid was going to go. Between flyovers from Colin's drone, and invisible stakeouts from me, we'd figured out that there was only one security guard on-site, and he was hanging out on the north end, at the road bridge. He was far enough away from the Well that all I'd have to do was climb over the fence a bit further down the line and sneak up on the Well from the south side. Ivy would be on standby in case anything went wrong, but if everything went to plan I should be able to make the sigl and slip away into the night without anyone noticing that we'd even been there at all. We decided that we'd do it on Saturday night, and took the Friday off to rest and prepare.

And then it all fell apart.

Colin and I were at Kiran's house when we got the call, celebrating Colin's exam results. All five of us were there—me, Colin, Kiran, Felix, and Gabriel. I still wasn't on the best terms with Gabriel after what had happened last year, but he was part of the group and by unspoken agreement we'd all decided to stop bringing up the subject. As was tradition when we were at Kiran's house, we were playing an old FPS game from our childhoods; it had a four-player co-op mode that was supposed to involve everyone working together, but (given how seriously we took it) mostly just led to people screwing up in entertaining ways.

"Okay, board it, board it," Colin was saying.

"We can't, the Hunters are still there."

"I thought Gabriel was killing them!"

"Uh, gimme a second, I need to grab a weapon and run back."

"Grab a—? You died, didn't you?"

"Just once . . ."

"Okay, screw it, I'm going for it. Leeeerooooy . . ."

"No, wait! It's going to—"

On the screen, the hovering blue tank spat out a huge ball of plasma. It hit Felix's character at point-blank range, and Felix and Colin's screens disappeared in the ensuing explosion.

"Dumb arse," Kiran told Felix as his character's body flew fifty feet and started bouncing.

"Hey, I got the tank."

I laughed and noticed as I did that my phone was buzzing. I pulled it out and walked to the other side of the room as Colin and the others continued to bicker behind me. "Hey, Ivy," I said. "What's up?"

Ivy's voice was tense. "The Well's gone."

"What? You mean the one . . . ?"

"*Yes*, the one in Dulwich. Where's Colin?"

"Wait." I muted the phone and called over. "Colin! We've got a problem."

Colin looked away from the screen with a frown.

COLIN AND I moved into the kitchen and closed the glass doors. From the other side we could still hear the sound of electronic explosions. I set the phone to speaker mode and put it on the dining table. "Colin's here," I told Ivy. "What happened?"

"I just did our evening check on that Well," Ivy said, her voice a little distorted. "And it's not there. Barriers and security tent are gone, and the Well's been drained."

"Are you sure?" Colin asked.

"I can tell the difference between a full Well and an empty one."

"What happened?" Colin asked.

"What do you think happened?" I said. My spirits had dropped as soon as Ivy had given me the news, and now they were at rock bottom. "They used it."

"I think it was today," Ivy said. "Everything looked the same last night."

"Must have been," I said. "Shit." It was infuriating. If they'd just waited two more days . . .

"Why'd they do it now?" Colin asked.

"Well, maybe they noticed *some* people snooping around," Ivy said.

"What's that supposed to mean?"

"You said the guard noticed when you did that drone flyby on Tuesday."

"I said he *might* have noticed."

"Well, looks like he did, doesn't it?"

"How do you even know it was me?" Colin demanded. "Maybe they spotted *you*."

"I'm not the one who decided to buzz the guy with a drone just because—"

"It doesn't matter," I interrupted. I'd been mentally speedrunning through denial, frustration, and bargaining before settling on acceptance. "For what it's worth, I doubt they saw either of you, or else they'd have bumped up the security. It's more likely they were going to use it anyway. We were on a deadline this whole time, we just didn't know what it was. Anyway, it doesn't matter. The Well's gone and that's it."

Both Ivy and Colin were silent. Colin and I stood around the phone for a few moments, lost in our own thoughts. A shout came from the living room, followed by a burst of laughter.

Ivy's voice sounded from the phone's speakers. "So now what?"

"We've got no choice," I said. "We're going to have to hit the one in Camberwell or the one in Greenford."

"But they're both terrible," Ivy said.

There had been a reason we'd chosen the Dulwich Well: it had been the most lightly defended. Both alternatives were significantly harder.

The Well in Camberwell was the weaker of the two. It was a permanent Well located inside a building used as a children's centre; apparently the corporation that owned it leased it to some education charity for ten months out of the year, then shut it down during July and August so that they could schedule their sigl-making operations. At a strength of C+, it was on the borderline of what I needed, but I was pretty sure it would be enough.

The Greenford Well was temporary. It was on the banks of the River Brent, just above Ruislip Road. A section of the riverbank had been fenced off with barriers and tape, with vague warning signs suggesting that it was being used for some kind of construction work. It was significantly stronger than the Camberwell one, at B-class.

Both Wells posed major problems. In the case of the Camberwell one, the issue was that it was a permanent Well. Permanent Wells represented a major investment for the Houses or corporations that owned them, and they tended to be well protected. In this particular case, the corp in question had covered the building with security cameras and had a guard inside the building to watch the monitors 24/7. There was no way to approach any of the doors without being caught on multiple video feeds.

The Greenford Well, being on a dark, overgrown section of riverbank, didn't have cameras, but it *did* have two security guards round the clock. Even more worrying, it had the second-lowest HTR time of any Well in the notes. That meant that the corp that owned it knew that it was vulnerable, and were ready to send a heavily armed response team at extremely short notice.

One had better electronic defences, one had better human defences. We'd have to decide which to face.

"So what's it going to be?" Ivy said at last.

I stood silently for a couple of minutes. "We check them out tomorrow and decide then," I said at last. I didn't bother to mention that we'd have to be faster next time.

THE FOLLOWING DAYS were tense. Scouting wasn't a game anymore; we'd been reminded that we were on a clock. Every time that I arrived at one of the Wells, my heart was in my mouth as I anxiously scanned for any sign that they'd drained the Well, and every time I'd relax as I saw the familiar glow of essentia. But each day they weren't drained made it that much more likely that the next time, they would be.

After each visit, we'd gather and discuss possible approaches and plans. I started carrying a folder to the Nelson with printouts of satellite photos and blueprints.

In the end it was Colin who came up with the plan. It was funny, because he'd been the least keen on the whole idea to begin with, but it was his idea that was the best one, and we spent a long time discussing and refining it before we decided to run with it.

We would make the raid on Thursday night.

Thursday 27th July. 11:10 p.m.

"FINAL CHECKS," I said through my earbuds. "We good?"

"Ready at the front," Colin said. I could hear the nervousness in his voice. Colin's part in this was crucial: if he couldn't lure the guard out, nothing else was going to work.

"And the drone?"

"I stashed it behind that fence."

"How's the side gate looking?"

"All quiet," Ivy said. She sounded even more tense than Colin.

"We forgotten anything?"

"Can't think of anything," Ivy said.

"I have to piss," Colin said.

"You'd better be fucking joking."

"I'm joking."

"God damn it, Colin."

"I thought you said no names."

"Oh, screw you."

"Can you two stop playing around?" Ivy said in annoyance.

I grinned for a second—Colin had eased my tension slightly, which was probably why he'd done it—but it didn't last. I pulled on my mask, took a breath, and triggered my sigls. "Here I go."

The Leytonstone raid had been a failure, but it had taught me some useful lessons. First lesson: if you want to break into a building, the best place to start looking is next door. This Well was inside a children's centre, with high walls, barred windows, and a ten-foot fence; all the climbing routes on the street side were risky and in direct line of sight of cameras. But the children's centre backed onto other buildings, and those were much less well secured.

For this part of the raid I was using what I'd come to think of as my "infiltration" set. Invisibility so that I wouldn't be seen, mass reduction to help me climb. On the south side of the children's centre was a row of terraced houses. I climbed a fence, crossed a garden, and scrambled up a tree until I was able to bridge across onto the roof of the children's centre's gym. The gym and main building of the children's centre formed an L shape, surrounding a playground. The playground held the Well; from my position, I could look right down the slope of the roof and into it. If I wanted, I could scramble across and drop down onto the Well right now.

But getting to the Well was the easy part.

In the corners of that playground were at least three cameras. The camera feeds went to a security office, and in that office was a security guard. As soon as I dropped into that playground, the cameras would broadcast my image to the screens, the image on the screens would be seen by the security guard, and the security guard would pick up his phone and call his office. And at that point we were screwed. I'd spent a long time refining this sigl design, and I'd practised and practised to make the process as smooth as I could, but even if things went perfectly I didn't think I could do it in less than an hour. Estimated HTR response time to this Well was twenty minutes. Which meant that as soon as that call was made, we were done.

This was the second lesson I'd taken away from that raid in March. When you were raiding a Well, the biggest danger wasn't what was there; it was that someone would raise an alarm. It didn't really matter who they escalated it to—the police, corp security, whatever, we couldn't fight any of them. Our only chance was to shape that sigl and get out before the response team arrived. Which meant stopping that alarm from ever being raised.

I made my way across the roof, skirting the Well and heading for the main building. In one of the building's corners was a small open window. I was glad to see no one had closed it since Colin's last drone flyby—I'd come prepared to break it if I had to, but this way was better. I scrambled up and slipped inside.

The interior of the children's centre was silent and dark. We hadn't been able to get blueprints for the place, but from studying the outside we'd been able to figure out more or less what the interior layout had to be, and I made my way down the corridor and to the eastern stairwell.

And stopped.

"Shit," I said quietly, looking up through the window in the door. Just visible in the dim light at the top of the stairwell was a small half dome. I pulled back and touched my earbuds. "Hey."

"Yo," Colin said.

"There's a stairwell camera."

"The same stairwell I'm getting in through?" Ivy asked.

"Yes."

"Can you get around it?" Colin asked.

"No," I said. Getting this far without running into any cameras had been hard enough; any alternate route would certainly run into more. "You think it'd see me?"

"In a stairwell?" Colin said. "Almost definitely."

My invisibility sigl hid me from visible light. Unfortunately, security cameras didn't *just* use visible light; the better models also used infrared, and according to Colin, these ones covered a part of the infrared band that my sigl didn't. We'd done some testing and Colin was ninety percent sure that they'd be able to see me.

"If I overcharged my sigl and moved fast?" I asked.

"Then you'd be a big fast-moving blur. That'd make you *more* obvious."

"Damn it," I said. "I, how long will it take you to get to the window?"

"You really need a better code name for me if you're going to keep doing this," Ivy said. She was trying to sound casual, but I could hear the tension in her voice. "Maybe sixty seconds."

"All right. I'll stay up here until go time. Shouldn't take me longer than that to get down there and get the window open."

"You know I can't guarantee how long the guy's going to be busy for, right?" Colin said.

"Just keep him there as long as you can," I said, and paused. Ivy was in position; I was close to position. "Everyone ready?"

"As I'll ever be," Colin said.

"Would it matter if I said no?" Ivy said.

"Just answer the question."

"Ready," Ivy said resignedly.

"Go," I said.

"Wish me luck," Colin said.

We'd hashed out this next part of the plan many times, and we'd always come back to the same sticking point. No matter what we did, there was no way we could make this work while the guard was in the security room. We had to lure him out.

Colin had landed the job. Despite everything, he'd been fairly confident that he could do it. As he put it, if there was one thing he was good at, it was pissing people off. The question was whether he could piss the guy off just enough to make him come out the front door, but not *quite* enough to make him call in backup.

I'd already decided that I wasn't going to listen in or backseat. I had my job to do; Colin had his. I'd just have to trust him.

I stood up there in the darkness, one hand on the door. A minute passed, then another. I clenched and unclenched my fist, trying to stay calm. Nothing to do now but wait.

My earbud buzzed and I heard a single word from Colin. "Go."

I was already moving, shoving open the door and racing down the stairwell. I paid no attention to the camera; if Colin had done his job, there'd be no one watching. Two flights down and I was at the window. It was white PVC, and I grabbed it and twisted the handle, hoping it would turn and I wouldn't have to break it.

It turned, and I pushed the window open and looked out to see Ivy was scrambling up onto the lower roof below. Dressed in black, with a ski mask, she looked *exactly* like someone breaking and entering, and I quickly scanned the street to see that it was empty. I reached down, caught Ivy's hand, hauled her up and inside—she was light—then shut the window behind her. The whole thing had taken less than ten seconds.

"Where?" Ivy whispered.

"Down," I whispered back.

The security office was on the ground floor. It was closed and locked, and I felt my heart skip a beat. The guard couldn't be inside, could he? If he was, he'd have seen us already—

No. Calm. Colin would have told us if the guy was already in.

My earbud crackled and I heard Colin's voice. "He's coming in."

I looked at Ivy and saw her nod. I signalled for her to back around the corner. She did, and I triggered my invisibility sigl once again, watching the world fade into blue.

We were only just in time. Less than a minute later, I heard the slam of the front door, then heavy footsteps. They grew louder and then the door at the end of the corridor swung open, revealing the bulky shape of the security guard. He was fiddling with his key ring and muttering under his breath, something about "bloody kids." He stopped in front of the security room and started searching for the right key.

I let my invisibility and vision sigls drop, pouring essentia into my strength and shadowman ones instead. The hues of the world changed, becoming redder and darker. Out of the corner of my eye I saw Ivy fade into black as she activated her own sigl, but all my focus was on the guard. I darted forward, moving quickly and quietly, and as he started to open the door I grabbed him by the shoulders and yanked him back.

The man was bigger and heavier than me, but I was ready for a fight and he wasn't. He staggered back with a shout, pinwheeling his arms, and recovered his balance just in time for Ivy to discharge her Life sigl into the back of his neck.

I'd known for a while that Ivy had a sigl that could stun

people, and one of the first things I'd asked her once we were on reasonably friendly terms had been how it had worked. Unfortunately, Ivy didn't know. She knew *what* it did, in general terms—it staggered and dazed people, and with repeated uses could even knock them out—but she didn't understand the theory. The more drucrafters that I met, the more I was starting to realise that my own approach to sigl design, where any sigl I carried was one that I understood inside out, was very unusual. Other drucrafters didn't make their sigls from scratch—they bought them or were given them—and they didn't understand how they worked because they didn't need to.

But while Ivy didn't know how her sigl worked, she did know how to use it.

The security guard jerked and fell. It took him a few seconds to shake off the daze and raise his head, and when he did he saw both me and Ivy, wreathed in shadow, standing above him and staring down.

"This is a raid," I told him. I tried to make my voice sound deeper and tougher than it really was. "We're here for the Well, not you. You going to put up a fight, or stay out of our way?"

The security guard's eyes rolled fearfully at us.

"I can't believe he didn't put up a fight," Ivy said as we walked back towards the security office.

"Most security guards are clock punchers," I told her. We'd locked the guy in the cleaning cupboard after relieving him of his phone and keys. "It's only the professionals you need to worry about."

"How did you know he wasn't one?"

"Professionals are expensive and corporations are cheap."

The door to the security office had swung closed and locked, but a minute's work with the key ring got it open. We pushed the door open to reveal a small, cramped office. Monitors split into cross-sections showed feeds from more than twenty cameras.

Ivy looked at the screens dubiously. "Should we delete the footage?"

"Do you know how to delete footage off security systems?"

"Not really."

"Neither do I. Just stay here and watch the monitors. I'll be at the Well."

I SLIPPED OUT into the darkness of the playground. The Well glowed blue white in my essentia sight, sending a thrill of nervous excitement through me. Ivy and I hadn't been able to find any sign that an alarm had been raised, and Colin was in position outside, ready to send up the drone. All that was left was to actually shape the sigl, and that was something I knew how to do.

"How many cameras?" I said quietly into my earpiece.

"I can see you on three," Ivy said. "Two close, one far."

I pulled out a small can of spray paint from where it had been weighing down my pocket, shook it up, and moved from camera to camera, spraying each one. Covering the fishbowl-like lenses took more paint than I'd expected, but with Ivy checking the feeds it was easy to know when I was done.

"That it?" I asked after doing the third.

"No, there's a fourth," Ivy said. "Far corner. You just showed up on it."

I sprayed that one too. "Now?"

"You're clear."

"Nothing on the monitors? No blinking lights?"

"Not yet."

"Outside?" I said.

"Dead," Colin said.

I took a deep breath. "All right, I'm starting. Don't call me unless it's an emergency."

"Work fast," Ivy said tensely.

I turned and walked to the Well. It was on the north side of the playground, under a tree, off to one side of the sandpit. I could feel the power inside it, potential waiting to be used.

I sat down, pulling off my ski mask and stuffing it into my pocket; I didn't want any distractions for this. I closed my eyes and sat still for sixty seconds, steadying my breathing. Then, I opened my eyes and began.

Within minutes, I knew this was going to be hard. It was the first time I'd ever worked with a Well of this level, and I hadn't realised how *forceful* I needed to be. My first attempt fell apart immediately, and only my experience saved me from wasting a disastrous amount of the Well's essentia right from the start. I had to slow down, treating the thick strands of essentia with a cautious respect. And this Well wasn't even B-class. I wondered what a really powerful one would be like.

Slowly the skeleton of the sigl began to take shape. I couldn't do the construct in one go; it was too big. Instead I had to focus on one section at a time, splitting my attention in order to keep the rest of it formed and steady.

It was the first time I'd ever really felt what it meant to have a Light affinity. Maria had told me that I had a talent for it, but I'd never noticed; Light essentia just seemed like the default to me, while the other branches all seemed to have a bunch of annoying quirks. Only now that I was pushing my abilities to their limit could I see the difference. The essentia of the Well seemed to obey my desires, moving when I needed it to move, staying quiet and still when I needed it to stay steady. The more I worked, the surer I became that my affinity, and the practice I'd put in, were the only reasons I had any chance of pulling this off at all.

But I *did* have my Light affinity, and I *had* put in the practice, and it *was* working. The shape of the essentia construct was growing in front of me, becoming thicker and brighter as I layered in the strands. I wiped my forehead, my sleeve coming away damp. It was exhausting, but it was exciting too. I was more than halfway done, and I knew that what I'd done was good. I just needed to keep going.

A fox barked in the distance. I shook the sweat off my hand, took a breath, and got ready for the second leg.

My earbud pinged.

I frowned. I didn't want to talk to Colin or Ivy right now.

It pinged again.

Damn it. I touched the earbud. "What?"

Ivy spoke into my ear, her voice tense. "The phone's ringing."

"What phone?"

"The guard's."

A second later I heard it too: a steady *bzz-bzz*. After a moment it stopped, then started again.

"That's the third time," Ivy said over the ringing. "Do you think it's . . . ?"

She didn't finish, and didn't need to. We were both thinking the same thing.

A wave of panic swept over me, and I felt the essentia construct tremble. Estimated HTR time for this Well was twenty minutes. I couldn't finish the sigl that fast!

No. Calm. "What time is it?"

"12:04."

"Okay," I said, thinking fast. "Okay. It could just be a check-in. This guy's shift is 10 through 6, right? Maybe he's supposed to check in every two hours?"

"Well, they're going to figure out something's wrong pretty fast when he doesn't pick up for the fifth time, aren't they!"

I hesitated. In the background, I heard the buzzing of the phone cut off once again, and my father's words ran through my head. *Be cautious. Nothing you can get from a successful raid is worth what a failed one can cost you.* If he were here, he'd tell me to get out and wait for another chance.

But there might not *be* another chance. It's one thing to be cautious when you know you can keep trying. It's another when you can't. That information of Charles's had a time limit, and our window was closing.

And I *needed* this sigl. If I left now, I'd be back where I started. Sooner or later, I'd have to face the Winged, and this sigl was my best chance of beating them.

Sometimes the smart thing is to back away. Sometimes you have to see the danger and keep right on going.

All that flashed through my mind in a few seconds. In the background, I heard the phone start up a fourth time. "All right," I said. "Wait twenty minutes, then get out."

"You mean—?"

"If they knew we were here, they wouldn't be ringing that phone, they'd be on the way already," I said tersely. "But they'll start moving soon. Make sure you're gone before they do."

"What about you?"

"I'll stay as long as I can. When the twenty minutes are up, call Colin and tell him to get the drone in the air."

"You'll get caught."

"I can turn invisible, you can't. Do it."

Ivy was silent for a second. "All right," she said at last and rang off.

I took a deep breath and turned my attention back to the Well.

The construct had frayed and started to come apart while I'd been talking to Ivy, and I had to spend precious minutes rebuilding it before I could start to make progress again. Once I did, I threw myself into it feverishly.

The construct grew faster this time; I was more used to the Well now and could go more quickly. The shape of the threads began to complete, a network of glowing light hovering just in front of me. My earbud rang and I touched it without breaking concentration. "Yes."

Ivy spoke. "It's twenty minutes—"

"Okay. Go."

"What about—?"

"I'll be fine."

I turned my attention back to the construct floating in front of me, giving it a final check. Structure looked good; nodes looked good. Capacitor was as big as I could make it. It looked as though there had been just barely enough essentia in the Well. It was time for the final stage.

I threw myself into it with everything I had. The construct stage of a sigl is all about being slow and careful, but to condense it you want to do it in a single smooth step, and I pushed myself to my limit. The construct pulsed with light as it spun and shrank, growing denser, more real. Dimly I was aware of a familiar voice talking, but I didn't have time to listen. All my attention was on shrinking that glowing ball, making it smaller and smaller and—

—with a final push, it was done. I felt the pressure as the finished sigl dropped into my palm. Small as it was, I still felt as though I could sense the extra weight. I swayed, a wave of dizziness rolling over me, nearly making me fall. I scrubbed at my forehead with my free hand and felt it come away wet.

Gradually I realised that someone was talking into my earbud. Colin. I tried to focus on what he was saying.

"... can you hear?" he was saying. "Stephen, can you hear? Get out. Get out now."

"What?" I said. I was still a little confused and catching up. "What's going on?"

"They're here, they're here in a van. Get out!"

Adrenaline flared through me, burning away my exhaustion. I scrambled to my feet, fumbling out my sigl box and placing the new sigl inside before snapping it closed and dropping it into my pocket. I turned back towards the main building. I should be able to get up and out through the window—

A voice floated out of the darkness. "Are you done?"

I stopped dead. "Ivy?"

I saw movement in the shadows. Ivy was there, in the corner. My heart rate jumped. "I told you to go!"

"You were still here," Ivy objected.

"That doesn't—!"

A footstep sounded from outside. A man's voice floated over the fence, deep and confident. "Hello?"

Ivy and I whirled, going silent. I looked left and right, my thoughts racing. Back inside? No, we'd left it too late. I could slip away invisibly, but Ivy couldn't.

One option left. I hit the button to switch off my earbud, then strode forward and grabbed Ivy's hand. "Come with me," I whispered. "Don't move until I tell you to. And *stay quiet*."

"Hello?" the voice called from over the fence. "Anyone there?"

"*Stay quiet*," I repeated, and pulled Ivy forward. Towards the voice.

The side gate to the children's centre was made of wire mesh.

It was heavily overgrown with shrubs and climbing plants, but I could still see glints of light from the other side, and I pulled Ivy into the corner nearest to the gate as I heard the rattle of a chain and padlock. I took a deep breath, pulled Ivy in close, and activated my invisibility and vision sigls.

The world faded, turning blue. Ivy had gone rigid, but blessedly didn't push me away or argue. A few seconds later, the gate swung open with a creak of hinges and a man stepped in, shining a torch.

No gun, was my first thought. The guy was big and bulky, and from the way his torch was up and scanning the playground, he was on the alert. But I couldn't see a weapon and he didn't have any active sigls, and that made me suddenly sure that, while they might suspect something was wrong, they didn't *know*. The torch beam swung towards me, and I froze.

Sapphire light washed over us. I blinked, dazzled, but the torch beam swept on almost instantly. The man did a slow sweep of the playground, the beam picking out the door, the climbing frame, the corner Ivy had been hiding in. I kept very still.

I heard the crackle of a radio and an electronic voice spoke from the direction of the man. "... you in?"

The man reached up with one hand; I was so close I could see him twist his neck slightly to speak into the radio. "Yeah, at the Well. Looks clear."

I could feel Ivy pressed against me. She was rigid and still, but I could feel the tension seeping through her. The man was maybe five paces away; if he moved in our direction, or looked at us too hard...

There was a garbled message from the radio.

"He's not picking up," the man said into his radio. "You want me to run a check on the Well?"

Oh shit. I could still see the Well in my essentia sight, but it was so faded as to be barely visible. Even a finder's stone would be able to tell that it was drained.

There was a pause, and I held my breath, then the radio crackled again. "No, get to—" there was a burst of static "—office. See what's going on."

"Roger that."

The man turned and walked away from us, past the Well and across the playground. He disappeared inside, the light of his torch flickering back and forth within the building.

I stayed still for three seconds more, then as the light of the torch disappeared I took Ivy's hand and led her out of the gate, the way the man had come in. She moved slowly, blindly, and it took a few seconds more for us to get out and into the street.

I looked up and down. No one in sight.

I dropped my invisibility. Colour flooded into the world, and I saw Ivy blink as she could see again. "Run," I hissed.

We took off down the road at a sprint. Somewhere behind us, from within the children's centre, I heard a shout. Neither of us turned to look.

We ran south, turning left and then right, leaving the Well and the building behind us. As I ran, I hit the button on my earpiece. "Colin," I said breathlessly.

"Are you out?" Colin demanded. "I just saw another guy run in the front."

"We're out, we're out. Pull your drone and get out of there, now!"

"I'm on it."

We disappeared into the night.

"Holy shit," Ivy said much, much later. "We actually did it."

"What, you were expecting to get caught?" I asked.

We were on Peckham Road, south and east of the Well. We'd kept running for quite a while, but once we'd put more than half a mile between us and our crime scene, we'd finally let ourselves believe that we were safe. Right now we were at a bus stop on the main road, waiting for the night bus that'd take us north across the river and into the West End.

"I didn't think we'd get *caught*," Ivy admitted. With her ski mask stuffed into her pocket and her sigls out of sight, she looked like an ordinary Londoner again. "I just thought something'd go wrong and you'd end up calling it off."

"Something *did* go wrong," Colin pointed out. With the drone stowed away in his backpack, he looked no more suspicious than Ivy. "I nearly had a bloody heart attack when I saw those men get out of the van."

"They weren't a real HTR team," I told Colin.

"They could have been," Colin said.

I didn't argue. Because, of course, Colin was right—the security company had treated that guy missing his check-in as something to investigate, and had sent a van with two guys. But they *could* have thrown the kitchen sink at us instead. It would have been an overreaction, but if they'd put two and two together a little faster . . . if they'd arrived a little earlier . . .

A lot of things had gone our way tonight. The window had been open. The street had been empty. The guard had chosen to chase Colin off. All of those things had been *likely*, but they hadn't been *certain*. But luck had smiled on us, and every time we'd rolled the dice, they'd come up in our favour. They wouldn't always.

"It's not always going to turn out that way," Colin told me, echoing my thoughts. "You know that, right?"

"I'm not planning on doing this again," I told him.

"Really?" Ivy said.

"What, you're disappointed?" Colin asked. "I thought you didn't like this stuff."

"Well, I still don't," Ivy said. "But come on, it was kind of exciting."

"Oh, bloody hell." Colin threw up his hands. "You're *both* adrenaline junkies."

"I'm really not," I told Colin. "Like I said, I don't want to do this again."

"Good," Colin said. "So we're done, right?"

"Well, I said I didn't *want* to, but I probably still will."

Colin gave me a look.

"I'm kidding," I said with a slight smile. "For now."

"What do you mean, for now?"

"Now I've got this sigl, I need to train with it. Set it into a ring, do some practice."

"So can you make me one too?" Ivy asked.

"You have got to be fucking kidding me," Colin told her.

"Hey," Ivy pointed out. "He's said it's easier the second time."

"I thought you wanted an invisibility one," I told her.

"That too."

"Isn't it my turn to get one next?" Colin said.

"I thought you said you wanted to be done with it?" Ivy said.

"We could still do *safe* ones."

"So does that make you an adrenaline junkie too?" Ivy asked innocently.

I laughed. Hearing Ivy and Colin argue back and forth, I felt warmth spread through me. You could tell from looking at them that they trusted each other now. And now that I thought about it, I trusted them too.

I've actually built something here. Three wasn't a big number, but it was a lot more than one. For the first time in a long while, I wasn't alone.

It was an odd, comforting feeling, like coming inside after a long journey in the cold. With a sigh, I leant back against the wall of the bus stop and closed my eyes. It had been a long night and the adrenaline crash was making me sleepy, but I wasn't worried. If I fell asleep before the bus came, one of my friends would wake me up so that I could get home.

CHAPTER 16

IT'S WEIRD TO go through a life-changing experience and then wake up the next day.

I opened my eyes that Friday with the feeling that everything was different. Our little group had planned, prepared, and carried out a raid. And it hadn't been a small raid—that sigl I'd made last night would probably have cost over £100,000 on the open market. It almost felt like I'd become a professional criminal, which was exciting and disturbing at the same time.

But I woke up to . . . a completely normal morning. The boiler in our house had finally broken down completely, and Ignas and the others were trying to pester the landlord into fixing it. Hobbes needed to be fed. The month's rent was due. I needed to go to the supermarket. There was a message on my phone from someone at House Ashford telling me about a Well survey next week.

It was all bizarrely normal, enough that it almost made me wonder if last night's raid had really happened. A part of me actually wanted to go back to Camberwell and take another look at that Well just to make sure that the whole thing hadn't been some very long, extremely vivid dream. I didn't, but I did look the area up on social media and news sites, looking for reports of a break-in. There was nothing.

But I had proof that the raid had happened: the sigl sitting on my bedside table. Now it was time to master it.

THERE'S A DIFFERENCE between being able to make a sigl, and being good with it. How much essentia to use, the best way to channel, what happens when you over- or undercharge . . . there are dozens of tiny little details that you have to get familiar with before you can really use it effectively, not to mention lots of mistakes that you only *know* are mistakes once you make them. It's like learning how to work a new phone, or drive a new car, and the only answer is practice.

First I had to mount it. As with the rest of my combat sigls, I went with a steel ring, the sigl slightly recessed so that it wouldn't be at risk of breaking from impact (sigls are very hard, and I've yet to see one shatter, but I didn't want this one to be the first). Next, I spent a while channelling into the thing and getting a feeling for how sensitive it was. With that done, it was time for field-testing.

Field-testing enhancement sigls is easy: you put them on and see what happens. Testing a weapon is a bit more awkward. Some practice in a darkened room confirmed that the thing would work, but what I really needed to know was what it would do to a living target, and that's not the kind of thing you can find out by shooting at a wall. I briefly considered seeing if I could find that raider gang who'd beaten me up in Stratford last year, and I was actually tempted until it occurred to me to wonder what would happen if I used it on them and it didn't work . . . or, possibly worse, worked *too well*. In the end I decided my least bad option was animal testing.

For my test location I went back to the Channelsea River. I found a nice, deserted spot a ways down the bank, across the water from the gasworks that I'd visited with Calhoun, then waited until dusk. Once the light was dimming and there was no one in view, I threw some bread on the riverside path, then backed off and waited. Hobbes had followed me and tried to eat the bread; I picked him up, backed off to his complaining miaows, and scratched him around the neck until he started purring. Then I waited. It didn't take long for a pigeon to flutter down and start pecking at the food. I lowered Hobbes to the ground—he immediately crouched down, zeroing in on the pigeon and going into stalking mode—and sighted on the bird. We were a little further away than I'd planned, so I decided to try the sigl at full power. I aimed at the bird as it pecked away at the food, channelled until the capacitor was full, and discharged it.

As it turned out, I'd underestimated how bright the thing was.

It wasn't as though I hadn't had warning. I'd used the sigl indoors and it had dazzled me, but I'd figured that had been because I'd been using it in an enclosed space. It wasn't. I'd done my best with the focusing lens, and according to my calculations, ninety-nine percent of the generated light should be landing on the target, but either I'd got a decimal point wrong somewhere or one percent of the sigl's power was a hell of a lot more than I'd realised.

The riverbank lit up in brilliant green. It looked like a giant laser, connecting my hand and the pigeon in a solid bar of light, and bathing the path, riverbank, and everything around us in dazzling emerald. I cut off the beam almost instantly, blinking against the afterimage; as the spots faded from my vision, I saw that the pigeon was lying motionless on the path.

Hobbes sprang forward and snatched it up in his jaws.

"Hobbes!" I hissed at him. "No!"

Hobbes turned to look at me, still hefting the pigeon, and gave a muffled "mraow."

"Put it down! No, don't run off, don't run off—!"

Hobbes ran off.

I swore, then realised that I'd drawn attention. Lights were coming on in the windows of buildings across the river, and I could hear voices drifting across the water. I turned and fled into the darkness. I kept running until the voices had faded away behind me, thinking as I did that it would have been *really* helpful to know exactly how long that pigeon ended up knocked out for.

I RAN SEVERAL more experiments over the next few days, with mixed results. As it turns out, it is very difficult to find somewhere in the middle of a city where no one'll notice a giant green laser. I eventually realised that I was making life a lot harder for myself by trying to do it at night—over the past few years I'd come to think of the darkness as an ally, but when you're trying to practise with a weapon that lights up the entire neighbourhood, the middle of the night is the absolute *worst* time to do it. Once I tried using the sigl in broad daylight, where the brilliant flash could be drowned out by the power of the midday sun, everything became much easier.

The good news was that the thing definitely worked. Birds and small animals dropped instantly when hit in the eyes, and poking them afterwards confirmed that they were unconscious. How long they *stayed* unconscious varied—the shortest time was under thirty seconds, the longest was almost an hour. I had the feeling that the duration was heavily dependent on small details like exactly where they were looking and how quickly they closed their eyes against the flash.

The effect didn't seem to cause permanent damage. I'd been a bit worried that I might be burning out the eyes of anything I hit, but after watching a dozen or so animals get zapped and then wake up and struggle back to their feet, I couldn't see any sign of it—they did seem a little shaky, but there was no indication that they were blind or anything, which was a relief. A bigger worry was how unpredictable the duration was. I didn't much like the idea of zapping someone and having them get up again twenty seconds later, but you couldn't have everything—besides, realistically, if I was shooting someone with this thing, I was going to be getting the hell out of there shortly afterwards, so whether it put them down for five minutes or fifty shouldn't make too much difference.

I also managed to figure out how to reduce the width of the flash. Apparently I'd been a bit too enthusiastic that first time—if I moderated the amount of power, and made an effort to channel the essentia in a focused line, I could narrow the beam a good deal. That said, even if it no longer looked like a giant emerald firework, it was still about a million miles away from subtle. If I triggered this, especially at night, I was absolutely guaranteed to catch the attention of everyone in the area.

But at the end of the day, these were niggles. I finally had the weapon I needed, and as day after day passed, and I became more and more comfortable with it, my confidence grew.

August came.

Colin, Ivy, and I kept our eyes open for any sign of fallout from our raid, but none came, and once a week and a half had passed we let ourselves relax. I suggested we meet up to celebrate, but Ivy said she was going to be busy. When we asked her with what, she said something about a family visit, then stopped answering her texts.

A JUDGEMENT OF POWERS

I saw a lot of Colin that summer. Now that he'd graduated and was looking for a job, he'd moved back in with his parents, meaning that he was living within walking distance again. In between hanging out and watching movies, Colin asked me to make him another sigl, which I agreed to—I figured that after that raid, he'd earned it.

In the end, after some discussion, we settled on a power sigl: a continuous Light sigl that drew on the wearer's essentia to produce a steady flow of electricity that could be used to power electronics. Electrical sigls were an area of Light drucraft I'd yet to explore, and I figured a power sigl would be a nice easy way to learn . . . which, as it turned out, was half right. I picked up the basics of electrical sigl design fast, and since power sigls worked just fine at D-class, we didn't have to do any more high-risk raids, which neither of us were really feeling up to at the moment. What *wasn't* so easy was fixing the sigl's output. Turns out that electronic devices have very specific power requirements, and if you connect them up to a power supply with the wrong voltage and current, it doesn't work very well. A channeller can adjust a sigl's output on the fly, but Colin *couldn't* channel, and figuring out a solution to that turned out to be a surprisingly difficult problem.

But while it was a problem, it was an interesting problem, in a subject I loved, that I had a friend to help me work on, and for me, the weeks that followed were happy ones. I'd wake up, do some locating in the morning, then head over to Colin's. We'd work on designs and try stuff out for a couple of hours, then go out in the evening to go to the pub or just get a takeaway and wander around the Plaistow streets, enjoying the warmth of the summer nights.

Things continued moving along in the background. I kept showing up on Mondays for my lessons with Magnus, occasionally seeing other members of my family. I started meeting up with Father Hawke again, reading the books he'd give me and discussing them afterwards. I didn't bring up the subject of my patron, but as he'd promised, Father Hawke didn't press me on it. I also got a message from my father—the email was extremely unspecific about where he was and what he'd been doing, but it did mention that he expected his work to be finishing up before the end of the month.

The prospect of seeing my dad again added to my good mood. Slowly the height of summer passed, the days cooling with the approach of autumn.

ON THE THIRD Saturday of August, I went to meet Bridget. I hadn't seen my half-sister since that botched raid in the spring, and she'd sent me a couple of messages hinting that she was bored and wanted company. I spent most of the journey there trying to figure out how to do that without giving too much away. I like Bridget, and she seems to like me, but she's sixteen and not exactly what you'd call reliable. Telling her the details of our latest raid didn't seem like the smartest idea.

But when I got there, Bridget seemed unusually subdued. She didn't question me about what I'd been doing or how the raiding group had gone since she'd left. She just said hello and lapsed into silence.

"Uh," I said. "You want to go to that café?" We'd met up at one of the north gates of Hampstead Heath, not too far from Kenwood.

"Not really," Bridget said.

"Oh," I said. "Okay." In the absence of any better ideas, I picked a path into the Heath more or less at random. Bridget followed me, eyes down.

"What's wrong?" I asked after we'd gone a little way. The sun was shining, but thick banks of cloud were drifting through the sky overhead. People were scattered across the paths and the grass, but the Heath is a big place and no one was close enough to overhear.

Bridget didn't meet my eyes. "There was a fight."

"A fight?"

"I was out in the kennels playing with the dogs."

I gave Bridget a confused look.

"And Mummy found me," Bridget explained.

I was completely lost. When Bridget had said "a fight" my mind had jumped to an image of something a lot more serious. "That started a fight?"

Bridget nodded.

"Um. Why?"

"She said I'd get messy and smelly for the party tonight," Bridget said. "And that I should have been studying."

"Studying with . . . ?"

"With Susan. My governess. And it wasn't even fair! I'd *done* my work. But then Mummy went back and made me go over all of it and said I'd done a bad job and called in Susan and told her she hadn't been teaching me well enough and then told me to do lessons for the whole afternoon before getting ready at six."

I wasn't quite sure how to answer.

"It's not fair," Bridget repeated. "I do the work Susan sets. Well, mostly. And I have lessons with Daddy. And I go to all the parties. But she's never happy."

"Why?"

"She'll always ask me questions afterwards," Bridget said. "About why someone is doing something or saying something, and what they wanted, and how I should treat them. And I never seem to give the right answer and she'll get angry and say I'm not trying hard enough."

"Does that happen all the time?"

"Sometimes . . . It's been worse the last couple of months.

Mummy keeps saying that things are different now because of Calhoun."

"Because of Calhoun? How?"

Bridget shrugged.

I cast around for a new subject. "How's Calhoun and Johanna's engagement going?"

"All right, I suppose," Bridget said. "Tobias thinks she's going to dump him."

"Wait, what? How would he know?"

"He snoops on them."

I rolled my eyes. *Of course he does.* "Do you think he's right?"

"No . . ." Bridget said. "I mean, I don't think so. It does sort of feel like Calhoun's keeping her at arm's length, but he does that with everyone."

"Oh," I said. "That reminds me. Have you guys found out anything else about that bomb?"

"The bomb?"

"Charles said back in the spring that he was having it investigated."

"I don't think they've found out anything."

"What, nothing at all?"

I'd asked the question casually. But Bridget shot me a peculiar look, a sort of darting sideways glance, then cast her eyes downward again.

"What's wrong?"

"Nothing."

"Who do *you* think did it?" I asked.

Bridget took a while to answer, and when she did, she sounded awkward. "Our House has a lot of enemies."

I frowned, but before I could follow up Bridget seemed to recover and started asking me about what I'd been doing, and my attention was diverted figuring out how much to tell her about the raid. But as we kept on walking and talking, the thought lingered at the back of my mind that she hadn't exactly answered my question.

It was the Monday after.

"...which finally allowed Walter Ashford to complete the purchase of the Bishop's Well in 1997," Magnus was saying. "House Ashford successfully achieved Lesser House status that same year."

"Why did it take so long?" I asked. "I thought you said they'd had the money for years."

"Assets above a certain level of importance are not for sale to anybody who just walks up and writes a cheque," Magnus said. "In the United Kingdom, ownership of a Well of class A+ grants you a seat on the Board, and, as such, any sale or purchase of such a Well requires Board approval. In the case of House Ashford, it was only Charles Ashford's previous work with the Board that enabled our House to complete the purchase."

"So if I had five million pounds and wanted to buy an A+ Well..."

"Try five *hundred* million," Magnus said with a slight smile. "But even if you had that much, no, you couldn't. You wouldn't know the right people to approach, or how to convince them. Charles was only able to do it by calling in a number of favours."

"So why do people even bother with A+ Wells? Wouldn't enough A's and B's add up to the same thing?"

"If all you want is essentia, then, yes. You can focus on temporary Wells, like a lot of the corporations, or you can build up a network of B- and C-rank permanent Wells, like a lot of the old Houses. But that doesn't get you a seat at the table."

I glanced at Magnus thoughtfully. There was something that

had occurred to me recently; when Tobias had first talked about the possibility of Calhoun becoming heir, he'd made it sound as though it was his generation that were the candidates: him, Calhoun, and Lucella. And he'd been right—when Charles had made his announcement, it had been Calhoun he'd picked.

But Charles had a daughter and a son-in-law. Why had he decided to skip them?

I opened my mouth, thinking about how to phrase the question.

The door swung open, and Magnus and I turned to see my mother step inside. "Oh, Stephen," she said. "You're still here." She looked past me to Magnus. "It seems like the sale of the Velbert Well is going ahead after all. We're probably going to have to fly out next week."

Magnus frowned slightly. "We?"

"It's Ariane Meusel. It'll look better if you're there."

"Why can't she come here if she wants a visit so badly?"

My mother glanced aside to me. "Oh, and Stephen, Anderson wants you to do a grounds course."

I frowned. Anderson was the head of security of House Ashford, and he'd never said a word to me about anything like that. "A what?"

"A course covering what parts of the landscape to avoid damaging so as not to disrupt a Well's essentia. All House Ashford security have to do one."

"That sounds completely pointless. I can *tell* when something's damaging a Well."

"Maybe, but Anderson's been complaining, so you're going to have to do it. Until you do, you won't be able to go on any more surveys."

"Oh, come on!"

"Go and talk to Clarissa, she'll see about booking you a slot," my mother said, and glanced back at her husband. "Magnus?"

"Yes," Magnus said resignedly and looked at me. "That's all for today."

It was a dismissal. I rose and left.

I walked down the mansion corridor in a grumpy mood. This "grounds course" sounded like a complete waste of time, and having to book it via Clarissa was two aggravations for the price of one.

I could completely believe that it was the kind of thing that Anderson would do, as well. The shaven-headed man had made it obvious by now that he didn't like me, and that's the kind of thing managers do with employees they don't like—they force them to follow all the most annoying and pointless rules in the hope that they'll quit.

I paused, my hand on the door handle. *But why's he doing it now?*

Doing some random training course because the boss says so sounded normal. It *was* normal. But somehow, something about it didn't quite fit.

Not too long ago, I would have shrugged it off and gone about my day. But over the past year and a half, I'd learned to listen to my instincts. Maybe it was time for my monthly visit.

"You didn't keep me waiting as long this time," I told Charles Ashford as I walked into his study.

"Given our previous meeting, it seemed fairly likely that this one would involve you rushing to me in a panic hoping for me to clean up your mess," Charles told me. As usual, he was writing at his desk. "But you don't look agitated enough."

"You are the last person on Earth I'd go to for help cleaning up a mess."

"Good," Charles said, turning over a leaf of paper. "So what is it this time?"

"I just got told that I can't go on Well surveys until I do a grounds course. Did you do that?"

"No."

"Did Anderson?"

"I believe Anderson did complain to Calhoun back in the spring about your lack of training. Although the deficiencies he cited were your skills in close protection and first aid."

"I didn't hear about that."

"That's because Calhoun told Anderson, in more polite terms, to stop wasting his time." Charles glanced up at me. "Who said you were being taken off Well surveys?"

"My mother."

Charles looked back at me for a few seconds, then returned his attention to his papers. "I see."

"You didn't give the order?"

"Security questions in House Ashford are delegated to Anderson," Charles said. "Day-to-day management is handled by Helen, surveys of new Wells are done by Calhoun. And so on. If there's a serious problem to be solved or a significant decision to be made, I'll step in. You being sent on a training course is neither of those things."

I made a face.

Charles signed the bottom of his sheet of paper, then put it on a pile. "Was there anything else?"

"What's a castle?"

"Go ask an architect."

"I'm not talking about buildings."

"Then what are you talking about?"

"Back in the spring, I met someone from the Winged," I said. I saw Charles stop and look up. "He said the Winged fought with some group called the Order of the Dragon over 'castles.' What did that mean?"

Charles studied me for a few seconds before answering. "Have you ever wondered why Britain has so many castles?"

"Not really."

"Look how many of the things there are," Charles said. "They'd be expensive to make even today. With the technology of their time, they'd have cost a fortune. So why did kings spend so much on them?"

"Because if you got attacked you could retreat into the castle and defend it."

"You think rulers nearly bankrupt themselves building last-ditch emergency defences?" Charles asked dryly. "Kings and prime ministers can barely be bothered to *maintain* things like that, much less build new ones. No, if a castle's only purpose was to defend, there wouldn't be so many of them."

"So why else would they build them?"

"Castles were tactically defensive but strategically offensive. A castle functioned as a base of operations from which a group of armed men could project power. An enemy wanting to operate in the area would be forced to lay siege to the castle and spend resources conquering it. If they didn't, the castle's occupants could sally out and raid them, withdraw back to the safety of the castle, then repeat the process later. Building a castle, or taking one, was a way to gain control of contested territory."

I frowned.

"Conflicts in the West today aren't fought over fortifications, they're fought over institutions," Charles said. "A bank, a media company, a branch of government. They function as control points. Take one, you gain influence. Take enough, you own the country. In the old days you'd do it by marching an army over and killing anyone who didn't do as they were told. Nowadays it's leveraged buyouts and media campaigns and the odd discreet assassination. But the principle's the same."

I looked at Charles.

"The Brotherhood of the Winged and the Order of the Dragon are locked in an endless battle for dominance, fighting on a thousand battlefields across the globe," Charles said. "The larger and more important any organisation, the more likely it is that it's under the influence of one or both of them. They're the puppet masters who sit behind the curtain, pulling the strings. We all live in their shadow, though not one in a hundred knows it."

I sat silently for a little while, thinking. "So which one controls us?" I said at last.

"House Ashford has members under the influence of both, but is owned by neither," Charles said. "Much of my time and effort is spent on keeping things that way." His lip curled slightly. "While you're busy with your raids and amusements."

I let the implied insult slide off. "You said once that the Winged would tear down House Ashford. Are the Order of the Dragon the same?"

"Less inherently hostile. Not any more benevolent. I wouldn't recommend going to them for help, if that's what you're thinking."

"I wasn't."

Charles had stopped writing; he seemed to be paying full attention to me. As I looked at him, it suddenly occurred to me that maybe my position towards him wasn't so different from his towards the cults like the Winged. It was a disturbing thought.

"Was there anything else?" Charles asked again.

I hesitated a second. "There's supposed to be a guy from the Winged taking an interest in House Ashford."

"A 'guy'?"

"All I heard was a name. Oscar."

Charles studied me.

"Is this something I should be worried about?" I said when he didn't speak.

"One of the few benefits of your current position is that questions like that are above your pay grade."

"Which means you're not going to tell me what's going on."

"If I ever do, it'll be because I'm expecting you to handle it. For now, you have neither the knowledge nor the responsibility." A corner of Charles's mouth curved up; it might have been a smile. "Enjoy it while it lasts."

I wasn't quite sure how to take that. I got up to leave.

"Oh, Stephen?" Charles said. He'd returned to his papers and didn't look up as he spoke. "You'll be accompanying Calhoun on his next couple of Well visits. The times aren't settled yet, so consider yourself on call for the next couple of weeks."

"I thought I wasn't allowed to—"

"I am countermanding that order. You are not to mention this to anyone else. Understood?"

I nodded slowly.

"Go."

CHAPTER 17

The last Friday of August started like any other day.

I woke up to bright sunlight and a clear blue sky. Hobbes slipped in through the window as I was getting dressed, miaowed at me until I fed him, then hopped onto the bed while I stroked him and listened to him purr. Then, in his usual catlike fashion, Hobbes decided that now he'd been given what he wanted, he was no longer interested in sticking around, so he left.

I went for a run in West Ham Park, passing the dog walkers and the crowds of little children, then went home to do what strength exercises I have space for in my little room. My strength sigl is a percentage increase, not a flat boost, meaning the stronger you are, the more it does. I'm never going to be stronger than some hulking six-foot bodybuilder, but you don't need to be stronger than a bodybuilder, you just need to be strong enough to deal with the guy you're fighting right *now*. Once I was done with my workout, I showered, had breakfast, and went out locating.

Afternoon found me talking over the phone to Colin.

"*Yes*, it matters if the voltage is wrong," Colin was saying. "You can't just plug a laptop into a random power supply and expect it to work."

"Look, I told you there was zero chance I was going to get the exact voltage you wanted on the first try," I told Colin. "Honestly, I think I did pretty well getting as close as I did."

"But you said I'd be able to change the output."

"I said you could change the sigl's output *if you could channel*. The fact that you *can't* is why I have to make all your sigls continuous."

"Can't you design it with an output dial or something?"

"It's a *sigl*," I said testily. As soon as I'd made the sigl Colin had asked me to mount it; after several headaches, I'd managed to figure out a way to fit it into a bracelet with a USB socket, the idea being that he could run a cable from the bracelet to his laptop or whatever. Now he wanted an output dial too? "It's a piece of aurum two millimetres wide. Where the hell am I going to put a dial?"

"This is bullshit," Colin complained. "I just want to be able to tell this thing 'okay, now output nineteen volts,' 'okay, now output twelve volts.' I can buy a gadget that does that for ten quid."

"Then *buy* your stupid gadget and plug it in between the bracelet and your laptop."

"That needs a converter, and the only one I've got is AC."

"What's AC again?"

"Alternating current. The way you do normal electricity generation is by spinning a magnetic field, and that produces a current that oscillates at a specific frequency. This sigl *doesn't* do that, so you get—"

"Hang on," I said. My phone had just buzzed, and I picked it up. As I read the message I frowned. "I might have to cancel tonight."

"What, your family again?"

"They want a Well surveyed," I said, scanning the message from Calhoun. "Something about checking out the damage from a raid."

"If it's been raided already, you think we could hit it too and they wouldn't notice?"

"I think I'm having a bad influence on you," I told Colin. "Anyway, the survey's at seven. I'll drop by afterwards."

THE MEETING PLACE Calhoun gave me was by the gasholders.

By the time I got there, it was an hour before dusk, the sun just barely visible above the tops of the trees. It had been a warm day, but with the approach of evening the weather had cooled; clouds were gathering in the west, turning the sky bloodred.

Calhoun's car showed up a few minutes after I did. The driver got out, looked around, then signalled; Calhoun and another man got out, and the three of them walked up to where I was waiting by the gates.

"Thanks for coming at such short notice," Calhoun told me, then glanced at one of his security men. "Take a look." The man nodded, unlocked the gate to the gasworks, and went inside.

"What's the story?" I asked.

"Cameras picked up a small group breaking into this place at around three a.m. this morning," Calhoun said. "We sent a response team, but the raiders fled as soon as they saw them."

"Raiders?"

"Or maybe bored kids," Calhoun said. "But if it *was* raiders, they had about half an hour undisturbed. We're here to see how much damage they did."

"Are you the House Ashford Well Inspector now?"

"First, I was on security, then it was the supply office, then it was surveys and shaping. All the ins and outs of the business." Calhoun glanced at me. "They'll probably do the same with you."

You haven't given up on that, huh? I thought.

The man Calhoun had sent into the gasworks came walking out again. "It's clear."

WE PICKED OUR way through the gasworks as the sun sank towards the horizon. The gasholders towered over us, rusting relics of a bygone age.

I found myself standing under the north-middle gasholder, staring down at the ground. There was a small Well here, just off the path, glowing yellow in my essentia sight. Behind was the pond at the centre of the site. The wind had dropped with the coming sunset, and the water was murky and still.

"Calhoun," I called.

Calhoun emerged, dust scuffing from his shoes as he crossed the path to me. "What is it?"

I pointed at the Well. "How's this look to you?"

Calhoun gave it only a glance. "Temporary Motion Well. D to D+."

"You said you hadn't stationed any permanent guards here because none of the Wells were ready to be harvested," I said. "Right?"

"This one developed faster than usual. It happens."

"I know. Why's it still here?"

"You mean why didn't they drain it?"

"You said they had a good half hour undisturbed. Isn't that more than enough for a little one like this?"

"Yes, and it's a pretty obvious spot," Calhoun said, glancing around. We were right on the main path. "Raiders wouldn't have missed it. Maybe they were just teenagers after all."

"I don't buy it."

"Why?"

"Because I *was* a teenager who grew up around here," I said. "And me and my mates *did* wander around getting into trouble. But we hung around places that were easy to get into. Not ones where you had to climb ten-foot spiked steel fences." I looked at Calhoun. "This place is in the middle of an industrial park with no guards. After work hours, it'd be totally dead. If"—I caught myself just in time; I'd been about to say "If I"—"some raider was looking for a low-risk Well to hit, this is exactly the kind they'd pick."

"So what does that mean?"

I looked around. The sun had disappeared behind the western trees, flooding the sky with red light. The air felt tense, silent.

"I think we ought to back off," I told Calhoun.

"Why?"

"I just don't like this," I told him. After I'd told my father about my side job as Calhoun's bodyguard, he'd spent a little while giving me advice about the profession. And one thing he'd told me again and again was to listen to your instincts. If something feels wrong, you back off *first* and figure out what's making you uneasy *afterwards*. "We're really exposed out here."

"We haven't finished the survey."

"Your car was bombed a few months ago," I pointed out. "I'd say the survey can wait, but it's your call."

Calhoun hesitated. The gasworks was quiet and still, but the sense of danger that had been growing at the back of my mind, the one that had been honed by my months as a raider, wasn't going away.

"All right," Calhoun said. He turned and called over to one of the security men. "Olly!"

The man approached and gave Calhoun an inquiring look. "Get Mike," Calhoun told him. "We're leaving."

The man nodded and took out his phone. "It's going to be difficult explaining this to Charles," Calhoun told me as we started walking back along the path.

"You can blame it on me," I said, scanning ahead. The path curved around the round artificial pond before winding its way towards the back two gasholders and the exit. Pretty exposed, not much cover. "Anyway, you were told to check this place out, and you did."

"Half of it."

Behind us, the two security men reappeared, walking briskly to catch up. My eyes swept back and forth, going from the pond to the looming gasholders to the trees to the dusty path. We were only a few minutes away from—

A red shimmer flickered ahead of me, fading in then out at the edge of my range.

My hand shot out and caught Calhoun's arm. "Stop."

"What?"

"There's someone here." I kept my eyes locked on the path ahead. That blur of Matter essentia had only been there for a few seconds, but I'd been keyed up and alert, just waiting for something to appear, and I'd recognised it as a transparency signal.

There was a moment of silence.

Then the air ahead shimmered and a figure appeared on the path, dressed in red. He pushed a set of goggles up off his eyes and onto his forehead as his invisibility faded away. "Ah, hell," he called over to us. "Busted, huh?"

Vermillion looked much the same as when I'd last seen him, with one difference: over his red silk shirt he was wearing military-style body armour. He began strolling towards us.

"Oh shit," I said quietly.

"You know this guy?" Calhoun asked.

"You remember when you came to see me in hospital?" I said, tension seeping into my voice. "This was the guy who put me there."

Calhoun's two security men moved up to either side of us, taking up protective positions. One of them looked at Calhoun; Calhoun made a hand signal.

"Well," Vermillion said as he came to a stop. "Have to admit, I wasn't expecting to run into both of you."

"Boss?" the man Calhoun had called Olly asked.

"Hold here," Calhoun said, then looked at Vermillion. "I believe you have the advantage of me."

"Oh, where are my manners?" Vermillion said with a smile. He gave a sweeping bow. "Knight-Apostle Vermillion, of the Brotherhood of the Winged, at your service."

Calhoun looked at Vermillion for a long moment. "So," he said at last. "This is what this is about."

"This is what this is about," Vermillion agreed.

The two men watched each other, and I looked back and forth between them. Calhoun was dressed in dark blue, his clothes contrasting with Vermillion's red. The air felt tense, brooding.

My thoughts were racing, cataloguing my tools. I'd brought my full loadout of combat sigls, and I was wearing my armour vest beneath my jumper. Neither of those things had done much good against Vermillion last time. The only thing I thought gave me a chance of beating him was my new sigl.

"So those raiders this morning were yours," Calhoun said.

"Not the most elegant way to handle things," Vermillion said, "but they did the job."

"To draw me out?"

"Just for a talk," Vermillion said. "Yeah, I could have made an appointment with your secretary, but it wouldn't have had quite the same impact, you know?"

"Before we get to that," Calhoun said, "I have a question for you."

"Okay, shoot."

"My sister. Lucella. What did you promise her to make her join you?"

Vermillion looked at Calhoun curiously for a second. "I . . . don't really know?"

"You don't know, or you won't tell me?"

"No, I genuinely don't know," Vermillion said. "If I'm getting called in, it's usually for the rough stuff, you know? Recruitment isn't really my ballpark." He paused. "Well, I should say it *wasn't* my ballpark. But what the hell? Diversifying, right?"

"If recruitment really was why you came here," Calhoun said, "then making an appointment with my secretary would have saved you a lot of time."

"Hey, let's not be too hasty. Let me give you the sales pitch. Who knows, I might change your mind."

"You want us to throw this guy out?" Mike asked Calhoun.

"You *do not* want to try and throw this guy out," I told Mike.

"Quiet, both of you," Calhoun said. "All right, Vermillion. Say your piece."

"Thanks." Vermillion glanced around. "You want to sit down? Find a bench or something?"

"Get to the point."

"Fine, fine. So I don't know what Byron told you last time, but I'm guessing he gave you the rundown?"

"He gave me his version," Calhoun said. "I made it my business to look you up afterwards."

"So you know what we are," Vermillion said. "What we can do." He looked straight at Calhoun. "We want you to join us."

"I already gave Byron my refusal."

"Don't be so hasty," Vermillion said, and reached into his pocket. I tensed, and felt the security man on my side do the same, but Vermillion's hand came out again holding only a silver pen. Vermillion spun it between his fingers as he addressed Calhoun. "Back when Byron came to you, you would have been barely out of uni, right? Still figuring out what you were doing with your life. But now you're the House heir, and you have to think like one. I'm guessing since then, you've learned how many more fish there are in the pond? All those corps and Houses your family competes with. Your position's good, but it's not *that* good. You could use some help."

"And I suppose you'd be happy to provide it."

"Why not?" Vermillion said. "You know we can do it. Favourable stories in the media. A word in the right ear when you need permission from the Board. Family rates when you buy and sell Wells. None of that kind of thing's your business now, but it will be. And when you're sitting on the throne, we can make your life a lot easier."

"You have a very different way of selling this than Byron," Calhoun said. He was watching the pen dance over Vermillion's knuckles.

"Yeah, Byron runs his mouth a lot," Vermillion said. The light of the setting sun flashed from the pen. "I think this is where I'm supposed to start talking about freedom and autonomy and all that crap, but I'm more the pragmatic type, you know? Deal with what's in front of you right now."

Vermillion's pen spun lazily, drawing my eyes. It was making it hard for me to focus and with an effort I pulled my gaze away. "Calhoun," I said.

Calhoun was staring at Vermillion.

"Calhoun!"

Calhoun started and looked at me. "Focus," I told him.

"No need to muscle in," Vermillion told me. He was smiling slightly, but something told me he was annoyed.

"I seem to remember that when I turned down Byron the first time," Calhoun said, "he told me that he wouldn't keep coming back."

"Oh, Byron didn't send me. It was someone else."

"Who?"

"You wouldn't know him. See, different branches of the Winged have different . . . philosophies, you could say? Byron, he's the softly-softly type. Likes to talk people into things. They say no, he'll make a big show of backing off and saying he respects their choice. Just his way of doing things, you know?"

"And the others?"

"The guy who sent me today, he likes to stay more behind the scenes," Vermillion said. "But he's more a believer in doing things the direct way. He wants what he wants."

"And right now what he wants is House Ashford?"

"Pretty much. So what do you say?"

Calhoun studied Vermillion for a few seconds. "My answer hasn't changed."

"You sure?"

"I don't like repeating myself."

"Is this because of Lucella?"

"If it was, that would be enough," Calhoun told him. "I saw what membership in the Winged did to her."

"Whoa," Vermillion said, raising the hand with the pen. "Look, Lucella was a few years behind me, but we've hung out enough for me to get a pretty good read on her. And I promise you, Byron did *not* need to offer her much. Don't get me wrong, he loves the whole seducing-the-innocent thing, but she *definitely* wasn't innocent and I don't think he had to do much seducing. Way I heard it, *he* was the one who eventually got tired of *her*."

"If you think talking like this about my family is going to make me more likely to co-operate," Calhoun said, "you are very mistaken."

"I'm just saying, from what I heard, she jumped in with both feet. Also, I hate to break it to you—don't get me wrong, this whole 'protecting your sister's honour' deal you've got going is a nice look, very classical—but she really doesn't feel the same way. Actually, last time we talked, she was kinda sorta hinting that she'd like me to kill you and make it look like an accident."

I spoke up. "Did you say yes?"

"Nah, she can sort out her own issues."

"I am well aware of my sister's 'issues,'" Calhoun said. "But she could have changed. Or she *might* have, if your 'brotherhood' hadn't twisted and poisoned her."

"Okay, this obviously isn't going anywhere," Vermillion said. "Maybe I should explain how—"

"No."

"What?"

"I'm not interested in how you think this would work," Calhoun said. "Or in becoming another of your pawns. Go back to whoever you work for and tell them no."

"It's not exactly—"

Calhoun interrupted him. "You can go now."

Vermillion stopped.

I glanced uneasily between Calhoun and Vermillion, one in blue, the other in red. Calhoun's expression was studiedly calm, but there was a set to his eyes, and something told me that he was angry. Vermillion's face was entirely blank.

"You're making a mistake," Vermillion said.

"I don't think so," Calhoun told him.

Vermillion studied Calhoun. His eyes were unreadable, flat. "Is that your final answer?"

"It is."

The gasworks was silent. The sun had disappeared and the light was fading from the sky. A cold breeze swept across the water, sending goose bumps over my skin.

Vermillion shrugged. "Have it your way." He slipped the pen back into his pocket, then made a small gesture towards us with a curved finger, like tapping on glass.

Movement flickered in the corner of my eye. I jumped to one side.

There was a loud, echoing crackle, like a dozen whips being cracked together, over and over again: *crack-crack-crack-crack-crack*. Calhoun's second security man, the one he'd called Olly, was standing on the left, and I was looking right at him as a puff of red came out of the side of his head and he dropped boneless to the grass. Invisible things hissed past me, one-two-three; essentia flared around Calhoun.

I looked around, panicked, heart racing. Both Calhoun's security men were down, and as I looked, I saw that a crowd of men had appeared out of nowhere. They were clustered on the wide dome at the centre of one of the gasholders, and there were dozens of them. There was someone behind, too, their face white and masklike, but my attention was focused on the fact that what looked like twenty of the men were holding guns pointed in my direction, and as I did they opened fire again.

Crack-crack-crack-crack-crack. I ducked, but as I did, I saw yellow light sparkle around Calhoun in my essentia sight, glowing pinpoints flaring. Each of those pinpoints was a bullet, its kinetic energy draining away as it came into range. Through luck or instinct, my jump had put me behind Calhoun.

I looked back; one of the security men, Mike, was moving weakly on the grass. "Calhoun!" I called frantically. "Back!"

Calhoun was facing our attackers, one hand wreathed with essentia; he gave me one swift glance and then withdrew towards me, not taking his eyes off the gunmen. Bullets continued to slam into his shield like pecks from some giant murderous bird. Calhoun kept backing up until the bubble of his shield engulfed all of us.

I crouched and channelled through my mending sigl, sending essentia down through my hand and into Mike. He'd been hit in the legs and blood was soaking his trousers; his breathing came in sharp pants, and he didn't speak as his eyes flicked between me and the men attacking us. There was another *crack*, and a bullet sparked into a star of yellow light right in front of my face; I flinched and kept on channelling.

"Enough," Vermillion called.

Crack. Crack. Crack.

"I said *enough*!" Vermillion yelled. "Hasan, tell them to stop shooting, you dumb shit!"

There was a shout from the crowd in a language I didn't know; the gunshots died away. There was a moment of silence.

"Finally," Vermillion said. He looked at Calhoun. "You fucking idiot."

Calhoun stood very still, his kinetic shield a shimmer of translucent light. Only his eyes moved, flicking from Vermillion to the gunmen.

"What did you think was going to happen?" Vermillion asked. "What do you think we are? A fucking telemarketing service? You thought you'd just keep saying no and we'd be like 'oh, that's a shame, well give us a call if you change your mind'? Is that it?"

I kept pouring essentia into the wounds on Mike's legs. It felt like the bleeding was slowing, but I didn't dare take my eyes off Vermillion.

"And you," Vermillion said, his gaze moving to me. "Why the fuck are you healing him? He's going to be dead in five minutes, same as you. Shit, I ought to cut his throat where you can see it just to make a point." He shook his head in disgust. "What a fucking waste. Both of you could have done so much, and now you're going to end up dead while your bitch of a cousin takes over your House. You know, I was *so happy* when I thought one of you was going to end up pushing her out and I wouldn't have to listen to her shit anymore. But you just had to be stubborn about it, didn't you?" He shook his head again. "Oh, screw it. Kill them both."

There was another volley of gunfire. Bullets flashed yellow in my sight, their energy converting into essentia.

"Not with guns, you morons!" Vermillion shouted. "He's got a ballistic shield, you think it's going to run out of batteries? Fuck!" He threw up his hands. "This is what I get for hiring locals. Go stab them to death. What, I have to show you how to knife someone too? I thought that was the one thing you idiots were good at?"

I saw scowls flash on the faces of the men, but they obeyed, moving towards us and spreading out as they did. Ten, fifteen, twenty. They moved to envelop us like a wolf pack surrounding its prey.

I rose, my movements jerky and quick. We were almost surrounded; only where the grass stopped at the pond was there a gap in the circle. Dark faces, dark eyes, cold and unsmiling. The last rays of the setting sun glinted on knives and handguns; some were taking out machetes.

My heart was hammering in my chest, my breath coming fast. I'd fought outnumbered before, but nothing like this. My eyes darted left and right, searching for a way out. There was nothing. Panic rose up inside me and I struggled to keep control.

Then a hand closed on my wrist, and I nearly jumped out of my skin before realising that it was Calhoun. He was holding my wrist with his free hand, maintaining his shield with the other. "Keep it together," Calhoun said quietly. His voice was steady. "We're going to get out of this. Okay?"

I looked at Calhoun in disbelief, opening my mouth to speak—*How can you be so calm, we're going to die here*—then my brain caught up and I realised he was saying it for my sake. A moment of shame flashed through me, and I drew a deep breath, struggling to get my fear under control. I didn't want to die here, stabbed to death for no reason—

Reason.

My mind flashed back two months to West Ham Church. Father Hawke's voice. *"Will you accept the task you've been given, or reject it?"*

My answer. *"How can I accept it if I don't even know what it is?"*

"Presumably figuring that out is part of the task."

I snapped back to the present. The men were still surrounding us, but for a second it felt as though I was standing outside myself, looking down on me and Calhoun standing back-to-back.

"Wait," I said. I felt dizzy. "This is it. Isn't it?"

I felt Calhoun pause. "Stephen?"

My mind was whirling. Essentia sight. The tools to make sigls, to bring me here.

Was that it?

The light of the sun was fading in the western sky. As I watched, one last ray of light slipped through the clouds and buildings, passing above us to gleam upon the clouds overhead. I stared up at it.

"Come on, guys," I heard Vermillion say, hidden behind the men surrounding us. "This isn't a spectator sport."

The first of the men stepped forward.

I stared up at the clouds, then brought my eyes down.

Something clicked into place inside me.

No. Not for no reason.

This is where I'm meant to be.

I took a deep breath and straightened up. All of a sudden my fear was gone. I looked around and I no longer saw a faceless, numberless army. I just saw a gang, like the ones I'd fought before. Better armed, ready to kill . . . but not as brave as they were acting. Otherwise they'd have rushed us already.

"I won't be able to keep you shielded once it starts," Calhoun said quietly. "Get in close if you can. Makes their guns useless."

I nodded without looking, then breathed in and out, letting the adrenaline rise up inside me. I could pick out every detail of the men around: the laces on their trainers, fingers shifting on their knives, eyes flicking back and forth. I reached into my pocket and slipped on my headband with its vision sigls, then flexed my fingers, feeling the essentia flowing through them, ready to be unleashed.

The light on the cloud above us was fading. I could feel my heart pounding. *Thump, thump, thump.*

Vermillion's voice rose up from beyond the circle, impatient. "What are we waiting for? Let's go!"

I felt Calhoun tense.

Thump, thump, thump.

The men on the left shuffled closer. They were only a few strides away.

Thump, thump.

Gunsmoke on the air. The scent of blood.

Thump.

The light above went out.

Essentia flared behind me; I felt the temperature drop and heard a choked scream just as the man on my right darted in. I triggered my new sigl just as his arm came up.

Green light exploded outwards, a beam of dazzling emerald connecting my hand with his face. It was the first time I'd used it on a human target, and the man didn't do any better than the pigeons. His legs gave way beneath him and he went sprawling at my feet.

I snapped my head back the other way just in time to see two others rushing me from the other side; I triggered my flash sigl and they staggered back, dazzled. I dropped one more with a beam, then I heard the *crack* of a gunshot and felt something whistle past and realised too late that I was outside Calhoun's shield.

No time to think. I dived into the crowd.

The world became chaos. The men around me turned, shouting, faces startled and angry; they smelt of sweat and cheap leather. I lasered one in the face, twisted, lasered another. A knife came out of the darkness and I jerked back, knocked the guy back with a slam, hit him with an emerald beam that made him drop. I was surrounded, but there were so many of them that they were getting in each other's way. Each had to hesitate for an instant before attacking, to make sure they didn't hit one of their friends. I didn't hesitate. Everyone around was an enemy and I fought with everything I had.

I blasted another guy in the face but it did nothing; he'd had his eyes closed and crashed into me, his hands grabbing for my shoulders and hair. I ducked, channelling into the Matter sigl on my right hand, then slammed punches into his body, jab-cross-jab, my right fist hitting like iron. He grunted and staggered back; I followed up with two more body shots and then an uppercut that snapped his head back and sent him tumbling to the ground. I spun to face the next guy and sent another green laser at his head, but he was turned away, running, and all of a sudden everyone was scattering. I looked left and right, searching for a target. No faces. *They're running. They're running! They're—oh, shit, now I'm out in the—*

Crack.

Something hit me in the back, like a narrow, incredibly hard punch. I stumbled and fell, but my blood was up and I reacted instantly, hitting the grass with both hands and rolling onto my back.

The man—boy, really—who'd shot me was right behind, handgun levelled in both hands. His eyes were wide with fear, and I had an instant to take in what felt like every detail: a kid my age, short black hair falling down over his forehead, light-brown skin, a wispy moustache and beginnings of a beard, narrow mouth, fat cheeks, black jacket over a grey T-shirt. He looked shocked that I was still moving and his gun was still aimed above me as he stared down at where I was—

He started to lower the gun and I fired a beam of emerald light into his face; he jerked and fell. I kept rolling, two complete turns, channelling through my invisibility and vision sigls, the world shifting from red to blue as I faded from sight. I scrambled to my feet, searching for cover; there was a thin tree at the edge of the pond and I darted to it, then crouched and held still.

The gasworks was chaos. Men were scattered across the floor, some lying still, others groaning and struggling to rise. One was screaming in pain, and his high, breathy shrieks gave an eerie, horror-like cast to the scene. The men who'd been fighting me were shouting, casting around; they'd lost track of me in the confusion and the fading light. I reached around to where I'd been shot, my fingers touching the armour of my vest. I felt a stab of pain, but no blood.

But it was Calhoun my eyes were drawn to. He was isolated, a lone figure in white and blue. Enemies surrounded him, weapons glinting in the dusk.

A man lunged, knife out. Calhoun twisted around the attack, moving with unnatural speed, green and gold essentia wreathing him as he hit the man with a palm strike to the chest. The man went flying as if kicked by a horse, slamming into the path to roll over and over. Gunshots rang out, yellow pinpoints sparking against Calhoun's shield; Calhoun pivoted smoothly and a cone of Motion essentia flared from his hand. The man who'd shot at him fell to his knees, his skin and clothes going pale as ice crystallised around him.

I caught a glimpse of Vermillion, his expression set and cold. He pulled down the goggles over his eyes, and vanished. I opened my mouth, about to call out to Calhoun—

"Hey! Hey!"

I looked around. One of the younger guys was shouting to the others. He had a gun out and he was pointing in my direction, staring right at me. As he kept calling, two others turned to stare as well.

Shit.

First one, then the others lifted their weapons, aiming in my direction. They were squinting in the dusk, and I held very still. Behind them Calhoun was still fighting. Maybe if I didn't move, they wouldn't be able to—

One of them called something and they started to move towards me.

Shit, shit, shit. I thought fast. I could drop one, but as soon as I fired the beam would show them all where I was . . . but there was no more time and the longer I waited, the worse it would get. I took a deep breath and threw myself flat.

One of the men shouted just as I fired, a beam of emerald light catching him right in the face. He dropped and I heard the *crack* of a gunshot and the eerie whiz of something ripping through the air overhead. The other two fired, but their shots went high; they'd been aiming for a standing target. I fired, tracked, fired again—

—and suddenly everything was still.

I twisted my head left and right, terrified that I was about to be shot in the back again, but there was no one there. A couple were running; everyone else was down. I scrambled to my feet, looking around; the ground between the gasholder and the pond was covered with bodies, unconscious or groaning and moving weakly, and I felt a moment of dizziness. The only ones standing were me and Calhoun. *Did we do all that?*

Wait. Me and Calhoun?

I looked up and ran a few steps towards Calhoun. He was looking from side to side, scanning for enemies; he glanced towards me with a frown, but I looked past him, searching—

A shimmer of red light, moving in. "Behind you!" I shouted.

Calhoun reacted instantly, spinning away. The red shape flew past; Calhoun raised a hand to strike—

Movement blurred at the edge of my vision and I jumped back just in time. A hand stabbed into the air where my neck had been half a second ago, Motion essentia flashing in a short, knife-shaped blade. I came down, twisting to face my attacker.

It was a man—probably. Blue jacket, slim build, vaguely androgynous. A white mask with eye slits but no mouth, the blank face staring expressionlessly. He was Vermillion's ally; I'd caught a glimpse of him before, but hadn't realised what I was looking at—

Then the figure blurred and lunged, impossibly fast, and in an instant I was fighting for my life. A fiery line scored across my forearm, followed by a numbing blow. I triggered my flash sigl and the figure checked, stumbling back a step, and I had an instant to register the purple aura around him. Dimension essentia. Time alteration—?

The masked figure came in again. His strikes were so quick that I could barely make out the weapon. Distantly I was aware of Calhoun and Vermillion fighting, but I couldn't spare even a fraction of a second to look; all my attention was on dodging the next attack, then the next.

A Motion strike hit my stomach, glancing off my armour. I staggered, throwing a slam blast at the figure, and saw them stumble. I tried my laser; the beam of emerald light splashed over the mask, but in the instant before I fired I saw him duck his head away, and as my eyes cleared from the flash, I saw a blur coming straight at my head. I jerked my head aside and felt something score along my cheek, then the figure's left hand snapped up and a burst of blinding light exploded into my face.

I cried out and jumped away, but it was too late. It was the same trick I'd used so many times, and even as my feet left the ground, I knew I was dead. My vision was darkness and sparks; it would take seconds for it to clear, and he was going to kill me before I had the chance. Time seemed to slow as I floated through the air, searching blindly for—

No. Not blindly. I could sense the glow of sigls, moving—

Thoughts flashed through my mind at the speed of light. Father Hawke, telling me how my gift worked. Data through the occipital lobe, a sixth sense. *Sixth*, not fifth. Not my eyes. I didn't need my eyes.

I shut my eyes, and saw. Light in the darkness, a human-shaped blur. The outline was purple, but it wasn't purple I was looking for; it was yellow, the light of that Motion blade that had nearly—

There. A narrow triangle of sparkling gold, extending—

My feet hit the ground and everything seemed to snap back to full speed. The blade flashed towards me and with the speed of terror I grabbed the hand that held it, my fingers clamping on to his wrist. I channelled through my Matter sigl, fusing my hand into a rigid shell, gripping his.

An instant later I was yanked forward, my arm jerked almost out of its socket. If I'd been holding on I would have lost my grip, but my hand was welded to the other boy's, and I couldn't have let go if I'd wanted to. We staggered and spun, neither able to get free.

The spots faded from my sight, and my vision returned just in time for me to see White Mask twist into a roundhouse kick. I yanked on his arm, and he overbalanced, hitting me with his knee instead of his foot, then he crashed into me and we both went tumbling to the ground. He twisted like a snake, getting behind me, his free arm coming around for a choke; I grabbed his arm before he could get it against my neck, and suddenly we both were still.

I was lying on my back, half on top of White Mask, my hands locked on to his wrists. The Winged strained to bring his forearms to my throat, pulling first left, then right, but he couldn't pull free. Hope soared within me as I realised that while this guy might be faster than me, he wasn't stronger . . . and now that I was on top of him, he didn't seem faster anymore, either. I looked down to see that the Dimension essentia that had been wreathing him was covering me too.

But I could see metal rings on the long pale fingers just in front of me. Sigls. The instant I let go of either wrist, he'd be free to use them to kill me.

White Mask's hands trembled, trying to reach me. As I fought to push them away, I was distantly aware of the battle on the path ahead as Calhoun moved like flashing light. Gunfire and thrown knives came stabbing out of the night, but Calhoun's kinetic shield stopped every attack, sending the projectiles tumbling to the ground. Vermillion was a red blur in my essentia sight; Calhoun blasted him with another cone of cold, but as the freezing mist cleared I saw that Vermillion's shape was still moving, seemingly unharmed. Calhoun raised his other hand and channelled, Light essentia stabbing out in a beam, and Vermillion shimmered and materialised, face twisting in pain as he raised an arm to shield his face—

White Mask's hand twisted towards me and Motion essentia speared from one of his rings. I jerked my head back, eyes going wide as I stared at the blade; it was the same sort of effect as my slam sigl, but it was the "same" in the way that a sword's the same as a butter knife. It would cut through my skin and flesh like paper. The blade disappeared, speared out, disappeared again, straining to reach my face. With trembling muscles, I forced White Mask's hand away, then looked back towards Vermillion and Calhoun and saw that Vermillion was—

—spinning his knife?

Vermillion had his fighting knife out and was twirling it around his hand and fingers, the blade flashing in the dusk. His movements were sinuous, graceful; *flash-flash-flash*. I stared at the flickering steel in growing fascination, then White Mask jerked his hand back towards my face and I snapped out of it, forcing his hand away. I shook my head quickly and looked towards Calhoun to see that Calhoun was doing—

—nothing. He was staring at Vermillion.

Dread spiked through me as I understood. "Calhoun!" I shouted.

Calhoun didn't respond. Vermillion took a step towards him.

"Calhoun! Wake up!"

Calhoun kept staring, hands by his sides.

Vermillion's eyes glanced towards me and there was something chilling in that look. He wasn't smirking or gloating; all there was in his eyes was the calculation of whether I could get to him before he could cut Calhoun's throat. It lasted only a fraction of a second, then Vermillion was back to focusing on Calhoun again, knife flashing through the air as he walked steadily towards him, step by step.

Panic rose up inside me and I knew I had only seconds. My eyes came to rest on the new sigl on my hand—but it was on my *right* hand, the same one that was keeping White Mask from stabbing me—

Vermillion stepped up to Calhoun.

I clenched my teeth, poured essentia into my strength sigl, and let my iron-fist sigl wink out.

My right hand softened, turning back into flesh. White Mask jerked, but the extra power from my strength sigl was just enough to let me force our hands away long enough to fire.

Emerald light bloomed like a star. The beam flashed between Vermillion and Calhoun, soaring up into the evening sky. It didn't quite hit either of them; neither was in the direct path of the beam, neither was looking in my direction. But it was enough to send them both stumbling back, covering their eyes.

But in focusing on that sigl, I'd lost my grip. White Mask's hand twisted back, and this time he finally had it pointed at my face. In my essentia sight I saw golden light flash through White Mask's finger as the Motion blade began to trigger.

I still had a grip on White Mask's left wrist, and, as the strike stabbed in, I yanked it across with the strength of desperation. White Mask's blade flashed towards my nose and struck his own hand instead, piercing through flesh and bone. Blood splattered on my face.

White Mask screamed. I shoved off, rolling to my feet.

I think White Mask could have killed me in that instant, but as I came up I saw him shimmer into a ghost of Light essentia and break into a run—directly away. He went darting down the path, invisible footsteps kicking up dust as he fled, his image blurring and vanishing as he passed out of my range.

I turned back to Vermillion and fired another beam of emerald light. Vermillion ducked away, closing his eyes, but before he could recover I felt Light essentia from behind me and Calhoun stepped up to my side, his sigl glove aimed at Vermillion. Vermillion spun away, ducking behind one of the gasholder pillars.

I stepped in next to Calhoun, getting under the protection of his shield, keeping my arm raised towards Vermillion. Calhoun did the same. The two of us kept our arms trained on where Vermillion would have to step as the Winged leant out from behind the pillar.

I saw Vermillion's eyes flick between the two of us, and even in the dusk and at this distance, I could read his thoughts on his face: Could he beat us on his own? It took him only an instant to make his decision. He faded from sight.

Calhoun and I fired, my green beam and Calhoun's invisible one spearing through the air. There was no reaction, and I focused on my essentia sight, looking for the telltale shimmer of Vermillion's transparency sigl. Nothing.

Everything was quiet.

I looked around. Our attackers were still scattered all over the gasworks. Most weren't moving, but some were starting to stir and groan, and I didn't know how long we had before some of them recovered enough to sit up and grab their weapons.

"We have to go," I said.

"I know. Find Mike."

For an instant I had no clue who Calhoun was talking about, then I remembered the man who'd been shot. I channelled through my vision sigl, feeling my sight sharpen as I scanned the bodies, looking for one in a suit—

I pointed. "There!"

Mike was still breathing, but his eyes were drooping and he seemed barely conscious. Calhoun sized him up at a glance. "You take the left side. I'll take the right."

Together Calhoun and I hauled Mike up. Even with my strength sigl and with Calhoun's help, I could barely manage it; the big man must have weighed almost as much as the two of us put together. I had to sling his arm over my shoulders, and even then it was a strain, but at last we managed to straighten up. I hesitated, glancing towards the man who'd been killed.

Calhoun's voice was tight. "Leave him."

We set off along the path, moving slowly and painfully towards the entrance to the gasworks. My eyes searched left and right, scanning for threats, and my back itched knowing how many enemies were behind us. If someone were to attack us now . . .

But they didn't. Slowly and painfully, we made our way down the path and out through the gate.

The yellow lights of the industrial road greeted us as we came out of the gate, death and violence replaced in an instant by a quiet nighttime street. The blood-soaked, wounded man between us felt jarringly out of place. Calhoun's car was mercifully close, and Mike gasped with pain as we manhandled him into the back seat.

"Mending sigl?" Calhoun asked.

"Yes."

"Stabilise him."

I got into the back with Mike. Calhoun slid in behind the steering wheel. The car's engine started with a growl, and I had one last glimpse of the metal fence of the gasworks before we pulled away into the night.

CHAPTER 18

THE INSIDE OF the car smelled of leather and blood. Calhoun was driving fast and I was thrown from side to side; I hung on the grab handle above the window as I tried to stem Mike's bleeding.

From up ahead, I heard the trill of a phone, followed by Calhoun's voice, clipped and sharp. "This is Calhoun. Get me Anderson." There was a long pause. "Anderson? It's Calhoun. We've been attacked. One in critical condition, one dead. Driving back to the mansion now, ETA thirty-five minutes. Have medical ready for when we arrive." Calhoun paused again. "No, I'm fine." Pause. "I won't, but Mike will. Get it done." Pause. "Good." Calhoun hung up and I saw his eyes glance towards me in the mirror. "How's he doing?"

"I'm not a paramedic," I told Calhoun, tension coming through in my voice. I had my free hand on Mike's right thigh, the green light of Life essentia pouring out of my sigl and into his flesh. I couldn't tell how many times he'd been hit, but there was a lot of blood. "How am I supposed to know?"

"Do we need to take him to a hospital—?"

"*Yes.*"

"Let me finish. Do we need to take him to a hospital *right now*? Because if we go to A&E, there's a chance the Winged will track us."

"Shit." I hadn't thought of that. "Um. No. Keep going. I can keep him stable that long."

"You sure?"

"Believe it or not, this isn't the first time I've had to use this sigl on someone bleeding to death from leg wounds."

Now that the rush of adrenaline from the battle was over, I was starting to realise how badly I was hurt. I had cuts on my forearm and cheek that were beginning to sting, and my muscles were aching from strain. My back was the worst, though. Every time I twisted or breathed in too deeply, I felt a flash of pain, and it was getting worse.

"So you know the Winged," Calhoun said.

I didn't look up from Mike. "Yes."

"And they were trying to recruit you."

"Yes."

"So that was what you meant that afternoon on the river when you said you had your own problems to deal with."

I focused on my channelling.

For a minute the only sound was the growl of the engine. Calhoun wasn't slowing down, and each time he powered around a corner I felt another flash of pain from my back.

When Calhoun spoke again, there was an edge to his voice. "You could have told me."

"Yeah, I suppose I could," I said tightly. I really did not want to be having this conversation right now. I'm not great with Life essentia at the best of times, least of all while being thrown around in the back of a moving car.

"It would have *helped*," Calhoun said, his voice biting, "to know what I was walking into."

"*I* didn't have any reason to think the Winged would be coming after me with a small army!" I snapped. "And they didn't! They were after *you*! All this time you've been bringing me along as a bodyguard, and you didn't bother to *mention* that you were being threatened with assassination by the most powerful cult on the planet? What, did it slip your mind?"

"They didn't threaten me, and that was the first time I'd ever seen that man."

"And when he said 'Is that your final answer?' you didn't take the hint? Do you not understand how dangerous these people are?"

"I'm not bowing down to some grubby little cultists!"

"You didn't have to swear your soul!" I snapped. "Just, I don't know, tell him 'maybe'! Stall for time! At least *try* to find some way through the conversation that doesn't end with them trying to shoot us all to death. You might be bulletproof, but we're not!"

Calhoun glanced back, his eyes flickering between me and Mike before a swerve made him hurriedly jerk his eyes back to the road, pulling the car level again. I saw him open his mouth to speak, then he seemed to check himself and closed it again. We drove the rest of the way in silence.

THERE WAS A small crowd at the Ashford mansion, and as Calhoun drove in through the gates they converged on us. Calhoun pulled to a stop and opened the door, stepping into a babble of voices; Calhoun cut them off with a gesture. "I'm fine. Help Mike."

Someone said something I couldn't make out. "Is Philip here?" Calhoun asked.

"He's still on his way."

"All right, get him to the Princess Grace. Take a car and . . ." Calhoun moved away and I didn't hear the rest.

The side door of the car opened and a man leant in, asking

questions. I answered mechanically, struggling to keep focus; several times he had to repeat himself. The adrenaline crash had hit, and I was exhausted and in pain. At last two men lifted Mike out of the car, and I was able to sink back into the seat and close my eyes.

"Stephen? *Stephen!*"

A girl's voice. I opened one eye and then closed it again. "Oh. Hi, Bridget."

"Are you okay? What happened? Are you hurt?"

"No. I mean, kind of." I tried to get out of the car; pain spiked through me, and I fell back with a hiss. "Shit, that hurts."

"What's wrong?"

"Uh," I said. "I'm not actually sure I can get up." My back had stiffened; I was still hoping it was just a bruise, but trying to slide out of the car hurt too much. "Help me out?"

"I thought you weren't going on these things anymore!" Bridget said as she pulled me out of the car. I had to grab on to the door to stop myself from collapsing to the driveway. "Mummy said you weren't allowed for some reason."

"Yeah," I said. I managed to haul myself up on the car and leant against its roof while I recovered. "Next time, I think I'll just do the stupid training course."

I heard a *thump* behind me.

I was still on edge and snapped my head around to look; the movement twisted my back and I clenched my teeth against the flash of pain, but what I saw drove it out of my mind. My mother was standing between us and the mansion. She was wearing a purple business suit that was lit up in yellow-gold by the house lights behind; a red first aid kit lay at her feet where it had fallen from her hands, sterile packs scattered on the bricks. But it was her face that made me stop dead. She was staring straight at me; her face was white, and on it was an expression of stricken horror.

"Oh," I said.

My mother was still staring.

"Uh," I said. "Okay, technically, none of this was my fault."

My mother didn't answer. I wasn't sure if she'd even heard me.

"Uh," I said again, and glanced from my mother to Bridget. I was starting to feel uncomfortable. "Why is she—?"

"You kind of look like a survivor from a slasher movie," Bridget told me. "You know there's blood all over your face, right?"

"Oh." I touched my face; my fingers came away sticky. "It's not mine. Well, most of it."

My mother spoke in a low, husky voice. *"What happened?"*

"Ah." I didn't really want to answer that question. "There was a problem at the gasworks. Calhoun'll give you the long version—"

"Why were you there?"

"Your dad sent me."

My mother stared at me, then, slowly, turned back towards the house.

Charles Ashford was standing there, hands clasped behind his back. My mother looked at him; he looked back. Neither said a word.

Slowly my mother turned back to me. "Are you hurt?"

"Not badly, I—oof!"

My mother had grabbed me and was holding me in a tight hug. Her grip was shockingly strong, enough to send a bolt of pain through me. "Ow ow ow, shit! Gently!"

My mother pulled away, gripping my arms and staring at me with furious intensity. There was blood smeared all across the front of her clothes, but she didn't seem to have noticed. "Hurt how? What happened?"

"Back. It was"—I caught myself just before saying "a bullet"—"just a bruise. But it really hurts, okay?"

My mother stared up at me. "There's a cut on your face."

"A cut—oh, right. That one honestly doesn't hurt so much—"

My mother pointed off to one side. "Hospital. Now! I'll get a car and a driver. You go straight there, and you *do not leave* without telling me first. Understand?"

"Okay."

As I turned away, Bridget still doing her best to support me, I glanced back and saw Charles Ashford watching me. His eyes rested on me, opaque, unreadable.

I ENDED UP in the same hospital Calhoun had sent me to six months back. They even got me the same doctor, Dr. Saini, who made several jokes about me apparently liking the place so much I couldn't stay away. After he'd reassured me that none of my injuries were serious and that I'd be fine by Monday, I took some painkillers, crashed into bed, and fell asleep.

I WOKE UP the next morning to good and bad news. The good news was that my armour vest had worked—the bullet that had hit me last night had left me with nothing worse than bruised ribs. The bad news: bruised ribs are *really* painful. My back had stiffened overnight to the point that I needed help even to get out of bed.

But drucraft healing is really good for those kinds of injuries, and the private hospital that the Ashfords had sent me to employed doctors with a full array of sigls for any injury you could think of, bruised ribs included. Two half-hour sessions plus a four-hour rest period between them was all it took to get me up and walking again.

Calhoun showed up in between my treatments. He didn't stay long before leaving to check on Mike, and by unspoken agreement neither of us brought up the events of last night. Still, it felt as though something had changed between us. I had the feeling that, sometime soon, the two of us were going to have a long conversation about our respective histories with the Winged, and what we were going to do about them. Before I did, I would have to figure out exactly how much I trusted the Ashford heir; in the past, my answer to that would have been "not much," but after last night I was starting to feel as though that might have changed.

EARLY AFTERNOON FOUND me standing next to the window in the hospital room, looking down at the traffic passing left and right along Marylebone Road. My room was high up, with an impressive view, but I didn't really see any of it. I was thinking about last night.

For a long time now I'd felt as though I was drifting. Sometimes it had been the kind of drifting where you're floating along at a steady pace, with plenty of time to look around. Sometimes it had been the kind where you're rushing down rapids, frantically staving off rocks. But I'd never felt in control, never known where I was going. Most of my friends, the people I knew, they had some idea of where they'd be two years, five years from now. I didn't.

Maybe that was why I tried so hard to make plans all the time. It gave me a goal. But eventually I'd reach the goal and I'd be back where I started. I didn't really have a mission, a purpose. The closest thing had been "find my father," and now that was done. Since then, I'd been casting about for something else.

Until last night.

That moment in the sunset, facing those men, had just felt *right*, as though everything had clicked into place. When the combat had started, I'd thrown myself into it with everything I had. No doubts, nothing held back. There'd been a purity to it, a focus, that I'd only ever found when I was trying my hardest to shape a sigl or going all out in a fight. I wanted to feel it again.

But although I could remember the feeling perfectly, I had no idea where it had come from.

I thought back to what Father Hawke had said about my gift, its purpose. Was that what this was about? But if so, I didn't know what had triggered it. Protecting Calhoun? Fighting the Winged? Saving someone's life? One of them, two of them, all of them?

I wasn't sure. But I *did* feel as though what I'd done yesterday was a step on the right path.

There was a knock at the door.

"Hello?" I called.

A nurse poked her head in. "Stephen Ashford?"

"More or less."

"There's a family member to see you. Are we well enough for visitors?"

"Sure."

The nurse gave me a brisk smile and vanished. I leant sideways against the wall and waited, keeping an eye on the door. I wondered if Calhoun had decided to come back . . . maybe he'd decided to have that conversation after all. Or it might be Bridget, or my mother—she hadn't come last time, but then it wasn't as though I'd told her—

The door opened and Charles Ashford walked in.

I stared.

Charles Ashford looked me up and down, then closed the door behind him. He was dressed in his usual well-fitting suit. "You seem to have recovered. Good." He turned the lock with a click.

I kept staring at Charles as he walked up to stand next to me. "You look surprised to see me," he said.

I took a few seconds to answer. "I'm surprised you've got the nerve to show your face."

Charles raised his eyebrows. "Who do you think's paying for your hospital stay?"

"You're the reason I *need* a hospital stay," I told him. "Or what, you're going to tell me it was all just a coincidence? You overrule your head of security and send me to that Well, and by *completely random chance* the Winged just happen to pick that one specific evening to try and assassinate us?"

Charles turned to gaze down through the window. From our height, the men and women on the pavement of the main road below looked like crawling ants; black birds the size of dots lined the opposite roof. "Why don't you tell me what you think was going on last night?"

"What was 'going on' was that Calhoun and I both came about one second away from having our throats cut. If things had gone just a tiny bit differently, you'd have woken up this morning to two dead security men and two dead Ashford family members. What I want to know is why you thought that was a good idea. And why the hell I should go anywhere on your orders ever again."

"Then I'll explain," Charles said. "I suggest you pay attention."

I stared back at the House Ashford head for a few seconds. "Fine."

"The Winged have been interested in House Ashford for some time," Charles said. "Until recently, that interest has taken the form of trying to steal away our members. However, at some point within the past six months we drew the attention of a different faction, who intend to take control of House Ashford directly. After some consideration, they chose Calhoun as their point of attack. Their plan last night was either to recruit Calhoun to their side, or, should that fail, to abduct or kill him. Had they been successful, they would have contacted me to demand I make Lucella the new heir."

"Lucella?"

"She's been involved in all this from the start. Oh, she wasn't there last night; apparently she's no longer *quite* that stupid. She spent the evening at a party in Bristol, taking care to be seen by plenty of witnesses."

"You told Lucella and Tobias that if anything happened to Calhoun, they'd get disinherited."

"Unfortunately, threats only work if you have power over the one being threatened," Charles said. "Lucella's new patron within the Winged could not care less how I assign family inheritance. If I'd refused his demands, other family members would have been targeted until I gave in. House Ashford is not large. Between our family and retainers, we can put up perhaps twenty to thirty people in an armed conflict. Narrow that to ones who'd stand a chance against a Winged elite, and you can count them on the fingers of one hand. The Winged can deploy ten times that many. In any kind of open conflict between us, we will lose."

Charles stopped and looked back down through the window, seemingly lost in thought. I was taken aback; I hadn't been expecting him to say it that bluntly. "Then why did you send us to fight them?"

"The Winged's specialty is manipulation," Charles told me. "Oh, they can call on plenty of brute force when they need to, but they tend to be clumsy with it. Certain actions on their part led me to believe that they weren't taking us very seriously. So I made sure Calhoun would have someone with him. Someone low-key enough that he wouldn't look like much of a threat, but who could throw a spanner in the works of their plan."

"Is that what I am in your books? Something to mess up your enemies' plans?"

Charles glanced at me. "Does that make you angry?"

"What do you think?" I said with an edge in my voice.

"I had to ensure the safety of the members of this family, while also ensuring that if a battle did take place, it would be one that we would stand a chance of winning," Charles said. "All while maintaining our normal day-to-day operations. If I could have done all that while sending ten boys like you and Calhoun to that Well, I would have. But I didn't have ten, I had two. So two it was."

"If things had gone a little differently, you'd have zero."

"I am aware."

"Does that bother you?"

"I made the choice I considered best with the resources available," Charles said. "If I'd been wrong . . ." He shrugged. "Perhaps someday you'll be the one sending men out and writing letters to their families when they don't come back."

I wasn't sure how to answer that. "You're making it sound like we won," I said after a pause. "I'm not so sure we did. There were two Winged vanguards, and both got away. Calhoun and I took down a lot of the gunmen, but I'm not sure that matters. I don't even think most of them were from the Winged."

"They weren't."

"So what's stopping them from waiting until that white-masked guy's hand heals up, then trying the same thing again?"

"A stupid enemy, if you defeat them, will come back and try the same thing again," Charles said. "A competent enemy will learn from the experience, then come back in greater strength. In this case, that would mean fifty hired thugs instead of twenty, and five vanguards instead of two. Enough that you and Calhoun would have no chance against them at all." Charles glanced at me. "Always assume your enemies are competent rather than stupid. That way, all your surprises will be pleasant ones."

I stared at Charles for a minute. "If they did that, we'd end up dead."

"Yes."

"Then what was the point?" I said. "If that's how it's going to end, why were we fighting last night at all?"

"House Ashford is no match for the Winged as a unified entity," Charles said. "Fortunately for us, large organisations are rarely unified. The Winged are not a monolith; they have factions and internal conflicts. One of those factions prefers to achieve its goals through soft power; another, smaller faction likes to achieve them through violence. Your victory in last night's skirmish embarrassed the 'violence' faction in quite a public way, and, right now, the rest of the Winged are busy laughing at them. In the long run that'll just make them hate us more, but in the short term it presents an opportunity."

"An opportunity for what?"

Instead of answering, Charles took out a phone and dialled a number. "Send him up," he told whoever was on the other end, then hung up.

I looked at him with a frown.

Charles nodded towards the door. "Go unlock it."

I looked back at him.

"Today, Stephen. Once you see who's coming through that door, perhaps you'll start to understand."

I kept frowning but did as Charles said. Then I walked back to the window and waited.

A minute passed.

The door opened and Byron walked in.

My hand flew to the pocket with my sigls.

"Relax, Stephen," Byron said soothingly. "I know you've had a stressful night, but there's really no reason to worry."

"You being in the same room is a *very good* reason to worry," I snapped. Byron was smiling, apparently in a good mood. It didn't make me feel any better, and I kept one hand on the sigls in my pocket, wishing that I'd never taken them off. "Why the hell is he here?"

Byron made an easy gesture. "It's considered polite to meet face-to-face when starting a business relationship."

I stared.

"Ah." Byron looked at Charles. "You didn't get to that part?"

I continued to stare at Byron, then, slowly, turned to Charles.

"Byron and I have come to an agreement," Charles said. "The Winged will ... conditionally ... support House Ashford going forward. As part of that, hostilities between our factions will cease."

My eyebrows tried to climb up off my forehead.

"Byron did, however, have two stipulations," Charles said. He glanced towards the other man.

"At the moment, your cousin Calhoun is the duly appointed Ashford heir, while his sister has been pushed to one side," Byron told me. "My colleagues and I feel that this is unduly harsh treatment for such a talented and promising young woman, and that Lucella should be brought back in consideration as a potential candidate. With the appropriate treatment that comes with it, of course. Attendance at public events, presentations to associates, that sort of thing."

My temper flared. "The reason she got 'pushed aside' was because—"

"And since our organisations will be working together more closely going forward," Byron continued, "I thought it would be appropriate for Charles to assign one of his family members as a liaison to the Winged." He looked at me with a slight smile.

I stared back at Byron, then looked at Charles.

Charles was looking at me too.

"No," I said.

The two men looked at me.

"You've got to be kidding."

"I'm sure you'll do an excellent job," Byron said.

"I am not doing this," I told Charles.

"You can and you will."

"His men were trying to kill us both just last night!"

"Point of information," Byron said, raising a finger. "Vermillion and Valefor were acting on Oscar's orders, not mine. I expressed the opinion that such an attack would be unwise; they elected to ignore me. Should our agreement go through, any further suggestions on my part will be a little more forceful."

I glared at Byron and Charles.

"Well," Byron said once the silence started to become awkward, "perhaps I should leave you to discuss things in private." He gave me another smile. "I'm looking forward to working with you." He left.

As soon as the door shut behind him, I rounded on Charles. "Are you out of your fucking mind?"

"Byron is one of the leading figures in the Winged's soft-power faction," Charles said. "The Cathedral, I believe they're nicknamed. They don't like assassinations. They much prefer backroom deals. Makes it easier to present themselves as benevolent."

"And you actually trust Byron to keep his word?"

"I trust him to act in his own interests," Charles said. "The faction in the Winged who were pushing for violence are Byron's rivals. Now that they've very publicly failed, he gets to step in, resolve the conflict, and claim all the credit. Also, if you'd been paying attention, you'd have noticed that Byron just put a leash on Lucella. Apparently this Oscar had bribed her over to his side. Now, if she wants to benefit from this new arrangement, she's going to have to go crawling back to Byron and do anything and everything he says. Byron gets to score points off his rivals, bring

Lucella to heel, and establish himself as the peacemaker, all without lifting a finger. I imagine he's walking out of this hospital in a very good mood."

"He's not our friend," I said angrily.

"The Winged are a power. Powers do not have friends. They have interests."

"And let me guess, I'm supposed to do this because it suits *your* interests."

"The interests of the family."

"If you care so much about your family, why didn't you make your deal with Byron *before* Vermillion nearly slit our throats?"

"We disagreed over price."

I stared.

"Byron's initial demand was for Lucella to replace Calhoun as heir," Charles said. "I refused; negotiations foundered. This morning I contacted him again and suggested, given recent developments, that he should reconsider his offer. He graciously conceded the point."

I looked at Charles for a few seconds, processing what he had just said. "Was that all this was?" I said at last. "A disagreement over price?"

"A conflict can end in one of two ways," Charles said. "Either one side crushes the other, or they come to a compromise. As I told you, in any extended conflict with the Winged, House Ashford would lose. This was the best realistically achievable outcome."

"You're acting like I've already agreed to go along with this."

"Refuse to do so," Charles said calmly, "and you'll make yourself an enemy of both House Ashford *and* the Winged. How long do you think you'll last? A week, a month? I'd say it's a toss-up as to whether the Winged will go after you first, or the other members of our family. I imagine they'd pick a softer target than Calhoun this time. Maybe your mother, or your sister. If one of them was killed or kidnapped, would you do something then? Or would you stand aside until they got rid of every last member of House Ashford, one after another, before finally turning their attention to you?"

I glared at Charles. I hated the way he was manipulating me, and I couldn't see any way out of it.

"You are not being sold," Charles said when I still didn't speak. His voice was a little softer, in the same way that iron's a little softer than steel. "I agreed to appoint you as a liaison, and that is all. If Byron demands anything beyond that, you are fully entitled to refuse."

It didn't make me happy, but it did cool my temper. "And Lucella?"

"Lucella's new position is primarily a matter of appearances. Attendance, presentations . . . everything to suggest that she's once again a candidate for heir. The title, however, remains Calhoun's. For now."

I let out a long breath and stared out of the window for a few seconds. "You once told me that the Winged hated the whole idea of Noble Houses. That if they ever took over House Ashford, they'd tear it down just out of spite." I looked back at Charles. "What makes you think they won't do that anyway?"

"By publicly agreeing to this arrangement, Byron has—to a limited extent—invested in us," Charles said. "So long as his position within the Winged remains strong, I expect the truce will hold. Should that change . . ." Charles shrugged. "Agreements are temporary things."

I was silent.

"Well," Charles continued when I didn't say anything more. "Once you're discharged, report to the mansion and we'll discuss your new duties." He walked to the door and placed his hand on the handle, then looked back. "By the way, did you ever figure out who was behind that bomb?"

I frowned at Charles. An image flitted through my mind; the odd, closed expression on Bridget's face when I'd asked her the same question. "No."

Charles just looked at me.

"Did you?" I asked when he didn't reply.

For a moment, Charles almost smiled. "Still a child." He opened the door and left.

I stared after Charles, listening to the sound of his footsteps fading away down the corridor before the closing door cut them off with a click. *What was that about?*

Then I shook it off as my thoughts went back to Charles and Byron. I remembered that time in Charles's study, when he'd told me he would do whatever it took for the House to prosper. The call with Byron, where he'd told me that he still wanted me in the Winged, and that he wouldn't wait forever.

They've been planning this a long time. How long had they gone back and forth, haggling? Until what had happened last night had given Charles his bargaining chip . . .

I thought of that desperate fight in the dusk, fear and pain and fury, life and death balanced on the edge of a blade. Then I thought of how Charles had described it. *A disagreement over price.*

Was that all it had been?

No.

I remembered that moment, staring up at that last ray of light shining upon the evening clouds. I still wasn't sure why I'd been given this gift, but it hadn't been to make Charles's already-rich family slightly richer. It had been for something more.

But what?

My instincts told me it involved opposing the Winged. The Winged had their vanguards, with their gifts. Normal people couldn't stand against them. Who could?

Drucrafters with gifts of their own. Like me.

So if Byron knew that I might be a threat, why hadn't he made any effort to get rid of me? Maybe he knew about my gift, but not why I'd been given it?

Maybe... but I found it hard to believe. Old and wily as Byron was, I felt he must have seen boys like me before. More likely he *did* suspect the purpose of my gift, and that was why he'd gone to so much trouble to bring me into his orbit. I remembered his confidence when we'd met last autumn, the way he'd treated my rejection like some sort of amusing challenge. Probably he was sure that, with time, he could turn me into another trophy for his collection. In his eyes, I was just a naive, gullible child.

Well, we'll see about that. Both Byron and Charles saw me as easy to manipulate, to control. And that probably *was* how I'd acted when we'd first met. But back then I'd been alone, cut off from my family, with no idea of my place in the world. None of those things were true anymore.

So I would give Charles and Byron what they wanted, at least on the surface. I'd become a member of House Ashford, and their liaison to the Winged. But my real allegiance wouldn't be to either. It would be to my purpose, and to whatever had given me my gift. I still wasn't sure what either of those things *was*, but now I had a way to find out. If yesterday had been a step on the right path, then all I had to do to find out where it led was to keep following it. Which meant doing more things like last night.

Hopefully without coming so close to death next time. Still, there should be some way to do it without putting myself in *quite* so much danger. Right?

Everything's going to be very different now. A lot of my old problems were about to disappear; a lot of new ones would take their place. I'd be able to ask for more from the Ashfords, but they'd also ask for more from me. I'd have to carry out my new duties while keeping my real motivations a secret from both Charles and Byron. And at the same time, I'd need to keep using my raiding group to build up my own strength, and that of my friends. I'd passed from one phase of my life and into another.

Better get started, then.

I took a last glance out of the window, down at the people on the street far below, then took out my phone and began searching through my contacts for Father Hawke's number. There was work to be done.

THE LETTER

(A page from Stephen's notebook. Decoded letter is in **bold**. *Italics are Stephen's commentary.*)

#17

Three letter blocks: read as page/line/word, right to left
Four letter blocks: read as page/line/word/part-of-word, right to left

primroses over

(indicates book cipher. PROBABLY doesn't mean anything else... unless double meaning? Can't see what that could be. Disregard for now.)

Stephen

(last word I didn't have to decode. Either to catch my attention or because Watership Down *doesn't contain the word "Stephen.")*

I hope you get this letter, but I know you probably won't. In case it isn't intercepted, I've included a way at the end for you to message me. Think carefully before you do. The men after me will watch you to get to me. If they ever realise we have a way to speak, they'll capture you.

(*usual substitutes: "letter" for "letters," "included" for "include," "capture" for "captured." Don't think I'm losing any additional meaning here.*)

Here's what you need to know.

The men after me are members of the Winged. Back when I was one of them, I thought it was just a secret society. It's not. It's a cult that follows a great bird spirit. I know it's hard to believe, but I promise you it's real.

(*Four letter block: "difficult" decodes to last four letters, "cult." "great bird spirit" . . . no idea. Decoding mistake?*)
(*Double-checked. Not a mistake.*)

The spirit is served by (?) that give gifts to those they favour. Those with gifts are the cult Owslafa. The only reason they don't rule the world is that they spend most of their energy fighting among themselves and against the other cult.

(*depending on how you count the hyphen, the (?) could decode to "some" or to "demons." From the context I think it's "demons."*)
(*Owslafa . . . doesn't sound good. Byron/Vermillion/Lucella?*)

I'm safe for now, but only so long as I stay hidden. I hope that you can stay safe and apart from all this. But it may be that one day the cult will come after you as well. If ~~him~~ this ever happens, message me. Frithrah Fiver at the usual place. I'll wait to hear from you.

(pretty sure "him" for "this" is a coding mistake. One instead of a four. NB: "demons" and "great bird spirit" do not follow this pattern. Suggests they're NOT coding mistakes.)
("Usual place": guessing it's our email provider. Could be FrithrahFiver@, Frithrah.Fiver@, Frithrah-Fiver@, etc. Send cc to all.)

I love you very much and always will. I hate not being able to see you. Take care of yourself.

Love,
Dad

GLOSSARY

affinity (branch)—A talent or skill with one of the six branches of drucraft. Almost all drucrafters discover that they have at least one branch that they find particularly easy to work with, and at least one branch that they find particularly difficult. A strong affinity allows a drucrafter to use and create sigls from that branch more easily and with greater effectiveness.

affinity (country)—A natural familiarity with the essentia found in the Wells of a particular geographical region. It's almost always much easier to shape a sigl at a Well in the country you grew up in. Country affinity doesn't matter much to drucrafters who live most of their lives in the same place but causes problems for "sigl tourists" who want to fly into a country, acquire a sigl, and fly out.

Ashford (House)—A Lesser House of the UK. Origins in Kent and Cornwall. Family crest is three blue keys on a white field with black chevron; family colours are blue and silver. A minor family of little importance until the previous Head of House, Walter Ashford (b. 1922), acquired a significant number of Wells in postwar Germany. Upon returning to England, the family gained an A-rank Light Well in 1986 and an A-rank Matter Well in 1991, and finally rose to Lesser House status upon negotiating purchase of an A+ rank Light Well in 1998 (The Bishop's Well). Current Head of House is Charles Ashford (b. 1953).

aurum—The raw material that sigls are made of, also known as solid essentia or crystallised essentia. It has a density of 8.55 grams per cubic centimetre, slightly denser than steel and about the density of copper or brass. If left untouched, aurum will eventually sublimate back into free essentia, though in the case of solid sigls this can take thousands of years.

Blood Limit—One of the most important principles of drucraft, the Blood Limit states that sigls are locked at the moment of their creation to the personal essentia of whoever made them. This makes sigls nontransferable: to anyone but their maker, a sigl is nothing but a pretty rock.

There are two ways to get around the Blood Limit. First, in creating a sigl, a drucrafter can choose to mix their own personal essentia with someone else's. The higher the proportion of the other person's personal essentia that they use, the more effective the sigl will be for that person, but the harder the sigl is to make. This is the method used by all commercial providers.

The second way around the Blood Limit is to use a sigl shaped by a close relative. The more closely related two people are, the more likely it is that their personal essentia will be similar enough that the sigl will accept it. This method works well between parent and child or between siblings, but its effectiveness drops sharply with more distant relations, and anything more distant than grandparent to grandchild or aunt/uncle to niece/nephew almost never works. This method has been one of the ways in which Noble Houses have preserved some measure of their strength down the generations.

Due to the Blood Limit, all sigls effectively have a finite life span. No matter how powerful a sigl may be, there will eventually come a time when every person capable of using it is dead, at which point the sigl is useless.

Board—The ruling body that governs all matters relating to drucraft in the United Kingdom. The Board has wide discretionary powers but is still subject to the authority of the Crown and functions in practice like a cross between a board of directors and the British Parliament.

Possession of a Well of strength A+ and above grants the holder a seat on the Board; as a result, the sale and purchase of these Wells in the United Kingdom is subject to special restrictions.

branch—Different types of Wells contain different kinds of essentia and produce different kinds of sigls. These are known in drucraft as the six branches, named after the sorts of things that can be done with them: Light, Matter, Motion, Life, Dimension, and Primal. Of all the branches, only Primal effects can be created without a sigl, and then only weakly.

channeller—A drucrafter capable of controlling and directing their personal essentia, allowing them to activate triggered sigls. Becoming a channeller is generally the point at which someone is considered a "real" drucrafter.

corporations—Most corporations are not involved in drucraft, but those that are have great influence in the drucraft world. Like Houses, corporations can buy, hold, and sell Wells, and are treated by governments as legal entities in their own right. The distinction between a corporation and a House can be fuzzy, though there is a noticeable difference in terms of organisational culture: Houses tend to be more traditional and are more strongly tied to their country of origin, while corporations are much more heavily focused on profit and are typically international, with relatively little connection to the countries they operate in.

drucraft—The art and skill of working with essentia. Drucraft consists of three disciplines: sensing (perceiving essentia), channelling (manipulating one's own personal essentia), and shaping (the creation of sigls).

drucrafter—A practitioner of drucraft. Typically used to refer to a channeller or shaper.

essentia—The raw energy that powers drucraft and creates sigls. Essentia is fundamental and omnipresent, flowing through the world in invisible currents. If depleted in any location, it naturally replenishes itself from the surrounding area.

Pure essentia is completely inaccessible to living creatures: they can no more tap it than draw upon the chemical energy in a lump of stone. However, over long periods of time, essentia can be shaped by the land around it, its currents converging at a location called a Well. The essentia in a Well is still mutable but will be inclined towards a certain aspect of existence, such as light or matter.

A living creature of sufficient enlightened will can shape

the reserves of a Well into a small piece of crystallised essentia called a sigl. Sigls have the power to conduct essentia, transforming its raw universal energy into a spell effect. Over a long, long time, the sigl sublimates back into essentia; this essentia is absorbed again by the land, and the cycle begins anew.

essentia capacity—The rate at which a living creature can assimilate ambient essentia into personal essentia, and thus make use of sigls. It is measured on the Lorenz Scale and is loosely correlated with height and skeletal mass; average adult essentia capacity in the UK is 2.8 for men and 2.4 for women. For a combat drucrafter, an essentia capacity of 3.0 and over is considered ideal, allowing them to use three full-strength sigls at once, while an essentia capacity of below 2.0 is considered crippling.

essentia construct—A sketch or sculpture crafted out of essentia. Making an essentia construct is the first step towards creating a sigl. Manifesters typically use essentia constructs as blueprints, allowing them to practise the important early stages of creating a sigl, as well as adjust its design before attempting the costly process of shaping it for real.

Euler's Limit—Sigls can only be created from essentia: many substitutes have been tried and all have failed. This means that the supply of sigls is limited by the supply of locations that possess a sufficient concentration of essentia to shape a sigl. These locations are called Wells.

Exchange—The oldest and best-known institute of drucraft trade in London, specialising in the sale of sigls to private individuals.

Situated in Belgravia, between Belgrave Square and Eaton Square Gardens, it claims to be able to supply any sigl in the world. Average sigl price is in the tens of thousands; top-end sigls are in the millions.

Faraday Point—The minimum quantity of essentia needed to consistently produce a viable sigl. Below this point, effectiveness falls off sharply: a drop of even ten percent below the Faraday Point usually produces a nonfunctional sigl. A sigl created at the Faraday Point is rated as D-class.

The Faraday Point is used to define the Faraday Scale. A Well with a Faraday rating of 1 can sustainably produce exactly one D-class sigl per year.

Faraday Scale—The most common measuring scale for Wells, used in Europe, Japan, Russia, Australia, India, and some parts of Africa and South America. The Faraday rating of a Well is a measurement of how many D-class sigls the Well can sustainably make in a year.

The Faraday Point is a "soft" limit and as such is not considered one of the Five Limits of drucraft (which are much closer to being absolute restrictions).

Five Limits—The five most significant limitations on drucraft. More than anything else, the Five Limits shape how the drucraft world operates. In brief, the Five Limits are:

Euler's Limit: Sigls can only be created from essentia.
Primal Limit: You can't use drucraft without a sigl.
Blood Limit: You can't use someone else's sigl.
Limit of Creation: You can't change a sigl after it's made.
Limit of Operation: A sigl won't work without a bearer.

While the Five Limits significantly restrict what drucraft is capable of, all five do have work-arounds and exceptions.

House—An aristocratic family of drucrafters, usually one that holds title to one or more Wells. In the past, the Great Houses of Europe had various special privileges under the law; while this is rarely the case nowadays, Houses still command great wealth and influence.

Drucraft Houses are primarily found in Europe and Asia. In countries without Houses, different institutions fill similar roles: in the United States, the place of Houses is filled by corporations, while in China, the main drucraft enterprises are all state owned. In the United Kingdom, the main significance of House status is that both Great and Lesser Houses are entitled to a seat on the Board.

House Ashford—See Ashford (House).

House, Great (United Kingdom)—A House in the United Kingdom that possesses at least one Well of S-class and above. At the time of writing, there are eight Great Houses in the United Kingdom: Barrett-Lennard, Cawley, Chetwynd, De Haughton, Hawker, Meath, Reisinger, and Winterton.

House, Lesser (United Kingdom)—A House in the United Kingdom that possesses at least one Well with a class of A+. The United Kingdom has between thirty and thirty-five Lesser Houses (the exact number is subject to dispute).

Houses that own no Wells of class A+ and above have no special legal status, though they will often take the title of "House" regardless, particularly if they held Great House or Lesser House status in the past.

kernel—A sigl's core, made out of the shaper or wielder's personal essentia. The fact that it is *their* personal essentia is the reason that the sigl will work for them and not for anyone else.

limiter—A device used by shapers to assist in creating sigls. Limiters give two advantages: consistency (sigls produced by the same limiter are always exactly the same, without the variation created by free manifestation) and reliability (shaping a sigl with a limiter is much less demanding on the user's shaping skills). Limiters are expensive to create, and as such are typically not cost effective unless the owner plans to produce many copies of the same sigl. The vast majority of sigls sold commercially are created with limiters.

Linford's—A drucraft corporation. Corporate headquarters in London; major regional offices in New York and Singapore. Primarily a locating company, they sell the majority of the aurum they obtain. They have a small shaping department but do not supply sigls to the Exchange.

Lorenz Ceiling—The maximum quantity of personal essentia that can be channelled through any sigl before its efficiency drops off sharply. Like the Faraday Point, this is a "soft" limit rather than a hard one. The Lorenz Ceiling is defined as a 1 on the Lorenz Scale.

The Lorenz Ceiling is not affected by a sigl's size. Larger sigls have more powerful amplification effects (allowing them to draw in more ambient essentia from the surrounding environment) but cannot make use of any more personal essentia than a smaller sigl can.

Lorenz Scale—A measurement of essentia flow, used to evaluate both a living creature's essentia capacity and also the amount of personal essentia a sigl requires to function at full output.

Most commercially created sigls are designed with Lorenz ratings as close as possible to 1. A sigl with a Lorenz rating of less than 1 will be less powerful but also less draining to use (this is more common with Light sigls, due to their generally lower power requirements). Sigls with Lorenz ratings of more than 1 are rare, since going above the Lorenz Ceiling brings greatly diminishing returns. A sigl with a Lorenz rating of 1.5 will be only marginally more powerful than one with a Lorenz rating of 1, despite being much more taxing on its bearer's essentia capacity.

manifester—A drucrafter capable of creating a sigl without assistance (i.e., without a limiter or similar tool). Becoming a manifester requires advanced shaping skills. Most drucrafters never become manifesters, although there is a growing feeling that limiters have become so widespread in the modern age that being unable to create a sigl without one is no longer a significant drawback.

personal essentia—Essentia that has been assimilated by a living creature and that has taken on the imprint of that creature's mind and body. With practice and concentration, personal essentia can be directed, controlled, and channelled into sigls to produce various effects.

Primal Limit—The second of the Five Limits, the Primal Limit states that it is impossible to produce any kind of drucraft spell without a sigl. Humans can assimilate free essentia into personal essentia, but without a sigl they can't transform that personal essentia into a spell effect. The one exception to this limit is (as the name suggests) Primal drucraft, which can be performed unassisted, although much more weakly than with a Primal sigl.

shaper—Any drucrafter capable of creating a sigl. In theory this is a neutral term, but in practice, if someone is called a "shaper," it usually means that they can't create a sigl without a limiter. Otherwise, they'll call themselves a "manifester" instead.

sigl (SIG-ul)—A small item resembling a gemstone, created out of pure essentia at a Well. Sigls convert their wielder's personal essentia into a spell effect and then pull in free essentia from the surrounding environment to amplify it. Larger sigls have a more powerful amplification effect, allowing for more sophisticated and complex spells.

Sigls, once created, can be used only by their makers, though there are some work-arounds to this (see **Blood Limit**). There is no known way to alter a sigl once it has been shaped.

Though commonly assumed to be a derivation of the Latin word for a seal ("sigil"), the word in fact derives from the Old English term for a brooch or gemstone.

sigl class / sigl grade—A sigl at exactly the Faraday Point is defined as being of D-class. The mass of the sigl doubles for each half grade above D (a D+ sigl has twice the mass of a D-class sigl, a C-class sigl has four times the mass of a D-class sigl, and so on). In ascending order, and counting half grades, the sigl classes are: D, D+, C, C+, B, B+, A, A+, S, and S+. "Class" and "grade" are used interchangeably.

sigl type—Sigls fall into two types: continuous and triggered. Triggered sigls require their bearers to consciously channel essentia into them and as such can only be used by channellers. Continuous sigls are designed in such a way as to automatically pull in personal essentia from their bearers, meaning that they require no concentration and can even be used by a bearer with no knowledge of drucraft at all.

sigl weight—In casual conversation, sigls are usually referred to by their class. However, when greater precision is needed (such as when they're offered for sale), they are measured by carat weight instead. A D-class sigl has a weight of 0.18 carats, or 0.036 grams, and has a diameter of about two millimetres.

tyro—The lowest rank of drucrafter, with no ability to control their personal essentia. The only sigls a tyro can use are continuous ones.

Well—A location at which essentia accumulates. Wells are categorised by branch; for example, a Light Well collects Light essentia and produces Light sigls.

Wells can be permanent or temporary. Permanent Wells replenish themselves over time, and, if properly tended, can be used year after year for decades or even centuries. Temporary Wells, on the other hand, are typically one-offs: they have only brief life spans and do not usually refill themselves when drained. The distinction between the two types is sharper at higher ranks than at lower ones: Wells of class A and above will typically have storied histories of hundreds of years, while a permanent D-class Well can appear with relatively little fanfare and may disappear almost as fast, particularly if roughly treated.

Wells are commonly described by their class, which indicates the maximum strength of sigl the Well can produce when fully charged (e.g., a C-class Well can produce at most one C-class sigl before it must be left to replenish itself). Where more precision is needed, Wells are measured on the Faraday Scale.

Benedict Jacka is the author of the Inheritance of Magic series and the Alex Verus novels. He's studied philosophy at Cambridge, taught English in China, and worked at everything from civil servant to bouncer before becoming a full-time writer.

Visit Benedict Jacka Online

BenedictJacka.co.uk
𝕏 BenedictJacka

Ready to find
your next great read?

Let us help.

Visit prh.com/nextread

Penguin
Random
House